About
Night of the Broken Glass

The power of this novel is its universality. In these stories, the reader is brought face-to-face with himself .... To be able to provoke this kind of response in readers is one of the highest aims of fiction, and Broner has hit the mark with deadly accuracy.

Sun Sentinel
Ft. Lauderdale, Florida

It's perspective is original and filled with promise.

Hadassah Magazine

Well written.

Washington Jewish Weekly

Broner successfully portrays the complexity of the times. By focusing on individual lives, he makes the astonishment and inertia of Jews at their persecution comprehensible .... His characters confront moral responsibility and raise questions that transcend anti-Semitism and the Holocaust.

American Book Review

An intensely moving novel .... Deeply engrossing in characterization, story line, and morals, the book will make readers ponder their own courage.

School Library Journal

There are moments when the reader is carried along on breathless empathy.

Woodstock Times

NIGHT
of the
BROKEN
GLASS

NIGHT
of the
BROKEN
GLASS

PETER BRONER

Station Hill

Published by Station Hill Literary Editions, a project of the Institute for Publishing Arts, Barrytown, New York 12507. Station Hill Literary Editions are supported in part by grants from the National Endowment for the Arts, a Federal Agency in Washington, D.C., and by the New York State Council on the Arts.

Text and cover design by Susan Quasha.
Cover photos by Vivian Huff.

Distributed by the Talman Company, 131 Spring Street, Suite 201E-N, New York, New York 10012.

Library of Congress Cataloging-in-Publication Data

Broner, Peter
　　Night of the broken glass / Peter Broner
　　　　p. cm.
　　ISBN 0-88268-132-X: (cloth) $19.95
　　ISBN 0-88268-141-9: (paper) $10.95
　　1. World War, 1939-1945—Fiction. 2. Holocaust, Jewish (1939-1945)—Fiction. 3. Germany—History—1933-1945—Fiction.
　　I. Title
　　PS3552.R64N54　1991
　　813'.54–dc20　　　　　　　　　　　　　　　　91-23312
　　　　　　　　　　　　　　　　　　　　　　CIP

Manufactured in the United States of America.

*To all who take risks
in defense of human decency and freedom,
this book is respectfully dedicated.*

Contents

NIGHT
of the
BROKEN
GLASS

I
1937 - 1939

The Silver Family

Time and again Emilia had been on the verge of telling him, but each time she had pulled back. Only last week she had come into the library where her husband was reading after dinner, determined to tell him everything. Sinking into one of the big leather armchairs, short, pretty, and compact, she looked, despite her forty-one years, almost girlish with her shy smile and charming dimples. She settled back in the chair but then remained silent, as if the wind had suddenly been knocked out of her, until her husband looked up and asked with an air of puzzlement:

"What is it, Emilia?"

"Samuel," she began.

"Yes, Millie?"

The reversion to her pet name reassured her but made going on more difficult. She looked at his dark, kindly eyes, at his somewhat crumpled, uneven face that she so loved. Seeing her hesitation, Samuel said:

"Would you like a glass of sherry?"

"Yes, that would be nice."

He fetched the bottle and two glasses and filled them.

"Just a little for me," she said. Her low tolerance for alcohol was proverbial in the family.

She sipped silently for a moment, feeling an impulse to run out of the room. What was the purpose of telling him now after all these years? she thought. She hadn't told him when it happened. Why now? On account of the Nazis, she answered her own question. On account of the boy's suffering. She reminded herself of Paul's ostracism, of his inability to join the Hitler Youth like all the other boys, of the beatings in school because he was a proud boy who refused to turn tail; most important: of the lack of a future for him in this New Germany that didn't permit even half Jews to enter the university or any of the higher professions.

"I'm worried about Paul," she began finally. "He's going through a difficult time."

"Yes," Samuel answered softly, suppressing the commonplace comment: Aren't we all?

"I know we're all going through hard times," Emilia continued. "Especially you because . . . ."

She began to stumble. She wanted to say: because you're a Jew. But why say the obvious? She pulled herself together.

"But it's harder on Paul," she finished.

"Why harder?" Samuel replied, his eyebrows knitting into a frown.

"Because he's not old enough to understand."

"He's seventeen. That's old enough to understand evil," Samuel muttered.

"Maybe he's old enough," Emilia conceded, "but he's—"

Again she stopped short. She had wanted to say: innocent. But that implied that her husband was guilty. She bit her lip. The simplest things were becoming so difficult these days.

"—but he didn't do anything," she finished lamely.

"None of us *did* anything," Samuel said with quiet emphasis.

"Please, no philosophizing, Samuel," she pleaded with sudden heat. "We're talking about our son."

Her vehemence startled Samuel. What triggered this sudden passion in a woman ordinarily so calm and even placid?

"I know we're talking about our son," he said gently. "And I didn't think I was philosophizing. But what do you mean by saying: he didn't do anything?"

"He didn't ask to be born into a Jewish home."

A shadow of a smile hovered for a moment on Samuel's lips.

"True, but what do you want me to do about it? I didn't ask to have Jewish parents either."

"Of course," Emilia replied stubbornly, "but there's a difference."

The words had slipped out and she regretted them at once. They had arrived at the crux of the problem. What would she say if he were to ask, What is the difference? For some moments both were silent while Samuel absent-mindedly fingered the pages of the book he had been reading. Then he said:

"What *is* the difference, Emilia?"

How could she tell him the difference without telling him everything?

"*Männchen* . . . ." she began, using the endearment which she used so rarely these days. But her voice trailed off.

"Yes?" Samuel said encouragingly.

Only five words remained: Five words that she could say or not say, but once said, they could not be taken back—*Paul is not your son!*

All these years I have kept the secret from you because I didn't want to hurt you, but now I can't hide it any longer: Because Paul is the son of as Aryan a man as you can find and a baron to boot. God is punishing me for my sin and there isn't anything I wouldn't do to make amends and humble myself . . . .

Tears had begun to run down Emilia's cheeks.

"Millie, what is it?" Samuel asked, startled.

She shook her head. What would she achieve by telling him? By trying to allay her guilt, she would, in the end, merely increase the sorry sum of her guilt. If she could convince the Nazis that they were persecuting one of their own, she would shout it from the rooftops, whatever the consequences. But as it was, what would she achieve by telling him except to wound a man already badly wounded.

"Forgive me," she whispered, "but I'm suddenly very tired. May I go to bed?"

"That drop of sherry hasn't—?" But he didn't finish the sentence. "You wanted to tell me something about Paul," he said.

"Another time," she said hoarsely, getting up.

But she knew there would be no other time.

◆ ◆ ◆

Emilia slept late next morning, which was unusual for her, and for the rest of the morning she stayed in her room. Downstairs she could hear Laura clearing away the dishes, but she didn't feel like facing her. Laura had never been a pearl of a maid, but lately a subtle, insolent sort of familiarity had crept into her behavior. On account of the Nazis that too, Emilia thought. There wasn't anything that wasn't somehow connected with the Nazis these days. For instance, in the way Laura said *we*. We who? It took Emilia awhile to realize that what the maid meant was *we Aryans*, Aryan Emilia Silver and Aryan Laura against Samuel Silver, the Jew.

She sat down in the armchair that faced the large window overlooking the garden in back of the house and took up her knitting. From the armchair she could look into the crown of a large elm tree that dominated the garden and was just breaking into leaves. She loved the tree, the garden, the room. It was her little kingdom, bedroom and living room combined, just as the paneled library downstairs was her husband's kingdom. How he loved his books, Emilia thought as she sat knitting. Evening after evening he buried himself in the library, now more than ever. The Nazis had something to do with that, too.

Emilia got up and went to a corner where a crucifix hung above a small altar on which she had placed a picture of the Madonna and knelt down in front of it. In former years the crucifix had faced the bed, but some five or six years after her marriage, when she had stopped going to church, she had shifted it to a less conspicuous place in the corner. Would the nuns have approved of that? Bless them, no. They scurried around the nunnery plus school where she had spent most of her childhood with crucifixes flapping forever against their white, starched collars. Once a quarrel had erupted among the girls over the question of what the nuns did with their crucifixes at night—did they or didn't they sleep with them?—until one girl courageously asked one of the sisters. When her father visited, she mentioned the incident to him, which made him bellow with laughter. His laughter had offended her. The girls could make fun of the nuns; they were devout members of the Church. But her father was a nonbeliever and had no such right. Worse, he was a *bon vivant* and ladies' man ever since her mother died when Emilia was seven. He had put her in a Catholic school to counterbalance his own philandering life in which there was no room for a motherless child.

After a while Emilia got up and began to pace restlessly about the room. How could she help her son, the half-Jew who was really an Aryan, without grievously hurting her Jewish husband? she thought. That was the insoluble predicament that had come to stand at all the entrances and exits of her soul, for she couldn't help seeing in the boy's persecution the staggering precision and adroitness of God's punishment. Her sin had brought her back to the Church that she should never have left in the first place, although her return was surreptitious because she couldn't help feeling that it must seem to her husband like a cruel underlining of their difference. God knew she didn't want to hurt him! If she didn't love him as much as she did, she could easily have left him. The Nazis welcomed Germans who left their Jewish spouses, holding them up as shining examples of fidelity to the glorious Aryan race.

So she had begun to sneak away to church until Father Sebastian, her priest, had urged on her the view that it was sinful to reproach herself for paying God his due of worship, however laudable her motives might be.

"My daughter, have you forgotten the martyrs of old who gave their very lives to worship our Lord Jesus Christ?" he would intone. "You cannot put your husband above God."

Emilia was grateful to Father Sebastian for putting it in this clear light. He was right. Putting her husband's feelings above God merely heaped another guilt on the big guilt she was already carrying, like a snail riding piggyback on another.

But how could she atone for her sin? She needed to do something for the boy who was being punished unjustly for her sin, she needed to save him—but how? The question tormented Emilia. Confessing her sin to her husband might be penance for her, but it would devastate him and do nothing for the boy. How could she convince the Nazis that Paul was innocent? Sometimes the thought occurred to Emilia that it was precisely the impossibility of proving Paul's innocence that was to be her punishment. But why was God punishing the boy when it was she who needed to be punished?

She had knelt down at the altar again and was praying fervently now.

"Dear God, show me the way, tell me what to do, visit upon me Thy wrath. I shall accept Thy harshest punishment humbly and willingly. Only don't punish the boy. And don't let me hurt my husband."

In moments of self-prostration such as these, Emilia sometimes wished that adulteresses would still be stoned as in Biblical times. That would have been a fitting atonement for her sin!

◆ ◆ ◆

Mr. Samuel Silver was sitting in the jewelry store that he had inherited from his father, which was in one of the better business districts of Munich, while Leopold was busy polishing some silverware.

"Leopold, that silverware is quite polished enough," Samuel remarked without annoyance. "You only polished it last week."

Leopold had been an employee in the business for over forty years. He was a bachelor in his early sixties, very proper, a bit self-important, but kindly.

"I know, Mr. Silver," Leopold returned, "but things get smudgy, you know, from handling—and such . . . ."

He fell silent. He knew and Samuel knew that there had been very little handling for some time now.

"Business is bad," Samuel murmured, skipping all the surrounding reflections, the connective tissue in which this thought was embedded. "And I guess it'll get worse before it'll get better."

"It's the economy," Leopold said, as if an analytical pronouncement would correct the problem. "Everything is going for guns and cannons. People have no time for watches and jewelry anymore."

Samuel smiled. "No time for watches. That's almost a pun, Leopold."

A customer came in, browsed around for a while, and presently departed without a purchase.

Yes, business was bad and going downhill. It was as if Samuel's Jewishness were a poison that had seeped into his very merchandise. Still, it wasn't money so much that depressed Samuel. Rather it was that he, Samuel Silver, German, patriot, cavalry officer in the First World War, believer in and admirer of German culture, intellectual and democrat, yes, fervent intellectual, ardent democrat, was branded an outsider, an exploiter, a conspirator against the German people . . . really, it was too ridiculous. How could a civilized nation suddenly turn on a segment of its people and brand them as lepers? If it hadn't been for the reality of the empty store, with its Star of David prominently displayed outside, he would have thought it an evil nightmare, for Samuel, even yet, was not quite sure what to do with the Jewishness that had so suddenly been thrust on him. Just what did it mean, being a Jew? Was it a race? a religion? a tradition? a common experience?

Was Palestine the solution then, as his daughter Sofie was telling him? Sofie couldn't wait until she could emigrate to Palestine with her Abraham. But a Jewish "homeland" was something Samuel had trouble imagining because it implied that he felt like a stranger in Germany, which just wasn't so. If anything, he felt like a stranger when importuned to feel like a Jew. Could Palestine, with the ghosts and relics of his forefathers, make him, the Jewish non-Jew, into a Jew?

How could he be expected to feel like a Jew all at once after living a lifetime as a German—or rather: as a human being? His allegiance had always been a broader one, beyond race or nation. Humanism, scientific humanism, that was his motto—the perfectability of man. What sort of a humanist and believer in man would he be if at the first setback he threw in the towel and abandoned his country? There had been regressions throughout history; it was part of the evolutionary cycle not only of man but of every species, of nature itself. But after every regression, there was a leap forward, a higher synthesis. Hegel had had the right idea. Better still, he liked to think of man's progress as moving up along a spiral staircase: At first blush, man seemed to be running around in circles, but in reality he was going up, always up.

His thoughts burrowed on. He didn't believe, couldn't believe, that the madness that had taken hold of Germany would last. It was a temporary aberration grafted onto the deep solidity of this country that had given birth to Beethoven and Goethe and Kant. One morning his fellow Germans would wake up and realize the error of their ways; they would see that their economic misery had led them to worship false idols, forsaking the gods of their forefathers—music, philosophy, litera- ture—and there would come a grand awakening that would sweep

Nazism away, as Moses had swept away the ikons of the Children of Israel. To emigrate meant running away from his homeland in its hour of need. It meant admitting as reality what was no more than a transient nightmare. It meant prying the leak open some more, instead of helping to plug it. To emigrate meant to admit defeat. It meant that all the values by which he had lived were, in the end, impotent and useless.

No, one couldn't emigrate away from all that. What was needed was a calm refusal to be stampeded into panic.

Presently his thoughts reverted to Emilia. How strange her behavior had become of late. Something was working in her, upsetting her. But what was it? At times she was almost short-tempered; she who used to be so easy-going and placid. And her renewed involvement with religion. There was something frantic and compulsive in the way she ran off to church these days, a tense, hysterical quality that went beyond mere piety. He watched her church-going with an increasing sense of dismay, sadness, and alienation. Two or three times he had attempted to talk to her about it, but she had reacted so evasively that it had only reinforced his feeling that her new-found religiosity was somehow turned against him. So he had dropped the subject and had retreated into himself.

Was this her way of telling him that she regretted having married a Jew? Was it her way of disowning him?

The thought was so preposterous that everything in Samuel cried out against it. Not his Millie! Not his devoted, faithful wife whose love he had never questioned!

But what else could it be?

◆ ◆ ◆

Paul and Herbert were leaving the school building together. From the school grounds there issued the sharp, monotonous one-two-three-four of a Hitler Youth leader drilling his group.

Herbert nudged him.

"Let's watch 'em."

"Nah."

"Come on, Paul. It beats the fuckin' circus."

Herbert Hoffer was the only friend Paul still had, different as their personalities were: Paul, athletic, tall, and handsome; Herbert, lean, rather stringy, and far from athletic; Paul, by nature self-confident and friendly, in the past a popular leader looked up to by his schoolmates; Herbert, disaffected and insecure despite his outward swagger, an unpopular boy who felt unwanted on account of his limp and, in fact, was not wanted; Paul, brought up in a cultured, intellectual, middle-class home; Herbert, born into a working class family that had very little involvement with culture.

What had brought the two boys together was their ostracism, Paul on account of his half Jewishness, Herbert on account of his limp which had made him the butt of cruel jokes and teasing all his life and had driven him to be an outsider. His limp was a birth defect, which one doctor had told his parents could be surgically corrected. But his parents were too poor to pursue the matter so that Herbert had come to accept his limp as a permanent part of his life, although it had made him cynical and had left him with a sneering attitude toward life that he sported like a badge.

It was a friendship of convenience; in short, the Jew in Paul and the limp in Herbert drove them into their unlikely friendship.

They watched the column of Hitler Youth boys swinging toward them in their khaki shirts and black short pants.

"Just look at the poor bastards," Herbert said with a malicious grin. "How would you like havin' the piss rushed out of you by one of them goddam troop leaders?"

I'd like nothing better, Paul thought. But he remained silent. And in another moment he felt ashamed even of the impulse. What would his father have said? Not only because his father was a Jew but because he hated regimentation and militarism of any kind. But what had the Hitler Youth to do with militarism? It was just fun and games and being one of the boys. Except he wasn't permitted to be one of the boys anymore, Paul thought bitterly. All of a sudden he was a dirty Jew who was supposed to go-back-where-he-came-from.

"Where do you think I come from?" he had yelled back in the beginning in a naive attempt to defend himself. "I was born in Munich just like you guys."

He had soon learned that logic was the last thing his tormentors were persuaded by. For that matter, he didn't even look Jewish, fair-skinned and light-haired as he was. Nor was he even sure what a Jew really was. The question had tormented him, but he didn't know where to turn for an answer. His father was too biased to be asked. As also his mother. One day he had screwed up his courage in class when the teacher had talked about "the unclean Jewish race."

"In what way are they unclean, sir?" he had asked.

The teacher took the question as an affront and told him to sit down. And then someone in the class yelled:

"Just look at your father, moron!"

Whereupon the class cracked up laughing.

Posing such questions had made him feel like a renegade. But soon his guilt feelings had turned into anger and resentment. In order to be a renegade you had to abandon something you belonged to and believed in, but he didn't feel that he belonged to the Jewish race, not like Sofie, his sister, who couldn't wait until she could emigrate to Palestine. For him to be called a Jew felt like something artificially grafted on, whatever it was.

If he was Jewish, why hadn't his parents, and especially his father, raised him as a Jew? Why wasn't his father going to synagogue? For that matter, why had he married his mother? Why wasn't he practicing what he was supposed to be?

The Hitler Youth column was marching straight toward them now. Paul felt an impulse to move behind Herbert to shield himself from his classmates' stares but didn't. As the column swung past, Herbert suddenly fell in line with it with puffed up chest and exaggerated step.

"One—two—three—four," he mimicked.

He returned to Paul with a self-satisfied grin.

"All for the greater glory of the fuckin' *Vaterland*," he sneered.

"Hey, cool it, will you?" Paul muttered.

Such remarks shocked Paul. For him the fatherland was something real, along with such values as honor, patriotism, glory, and loyalty. Honor, in particular, loomed large in Paul's scale of values—as also in Hitler's speeches. Much as he tried not to, he couldn't help thrilling at the *Führer's* rousing oratory.

"Left face!" the Hitler Youth leader called out.

One of the boys marched blithely to the right.

"Column halt!"

Red-faced, the offender rushed back to his place while his comrades snickered, shifting uneasily on their feet.

"Wake up, Bauer!" the leader bellowed. "And the rest of you clowns too—what do you think this is, the boy scouts?"

The column swung into motion again.

"Come on, let's go, Herb," Paul said, beginning to move away.

"What's your damn rush?" Herbert grumbled.

He trailed behind Paul, regretfully looking over his shoulder.

In his heart Herbert, too, envied the boys and would dearly have loved to join. But so convinced was he that he would be rejected on account of his limp that he forestalled being rejected by rejecting first. It left him free to sneer at them, at least.

◆ ◆ ◆

Paul used to enjoy school, though he was no more than an average student. What he enjoyed wasn't so much the classes and learning but all the other stuff: the camaraderie, the sports and pranks, even the fighting, at which he was good. He had always been popular. Now he had to drag himself out of bed in the morning because all that was left was learning.

"Adventures of the mind can be exciting too," Samuel would say to him when he complained that he was shut out of everything. "Use this difficult time to your advantage, Paul. Remember: Knowledge is power." It was one of Samuel's favorite maxims.

"For me there are only adventures of the body and senses," Paul would counter resentfully. "Not books and philosophy."

That was the problem with the new generation, Samuel thought. Everything had to be physical, capable of being touched and handled. For him, learning, and especially philosophy and literature, had always possessed its own reason for being and needed no ulterior compensation. But then Paul had a different personality. Samuel had to remind himself of that again and again. Paul wasn't an introvert like himself. He was an extrovert who needed action and interaction. Even his appearance underlined their differences: fair skin and light hair—who had ever had light hair in his family? Paul possessed all the outgoing gifts that impressed people, in contrast to himself who was of a scholarly nature, unathletic and stockily built, and by now a bit paunchy and showing his forty-three years. Amazing how different a son could be from his father in both personality and appearance, Samuel reflected time and again. It was as if the parents' disparate blood clashed in the boy's veins so that he had been born only with his wife's blood, in contrast to Sofie in whom their blood intermingled without difficulty.

The truth was—in quiet moments Samuel had to admit it to himself— that his feelings for Paul were ambivalent. He loved the boy, yes; but he never felt entirely at ease with him. There was something unfamiliar and alien about the boy that both attracted and repelled him, in contrast to Sofie who was like an open book, well known and familiar.

Yes, in quiet moments Samuel had to admit to himself that he did not feel very close to his son. It accounted for his constant attempts to make restitution in an effort to bridge the gap and make up for something that he felt was lacking in their relationship, the kind of deeper bond that should exist between a father and son. Yet, paradoxically, this very lack made their relationship more interesting and challenging.

It was a complex, difficult, ambiguous relationship that the advent of Nazism had made even more difficult, Samuel reflected. But then life itself was a complex, ambiguous, and paradoxical affair . . . .

◆ ◆ ◆

To counteract the unrelenting Nazi indoctrination that students were receiving in school, Samuel had attempted to involve Paul in discussions about his studies, especially in the social sciences, selecting appropriate books from his own extensive library to acquaint Paul with non-Nazi points of view. But from the start he had run into unexpected resistance as Paul would defend his teachers' explanations.

"Why won't you, if not believe me, at least consider the possibility, Paul," Samuel would counter, "that what you are being taught in school is open to question."

"Because you're not a history teacher" (or whatever subject they were discussing), Paul would reply sullenly.

"But remain *open*, Paul," Samuel would urge. "Human knowledge advances by considering different points of view."

It was the sort of tone Paul feared most, this urgent, kindly pleading, those probing, sincere eyes before which he always felt defenseless and vaguely ashamed because they pulled him back to the time when he had admired and respected his father for his fairness, his patient kindliness, his even temper, his warmth. He had felt secure with him. It added to his bitterness and struggle that the very fountainhead of his security, his father, had suddenly become the cause of his insecurity and unhappiness, relegated as he was to third-class citizenship for reasons he could not really understand or accept.

The truth was that Paul, feeling neither Jewish nor permitted to be a German, oscillated wretchedly and guiltily between the two.

"I am open!" he would cry stubbornly. "It's you who is stuck in old views. Hitler is trying to create a New Order."

"Of suppression and violence."

"No, of honor and self-respect!" Paul would exclaim heatedly.

Hadn't Germany been treated unfairly at Versailles? Didn't Hitler merely want to rehabilitate the country and restore it to its rightful place among nations? Didn't he want to return a sense of hope and self-respect and honor to the German people?

Paul's defense of the Nazis was his way of remaining somehow still a part of the New Germany from which his paternity excluded him. It gave him, moreover, a certain arrogant pleasure. He would demonstrate that he was bigger than his hurt and could give the cause itself its proper due! He wasn't going to condemn all the palpable accomplishments of the Nazis merely because he wasn't invited to participate. One of the problems in the world was that everyone always acted merely out of their own narrow self-interest. He wasn't going to be like that.

"How can he talk that way?" Samuel would later say to Emilia. "Is he blind? Can't he see what the Nazis are doing?"

"He's a boy, Samuel. He's upset that he's being excluded and can't join the Hitler Youth like all the other boys."

"But why would he *want* to be included? Sofie doesn't want to be included."

"Sofie is happy being Jewish. Paul isn't."

"Anyway," Samuel would say, withdrawing from the conversation, "this sort of reasoning is bad because it merely bemoans the fact that Jews happen to be excluded instead of condemning the Nazis for an evil philosophy unworthy of civilized men."

◆ ◆ ◆

"And she came and saw and conquered," trilled Sofie.

"What the hell's the matter with you?" Paul growled. "What's makin' you find the world such a great place this morning?"

"Great place, make haste, make space," sang Sofie.

She had received word that her emigration papers were soon to be approved. Sofie was nineteen, two years older than Paul, on the stocky side, and looked like her father.

"Jesus Christ!" Paul shouted. "Will you shut up already?"

"When are you coming down for breakfast?" Emilia called from downstairs.

"Coming, mother, coming. *And she came and saw and conquered,"* sang Sofie, disappearing slowly downstairs.

"Silly bitch," Paul muttered after her.

"And I don't mean to make an exception of you either, Mr. Slowpoke," Emilia called up to Paul.

Samuel was already at the breakfast table, his napkin tucked into his vest.

"Is the world just generally so beautiful or is it your particular experience of it this morning that makes it so lovely?" he inquired good-naturedly of Sofie.

"Both, *Papchen.* Both. Because I'm going to leave soon."

"I'm happy for you," her father said.

"And it could make you happy too if you'd just make up your mind to leave this—dump of a country."

Laura came in with the eggs and coffee. Emilia touched Sofie's arm and threw her a warning look.

"That's one of the reasons I'm leaving," Sofie said under her breath after Laura had left. "You can't even speak your mind in your own home anymore."

"How much longer does Abraham think it'll take for the exit permits to come through?" Samuel inquired.

"A month or two."

Samuel was silent.

"I wish, I wish you people—" Sofie began.

"Just don't start warbling again," Paul interrupted sourly.

"—would reconsider," Sofie finished. Then she snapped at her brother: "Just because you're a sourpuss you don't have to spoil everyone else's fun."

"Fun, man," Paul muttered, screwing his eyes heavenward.

"Yeah, fun, man," Sofie mimicked belligerently. "If you still know what the word means."

"*Kinder, Kinder,*" Emilia interjected. "Why do you fight all the time?"

"He's turning into a misanthrope," Sofie said importantly.

"A what?" Paul said.

"Oh, shut up," Sofie snapped.

"Better anyway than dying of thirst in the middle of the desert," Paul replied aggressively. "I hear there isn't even water where you're going—what country did you say you're going to again?"

This, Paul knew, would infuriate his sister. Sofie leaned forward, deepening the folds thrown across her bosomy breasts by her somewhat tight dress.

"P-a-l-e-s-t-i-n-e," she ejaculated slowly and fiercely. "Where your forebears came from too, believe it or not, Mr. Aryan-looking Jew."

"*Kinder, Kinder,*" Emilia intoned plaintively. "Haven't we got enough problems without you fighting all the time?"

Baron Otto von Hallenberg

Baron Otto von Hallenberg, a tall, erect, slender, Nordicly handsome man, elegantly dressed in a light gray overcoat with hat and leather gloves to match, walked hurriedly through the large entrance hall of his manor.

"Schulman, is the Mercedes ready?" he called to the chauffeur who stood uniformed and ready, cap in hand. "We're driving to Munich right away."

"Will the Baron be home for supper?" inquired a maid trailing a step behind him. "What shall we tell the Baroness?"

"Tell her—" the baron began.

But the baroness herself had already appeared at the top of the stairs. She was a handsome, slightly heavy woman with black hair combed back severely.

"Are you going on business, Otto?" she asked.

It was a habit of many years' standing that the baron went to Munich on Fridays, not counting his other business trips which took him all over Germany in connection with the family's extensive manufacturing and real estate holdings, among which his stud farm was a mere sideline, a hobby more than a business.

"Of course it's business. I wouldn't be going to Munich on a Tuesday otherwise, would I?"

His tone was well-mannered, to others it would have seemed pleasant. But Olga von Hallenberg could pick up the irritable undertone. When people commune in silences, even a whisper can be ear-shattering.

"I'd love to go with you," she said.

Her voice was neither pleading nor reproachful because she was too proud for both.

"Some Saturday soon we'll go to the theater again," the baron said absent-mindedly without looking at his wife. "Better not count on me for supper."

It wasn't clear whether he was addressing the maid or his wife.
Then he was gone.

◆ ◆ ◆

As the Mercedes swung into the main highway to Munich, urged
forward like a sleek race horse by Schulman who crouched with seeming
carelessness behind the wheel, the baron relaxed into the plush upholstery of the elegant vehicle while his thoughts floated free. The physical
movement always induced in him a sense of contentment so that it was
with regret that he would see the first houses of Munich appearing after
half an hour or so. He liked Munich, though he didn't relish crowds. A
stranger's elbow in his ribs, an accidental shoe on his toes—these the
baron experienced like personal affronts, however profusely the offender
might apologize. He didn't even like shaking hands—the deplorable
European habit of acquiring other people's germs, his father used to say.

It wasn't until they approached the Sendlingertorplatz, one of Munich's busiest squares, that his thoughts reverted to the business at hand.
Why had the lawyer called him? What was so urgent that it couldn't
have waited until his regular trip to town—although he welcomed the
extra trip because it gave him a chance to see Ingeborg. He suddenly
felt a lively anticipation at the thought of dining out with her, afterwards
returning to her apartment, and considered the various restaurants they
might visit. He liked to rotate his restaurants—like his women.

He chuckled. That wasn't really true anymore. He had been with
Ingeborg for two and a half years now, the longest time he had been
with any mistress. But time was a funny, elastic thing. One could have
a brief affair and yet remember it a lifetime. Rosanna, for instance. And
even more so, Emilia. How brief that relationship had been and yet how
intense! Even now when he closed his eyes, he could see Emilia's face,
the innocence, the freshness, the little dimples, the clear, trusting eyes.
For years he had remembered her vividly, until she had finally faded
into a nostalgic tug, pleasant rather than painful.

Ingeborg wasn't in that class at all. She was and would always
remain a kind of fling, an agreeable diversion. He knew that and
Ingeborg knew that. Still, she was exciting and could be charming in
bed. The baron smiled. But why did he continue to want women other
than his wife? After all, he was forty-two and should be settling down.
His wife was more handsome, more impressive, and certainly more
intelligent than any of these women. He felt a twinge of guilt. He
should take her to Munich more often. He had felt her silent reproach.

She felt cut off in the country, alone with the three girls.

"Sir?" Schulman was saying.

He was holding the car door open, cap in hand. They had arrived at the lawyer's office.

"Thank you, Schulman," the baron said. He held on to his hat as he stepped out of the car. "I expect to be about an hour."

◆ ◆ ◆

"Would you like a massage, ma'm?" Marianne offered after the baron had left.

The baroness threw her maid a grateful glance, wondering how much of her feelings she divined.

"That's a nice idea, Marianne," she said.

Marianne had a way of saying the right thing at the right time in the right way. It was amazing how insightful this simple, almost uneducated country girl could be, the baroness reflected as she preceded Marianne to her own quarters. The girl had intuitive tact, what one called diplomacy in the world of politics.

They had arrived in the small dressing room adjoining the baroness's bedroom. The maid spread a large beach towel on the narrow couch while the baroness undressed.

"Help me with the bra, Marianne," the baroness said.

Marianne undid the hooks and the baroness lay down on her stomach. As the maid's soft, nimble hands began to massage the tight muscles around her neck, she could feel the tension beginning to melt from her muscles. But what good was that in the end? the baroness thought. You couldn't massage the tension out of the brain; you couldn't massage the sorrow out of the heart. Why had he gone to town today, breaking his usual routine? Had he met a new woman? Or was he still "faithful" to that little sycophant of a tart with her watery blue eyes—what was her name again? But the principal problem wasn't even his unfaithfulness, which he took little trouble to hide, nor the loneliness of country life—the principal problem was that she hadn't given birth to a son, for in this one sorrow lay the beginning and the cause of all the others. They had three girls, aged eight, eleven, and thirteen, who were the joy of her life, but he had wanted above all a male heir to perpetuate his ancient lineage.

She felt Marianne's hands along her spine, the heel of her palms and thumbs performing a little minuet while the four fingers of each hand encased her back.

"A little higher, Marianne," she said.

"Yes, ma'm."

"Do you like massaging me?"

"Yes, ma'm. You have a lovely figure."

"Thank you."

She was on the verge of adding, I wish my husband thought so too but caught herself in time. How long had it been since he had last come to her bedroom—three weeks? four? She couldn't remember. Did he think a woman of thirty-eight was past love-making? But then he had never really understood much about women, for all his vaunted male pride in thinking that he did. Yes, her figure was still good, despite three children, only a little heavy around the stomach. You would think all the riding she did would help more with that.

"It's my stomach," she said. "I should exercise more."

It was with her hysterectomy, six years earlier, that their estrangement had begun. Had it not been for the baron's Catholicism, he might have divorced her, though there was some loyalty and affection left still. But in a Catholic peerage divorce was unthinkable, never mind how many mistresses the man might maintain on the side. That was different from the more relaxed Protestant nobility of the north from which she sprang.

She felt Marianne's fingers on the soft side of her breasts which her position had pushed out sideways. Where did the girl get those immensely gentle, knowing hands? she mused. She suddenly felt herself becoming hot all over and, to her surprise, heard herself emitting a soft moan.

"Have I hurt you, ma'm?" Marianne inquired solicitously.

The baroness sat up abruptly.

"No, Marianne. I'm fine."

Then, with a harshness born of shock and embarrassment, she added rather curtly:

"That will be all for today."

◆ ◆ ◆

"My dear Baron," the lawyer exclaimed, precipitating himself toward the baron with outstretched hands. "It's good to see you. I'm sorry to be the cause of a special trip to town."

Dr. Metzner grasped the baron's hand before he had a chance to remove his gloves.

"Not at all," the baron said graciously. "I'm always delighted to come to town. Munich is such an exhilarating city."

"Ha, ha, ha," the lawyer laughed in his half-hearty, half-theatrical manner. "One wouldn't think so the way you bury yourself on that beautiful estate of yours. Sit down, my dear Baron, sit down."

It was typical of the lawyer to mix a criticism with a compliment. It made it difficult to be offended by him—or to really like him either. The baron took his gloves off and sat down, anticipating with some distaste the handshaking ritual to come upon departure, but it would be rude to keep his gloves on.

"Actually, the matter concerns your wife," Dr. Metzner continued, settling down behind his desk. The light came from behind the lawyer's back, silhouetting his head and hiding his features. The effect made the baron somewhat uncomfortable, as if there was something in the man that needed constant watching. "But I thought it advisable—hm—to discuss it with you first."

"I understand," the baron muttered.

He crossed his legs and lit a cigarillo.

"As you know, ever since the arrest of the Baroness's father and his subsequent unfortunate demise, there have been certain, shall we say, difficulties with the estate that, you will recall, you kindly asked me to take in hand."

The baron nodded with a touch of impatience. Lawyers had this deplorable habit of reiterating well-known facts in their mania for exactness.

"I have now received a decisive communication"—the lawyer drew a letter from a folder on his desk—"and I'm sorry to say it's not very encouraging. The Government takes the position that inasmuch as Freiherr von Wedlingen was, what it terms, an Enemy of the State, certain additional taxes and fees are to be levied against his estate."

"I see," the baron said, making note of the tiny shift in language that gave away so much: As recently as three months ago Dr. Metzner had still spoken of "the Nazis" whenever he referred to the authorities, now it had suddenly become "the Government." He took the letter proffered by the lawyer and read it through carefully. Then he inquired matter-of-factly:

"What can be done about it?"

Dr. Metzner rotated his chair so that his features shifted back into the light, like the moon after a partial eclipse. Curious, thought the baron, how some corpulent people were constantly on the move, as if to exercise in preparation for the next opulent meal.

"Well sir," the lawyer said crisply, "you can appeal the decision in the courts, of course."

Another interesting shift, the baron thought. In the past the lawyer had always spoken in terms of "we." Now it was suddenly "you."

"What portion of the estate are we talking about anyway?" the baron asked.

"That's difficult to say. The taxes and fees depend on the size of the estate. But it may be considerable, considerable. Possibly as much as two thirds."

"Two thirds!" the baron exclaimed. "Why, that's—" He wanted to say expropriation but swallowed the word. "Punishing Enemies of the State is one thing," he said after a moment. "But why do they want to penalize their innocent offspring?"

Dr. Metzner smiled somewhat pained.

"I can't answer that, my dear Baron."

"And what are the chances of winning an appeal?" the baron asked. "Or at least of decreasing the size of the—the taxes."

"That's the crux of the matter, isn't it," the lawyer said with a self-satisfied air, "and the reason why I called you."

He rotated his chair again, disappearing once more into silhouette. The baron suddenly became uncomfortably aware of his own exposure to the light, which fell squarely on his face. No doubt the lawyer had purposely arranged his desk that way, he thought, annoyed.

"Frankly," the lawyer continued, "it all depends on the character of the appellants."

"We are hardly in need of character references," the baron said drily.

"Ha, ha, ha!" the lawyer cackled with forced gaiety. "You hardly are, my dear Baron, you hardly are! But I'm afraid you're missing the point. What I have reference to is the *political* character of the appellants—because, though your wife would technically be the one to appeal, the court would presume you to be the main appellant both by virtue of your status as her husband and your status as the head of one of the oldest and most respected families in the country."

"I'm afraid I *am* missing the point, Dr. Metzner," the baron said with a touch of impatience.

"The point, my dear Baron, is that the political character of the appellant is all-important in cases involving confiscation—I mean, taxation," the lawyer corrected himself quickly, "of property belonging to someone considered antagonistic to the State. The reason is that the Government is understandably reluctant to see property belonging to an Enemy of the State pass into, shall we say, politically indifferent hands. On the other hand, the court will view with much more favor an appeal coming from an outspoken *supporter* of the State."

Why did he keep saying "the State," the baron thought irritably, when

he actually meant the Nazi regime. Was he implying that he was less
devoted to the fatherland than the lawyer, he whose family had served
the country honorably for centuries while the lawyer's forebears were
mere untraceable smudges in history? He suppressed the temptation to
make a point of it and said instead:

"And you deem me to be an insufficiently outspoken supporter?"

"I'm afraid so," Dr. Metzner said with unexpected bluntness, all
smiles now. "Unless you joined the Party since I last had the pleasure
of seeing you, my dear Baron. Have you?"

"No."

"That, my dear Baron"—the lawyer's tone was calculatedly affable as
if he were discussing the most commonplace matter in the world—"is
what I wanted to discuss with you—provided you wish to appeal, of
course. To be candid, your appeal doesn't stand a ghost of a chance
without a more decisive act of friendliness on your part, if you get my
meaning. Not that you are unfriendly, don't misunderstand me," he
added quickly, "but your chances need improving, and the best way to
improve them is to join the Nazi Party. In fact, if you permit me to say
so as an old acquaintance, even without this particular matter it would
altogether rebound to your benefit to join the Party, my dear Baron."
He paused and then added with emphasis: "I have."

"My family has never been in the habit of joining a cause for mere
personal advantage," the baron said stiffly.

But he regretted his words at once. What need was there to reveal his
feelings to this man, or to any man, for that matter? A forced smile
spread on the lawyer's face, and a cold silence settled between them.
Presently the baron got up. The lawyer jumped up as well.

"No offense meant, my dear Baron," he exclaimed, rounding the desk.
"A lawyer may be forgiven if he now and then tries to counsel an old
client in matters not strictly in his purview—for his own good."

"Thank you, Dr. Metzner," the baron said drily as he moved toward
the door. "I'll be in touch with you about the appeal after discussing it
with my wife."

"Whatever your decision, it has been a pleasure to be of service to
you," the lawyer said obsequiously, accompanying the baron to the door
where he extended his hand. "As always, my dear Baron."

◆ ◆ ◆

A week went by and still the baron had not discussed the appeal with
his wife, for he was intensely conflicted about the inheritance. On the

one hand, he was too proud to let his wife know that he wasn't prepared, despite his wealth, to relinquish her inheritance without a fight. On the other hand, there was the issue of joining the Nazi Party.

As far as he was concerned, the Nazis were a presumptious, pushy, ill-bred rabble, mere upstarts with whom he had promised himself not to tangle. It wasn't even their goals that he found so objectionable as the vulgar, rabble-rousing way they went about achieving them. Take the problem of the Jews, for instance. Yes, the Jews were a foreign people who should go back where they came from, wherever that was. But that didn't justify the way they were being treated. What needed to be done could be accomplished in an orderly, life-and-property-protecting manner, even if some expropriation were in order.

The truth was that the baron was a conservative in the truest sense of the word: to conserve, protect, perpetuate. He could forgive many things but not destructiveness and ill manners, because for him manners were not mere superficial social conventions but the gateway to a person's character, the window to his soul. One could dress up words, one could even dissemble feelings, but one could not disguise these subtle stitchings of one's soul.

Finally, there was also the matter of Freiherr von Wedlingen's character. His wife's father had always touched a deep, visceral chord of antipathy in him, so that the prospect of fighting for the man's property was distasteful. The Freiherr's boisterous, boastful bravado and heavy-handed sense of humor had always seemed distressingly boorish to him, being a reserved man himself. When the Freiherr was arrested and committed to a concentration camp in late 1935, he had felt a pinch of secret, malicious satisfaction, though he didn't approve of the imprisonment, of course.

"If he had just kept his mouth shut," he had said to his wife at the time. "What need is there for such empty bravado?"

"Bravado, if my memory doesn't fail me, my dear Otto, means false or pretended courage," the baroness had replied tartly. "Father wasn't awarded a medal for bravery in the Great War for nothing, you know."

"I hope not," the baron couldn't help commenting with a touch of sarcasm.

In the baron's harsh opinion, it was pure and simple garrulousness, not some forbidden political activity, that had brought the Freiherr to a concentration camp. He had blabbed without discretion, holding forth to all and sundry, needling and boasting and swaggering, braggart that he was, until the Nazis, exasperated finally by his impudent stings after more than one warning, indeed with more forbearance than the baron would have given them credit for, finally put away the old, high-living, merry-making braggart who never thought that they would touch a bearer of a medal of honor and kept shouting impertinent insults even as he was being unceremoniously hauled away.

The Freiherr's death was another matter. The Freiherr had been only fifty-nine and until then in the best of health. Nine months after his imprisonment he was suddenly discharged. It never became entirely clear what had happened, except that he had received a severe beating, including several blows on the head, which had brought on complications leading to his discharge. The Freiherr himself had looked upon the beating as a stroke of good fortune since it had brought about his release, but ever since then he had suffered from severe migraines. Then, one morning, two months after his discharge, he had had a cerebral hemorrhage, and before he could be got to the hospital, he had been dead.

A week went by and still the baron kept using one excuse after another to postpone the inevitable discussion with his wife. Finally, one evening after supper, he asked her to his study. He led the way, politely opening the door, and she passed inside and sat down on the sofa in front of the large fireplace, calm, elegant, and self-possessed, her black hair pulled smoothly back, her dark eyes resting questioningly on him, her sensuous lips parted slightly as if about to open for a kiss. But the baron didn't connect her mouth with kissing anymore. Instead, it reminded him of her tendency to drink, which the baroness did rather more of late than she admitted even to herself. It did not endear her to him, much as he liked to bolster and refine his own meals with a good bottle of wine.

He had remained standing in front of the fireplace.

"Would you like something to drink?" he inquired, though at once reproaching himself for the offer.

"Why yes, that would be nice," the baroness said. "A Benedictine, please."

As he went to the bar and poured her a glass of the liqueur and himself a cognac, his wife absorbed the room into herself, this world which she would no more have entered without his permission than she would have rummaged through his drawer of underwear—an apt comparison considering that the baron regarded his study to be as intimate a part of himself.

Although he called it his study, suggesting an intimate room, it was actually a very large room. But it retained an air of intimacy because of the many areas and rooms-within-rooms into which it was divided: here a sitting area encircling the large fireplace; by the huge picture window facing out into the rose garden, a large desk flanked by filing cabinets; in another corner, a reading area surrounded by high, old-fashioned bookshelves; in yet another corner, a small bar. The baron always entered the room with a sense of reverence, for here was spread out along the walls the illustrious history of his ancestry: somber, majestic men dauntlessly carrying heavy duties of state, their portraits hanging amidst ancient swords and rifles and silent, antlered heads of animal trophies and, interspersed through it all, framed letters of praise and elevation written by kings and ministers to his forebears, along with the hundred and one other mementoes accumulated over generations of distinguished service. Yes, here lay the heartbeat of what he and his ancestry stood for, a tradition which he had the duty and honor to preserve, perpetuate, and defend.

He brought the glasses back to the sofa and sat down in one of the armchairs and for some moments they indulged in small talk while the baroness sipped her liqueur, feeling the glow spreading pleasantly through her body. Still the baron hesitated until a silence finally settled between them. Suddenly the baroness laughed.

"It seems to be a difficult matter, Otto."

He looked up from his glass and gave a forced smile, experiencing her laughter as if a stranger had suddenly fingered him familiarly. She had this precipitous, unsettling, deep-throated laughter that sometimes sounded more like a growl.

"I realize my hesitation must seem strange to you, Olga, but I hesitate because I know the subject to be painful for you."

"Oh?"

"It involves your father—and your inheritance."

"I see."

"You will recall my unexpected trip to town last week. Dr. Metzner called and asked to see me."

"He should have asked me to come along too," the baroness interjected, piqued. "It is my inheritance, isn't it?"

"He called," the baron continued, sidestepping the question, "because he had received word that . . . but let me show you the letter."

He got up and fetched the letter from his desk while the baroness drained her glass. The warm, pleasant glow had suddenly given way to a heavy feeling.

"Would you mind pouring me another?" she asked when he returned.

"Please give this matter your fullest attention, Olga," he said with a touch of reproach, handing her the letter.

"Don't worry, I won't overindulge," she replied with a mixture of banter and irritation.

He went to pour her another without answering, while the baroness sat with the letter on her lap as if needing some moments of silence and concentration before plunging into it. Finally she took up the letter and began to read. But in a moment she put it down again and exclaimed:

"The nerve! To call papa an Enemy of the State! He received the *Ritterkreuz* in the Great War and they have the gall to lecture him about patriotism!"

"It can hardly be a lecture, Olga, since your father is dead."

"Yes," she exclaimed heatedly, "killed by them! murdered by them!"

How aggressive she had become of late, especially when drinking, the baron thought. That's why he didn't want her to drink.

"Olga, there's no use fighting old battles over and over. And do lower your voice, please. There's no need for the servants to hear. Anyway, that's not the issue. Bravado isn't going to get us anywhere—"

"Bravado!" she interrupted, the word only serving to ignite old arguments. "Are you implying—"

"I'm not implying anything!" he cut her short, his annoyance plainly showing through for the first time. "Let's not get into all that again. It's one area where we just don't see eye to eye."

"Only *one* area?"

The baron looked at her, brought up short by her sarcasm. Why did she have to rip things open instead of letting them rest? He looked out of the window, wishing that he could get away.

"Go ahead," the baroness muttered.

"What?"

"Run away."

It was her most galling reproach, that he liked to bury his head in the sand. How well she read him still, had always read him. If anything, their estrangement had only sharpened that ability. With a sinking feeling, he felt himself drawn back into ancient arguments. He pulled himself together.

"Olga, what's the use of all this? We have a decision to make. At least read the letter first."

She quickly finished the letter.

"The gangsters!" she exploded. "Didn't they do enough to him when he was alive? Now they want to take away his property too. But I won't let them!"

"The question is: How do you propose to stop them?"

The baroness was silent for some moments.

"Don't we know someone with influence? These things always get fixed by pulling some wires behind the scenes."

The idea did not appeal to the baron. Begging for favors or special intercessions went against his grain. The von Hallenbergs had never needed to do that. But he had to admit that the idea had merit.

"Martin Hammerschmidt maybe. He has a lot of contacts," he said. "Or Werner, of course. He's offered his help more than once."

Werner Strapp was an old boarding school friend of the baron's whom the baroness had always disliked for his brashness even before he joined the SS. He was a major or colonel by now. She had never been able to understand her husband's inexplicable fondness for the man.

"He'll only try to get you to join the Nazis," she said. "As he's been trying since 1930."

"Funny you should say that," the baron said, glad that she had provided an opening. "Because the lawyer suggested the same thing."

The baroness bristled. "He's another mealy-mouthed . . . !" She swallowed the word.

"Maybe it wouldn't be such a bad idea, Olga."

"Otto, how can you say that?" she cried reproachfully.

"I know. I don't relish the idea either," the baron agreed, his own frustration pouring out. For the first time, he felt a sense of solidarity with his wife. One thing they had always shared was a distaste for the Nazis, much as their reasons differed. "But Metzner feels our position is pretty hopeless because I'm not a good, solid prop of the National Socialist regime."

"I hope you told him to go to hell!"

"I told him I wasn't in the habit of joining causes from mere motives of personal gain."

The baroness stared out of the window. A look of sadness had come over her face.

"What's become of our country, Otto? Our judiciary used to be the fairest, the most impeccably honest in the world. It's become an ugly country to live in," she murmured, "to raise children in."

The baron remained silent, torn between his own distaste for the Nazis and disapproval of his wife's sweeping condemnation. Finally he said:

"The Nazis are a passing phenomenon, Olga. Germany endures."

"Everything is a passing phenomenon. But while it lasts . . . . " She made a vague gesture.

"There's no use theorizing, Olga. We're facing a concrete situation and have to come to a decision. What do you propose to do? Bear in mind that our chances of winning an appeal without my joining the Party are, according to Metzner, very poor. We might wind up merely throwing good money after bad."

"We can take the legal costs out of what I get."

"That's not the point," the baron said tartly. "I'm not expecting you to carry the costs."

"Of course you won't join the Nazis just to win an appeal!" the baroness exclaimed.

"We haven't yet decided to appeal."

"But we are going to appeal!" she cried heatedly. "Do you think I'm going to let them have a penny of papa's money if I can help it?"

"As a matter of principle, eh?" the baron muttered.

But he felt a sense of relief at her decision.

"I'll let Metzner know in the morning," he said presently.

Paul

They were as yet moving at a distance, so distant they might have been just any group of five boys on the way home from school, except that there was no horseplay among them and there was a grim quality in the way they advanced behind Paul. Paul recognized two boys from an upper class. The other three were strangers to him.

He turned a corner and again a corner and yet again a corner, but the boys kept right on behind him as if he were towing them behind on an invisible chain. No, there could be no doubt about it anymore. They were after him. He could continue to walk around the busy streets of town until they grew tired of following him. Or he could jump on a streetcar as it began to move away. But he wouldn't run away. He had never run in his life and he wouldn't now. He could defend himself. They wouldn't all jump him at once but would choose the strongest among them. Let them. He was a good fighter, one of the best in school.

Pedestrians were beginning to thin out as he approached the Isar River and began to ascend on the other side through a strip of park running along the river. If he could reach the Maria-Theresia-Strasse running parallel to the river higher up, he would be safe. He listened intently for footsteps and sneaked a look behind, feeling tempted to accelerate his pace but restrained himself.

Suddenly he heard rapid footsteps behind him.

He stopped and turned around as the five boys surrounded him. A tall boy whom he didn't know stepped forward. He was taller and more heavily built than Paul.

"So you're a dirty Jew," he said tauntingly.

"Fuck you," Paul flung back aggressively. "My mother's as Aryan as yours."

"Then she's a dirty whore spreadin' her legs for a dirty Jew."

Paul had heard that one before and didn't react. They were circling each other warily now like gladiators. Presently the boy lunged forward, and Paul could feel his strong arm tightening around his neck. He tried to break loose but couldn't.

"Look at the dirty Jew! His face is turning as red as a beet! He's gonna croak!" the boys jeered.

Finally Paul managed to maneuver one leg behind his opponent's legs so that both toppled to the ground. Paul was on top now and got the boy from behind in a full nelson. Failing to free himself, the boy suddenly grabbed Paul by the testicles and squeezed hard. Paul cried out in pain and kicked him with his knee.

"He's fighting unfair!" the boys cried. "Get the dirty Jew! The filthy bastard!"

One of the boys kicked Paul hard from behind, loosening his hold so that his opponent was able to free himself and jump up. So did Paul.

"Kick me, will you!" the boy panted. "You'll regret that, filthy Jew!"

He rushed forward and threw his full weight against Paul. As Paul staggered back, he stepped on the foot of a boy who howled and punched him and shoved him on to another boy who punched him in his turn and shoved him on. Paul now found himself tossed around the tight circle of boys, each of whom added another blow.

But by then Paul no longer fought back. He had covered his face with his arms to shield himself, his nose bleeding, his eyes rapidly swelling shut, tears blurring his vision not on account of the pain, which was irrelevant for the moment, but because of the unfairness and injustice of it all.

♦ ◆ ♦

"What happened to you?" Sofie cried, half sarcastically.

She thought that Paul had got into another scrape. Her exclamation brought Emilia out of the kitchen.

"*Junge!,*" she cried in alarm. "What happened to you?"

Paul was standing in the middle of the living room, his arms dangling by his sides, his back a little stooped, not like an old man who lacks the strength to keep it straight but like a young man who lacks the desire to, which is worse.

"They jumped me."

"Who jumped you?"

"Boys. Older boys. Five of them."

"Five boys? For what reason? Why?"

"Because he's a Jew, that's why!" Sofie interjected.

"Five boys don't attack a single boy without a reason," Emilia insisted.

"Nazi pigs do!" Sofie exclaimed, for once on Paul's side.

"They followed me halfway across town waiting for a chance to jump me."

Emilia began to bustle about, avoiding the deeper issue as she marched Paul to the bathroom.

"Always getting into fights," she grumbled while she dabbed at his cuts and bruises with a wad of iodine. It was easier to deny the reality by blaming Paul. "You know how papa hates fighting. He isn't going to be pleased with you at all."

"But I didn't do anything!" Paul exclaimed. "How can you defend them? Ouch!" he yelled, reacting to the iodine.

"Yeah, he did something: He did being a Jew," Sofie sneered.

She was leaning against the door of the bathroom.

"I'm not even a Jew," Paul said angrily. "And I belong here just as much as they do. Is it my fault father is a Jew?"

"Boy, you're the dregs," Sofie exclaimed contemptuously.

She turned around and walked away.

"You should be proud of your father," Emilia said reprovingly. "He's a fine man."

At the dinner table Samuel wanted to know what had happened. Paul related the incident again.

"And I didn't do anything to them," Paul said defensively. "I didn't provoke them."

"I'm sure you didn't," Samuel said reassuringly.

"Mama acts as if it was my fault."

"You don't have to do anything," Sofie said bitterly. "Being a Jew is quite enough, thank you. Boy, if you people just wouldn't be so dense about Palestine."

"Go to hell with your Palestine!" Paul snapped. "We belong here."

"Sure, like a goiter on a neck."

"*Kinder*, please," Emilia admonished.

After dinner, Samuel invited Paul to the library for a talk. Sitting back in his leather armchair, which made a sighing sound as he settled into it, Samuel studied his son. His black eye made his face look lopsided and the three bandaids tilting at haphazard angles made him appear slightly ridiculous. For a brief moment a smile wanted to break through the basic grimness Samuel felt. Such fair skin and light hair and he gets beaten up as a Jew! He felt a surge of compassion for the boy, as if his fair skin sharpened the injustice of being beaten up as a Jew, a thought that annoyed him in another moment because of its unspoken implication that looking more like a Jew would have justified the beating.

"None of us has done anything, Paul," he said, taking up the thread of the conversation again. "That's the tragedy. And that's why I keep asking you to take your studies more seriously," he continued. "As I've said so often, knowledge is power."

But even as he said it he wondered, power to do what? to withstand the injustice of an insane world?

Paul shifted uneasily in his chair.

"What has knowledge to do with it?" he said. "It all boils down to force."

He felt disappointed and vaguely betrayed. They didn't have much to say to each other anymore but was that all his father could say to him, to grind his old saws even now?

"Force breeds force," Samuel replied. "That has never solved anything."

"So what should I have done?" Paul bristled. "Lain down and let them beat me up?"

Samuel could feel the boy's outrage, which made him retreat into his own bafflement. The question went straight to the heart of the eternal dilemma of violence. He thought he had known the answer—that rational, temperate, well-intentioned communication could hurdle all differences between men of good will because man was a rational creature, not a snarling brute of an animal. He had passionately believed this all his life, but somehow he no longer trusted it now.

"I grant you it's a difficult question," Samuel murmured, his voice trailing off. "I wish I knew the answer . . . ."

◆ ◆ ◆

For Samuel the bitterest thing was to know that he was the cause of it all; not a legitimate cause, of course, not a cause in a more mature society and in a saner world, but that didn't change the bitter truth. He could not shake the thought that Paul was being punished in the most literal sense for the "sin" of his father. He must hate me, Samuel thought one day with a shock. And then an even more shocking thought flashed through his mind: And Emilia too! They must all hate me! Only Sofie had grown closer and she was leaving. How easily his feelings flowed toward her, while with Emilia and Paul everything was becoming more and more tangled and unwieldy.

The relationship between father and son had continued to deteriorate, becoming increasingly strained and finally antagonistic as Paul found himself in a reality that overwhelmed him, while Samuel at least had the mental and emotional armament of his education and maturity.

Paul—tall, strapping, Aryan-looking, extroverted, popularity-hungry Paul—had no such defenses.

The hidden source of Paul's feelings exploded into the open one day at the dinner table at the end of a long discussion about racial purity. Samuel argued that it was a false concept lacking any scientific basis, while Paul obstinately threw in one Nazi argument after another until Samuel, shaking with exasperation, finally fetched a book from the library and put it on the table.

"There, read that, Paul! It's by a Nobel prize-winning scientist of international reputation! It'll tell you how much purity there is in our blood!"

"I don't care about your books!" Paul cried, pushing the book away. "I don't care what they say! You're a Jew, so you can't help being biased! But one can be big enough to admit others are right even if that leaves one out in the cold! Maybe Germany *is* better off without Jews!"

Samuel sank back in his chair, struck silent, while Paul jumped up and ran out of the room. Emilia sat mutely next to him, torn between sympathy for her husband and her own secret knowledge.

"*Männchen*," she murmured, putting her hand on his. "*Männchen* . . . ."

It was the last time Samuel attempted to discuss anything of the sort with Paul. Their coolness now turned into outright alienation.

◆ ◆ ◆

Paul's estrangement from his father brought him closer to his mother. Emilia had always doted on the boy, and these feelings were now compounded by her own sense of guilt and by Sofie's emigration, which had meanwhile materialized. The family's changed fortunes also increased their closeness because it brought with it certain practical consequences.

Laura had been discharged by Emilia with mixed feelings of regret and relief; various luxuries had been sacrificed—the car had been the most painful—and some belt-tightening had become necessary all around. In fact Emilia now had to figure her expenses with an entirely unaccustomed degree of exactness, and not only did the cooking now, which she had always done, but the shopping and house cleaning as well. Even Sofie was no longer there to help.

One day, on coming home from school, Paul found himself walking behind a perspiring woman who was struggling with a load of shopping bags that were obviously much too heavy for her. Suddenly, on coming abreast of her, he recognized that it was his mother!

"Mama!" he cried. "Let me help you. Why are you carrying such heavy stuff?"

"Did you think our meals walked into the house on their own?" Emilia responded with a rueful smile.

But she readily surrendered her load, happy to be helped and even happier that he recognized the situation.

"Why didn't you ask me to help?" he said reproachfully. "I can do the shopping."

"You?" she said dubiously. "Anyway it's nice of you to offer."

But he insisted. Paul was like that. Once he made up his mind that something was right, he stuck stubbornly by his guns. Honor and loyalty and fairness were important to him, and once he gave his word, nothing could induce him to break it.

What they worked out was that henceforth Paul would buy all the heavy, bulky supplies on his way home from school.

♦ ◆ ♦

Paul's loneliness had made him draw closer to yet another person: Herbert, the classmate with the slight limp whose sneering attitude had earned him several beatings from the Nazis.

The first time it happened, he sported his black eye and swollen face almost proudly.

"Guess what happened to me," he said to Paul.

"What?"

"The Hitler Youth bastards beat me up."

"I can see that. But why?"

"Why, nothin'!" Herbert trumpeted. "I made a comment about the Hitler salute, that's all."

"What did you say?"

Herbert had only been waiting to tell him.

"That pretty soon their arms are gonna get stiff from all their salutin', and what were they gonna use then to jerk off!"

"Jesus, Herbert, you didn't say that!"

"Sure did," Herbert replied proudly.

Herbert thrived on misfortune. It was for him a kind of badge, proof positive that the world was as rotten as he claimed it to be—or rather, as he expected it to treat him.

After a second time, however, even Herbert began to pipe down. It was a severe beating that made him limp about in earnest for a couple of weeks. It had been administered by two SS men who warned him that next time he'd get a *real* beating if he didn't shut up.

"Man, the walls are gettin' to have ears nowadays, I tell you," was all Herbert would say about it to Paul.

After that he kept his mouth shut, except toward Paul, whom he considered safe and nonthreatening because he was a half-Jew. Not because Herbert liked Jews—far from it—but because it made Paul an outcast like himself. What was more, Paul was an outcast for life, by definition, absolutely and irrevocably, and thus was unable to change course and reject, abandon, or betray him—and that was of supreme importance to Herbert.

Paul discovered his friend's true feelings toward Jews one day when he asked him how he thought Jews were different.

"Their pricks are different," Herbert said.

"People don't run around with their pricks hanging out," Paul objected. "And what about Jewish women?"

"Jews are smelly and money grubbers, and they're out to do Germany in."

"Do you really believe that?"

"Sure, I believe that. Besides, they don't belong here."

"Why shouldn't they belong here just as much as you if they were born here?"

Herbert shrugged. "They just don't."

"Tell me, Herbert," Paul persisted. "Why do you associate with me if you believe all that?"

Herbert laughed.

"I don't think of you as a Jew. They could stick you in the *Leibstandarte Adolf Hitler** and you'd never stand out."

◆ ◆ ◆

Paul had begun to frequent the Hoffer home, usually after school since the Hoffers lived but a short detour from his own way home. Mrs. Hoffer was a bluff, straightforward, hearty woman who had no use for anti-Semitism, in contrast to her husband, a burly, rather bitter factory foreman who was rarely at home when Paul visited. It was a noisy

---

* An elite Nazi SS unit composed of particularly Aryan-looking men.

household, with the parents barking at each other or, in unison, at the children, of whom there were five (Herbert was the oldest), which kept them forever on the brink of poverty, a circumstance Mrs. Hoffer very much resented.

Paul liked Mrs. Hoffer and was grateful to her for making him feel at home, almost the only home where he was still welcome; but there soon emerged another reason for his steady visits: a sister of Herbert's named Erika.

Erika was fifteen, a girl whose rapid blooming had left her with an array of features that didn't quite fit together yet. Her breasts had blossomed disproportionately while her legs were still girlish and stringy; her eyes had the shy, frightened look of a child, while the rest of her face, and especially her lips, had curved out sensuously. But Paul was blind to this admixture: to him she was the loveliest girl in the world!

Erika was rather shy, in contrast to her brash brother, and, in the presence of this tall, handsome young man, quite ill at ease, although no more so than Paul. Both were so ill at ease, in fact, that for some time neither realized how uneasy and infatuated the other was. It was Mrs. Hoffer who unwittingly broke the impasse with a teasing remark that made Erika blush fiercely and sink into a flustered silence, which suddenly made Paul realize that his own tongue-tied infatuation was being reciprocated by the girl. When their eyes met soon after, they did not hasten on but lingered for a moment for the first time.

After that, Paul came almost daily after school. Usually Erika was already at home waiting anxiously for Paul behind a thin disguise of nervous activity.

Mrs. Hoffer had seen what was happening to the two young people even before they had properly realized it themselves. Generous and outspoken, of a faded prettiness, somewhat malodorous from garlic and onions that lodged in her hair and clothes and indeed in the whole apartment after years of steady use, she liked the tall, handsome, rather shy boy and threw no obstacles in the way of their courtship. On the contrary, she enjoyed it vicariously because it replaced the courtship she had never had by becoming pregnant five months after meeting her husband, whereupon they had rushed into marriage.

Erika was, like Paul, of an athletic disposition. She loved to hike, to bike, to climb—in fact, most of the things Herbert did not like to do or could not do very well on account of his limp. But he would tag along, and for a while they formed a harmonious threesome. Paul and Erika were as yet too shy to want to be alone. How much easier to touch each other under the guise of an activity or game that permitted no follow-up!

As spring veered toward summer, however, their local excursions through the English Garden and along the Isar River gradually lengthened and turned into daylong bicycle trips into the surrounding countryside. Finally one weekend they received permission from their parents to make an overnight camping trip into the Bavarian Alps and sat talking by the campfire far into the night. When Herbert finally fell asleep, Paul and Erika walked to a ledge overlooking the valley, and there Erika put her head on Paul's lap and they kissed for the first time. And then they continued kissing and caressing without talking anymore at all.

It was the first sexual encounter for both and kissing and caressing were quite enough.

◆ ◆ ◆

After that, Paul and Erika's love (to use the term they used to describe their feelings) prospered as it unfolded with intense glances and touchings fraught with untold meanings and longings.

Their excursions into the country now became more frequent, encouraged by both families, though for different reasons. Emilia was happy that the frequent contacts with the Hoffers, which she might have frowned on in other times, took Paul's mind off his ostracism, while for Mrs. Hoffer their courtship had become a frankly vicarious experience. Let the girl have some fun, she thought, she had never had any; as long as she took care of herself. To this end, she took aside Erika, who looked up to her mother and was quite dependent on her, and instructed her in some rudiments of birth control which was, considering the time, quite a brave and unconventional thing to do. The deep blush on Erika's face, coupled with her confusion, convinced Mrs. Hoffer that she had reached her daughter before anything had happened, except in the girl's steaming imagination.

So the night arrived, a cloudless, starry summer night, when Erika and Paul found themselves bedded down together in a vast open field, alone for the first time because at the last moment Herbert had developed a mean sore throat and couldn't come along, their bicycles leaning intimately together, silhouetted against the mountain range toward which they were cycling, and there they finally came together.

If only well-meaning, vicarious-living Mrs. Hoffer had known how copiously and uncontrollably Paul flowed into Erika that night under the starry, glorious sky—fortunately without mishap!

◆ ◆ ◆

The relationship with Erika now dominated Paul's life completely. From one tryst to the next he would daydream and fantasize about her: How they would meet in their secret hiding place along the Isar River where they had hacked out a place for themselves in the dense underbrush, there to bed down trembling amidst the fragrant leaves; how their mutual sexual explorations were becoming ever more courageous and exciting (oh, if people only knew how exquisite their sexual encounters were!), and from there his fantasies would kick free: to next summer's planned bicycle trip through Austria, Switzerland, and maybe Italy, to years hence when, miraculously rich, they would travel to exotic places like South America or the Caribbean . . . oh, there was no end to what they would do!

The only thing Paul never fantasized about, interestingly enough, was getting married.

Meanwhile Erika was maturing and rounding out incredibly. From an awkward half-woman, she had blossomed into a lovely, fresh, bursting young woman who attracted admiring, jealous glances wherever she went.

"Why do people *stare* so?" she would whisper with a delightful mixture of naive shyness, cocky pride, and baffled wonderment that she, who had not so long ago stood despairingly in front of her mirror wondering whether she would ever grow into a mature woman, was all at once attracting so much admiring attention.

"Why?" Paul would whisper back lustily. "Because you're beautiful, that's why!"

"Me?" Erika would giggle, pleased and incredulous at the same time.

"Yes," he would declare solemnly. "You *are* beautiful."

It was a heartfelt tribute that Paul never tired giving, mixed as it was with honest admiration and boastful self-congratulation that so lovely a girl had deigned to give herself to him.

◆ ◆ ◆

Meanwhile Emilia was becoming more and more preoccupied with her son. The indignities heaped on her husband were awful, but the indignities heaped on Paul made Emilia suffer even more. For her husband was an adult, after all, and he *was* a Jew so that the persecution, dreadful as it was, was at least directed toward the right person. But Paul—Paul was innocent!

As for Samuel, despite the buffeting that he was receiving at the hands of his wife and son, from his declining business, and from the virulent anti-Semitism spreading throughout the country—despite all these, he struggled to stand by his humanistic values, be they ever so much trampled underfoot by others, and to maintain some sort of equanimity. He couldn't shout his beliefs from the rooftops, he couldn't shout them anywhere, in fact. But the crucial thing was to hold on to them as best one could, even if one merely whispered them in one's heart. For what kind of response could a Jew, or any human being, for that matter, make to brute force without jeopardizing the very values for which one was making the stand in the first place?

It was Samuel's way of saying No to what was happening, for he was not a man of action, nor did he pretend to be.

To Join or Not to Join

The baron's thoughts and feelings now collided in anxious conflict around the question of joining the Nazi Party. When he had called Dr. Metzner to tell him to proceed with the appeal, the lawyer had inquired:

"Have you given some more thought to the matter of your—hm, political credentials?"

The baron knew well enough what he was referring to but replied:

"What credentials?"

"The matter of joining the Party."

"I've given it some thought. But I've decided to wait."

"Wait!" the lawyer exclaimed with unexpected impatience. He reined himself in. "The court won't reverse itself once a verdict has been reached. I'm sure you understand that."

"I do," the baron replied tartly.

"I can't impress on you sufficiently the importance of what I'm suggesting," the lawyer said once more before hanging up.

The fact was that joining the Nazi Party was distasteful to the baron. True, Germany was steadily becoming more powerful—no patriotic German could remain indifferent to that. But that didn't mean one needed to become a bedfellow of the Nazis, who were and would always remain an upstart, vulgar rabble, however much they might deck themselves out in assumed finery.

The baron did not view himself as a politically minded man and considered politics the excrescence of a nation's life. But the inheritance had suddenly moved the Nazis into his front parlor, so to speak, where he needed to deal with them.

There were two ways of proceeding with the appeal: He could join the Nazi Party or he could try to get some person of influence to pull some wires behind the scenes, an approach which repelled the baron. Still, it was the lesser of two evils. But whom did he know who had sufficient influence? He had always liked and admired Werner Strapp, his former classmate, but the thought of asking an SS officer for a favor was distasteful. The other person who seemed to have excellent contacts was Martin Hammerschmidt. He would visit him, he decided, on his next trip to Berlin.

Martin Hammerschmidt was the owner and director of the *Hammerschmidt Schuhwerke, A.G.,* one of Europe's larger shoe manufacturing concerns. The baron had originally met him through a business loan and still had dealings with him from time to time, which, indeed, was the professed reason for his visit.

Martin Hammerschmidt lived with his wife and two children in an impressive villa on a knoll overlooking Erfurt, a pleasant town in Central Germany. He was a handsome, well-groomed, immaculately dressed man in his late forties, who displayed an air of wealth without flaunting it. Truly rich people had no need to advertise their wealth, the baron liked to say.

The two men settled down with cigars and brandies after dinner in the lavish living room.

"Well, and how is business these days, Martin?" the baron inquired jovially.

"Couldn't be better, Otto. In fact, if anything worries me, it's that business is almost too good."

"What a pleasant worry," the baron smiled. "But why does that worry you?"

"Because more and more of my shoe production is going to the Armed Forces. You know, they say an army travels on its stomach. But it travels on its feet as well." Martin blew a smoke ring and followed it pensively. "Do you think we'll have war, Otto?"

"I don't think anyone wants to push it that far," the baron replied noncommittally.

"The Nazis have some good ideas," Martin continued thoughtfully. "But I sometimes wonder whether Germany couldn't regain its rightful place in a less—strident manner."

"Hitler's *modus operandi* is at times a bit unsettling, isn't it?" the baron chuckled pleasantly.

He wasn't going to voice his real opinions. What did he really know about Martin Hammerschmidt? That he was a genial host, an engaging conversationalist, and a charming man, absolutely trustworthy in business affairs, but he knew nothing about his political convictions. For all he knew he was a staunch member of the Nazi Party. He certainly seemed to have important friends and to hobnob with highly placed officials.

It wasn't until late in the evening, when both men were feeling mellow, that the baron finally broached the real reason for his visit.

"You seem to have influential contacts all over the country, Martin," he ventured.

"Not all over the country. Mostly in Berlin. Can I help it that everyone wants shoes—especially the Nazis?" Martin laughed. "Besides, my wife loves to give parties."

"Did you happen to know any influential people in the Ministry of Justice who are looking for shoes?" the baron laughed.

Martin thought for a moment.

"Not any more. I used to know someone close to the minister but he retired last year and promptly died. But why do you ask?"

"Oh, nothing," the baron said lightly. "We're involved in a little unpleasantness, that's all. But it's nothing of consequence. I just thought I'd ask."

◆ ◆ ◆

The week he visited Martin Hammerschmidt, the baron missed his weekly trip to Munich. When he called Ingeborg the following week, he noticed at once that she was in a "difficult" mood.

"At your command, *Herr Baron*," she snapped, parodying a rookie facing a general. "I'll snap to obedient attention the minute *Herr Baron* arrives."

He laughed embarrassedly. Scenes of any kind embarrassed him. One had to discipline one's emotions and not let them run wild.

"Really, my dear Ingeborg," he said to her later that evening, "just because I don't come to town for a week is no reason for you to carry on so. I do have other obligations, you know."

"You don't have to rub it in," she said aloofly.

The baron didn't like Ingeborg's periodic rebellions, as he called them, when she would deliver two-edged allusions loaded with hidden reproaches. He liked his women well behaved. He had to chuckle. Well behaved—that was hardly an appropriate description of Ingeborg. Yet, when all was said and done, Ingeborg interested him precisely because she was outspoken, impulsive, spontaneous—and inconsistent.

"Consistency—what's that?" she would say with a straight face when the baron tried to point out her inconsistencies. But a moment later she would nudge him playfully: "Life is like that, Ottchen. All jumbled up. It's not my fault."

The baron had met Ingeborg, a divorcee, at a *Faschingsball* where she had been dressed up stunningly as a fairy queen. He had been attracted to her at once. She was pretty, with a taut, slim figure, in contrast to his wife who was beginning to put on some weight. But then Ingeborg was only twenty-nine and had had only one child, a seven-year-old girl.

Sometimes the baron toyed with the idea of making Ingeborg pregnant in the hope that she would give birth to a son whom he could then raise as his own. He trusted himself to be able to get his wife to accept such an arrangement—for that matter, he wasn't sure that he would give her any choice. But when he had tentatively broached the subject on two or three occasions, Ingeborg had stated categorically:

"No more children for me. Not with a husband and certainly not without one."

"But what if you wouldn't have to raise the child?" the baron had ventured.

"A woman who gives up her children is a monster!" Ingeborg had pronounced with conviction and finality.

Actually, though she grumbled about it at times, Ingeborg liked the freedom their once-a-week relationship gave her and was even rather faithful and committed to the baron, although he was the last one to whom she would have admitted it. She would have preferred to have been known as a virtuous woman, but, since this wasn't feasible, it was as well to be the mistress of as notable a personage as possible.

◆ ◆ ◆

Several weeks passed and there was no further word about the appeal. The baron contacted Dr. Metzner several times, so much so that impatience began to ooze through the lawyer's outwardly obsequious manner.

"These matters take time, my dear Baron."

"How much time?"

"I wish I knew. Six months—nine months—a year? It all depends on the larger picture, if you know what I mean. Have you had a chance to think over what we've been discussing?"

"Yes. But I'm afraid the answer is still no."

"A pity, my dear Baron. A pity," the lawyer said coldly.

The larger picture, the baron reflected. Yes, it all depended on the larger picture. But the larger picture had nothing to do with the Nazis. It had to do with the soul of Germany, with Germany the *Vaterland*, not with the Nazis, who were a passing phenomenon. For him nothing as fleeting as a political party could tarnish this holy concept of the *Vaterland* for which his forebears had labored and bled and of which he, Baron Otto von Hallenberg, was presently the only trustee, the sole bearer of an illustrious name that placed upon him a commitment and obligations to which he was married as intimately as to his own skin.

Nevertheless, the lawyer's insistent importuning finally provoked him to visit Werner Strapp—if not to ask him for help yet; rather, well, to explore the feasibility of possibly calling on him for assistance at a later date.

Werner was pleased to hear from him and invited him to his home, a small, elegantly furnished apartment overlooking the English Garden on one of Munich's more expensive residential streets. On opening the door, he boomed:

"*Heil Hitler*, Otto—or must I still say *Grüss Gott*?"*

He extended his hand and the baron grasped it, one of the few men whose firm handclasp he enjoyed.

"Sit down, sit down, Otto," Werner exclaimed warmly in his staccato manner.

Werner was somewhat shorter than the baron but appeared taller because of his broad, muscular build in contrast to the baron's slender figure.

"How about some genuine Russian vodka?" Werner boomed. "Try it. Excellent stuff." He poured two glasses and brought them over. "One thing the Russkies sure know how to make."

"Doesn't that make you suspect as a Communist sympathizer?" the baron joked.

"Ha, ha, very good," Werner guffawed appreciatively, waving his hand. He wore no jacket, and the sleeves of his white shirt were rolled up almost to his elbows, revealing his hairy, muscular arms. "But once you get to my elevated position, you can even drink Russian vodka with impunity! *Heil Hitler!*"

He downed a generous gulp and for a moment lapsed into silence as he felt the liquor settling. There was something virile and decisive in Werner that the baron had always liked and admired, a man on the go, charged with energy and enthusiasm, one of the very few people by whom the baron felt a little intimidated, as if in the presence of a primordial energy that antedated even his own ancient lineage.

"So what have you been up to, Otto?" Werner resumed. "Long time no see. Why aren't we getting together more often? Are you still sitting

---

* The common German greeting.

in that lovely, moldy mansion of yours? Why don't you come down from your ivory tower and join us? We're going places, Otto."

The baron laughed, strangely unoffended by the numerous familiarities punctuating Werner's speech.

"You must come and spend a weekend with us some time in our moldy mansion," he smiled.

"Would love to, would love to, by God!" Werner exclaimed in his staccato manner, his hand slicing the air. "If only I had time. How's the missus and the girls?"

"Fine, fine."

"You've got the greatest little girls, Otto—I envy you. I mean it. That's one thing I miss about this way of life: I never seem to have enough time for little girls, for a family."He laughed and waved his hand. "All I've got time for is the grown-up variety and even with them only on the run, always on the run."

"I'd settle for a boy."

"Hm. Yeah. Family tree and all that. I understand," Werner mused, stilled for a moment in his vigorous onward rush. "For us poor bastards a name's a name, something to call us by. None of that burden of preserving an ancient family tree and all that. See what advantages we poor bastards have?" he exclaimed, waving his hand.

"I thought one of your Party's objectives was to further everybody's family tree and see that it's pure."

"We-ll."Werner stared at him for a moment. "Between the two of us, I don't much go for that racial stuff. We'll outgrow that sort of thing. We're all mixed breeds, mongrels, as far as I'm concerned—well, maybe not you but that's, if you pardon my saying so, why you're dying out."

"I'm still quite alive, thank you," the baron smiled.

Astonishing, he thought, what this man could say to him without making him feel offended.

Werner took another gulp.

"So you're keeping busy, eh?" the baron said to change the subject. Pretty soon your *Führer* won't be able to run Germany without you anymore."

"Ha, ha! Not quite!" Werner guffawed appreciatively. Then he wagged his finger at the baron. "And don't think I didn't get that little dig—*your Führer*! He's your *Führer* too, Otto. You're just taking a little longer to find out that he is. But you will, you will. And even if you don't, he'll still be your *Führer* because you'll have to follow him whether you want to or not."

"A monolithic society, eh?"

"Let's cut the crap, Otto. A society is always monolithic, meaning that some people run the show. The only question is: Who runs the show and what kind of show do they run? Even this Jewish thing—"Werner sliced the air disparagingly, "it'll pass."

"You feel it isn't an integral part of Hitler's program?"

"By God, it isn't, Otto. His program is bigger, much bigger than a bunch of grimy Jews. Anyway, it's academic because the problem will soon liquidate itself. Once the bulk of the Jews have emigrated—as they will—vere's zee problem?" He spread his arms wide in broad caricature of a Jew. The baron grinned.

"May I ask, Werner—if it isn't an indiscreet question—what is your job at the moment?"

"Not at all, not at all. I'm on the personal staff of the *Gauleiter*.* A sort of man Friday, you might say. Gives me a lot of leeway—and power." He laughed his disarming, staccato laugh.

Now would be the time to ask for help, the baron thought. But instead he said blandly:

"Sounds important."

"It is."

Werner looked at the baron silently for a moment. Suddenly he said: "Seriously, Otto. When are you going to join us?"

The baron tried to shrug the question off flippantly.

"Can you give me three good reasons why I should?"

"With pleasure, Otto. With pleasure. Three, five, however many you want. In the first place and most importantly," Werner began to enumerate on the finger of his hand, "because our cause is *good* and *just*. We're sick and tired of being the trampling ground of Europe, which we've been now for hundreds of years. We're going to raise Germany up to where she rightly belongs: among the *big* nations of the world—and we're *doing* it, not just talking interminably about it like those mealy-mouthed democratic Weimar politicians who called themselves the friends of the common man but let him starve in the gutter. We're doing something for the common man, by God, Otto, not by pitting one class against another like the Communists but by raising them *all* up. That might not be important to you with your blue-blooded lineage, but it's where the action is, because we're living—excuse the cliché —in the age

---

* A Nazi Province administrator.

of the common man. You noblemen have had your day. You know that. I don't care whether it's aristocracy of birth or of wealth or what have you. Well," he broke off abruptly, "enough of that."

"Is that one reason or a dozen?" the baron said with a forced smile.

"I'll be generous: just one. The big, crucial one that makes us irresistible."

There was no humor in Werner's expression now, no twinkling in his eyes, only the raw, ruthless thrust of his fanatic devotion and conviction.

"But I'll give you an even better reason as far as you personally are concerned, Otto," Werner resumed soberly after a moment, taking up a second finger. "The best way to preserve that family honor and tradition of yours that you prize so highly is to join us. You know why? Because it is us Nazis who care about the German tradition and culture that you are so proud of. Why would we wish to destroy you? We want you to *join* us. We want you to help us spread your heritage, *our* heritage. We *want* you to join us. Because we *need* you, we need your honor, your prestige, your integrity to make Germany great!"

He was silent.

"You sound extraordinarily flattering, Werner; in fact, downright eloquent and almost convincing," the baron said. "But some diatribes I've seen in the press against us don't show much need for us or much desire to have us."

For the first time Werner exploded.

"Because you want to keep your tradition all to yourself instead of sharing it with us! Because you look down on us as rabble! That's why you force us to take your tradition away from you by force. Stop protecting yourself and think of Germany! Stop being such damn snobs and you'll see with what open arms we'll welcome you!"

They were both silent for some moments. The baron wanted to get up—his pride told him to get up—but he felt riveted to his chair. Werner was staring intently into his glass.

"Besides, look at it from a strictly selfish point of view," he resumed. "You and your family have much more to lose than most because your wealth adds an extra measure of vulnerability. Have you ever thought of that?" A smile spread on his face. "You know, on the theory that if you can't lick 'em, join 'em?"

"That almost sounds like a threat, Werner," the baron said with a touch of haughtiness. "I was more impressed with your argument that you need us to make our *Vaterland* great."

Werner disregarded his haughtiness. Leaning forward he said with soft intensity:

"We would fete you, Otto. We really would. Because we need names like yours on our side. We'll make it worth your while, believe me—just as we'll make it doubly hard for you if you refuse. I'm speaking to you as a friend now, Otto, not as a Nazi."

No, the baron thought, for the first time you are speaking entirely as a Nazi. But aloud he said:

"Thank you for your honesty, Werner."

Werner made a vague gesture and gulped down the rest of his glass. For some moments he was silent.

"Well, now," he said finally, returning to his former affable manner. "Tell me: What brought you here? Anything I can do for you? I would, you know. Because I've always had an inexplicable fondness for you stiff-necked rascal."

"Thank you, Werner," the baron said somewhat stiffly.

Now would be my chance, he thought. But he couldn't bring himself to ask, especially not after Werner's blunt words. Instead he said:

"But I appreciate your offer. Maybe I'll take advantage of it some day."

◆ ◆ ◆

One day soon afterwards, Dr. Metzner called and requested to see both the baron and the baroness. The baroness was delighted to go to Munich.

"Let's make an occasion of it, Otto, shall we?" she suggested. "I haven't been to Munich in ages."

"We could do that," the baron agreed unenthusiastically, seeing his rendezvous with Ingeborg vanishing.

"Where shall we go? to the opera?" the baroness asked.

"Whatever you like. Just make the arrangements."

The baroness dressed with elaborate care for the occasion. When she came down from her rooms—the baron was waiting for her at the foot of the broad staircase—she looked resplendent. She could still look like that, the baron thought with a touch of admiration, feeling a stirring of his old feeling for her, of admiration mixed with desire, the way he had felt in the beginning and well into the fifth or sixth year of their marriage. He had been faithful then. Until Olga, his adored Olga, suddenly couldn't conceive anymore. Suddenly Olga was sterile, barren, as effectively as if her ovaries had been ripped out of her, as later indeed they were, so that even the possibility of making her pregnant was taken away, which made him feel altogether like a eunuch. It was then that the procession of his mistresses had started.

"You look lovely, Olga," he said.

"Why, thank you, Otto."

For once she felt that he was really looking at her and absorbed his attention like parched earth absorbing rain.

Of course, that wasn't the way the baroness saw it. He was aware of that. As she saw it, his withdrawal and infidelities had come first, before her vain attempts to become pregnant again. That was what had started the disintegration of their marriage. How otherwise account for her sudden inexplicable inability to become pregnant again, she who had conceived so readily the first three times? It was then that she began to drink and put on some weight as she abandoned most of the sporty activities that had until then kept her trim. And then even her interest in the household began to wane as she turned more and more responsibilities over to the housekeeper. Something of a personality change had taken place, which had alienated the baron further and had driven him deeper into his extramarital diversions. The baron felt bitter about it. Indeed, angry. That was what got in the way whenever he felt a stirring of his old feelings for her.

He had taken his wife's elbow and was steering her toward the main entrance where the Mercedes was waiting and opened the door for her. But already it had once again become a mere gesture of perfunctory politeness.

◆ ◆ ◆

Dr. Metzner made a great show of wordy delight to see the baroness again, to which she responded graciously, though she had no great liking for the lawyer either. It annoyed the baron. Was she really taken in by all this verbose claptrap?

"Well, now," Dr. Metzner at last began, settling in behind his desk. "I'm finally able to report what I think we might, with due guardedness, call a positive development."

It was amazing what circumlocutions lawyers could dream up, the baron thought irritably. He ought to have been a Jew with his craftiness.

"How nice," the baroness said.

"I don't want to be too optimistic," the lawyer added at once, "but, with some guardedness, as I said...."

The baron noted with satisfaction that he broke off somewhat flustered, having run aground on a repetition which, in Dr. Metzner's demanding view, was an oratorical faux pas of the first order. Perhaps because of it he now proceeded without further flourish.

"The court wants some additional documentation about the Freiherr's *past*."

He paused with some emphasis in order to let the point sink in, which neither the baron nor the baroness really grasped. Failing to elicit a response, the lawyer continued:

"You will recall that in my affidavit I made an enormous point of highlighting the Freiherr's valiant decorated military service as a battalion commander in the Great War. If I had said any more, if I may say so myself, I would have had to serve up a twenty-one gun salute!" The lawyer abandoned himself to a self-admiring cackle.

"It's no more than the truth," the baroness observed drily.

"Of course, of course, forgive my levity, my dear Baroness; I don't mean to denigrate your worthy father in the least. Anyway, it shows that the court is not dismissing the case out of hand and is taking his positive side into serious consideration, not just his later—hm—difficult behavior."

"Difficult? How so, my dear Metzner?" the baroness blandly picked up the lawyer's word, dropping the "doctor" from his name. The baron could tell that a watchful, ready-to-pounce attitude had crept over her.

"Yes, difficult," the lawyer repeated, missing the change in her tone. "Although I can understand that a daughter's laudable affection for her father might dispute the word. But shouting insults at the Nazis and punching a respectable Party official in the face can hardly be called anything less than difficult—almost, one might say, provocative."

"He was drunk," the baroness observed tartly.

"Quite so. But *in vino veritas*, as they say. One must be fair, my dear Baroness," the lawyer persisted to the baron's surprise. "A long string of destructive behavior preceded that final fracas—*self*-destructive behavior, Baroness."

The baroness remained silent. Her face had suddenly changed. Her smiling mask was gone and had been replaced by a brooding expression.

"Yes, that he was," she murmured.

"And such a gallant officer too," the lawyer commiserated, shaking his head. "It pains me to think of it."

His words and manner struck the baron as bathetic and deepened the annoyance he felt at the lawyer's pushy, verbose assumption of familiarity, although he actually agreed with him. The realization suddenly struck him that almost all his dealings with the lawyer left him in a rather ill-tempered mood regardless of the substance of their meetings. Then why did he continue to retain him? Because the man was, for all his pompous verbosity, one of the best lawyers in Munich.

"To get back to the business at hand," the baron interjected. "You were saying that the court wants further documentation."

"Yes, my dear Baron, they're suggesting some very specific things." The lawyer picked up a letter that had been lying in front of him. "It might require a bit of leg work but I think it more than worth it."

The rest of the meeting dealt with the various items requested by the court and with how to assemble the information as expeditiously as possible.

◆ ◆ ◆

One day the baron arrived half an hour early at Ingeborg's apartment and heard a male voice inside. He stopped, without ringing the bell, and listened for a moment, feeling an involuntary twinge of jealousy when he heard Ingeborg's lighthearted, amused laughter, but he suppressed the feeling at once. It was ridiculous to be jealous of a woman like Ingeborg. For that matter, jealousy was altogether an emotion beneath his dignity. He composed his face and, putting on it the slight, rather supercilious smile that he could affect so well on demand, rang the bell.

Ingeborg opened the door in a chic gown that he himself had given her, her hair piled high on her head. She looked lovely.

"My dear Baron," she cried theatrically. "You're early. But do come in."

Her theatrical tone and manner revived his suspicion. Nevertheless he stepped up to kiss her, as was his habit. But Ingeborg stepped back, jabbing her thumb over her shoulder to indicate that there was someone in the living room. Then she preceded him into the living room.

"Otto, I'd like you to meet Johann Stantke, a tenant in the building. Johann, this is Baron von Hallenberg."

"How do you do," the baron said, inclining his head slightly.

"Grüss Gott, Baron," the man said in a friendly but unceremonious manner.

He was a man of middle height, on the slight side, with blond hair, a fair complexion, and blue, childlike, luminous eyes which lent him an air of transparency, as if he were lit up from inside. He faced the baron in a relaxed, unself-conscious manner, a friendly smile on his face that conveyed an air at once self-assured and self-effacing. There was something so disarming about the man that the baron felt ashamed of his narrow-minded, unfounded suspicion.

"Johann came down to get some aspirins for his wife," Ingeborg explained. "She has an abscessed tooth and her dentist is out of town until the day after tomorrow."

"Isn't that the way it always happens," the baron said politely.

The man remained silent, as if not quite knowing how to participate in such social chitchat.

"Sit down," Ingeborg exclaimed, addressing the baron. "I'll be ready in a jiffy."

"These jiffies have a way of stretching with you," the baron replied jovially, surprised at his directness in front of this stranger, he who was always so reserved and correct.

"I made some soup for Hannelore," Ingeborg said, turning back to Johann. "How is she?"

"The doctor says it's anemia."

"That's nothing very serious, Johann," Ingeborg said reassuringly. "Just see to it that she eats right. Hannelore is Johann's daughter," Ingeborg explained, turning to the baron. "I'll be right back."

She disappeared into the kitchen. There followed a silence that the baron found uncomfortable, but Johann remained standing unself-consciously in the middle of the room without seeming bothered. Suddenly he said:

"Ingeborg is such a good person. She's always ready to help."

The baron had to smile. Good-natured, generous, lovable—yes. But a *good* person? That was hardly the way he would describe her.

"An admirable view," he observed noncommittally. "And surely a rarity these days."

"Oh, I don't know," Johann said unpretentiously. "Most people are good—or at least try to be."

Was the man a simpleton? the baron wondered. And yet with what faith and quiet self-assurance he was saying these simple things. He suddenly found himself wondering what the man might say about the Nazis and felt an impulse to ask him. But then the very impulse annoyed him. People had been known to lose their jobs and worse for asking such questions. It was amazing, the baron thought; there was something about this simple, unassuming fellow that pulled one involuntarily into a deeper level of honesty. For a moment their eyes met, calmly and straightforwardly. Amazing that too, the baron thought, making no effort to avert his eyes, because he disliked eye couplings almost as much as shaking hands.

At this moment Ingeborg returned.

"Here," she said, pressing a covered jar into Johann's hands. "I made it only this morning. Chicken soup. Just let me have the jar back. And here are the aspirins. I do hope Maria will be better."They began to move toward the door, Ingeborg's hand resting lightly on Johann's arm. "Maybe I can go to the dentist with her if she lets me know the time."

Again the baron felt a twinge of jealousy. What was it about this man that drew Ingeborg out so much? She was never anxious to please him like that.

"You're very kind," Johann said. They had arrived at the door, and he took her hand and pressed it. "Thank you so much."

"My pleasure, Johann," Ingeborg laughed.

Ingeborg and the baron walked silently to the car, which Schulman had parked as usual around a farther corner in order not to attract undue attention. Settling into the comfortable car, the baron felt the luxurious upholstery enfolding him like an embrace.

"A queer fellow," he commented.

"Who?" Ingeborg asked absent-mindedly.

She was looking out of the window, watching the pedestrians and bicyclists streaming past. How different the world looked from a car; how different not to be walking or riding in a streetcar. She snuggled deeper into her corner.

"The fellow in your apartment. What was his name again?"

"Oh, you mean Johann," she said. But she didn't add, Yeah, isn't he a queer fellow.

"Where does he live in the building?"

"On the last floor. In the attic apartment. They're not very well off."

"What does he do?"

"He's a streetcar conductor."

"You never mentioned him before."

Ingeborg laughed.

"There are a lot of people I know I haven't mentioned to you, my dear Otto. What do you think I do all week? Sit home and twiddle my thumbs waiting for you?"

The baron remained silent, annoyed by her tone, but he was hardly in a position to complain unless he was willing to give her more time, which he wasn't. His annoyance latched on to Johann.

"I'd be a little careful, all the same."

"Careful with Johann?" Ingeborg exclaimed with a mixture of amusement and irritation at the implication that he had a right to supervise her life. "Why?"

"He seems somewhat simple and almost too—honest," the baron said vaguely. "People like that spell trouble."

Ingeborg laughed.

"Johann is one person you *don't* have to be careful with!" she said with conviction. "He brings out the best in people."

"A laudable trait," the baron observed sardonically. "I wonder how he does it?"

"Simple," Ingeborg exclaimed gaily. "He tells everyone how wonderful they are. You can't behave badly when someone tells you how wonderful you are!"

"I'll have to try that some time," the baron said with a forced smile.

They rode along silently for a while. Suddenly Ingeborg snuggled up to him and pressing her breast against his arm whispered:

"If I wouldn't know better, I'd almost think you were jealous, Ottchen."

The Newspaper Article

I t was the newspaper article that finally brought Emilia's anguished struggle to a head, aligning the various forces in the Silver family into new configurations, like a magnet thrust into a scattered pile of nails. Until then she had spun her wheels in a vacuum of doubt, guilt, and despair. But the moment she began to read the newspaper article, she felt the blood rushing to her head, and by the time she had finished reading it, she was trembling all over.

Paul had been given the article by Herbert who had handed it to him with a mysterious leer.

"Here, read this," Herbert had said.

He stood over Paul while Paul raced through the article, only half understanding it in such a rapid, distracted reading.

"Get it?" Herbert grinned.

"N-no," Paul muttered.

"What is there to get, dummy? The gal got laid by a stud who wasn't her husband, and when she got a big belly, she palmed the bastard off on her husband, see?" He poked Paul in the ribs. "First come, first served, you know."

"So what?" Paul said aggressively to hide his confusion.

"Kind of interesting, ain't it?" Herbert's leer broadened. "There could just be something in it for you."

"For me? What are you talking about?"

"Jesus, are you dense!" Herbert exclaimed, exasperated. "It could just be, couldn't it? Maybe you're from a first marriage or adopted or somethin' . . . ." He grinned insinuatingly. "You just don't look anything like your old man, do you?"

At home Paul read the article again. It told of a German woman whose Jewish husband had died and whose son, a lawyer, had lost his position on account of his half-Jewish background whereupon the woman petitioned the *Deutsche Rasseamt*, the German Race Office, to declare her son an Aryan, claiming that he was the illegitimate child of an Aryan and hence non-Jewish. The son was thereupon reinstated in his job with full honors, and Dr. Goebbels himself praised the woman for her courage in stepping forward to uphold the purity of the Aryan race, etc. etc.

Paul reread the article twice before he really grasped all the implications, being rather naive and unsophisticated in sexual matters. Then he stuffed it away under some magazines in his room, and it was there that Emilia found it.

◆ ◆ ◆

After reading the article, Emilia fled to her room as if someone were pursuing her. How had Paul found out? How had he discovered her shameful secret? It was a while before she calmed down enough to realize that there was no way Paul could have found out because even the baron knew nothing whatever about Paul, although if Paul had been lined up alongside him, the similarity would have been too striking to ignore.

At least that's how she remembered the baron. She had long ago destroyed the only picture she had possessed of him, but she had occasionally come across a picture of him in the newspapers or magazines and had saved one whole magazine, which couldn't arouse any suspicion, because it had a picture spread of the baron and his family, estate, and horse farm. He still seemed to look very much as he had looked then and as Paul looked now: tall, slim, and handsome, aristocratically self-assured, impressive not only on horseback—the way he had first come upon her—but on the ground too.

The baron wouldn't touch her now, Emilia suddenly found herself thinking, fortyish and a bit heavy as she was, although her body was still firm and attractive. She felt a sudden urge to look at herself in the mirror but suppressed it.

Strange only that he had had no son, Emilia reflected.

She sat staring out into the garden, trying to bring some order into her agitated feelings. And then it suddenly hit her: This was no ordinary newspaper article nor her coming upon it a mere accident! No, it was an indisputable sign from on high, an omen such as she had pleaded and prayed for! Here finally God revealed how she could rehabilitate Paul, here finally she was shown both her punishment and her expiation!

Oh, God, she prayed, kneeling down before her altar, bravely I shall take upon myself Thy punishment, humbly praising Thy name for showing me at last a way to save the boy! I shall not shirk or dodge my punishment!

She was sobbing ecstatically now as she prostrated herself fervently on the floor.

◆ ◆ ◆

Emilia's struggle now began to focus on how to carry out this new plan without hurting her husband—because she was determined not to hurt him if at all possible. The question was: How?

She agonized over this for days until the idea flashed into her mind that she could present it to Samuel as a ruse to help Paul without broaching the broader question of her infidelity; in short, as a clever plan to outwit a fate their son did not deserve. Would we have put him into the world, Samuel, she would argue, if we had known that the mere circumstance of your paternity would condemn the boy to an inferior, persecuted status? And she would answer her own question fervently and with utter conviction: Never!

Yes, she would tell her husband very simply, very straightforwardly, that they needed to do this for the sake of the boy, indeed *owed* it to him for he was not to blame for his paternity—no, that was putting it too crassly because it made it sound as if she was placing all the blame on her husband—but wasn't he to blame? . . . . Her thoughts became confused. No, it was she who was to blame, she who was the mortal sinner, the adulteress.

She knelt down at her altar and bowed down before the picture of the Madonna. Mary, Holy Mother of God, she prayed fervently, Thou who art a woman and understandest the weaknesses and sins of the flesh . . . she stopped, flustered, as she remembered that the Immaculate Conception lifted Mary above all possibility of infidelity. Mother of God, forgive me, she whispered hoarsely, becoming more and more confused.

She got up and stared down into the garden that she so loved but that now no longer seemed to provide a refuge and forced her thoughts back to the primary issue. The way she would put it, she decided, was that the boy was simply not to blame for being born. That would put the blame evenly on both parents. We have to do something, Samuel, she would say, to save the boy from the half-life half-Jews are condemned to live in this strange New Order, this horrible New Germany.

It was an approach that seemed to Emilia irrefutable, even while it detoured around a full confession. God knew it wasn't for her own sake that she shrank from such a confession—not for her own sake . . . .

◆ ◆ ◆

Emilia's return to Catholicism had become coupled with a growing superstition that had always lain dormant in her but was lately assuming a disproportionate importance in her life, for Emilia was essentially a simple woman for whom her husband's philosophical and moral torments were often complex abstractions that swam about on an intellectual (she was almost tempted to say: ineffectual) surface, like toy boats wafted about without a propulsion or meaning of their own. Yet for all her periodic irritation at Samuel's complexifying tendencies, when all was said and done, it was precisely this propensity to ferret out each moral wrinkle and endlessly knead the ins and outs and whys and wherefores of things that had initially attracted her to him and that she still admired and loved because it gave her a sense of security.

Her superstition wasn't the usual garden variety kind of superstition, as Samuel called it. Rather, it was the kind that sees in insignificant events—a dish falling out of her hand and breaking or a glove being undiscoverable when she wanted to go out—a momentous reprimand for something done or left undone or an ominous portent of things to come.

"As if God has nothing better to do than break dishes and lose gloves," Samuel would say, laughing.

"It's His way of making His wishes known to us," Emilia would insist, stubbornly clinging to her conviction that an invisible umbilical cord connected every human being to his Maker through which He revealed Himself with signs and portents.

"You mean God—God the Omnipotent, the Omniscient, and Omnipresent—cannot find more direct and effective ways to make His wishes known than by breaking dishes?" Samuel would exclaim, shaking his head. "Why, that borders on blasphemy!"

"Everything is always so rational and cut and dried with you!" Emilia would retort. "God works in mysterious ways."

"Mysterious, yes," Samuel would mutter. "But not with this cosmology of charms and omens."

◆ ◆ ◆

"I don't like letting you stay on alone in the store, Mr. Silver," Leopold remonstrated. "You go on home. I'll lock up."

It was a protest that Leopold had repeated for months now whenever Samuel wanted to send him home before leaving himself. Leopold knew that Samuel's stated reason for staying open late—namely to make up for bad business—was a ruse. There was nothing to stay open for because he hardly ever sold anything after Leopold left. In fact, they sold very little at any time.

The truth was, though he would not have admitted it to Leopold, that very often Samuel simply locked the door after Leopold left and turned out the lights. Then he would sit looking out on the street and at the people stopping now and then to ogle his wares, despite the Star of David prominently displayed outside the store, unaware that they were being observed from inside by a man who scrutinized them with a mixture of curiosity and fear as he tried hard to understand what had suddenly turned these people against him, these people among whom he had grown up, whose language was his mother tongue, who had always in the past been so familiar and friendly.

For all that, he couldn't help noticing that Leopold's insistence on letting him lock up was becoming more and more ritualized and perfunctory. His heart seemed to have gone out of his offer, as out of so much that had existed in their relationship. Because too much was lately avoided between them, too much remained unspoken. A silent uneasiness had settled over the relationship which pained and embarrassed both, with the result that they were particularly solicitous toward each other, which only increased the strain between them.

Samuel could feel the struggle in Leopold to retain the simple, uncomplicated warmth that had grown up over forty years of mutual trust and intimate association with the Silver family. Sometimes he felt downright sorry for the old man who was the picture of kindliness with his bushy, unwieldy eyebrows and crooked features that gave his face a somewhat mashed impression, as if someone had unwittingly stepped on it, especially when something troubled him as it troubled him now, at which time his eyes almost disappeared in their sockets, like two snails retracting into their houses.

Not that Leopold had become a Nazi. But he was a conservative man, a thoroughly conservative, patriotic, kindly old man who couldn't help being thrilled by the evidence of rejuvenation that he saw all around him. The truth was that Leopold had never thought of the Silvers as Jews so that it embarrassed him to be reminded of it because it roused certain unconscious, negative feelings about Jews in general, feelings that had survived intact precisely because he did not think of the Silvers as Jews.

It was all very difficult and confusing.

At times Samuel felt sorry for the old man, so sorry that he wanted to take Leopold in his arms and embrace him to convey to him the simple truth of his affection, the simple truth of human equality and dignity that made their struggle such a sorry and unnecessary mess. But he knew that the problem was more complicated than that, and that the evil could not be disarmed with a mere embrace.

Yes, it was all very difficult and confusing.

The final irony was that Samuel really couldn't afford Leopold any longer, because the business hardly supported even his own family anymore. But how could he discharge a man who had been with his family for over forty years and depended on him for his livelihood? He couldn't know that Leopold's savings, accumulated and invested diligently over a lifetime of bachelorhood, were quite enough to keep him modestly for the rest of his life and that often Leopold himself wanted dearly to leave his employment in order to escape from all the troubling thoughts and feelings it entailed—in short, that he was in his turn only staying on out of loyalty to Mr. Silver!

So even as simple and seemingly untouchable a relationship as this, thought Samuel sitting in his darkened store, can become poisoned. But was that surprising when even his marriage was slowly being poisoned?

Once more his thoughts had arrived at the pivot around which everything revolved these days. It was the principal reason why he now stayed on so often in the store in the evening. The horrible truth was that he couldn't face home! Even in his beloved library, the fortress of his soul, he would find himself wandering restlessly along the shelves stacked high with books, unable to settle down. The feeling that he was the cause of so many difficulties consumed him and gave him no peace. He loved his wife, still and always and sometimes almost more fervently on account of the split between them because it brought what they no longer possessed into bolder relief. Sometimes he experienced his love like a downright physical ache, a feeling compounded of longing and loneliness, of need and physical desire too, rare as their sexual intimacies had become, as if each shied away from desecrating this most intimate of all encounters with the disharmony that now prevailed between them. His family life had lost its naturalness and had suddenly become stark and oppressive.

Samuel sighed, got up, and left the store, double-locking the door. Pocketing the keys, he reluctantly faced the street. Should he walk or take the streetcar home? Every evening, and morning too, he now asked himself that same anxious question because the streets that had all his life been so friendly now seemed hostile and forbidding. The knowledge that one was no longer wanted and was denied the right to be a full-fledged human being was a sly, pernicious poison that slowly undermined one's mental and emotional health because it followed one about day after day like one's shadow.

It was as if he were walking through an increasingly strange town, as in a nightmare.

◆ ◆ ◆

The time Emilia chose for the difficult confrontation with Samuel was one Sunday morning after breakfast, a time, still, of relative serenity in the house. Paul was spending the day with Erika.

"*Männchen*," she began bravely, using the pet name that she used ever more rarely these days, "there is something I must talk to you about."

"Yes, Millie?"

"There's the matter of the boy—Paul," Emilia said, naming him as if to prevent some possibility of confusion. "I'm worried about him."

"Why?"

"I've been watching him. He's unhappy."

"He seems happier to me than he's been in a long time. Ever since he's been going with Erika."

Paul had introduced Erika to them, and they had both liked her.

"Puppy love," Emilia said dismissingly. "That'll pass. I'm talking about his future. What future does he have in Germany?"

"What future do any of us have here, I wonder."

"But it's different with the boy."

"In what way is it different?"

Always they arrived at the same point: Paul's difference. It had become a sort of watershed between them from which their thoughts and feelings flowed in opposite directions. But Emilia had made up her mind to confront it head-on this time.

"I've given it a lot of thought, *Männchen*," she said. "I think I know a way to give him back his future."

He frowned. "By sending him to Palestine?"

He sometimes wondered whether he shouldn't simply use his authority as a father to force Paul to join his sister. But force and pressure, even under these circumstances, were distasteful to him.

"No," Emilia said. "I've got something else in mind."

"And what is that?"

Emilia took a deep breath.

"I've heard that mothers can declare their children—I came across such a case in the papers just the other day—declare their children to be—Aryans."

Samuel looked at her blankly. His brain seemed momentarily to short-circuit.

"I don't understand. What kind of cases?"

"Of—illegitimacy," Emilia blurted.

"Are you saying—Paul isn't my son?" Samuel asked incredulously.

"Of course he's your son!"

"Then what are you saying?"

"I'm talking about a formality, *Männchen*. A mere *formality*."

"What is a formality?"

"To declare that he is not your son."

"But you just said he is."

"You and I know that. It's just so we can declare him to be an Aryan."

The enormity of the proposition now finally sank in on Samuel. He ran his hand across his eyes as if to wipe away what he now finally understood, while Emilia sat staring out of the window, overcome herself suddenly not only by the enormity of the proposition but by its irreversibility. A long silence settled between them. Finally she said plaintively:

"It's only a ruse, *Männchen*... it doesn't change anything between us... it's for Paul's sake."

Words that Samuel wanted desperately to believe, but a voice shouted inside him: No, everything has changed irrevocably!

♦ ◆ ♦

Although their talk seesawed back and forth awhile longer, nothing more of substance was said. Samuel presently retired to the library, while Emilia went to her room, each requiring time to assess and assimilate what had happened, only to be driven together again in the late afternoon, each flagellated by his own knotted feelings.

One thing was clear to Samuel: Emilia's proposition proved that she regretted having married a Jew. Who could blame her? To be married to a Jew in Nazi Germany was tantamount to having a chain around your neck. It meant giving up life as it should be lived. Yet for all that, he believed Emilia's declaration that Paul was his son. The thought that an actual infidelity had taken place was as outlandish and incredible to him as his wife's proposition, since she had always been the picture of devoted faithfulness and domesticity. He therefore tried to argue the case on its merits as an impersonal stratagem to outwit the Nazi enemy, although his personal feelings of betrayal and hurt broke through again and again. Let's leave aside, he argued, the question of what people will think of you, or of me, for that matter; let's even leave aside what Paul will think of you—

"Have you discussed this with Paul, by the way?" he interrupted himself.

"No," she replied, "I didn't want to discuss it with him before I had discussed it with you."

"What makes you think he'll go along with it?"

"It's not up to him!" Emilia exclaimed. "I'm the one to carry the—the—shame!"

"Let's even leave aside," Samuel continued, slightly raising his voice as if to silence his wife's foray into personal feelings, "whether you or we could get away with it, which I seriously doubt—the pivotal question which you haven't addressed at all, it seems to me, is: Do we really *want* our son to become a full-fledged member of a society that is as immoral and as vicious, corrupt, and evil as the Nazis—"

"Samuel, please, no philosophizing," Emilia interrupted. "It's not a question of the society. We're talking about our son."

"I know we're talking about our son," Samuel replied with some heat. "But why should we deny our identity to please a vicious system?"

"You never much cared about being a Jew."

"But I never denied being a Jew either. You can't separate the boy from the system you want him to become a part of. Maybe it's good that we're not part of the system. Maybe we should be *proud* that we're not part of this evil system!" Samuel cried with uncharacteristic vehemence.

Emilia sat with her hands pressed against her head.

"Please, please, please, Samuel," she ejaculated hoarsely. "For once stop moralizing."

It was then that Samuel's pretense at objectivity and rationality collapsed in the face of his tremendous hurt and sense of betrayal because he felt that his wife had violated a trust that could never be repaired.

"What possessed you, Emilia . . . how could you . . . for such a—a hollow victory . . . ."

He felt himself overtaken by sobs. But not wanting to give in to them, or share them, or even to have them seen as putting unfair pressure on his wife, he averted his face and jumped up and hurried out of the room.

◆ ◆ ◆

Emilia was close to despair. Her beautiful scheme to enlist her husband's cooperation without hurting him was badly miscarrying. Although she did not follow the precise convolutions of his mental and emotional processes, she needed only to look at his face—his growing pallor, the spreading rings under his eyes and, above all, the deepening sadness in those eyes—to feel a stabbing pain and a profound sense of guilt. What was she doing to this loving, devoted man whom she loved as much as ever, despite the hurt she was inflicting on him?

It was not the last time they spoke of it. Far from it. The issue came to dominate almost everything between them, at times seemingly tottering toward some sort of resolution, only to drop back again to where it had started, getting precisely nowhere. And even when they didn't speak of it, which happened more and more often, the silence at times stretching through whole days except for the most pressing day-to-day matters, even then the subject lay heavily between them.

There were times when Emilia felt like backing away from the whole undertaking. When she felt that way, she would suddenly grow tender and embrace Samuel, or she would all at once burst into tears, mumbling some incoherent words, or even feel tempted to get down on her knees to beg for his forgiveness. At other times, giving way under the stress, she would suddenly flare up in uncharacteristic outbursts of temper.

At yet other times, however, her harrowing sense of sin, coupled with her religiosity, kept her glued to the conviction that she needed to push forward with her plan irrespective of consequences. At such times, she considered even her husband's suffering but another deserved affliction, since it increased her own agony as well.

Yes, God was punishing her in many ways for her infidelity.

Father Sebastian didn't help matters. As he saw it, compared with Eternal Life, what did this life's puny trials and tribulations amount to? It was Father Sebastian's personal answer to the growing evil that surrounded him. Since he couldn't raise his fist against Caesar, he reasoned, he needed to labor that much harder to increase God's Kingdom.

When Emilia came to him in growing torment of spirit, he would try to comfort her, yes; but his message was always the same: God is pointing the way, my daughter; you are still trying to find a way around your sin, but He's not permitting you to escape any longer.

It repeated, with a priest's empowerment, precisely what Emilia was daily telling herself.

Thus it was that Emilia was forced by slow and relentless degrees to the harsh decision that the only way out of her dilemma was to fully confess her adultery to her husband: He could not then in good conscience stand any longer in the way of Paul's complete rehabilitation!

◆ ◆ ◆

About this time, before Paul had any idea that his mother had found the newspaper article, let alone what it had triggered in her, Paul asked his mother one day:

"Mama, how come children can look so different from their parents?"

Emilia looked up, startled.

"Why do you ask?" she demanded.

"Just wondering."

"It's because parents aren't the only ones who influence how children look. For instance, you look the spitting image of my grandfather on my mother's side."

Paul had hardly ever heard a word about this grandfather.

"Who was he?" he asked.

"He was an army officer."

But a week later, when Paul wanted to know something more about this grandfather, his mother replied absent-mindedly:

"I never knew him."

"But you said I look like him?"

"From pictures," Emilia said quickly. "And my mother always said so."

"Do you have any pictures?"

"No. Grandmother had all the pictures."

His mother seemed evasive and soon changed the subject, and Paul didn't press the issue.

Although Paul had no idea what agitated his mother, he couldn't help noticing that something was amiss between his parents. The atmosphere had become too charged, which stood out all the more since the atmosphere in the house used to be one of quiet harmony because Samuel was a quiet man and it was he more than anyone else who had stamped his character on the household.

"What's going on, mama," Paul would say. "It's getting to be like a morgue around here."

Emilia's vague respondent mutterings—things like "the times," "the spreading anti-Semitism," "business is bad," etc.—didn't truly clarify matters. But they satisfied Paul because his energy was focused predominantly on Erika, which shielded him, for the time being, from the full impact of what was happening in his own family and in the country and the world at large.

◆ ◆ ◆

Until Paul and Erika's sexual explorations led them to seek privacy, the happy threesome that they had formed with Herbert had been welcomed by them because it had provided them with an umbrella under whose protection they could safely inch their way toward each other. Once they became sexually involved, however, Herbert's presence became increasingly irksome, which they let Herbert feel in various subtle and not so subtle ways, which, in turn, triggered some unexpectedly violent feelings in Herbert.

The most influential circumstance in Herbert's life had always been his limp, which had become inflated in his mind, out of all proportion to its severity, into a drastic, lifelong impairment. It had resulted in a pervasive sense of inferiority and put him on a perpetual war footing with the world in order to forestall what he perceived everywhere as possible or imminent rejection. It was the secret reason why he sneered at the Hitler Youth, much as he would have loved to join it, convinced that he would be rejected. The best defense is offense, they say.

Herbert was proud to have brought Paul and Erika together, for he had always secretly admired Paul even before they had been thrown together by their ostracism, and he consequently arrogated to himself certain proprietary rights in their relationship. Their first muted efforts to signal to him that he was unwanted therefore flew by him without making any impression. Even when they pre-arranged on a number of occasions to get away from him after starting out together, Herbert dismissed their disappearance as a game and a joke. Finally, Paul took Herbert aside one day.

"Hey, man," he said, "how about, you know, we'd like to be on our own a little more often. Give us a break."

"Sure, man, sure," Herbert assured him, winking. "I got'cha."

But he didn't get it and continued to tag along wherever they went.

Matters finally came to a head one Sunday when Herbert insisted on accompanying them on a bicycle trip that they had specifically organized because Herbert had told them that he had other plans for the day. Paul didn't say anything, but once they gained the open countryside, he stopped his bicycle and dismounted. Surprised, Herbert and Erika stopped too.

"What's up, man?" Herbert demanded.

Paul approached Herbert with an ominous expression.

"You said you had other plans," Paul said.

"I did. But they changed."

"But we made *our* plans on the basis of *your* plans," Paul said aggressively, "and ours didn't change."

Herbert's face clouded over.

"I have a right to be here," he muttered.

"No, you don't!" Paul exclaimed. "Not when you're not wanted!"

"But I—I got you hitched," Herbert stammered, his face working now with a helpless expression.

"You're sticking to us like glue!" Paul shouted. "When are you gonna understand that we want you to beat it?"

Herbert stood, fighting back tears. Then he turned and walked away with his bicycle while Paul and Erika stood looking after him, Paul now with a twinge of guilt. He turned to Erika.

"I'm sorry but he's really become such a nuisance—"

It was at this moment that the stone struck him full force on the chest. He turned back to Herbert and saw him standing down the road, red-faced and shaking his fist.

"You son of a bitch! You cocksucking, motherfucking bastard!" yelled Herbert. "I'll get you for this!"

Then he mounted his bicycle and pedalled furiously away.

After that Herbert did not bother them anymore and refused to join them again even when they invited him, which they did on a number of occasions. Paul was baffled by the abruptness of the change and tried several times to set things right between them, feeling intuitively that he had inflicted a hurt on Herbert that went far beyond his intention. But Herbert rebuffed every attempt he made. Finally one day Paul tried to apologize outright.

"I'm sorry, Herbert. I didn't mean to hurt your feelings. We just wanted a little more time for ourselves and—"

But Herbert didn't even let him finish.

"Save your words, Jew-boy!" he sneered. "You got no power to hurt me. I hope you croak in your own shit, filthy kike!"

That closed the door once and for all between them.

◆ ◆ ◆

The rift did not affect Paul very deeply for he had always considered their friendship a product of circumstances rather than true affinity. Anyway, he felt much less in need of Herbert's friendship now that he had Erika.

For Herbert the rift was much more difficult. He had considered Paul the best friend he had ever had, which only served now to intensify his hatred and thirst for revenge. He consequently began to harass Paul wherever and whenever he could, driven by a burning desire to get back at him which even drove him to question his assumption that he could not join the Hitler Youth. Much to his surprise, it turned out that he was able to join without any trouble!

It changed Herbert's outlook overnight. He thrived in the Hitler Youth. To have a place in the scheme of things and be accepted at last! His very anonymity in uniform assured him of an acceptance and respect that he profoundly craved.

His harassment of Paul now turned ugly. On a one-to-one basis, Herbert knew that he was no match for Paul. But Herbert now moved in a pack that Paul knew he could not fight, so that he sidestepped every confrontation, pocketing insults and provocations, much as they hurt him at times. But to counter aggression with aggression was precisely what Herbert wanted and this would have been self-defeating and stupid.

On only one occasion did a group of Hitler Youth boys catch him unawares and roundly beat him up, egged on by Herbert. It was a severe beating that kept Paul out of school for two days.

Herbert gloated over it with conspicuous satisfaction.

◆ ◆ ◆

Once Mrs. Hoffer's repressed longings had found some vicarious discharge in her daughter's love affair, second thoughts began to trouble her, intensified by the young couple's ardor, which threatened to lead precisely to the kind of thralldom—early marriage and children—that Mrs. Hoffer felt had ruined her own life. In addition, Paul's half-Jewishness affected his ability to make a living in Germany and that was a serious matter indeed for Mrs. Hoffer, who, though not an anti-Semite, had always chafed at the penny-pinching, working class status that held her down.

Mrs. Hoffer's cooling enthusiasm led her to snipe at Paul, which upset Erika because her mother's approval meant a great deal to her. One day when Mrs. Hoffer made a derogatory, off-the-cuff remark about Paul, Erika exclaimed:

"You used to fall all over yourself saying nice things about Paul."

"Well, I know he's Prince Charming and all that, but he's human, ain't he?" Mrs. Hoffer countered placatingly.

But Erika was hurt and pressed the point.

"What's with you lately, mama? What's changed your attitude?"

"What attitude?" Mrs. Hoffer replied evasively.

"To Paul."

"I ain't changed my attitude."

"Yes, you have."

"Well, facts are facts."

"What facts? Will you stop beating around the bush?" Erika cried.

Finally, Mrs. Hoffer took the plunge.

"Well, you two are gettin' awful serious."

"You want me to—to—be intimate without being serious?" Erika said aggressively.

"Don't be smart with me," Mrs. Hoffer exclaimed. "But that don't mean you gotta sprint up to the altar right away."

"We never talk about marriage."

Which was true, though Erika, in contrast to Paul, certainly day-dreamed about it.

"I'm sure glad you haven't, because if you do, you'd better consider . . . ."

She stopped.

"What?"

"Well, since you wanna know," Mrs. Hoffer blurted, "Paul ain't got much of a future in Germany, has he?"

It was the first time that her mother had referred to Paul's Jewishness.

"So that's it!" Erika cried, her eyes filling with tears. "Are you joining them too?"

"I ain't joinin' nobody," Mrs. Hoffer said stubbornly, "but facts are facts."

"Paul isn't Jewish anyway. He's half-Jewish."

"So he's half-Jewish. Big deal!" Mrs. Hoffer cried, her pent-up concern, ambivalence, and frustration suddenly pouring out. "You think those screwball Nazis are—" she suddenly dropped her voice to a frightened whisper, "gonna stop at half-Jews?"

It was that frightened collapse of her voice that impressed Erika more than any reasoned argument, and it henceforth hung like a pall over her relationship with Paul.

◆ ◆ ◆

If Emilia thought that the pain and struggle of arriving at the decision "to tell all" would make the telling itself easy, she was mistaken, because for a while she could not bring herself to do it and many a fervent prayer for help crossed her lips before she was able to mobilize her courage.

Then one day—it was a Sunday in September 1938 when Paul and Erika had gone away for the weekend—she arose early, when it was still dark, with a sense that this was the day and that no further prevarication was possible. She knelt down before the small altar in her room and remained kneeling for almost an hour in intense prayer, importuning God to soften the blow for her husband. When the sun rose, she took a bath and put on a white dress, with some awareness of the irony but not of the deeper significance; namely, that she was engaged in a rite of purification. Finally, she sat quietly by the window of her room, without reading or knitting or being conscious of anything at all, waiting for the time to pass until she would hear her husband arising and could prepare breakfast.

During breakfast she remained unusually quiet. When it was over she finally said:

"Samuel, I need to talk to you."

Her voice was calm, almost ponderous, and her expression was solemn, all of which was unusual for her, so much so that Samuel looked up surprised and waited. Some moments passed before she continued.

"I have never lied to you, have I, Samuel?"

"Not to my knowledge."

"I have always told you the truth . . . ."

Her eyes suddenly filled with tears.

"What's the matter, Millie?"

It was so difficult, so horrendously difficult still. She pulled herself together.

"Except one time," she whispered.

He felt a cold shudder trickling down his spine. They both sat silently for some moments.

"Samuel," she said at length slowly, staring fixedly at the table. Only five words remained. Such a cataclysmic fact and it required only five words to say it. "Paul is not your son."

Samuel sat as if all life had suddenly been sucked out of him.

"Say something, Samuel," she whispered hoarsely.

Still he didn't move or speak, not because he wanted to shield her, or even himself, from the comfort of harsh words, but because the matter was beyond words altogether, the very intensity of his stillness being a measure of his shock and pain. So again it was she who continued.

"It happened the summer you were in England for your father and the business—when I stayed at the Starnberger Lake . . . ."

And then the whole story flooded out, as she had told it to him in her mind countless times, except this time he was sitting in front of her in the flesh, listening silently, slumped forward a little, without comments or questions or even lubricating movements of the head or hands to indicate that he was listening, and yet listening as if his whole body had been transformed into one large consuming ear:

It was a short affair, Samuel, brief to the point of being a fling, but such a word makes me flinch because I'm not that sort of woman; I'm not and wasn't then, believe me, even if the baron overwhelmed me with his charm and title and his three hundred year old mansion and his Teutonic good looks, sitting tall and erect on horseback while I was playing in the grass with Sofie, who was only a baby at the time. I kept Sofie between us like a shield, thinking that a man's motives must be pure when another man's child was crawling all over between us. And yet when the moment came, I didn't put up much resistance. It happened in a motorboat out on the lake at night, forgive me that it all sounds so trite and sentimental, but I was romantic then and only twenty-two. Afterwards I cried and saw your kind face and eyes as you stood before me looking sad and crumpled as if you had just got up, which is the only time when you don't look intellectual. Isn't it strange that I married you for all the things that appeared to me suddenly, in the baron's presence, a liability? Your kindliness and composure and cultured intellectualism—even your age, though you were only one year older than Otto—but how much older and wiser you have always seemed to me with your Jewish seriousness. With Otto I was lighthearted and gay, I could laugh and romp about, because, by comparison with you, he was a boy. Your seriousness has always forced me to be sedate—but have I told you well enough, *Männchen*, that I married you because I have always felt protected with you; you gave me a feeling of security that I so sorely lacked ever since my mother died when I was seven—all these things suddenly seemed to be turned upside down and inside out. I'm not criticizing you, my dear; today, and really always, I have known that I would not want to be with any other man, would not want you to be different; I'm only trying to explain why Otto turned my head. And even then, when the moment came to make a decision—it was not Otto who sent me away, but I myself who went. Yes, love. It was the only thing that gave me the feeling that I was not altogether an abominable and wretched woman: because I decided to stay with you of my own free will, despite Otto's infatuation and love—I do believe he might have married me. That was a proof of my love, wasn't it? a stronger proof even in some ways than when I married you as an inexperienced virgin, because now my love had been tested and had been found to be true. At least that's how I reasoned at the time. Still I didn't tell you, afraid of losing you and seeing no need to tell you—would you have left me or would you have forgiven me?

I didn't know, I didn't know and yet I wished so dearly to be forgiven . . . .

And then, when my period didn't come, I still saw no reason to tell you because by then you had returned. It was the only month when you and Otto had shared me, and I hoped desperately that it was your child that was growing in me, as by rights it should have been. Do you remember how passionately I took you into me at that time, as if by taking you into me again and again I could ensure that it was your seed and not the other man's that was coming alive in me? This torment went on for nine months, and even then it didn't immediately end because a newborn is like an empty canvas, and only slowly, as his hair grew and his features assembled themselves, did it become clear that you were *not* the father, and by the time Paul began to walk, the earmarks of his paternity were unmistakable . . . but by that time, love, I had lived with this struggle, this lie, this sin for so long that, well—I couldn't tell you any longer.

Emilia's tale was finished, and she sat, spent and exhausted.

The silence lasted.

"Please, say something, Samuel," Emilia whispered finally. "Reproach me, yell at me, beat me—anything . . . ."

Sobs choked off her voice. And then the whole desperate torment of her struggle broke forth in an outpouring of tears that Samuel made no attempt to stop or stifle because he experienced her tears like a purification not only for her but for himself as well, the tears opening a chamber in his heart that had remained locked since her "proposition" weeks before—a chamber of understanding and compassion, if not yet of forgiveness.

◆ ◆ ◆

The revelation stunned Samuel, of course. It was not so much the infidelity as such, for after all it had happened eighteen years earlier, as the deception, the betrayal of trust—slipping another man's child knowingly into his family, like certain birds that slip their eggs into another bird's nest.

All the years of frustration and self-reproach for being an insufficient, a conditionally loving father now came back to him—now that a reason and justification had at last been found. No wonder he had struggled with ambivalence toward Paul. No wonder the boy had sometimes seemed to him like a different species altogether, not only physically, although physically it was most apparent, but in his character as well and even deeper, in the very marrow of their respective natures where the basic vibrations of life are orchestrated— it was there, at the very source, that the two, father and son, purported father and purported son, differed fundamentally . . . .

Samuel now became aware of a good deal of anger at his wife, which added to his agitation because he had always considered himself a rational man not easily given to anger. How dare she have subjected him to all that? Because his ambivalence was tied to being Paul's natural father. Without his paternity he could have accepted their differences far more easily.

But what about his positive feelings toward the boy? Was he forgetting those in the onrush of his anger? Despite their friction, despite their differences, who knew, maybe just because of them, he became aware too of how much he loved the boy! Maybe their very friction had been the manure that had fertilized their relationship, making the boy more important and in some ways more beloved almost than Sofie, toward whom his feelings had always flowed so freely and easily.

Samuel's feelings were in turmoil as layer upon complex layer of emotion began to surface.

But the boy's half-Jewish status was the most important immediate issue. Emilia had shown him the newspaper article, and he was aware that she was waiting for an answer, although she had not asked outright for one. But for days he found it impossible to speak to her, overwhelmed by his agitated feelings, so that it was Emilia herself who finally broached the subject again.

"May I go ahead now, Samuel?" she asked.

"You don't need my approval. Why are you asking me?"

"I don't need your approval for *them*. But I need it for me, Samuel. I need your blessing."

"My blessing!"

Tears started to his eyes.

"I know it's asking a lot," Emilia whispered.

"Too much!" Samuel blurted, turning away.

◆ ◆ ◆

But as the days went by, all that before had seemed to Samuel insensitive and disloyal on the part of his wife, a misguided obsession to join a cause that was utterly evil, gradually began to appear in a new light. She had not been insensitive. She would not have pursued this strange proposition had not the truth wanted out.

Nor was her request to have Paul declared an Aryan a betrayal, not that part of it, for it was the simple truth. It was good to know that much, at least, because it had been the sense of being betrayed and denied that had been hardest of all to bear.

Gradually Samuel even became aware of a certain sense of relief, as he began to understand Emilia's new-found religiosity with its driving need for atonement and penance. Most important, the whole question of whether she regretted having married him because he was a Jew evaporated in the face of this new revelation and her expression of love.

Suddenly all the things that had so upset him before became comprehensible because it was the truth, and that changed everything. To suppress the truth of the boy's *non*-Jewishness would have been as wrong as it would earlier have been wrong to suppress the truth of his half-Jewishness. Even the matter of joining the Nazis needed to be seen in a different light. Not every German automatically became a Nazi, nor need the boy become one. One could choose to become a Nazi, or not.

Thus, all the arguments that Samuel had previously marshalled against declaring Paul an Aryan collapsed one by one. No, he had no right to keep the boy from being what he was, regardless of the pain or consequences.

One evening about two weeks after the fateful revelation, Samuel called Emilia into the library and said to her:

"I know you've been waiting for my answer, Emilia. I'd like to give it to you now."

"Yes, Samuel?"

"You can go ahead."

"Thank you, *Männchen*," she whispered, her eyes filling with tears.

But she continued sitting, looking at him still, waiting, so that he finally added slowly:

"With my blessing."

The Decision

The gathering of the documentation in regard to the past of the baroness's father proved more laborious and time-consuming than expected but was after some weeks finally accomplished. There now followed another period of waiting, lasting well into the summer of 1938 while the annexation of Austria took place and it was becoming more and more apparent that the Nazis were not only here to stay but were marching forward with mounting confidence and success.

From time to time the baron called Dr. Metzner to inquire how the appeal was progressing, but for a long time there was nothing to report. On one such occasion, Dr. Metzner said, "Of course I can't say I'm surprised," and again brought up the matter of joining the Party.

That evening the baron said to his wife:

"Sometimes I wonder whether we shouldn't listen to Metzner. After all, he has no axe to grind and should know what he's talking about. And the Nazis do have some good points," he added thoughtfully.

"Do they?" the baroness replied caustically. "That's like saying a killer loves little children."

"Come Olga, they're really not as bad as all that."

"What they did to papa was as bad! What they do to Jews and political enemies is as bad! God only knows who else they'll kill before they're through."

"Please lower your voice, Olga," the baron said, lowering his own. "There's no need for the servants to hear. Or the children, for that matter."

"Why shouldn't they learn what kind of a country they're growing up in?" the baroness shot back heatedly. "That you would even consider it."

The baron remained silent, embarrassed by her outburst. Why was she so exercised? Only ill-bred, vulgar people like the Nazis wore their emotions on their shirtsleeves.

"We seem to be drifting further and further apart," the baroness said after some moments.

"I can't say I'm aware of it."

They were silent. At length the baroness said gently:

"Do you know how long it has been since you've come to my rooms, Otto?"

He shifted uncomfortably. "Maybe tomorrow, Olga."

As for joining the Party, the baron came to no decision. And thus, in effect, came to a decision: namely, not to join.

◆ ◆ ◆

Then one day Dr. Metzner called the baron and asked to see him without delay. When they had settled down after the usual formalities, the lawyer said:

"I thought the matter too delicate to discuss over the phone. I have heard—through personal connections—that the appeal isn't going well at all and will in all likelihood be turned down—*unless!*" the lawyer hastened to add, raising his hand as if to ward off the baron's interruption, "a greater readiness to join the cause can be demonstrated on the part of the beneficiaries."

"Really," the baron said stiffly.

"Baron," the lawyer said bluntly, all at once dropping his unctuous circumlocutions, "you must join the Party post-haste if you still want to have a ghost of a chance to win the appeal."

He stopped with the air of a man who has said all there is to say, leaving the baron to stew in his own discomfort. It was the discomfort of a man who had known for some time about the possibility of an event but had discounted it, only to find that it was suddenly upon him with a vengeance.

"May I ask on what authority you know this?" the baron asked.

"The best, I assure you, the very best, my dear Baron, although I'm not at liberty to disclose it," the lawyer said, returning to his usual manner. "You must understand that the court needs to cover itself—vis-à-vis, shall we say—higher authorities—if queried... you understand?"

"I do. But is there any assurance we will win if I do join?"

"I'm afraid not, my dear Baron. These things don't get spelled out in a contract, you know. But it's—let's just say it'll increase your chances one hundred percent."

"In other words, you're asking me to buy a pig in a poke."

"That's not the way I would put it," the lawyer said with a frozen smile. "I would also remind you, my dear Baron, that you are hardly in a position to bargain."

"Is there no possibility of influencing the outcome—more directly?" the baron hazarded.

The last remnant of the lawyer's smile disappeared from his face.

"Baron," he said and now his tone and words were unmincingly blunt, "we are dealing with an honorable German court. I will choose not to have heard the last question."

The baron himself felt surprised by his proposal. He could not recall ever having tried to bribe anyone—that was beneath his dignity. He suddenly felt a keen discomfort. How could he have permitted himself to bargain like a Jew?

"Give it some thought, Baron," the lawyer said, making a motion to terminate their meeting. "Some *quick* thought, because time is of the essence."

The baron could not help noticing the unceremonious dropping of the unctuous "my dear." Indeed, there was suddenly in the lawyer's tone and manner a blunt directness, as if he no longer found it necessary to sheathe his fangs. Subtly the tables seemed to have been turned.

♦ ◆ ♦

That evening the baron got rather drunk in Ingeborg's apartment, a rare occurrence with him, so much so that Ingeborg felt it necessary to accompany him back to the car where Schulman was waiting, patient Schulman who whiled away the long hours of waiting by fantasizing about his master's sexual exploits in raw detail. On the way home, the baron slept while loyal Schulman navigated through the night with echoes of orgiastic fantasies lingering in his mind. Arrived home, he awoke the baron, who was roused only with effort, and helped him upstairs to his rooms while the big, ancient house creaked quietly all around them.

But next morning the need for a decision stood as starkly as ever before him—in fact, a little more painfully so on account of his hangover—brooking no further equivocation or postponement.

The baron didn't like decisions, hard and fast decisions that could not be reversed or backed out of or overturned.

He now became aware of something he had strenuously tried to deny before: that, far from being indifferent to his wife's estate, he cared very much for it! The prospect of losing two-thirds of the estate suddenly jarred him to such an extent that it became clear to him that he was by no means ready to give up the estate without a strenuous fight.

♦ ◆ ♦

The baroness rang for Marianne. When she came, she curtsied, somewhat perfunctorily, looking neat and pretty in her black uniform and small white apron. How nice she must look in a colorful dress, the baroness thought.

"Would you like to be massaged, ma'm?" Marianne inquired.

The baroness nodded gratefully. Always Marianne had this intuitive tact, making it sound as if it were her own idea rather than the baroness's. She wouldn't have admitted it to anyone—she hardly admitted it even to herself—but time and again after lunch, with its attendant glass or two of wine, which she and the baron never took together even when he was at home, there now ensued this little struggle as to whether she should call for Marianne or not. It was ludicrous. Sometimes the baroness thought that she would simply incorporate the massage into her daily routine—the girl clearly enjoyed it, besides it took her away from more onerous chores—but her pride always held her back.

Marianne unhooked her bra, and she stood for some moments looking at herself in the full-length mirror.

"I think the massage helps keep my weight down," she said pensively. "What do you think, Marianne?"

The maid appeared behind her in the mirror, looking at her mistress in the mirror as if looking at her directly would trespass on some forbidden boundary.

"I think so, ma'm."

"Only my stomach. Alas, a woman's Waterloo."

"Her what, ma'm?"

"Defeat," the baroness said, stretching out on her stomach on the narrow couch.

"Maybe massaging the stomach would help," Marianne offered as she began to massage the baroness's back.

"Do you think so?" the baroness said, closing her eyes as she abandoned herself to the soft, rhythmic stroke and kneading of the maid's deft, gentle hands. It was a sensation akin to floating on a slowly moving river and brought with it a feeling of surrender and security that reminded her of her childhood. As a child, an only child, she had felt like that: protected and secure, knowing that everything was all right because her parents, and especially her father, were there. Maybe that was the secret link that made the massage such a deeply comforting experience.

"What kind of a childhood did you have, Marianne?"

"Nothin' special, ma'm. Just a childhood."

"Was it happy?"

"I guess so. I don't rightly remember. A childhood's a childhood."

"Ah, you're wrong, Marianne. It's a golden time. The trouble is, we don't realize it."

The maid's palms and nimble fingers continued to massage her back, grazing the soft sides of her breasts. The touch reverberated in the baroness, though it was no more than a fleeting touch.

"We take a lot for granted, that's the trouble," the baroness mused. "That is, what we have we take for granted, what we don't have—*that* we keep complaining about."

"Yes, ma'm."

The baroness could tell that Marianne hadn't understood. She was a sensitive, tactful girl, but that didn't mean she was sophisticated or even very bright. How strange, the baroness's thoughts drifted on, that Marianne didn't seem to have a boy friend. Could she really still be a virgin at twenty-one? They said girls from the lower classes lost their virginity early. Maybe the girl just wasn't letting on. Under her surface amiability, there always seemed to lurk something hidden and secretive. The thought that she had a boy friend sent a jolt through the baroness that she suppressed at once. Why shouldn't she have a boy friend?

"Shall we try the tummy, ma'm?" Marianne asked.

The baroness rolled over on her back and closed her eyes, aware that Marianne was now seeing the whole of her, not only her exposed breasts but the cushion of pubic hair hidden under her brief, sheer panties. It was a strange feeling, at once exciting and unsettling. What was Marianne thinking? She felt Marianne's gentle fingers moving down along her body, felt her fingers coming closer and closer to the area of her pubic hair and then felt her hands leaving her stomach and alighting with quick chopping, kneading motions on her upper thighs, working downward toward the ankles and finally the soles of her feet, where they lingered with a soft rubbing motion that was intensely pleasurable. And now she became conscious of Marianne's rotated perspective as she stood at the foot of the couch and looked up at her past her slightly spread legs.

She felt herself tensing and, opening her eyes, sat up.

"Thank you, Marianne," she said with unintentional curtness. "That was very good. We must do it again soon."

◆ ◆ ◆

That Saturday the baron informed the baroness that the appeal appeared lost. She received the news silently but turned quite pale. Finally she said:

"Can the appeal be appealed?"

"Theoretically, yes. But Metzner considers that utterly futile."

After a moment he added:

"There is one more thing we could try though: Werner Strapp."

The baroness tensed.

"I know how you feel about him, Olga. But he does have the ear of the *Gauleiter*. And he did offer to help."

"You know what he'll demand."

Yes, the baron knew. But now the battle was joined: It was the estate or joining the Party.

"The price is too high, Otto," the baroness added.

He took a deep breath.

"I don't think so, Olga."

The words had come out spontaneously, but the minute they did, he felt comfortable with them. No, the price was not too high if it would save the estate! It was false pride that had kept him from joining. The Nazis had accomplished a good many worthwhile things and would accomplish more if given the chance. By joining he would have some input, as Werner had said, instead of watching from the sidelines. Was the *Vaterland* not worth this sacrifice, this *Vaterland* that was as much his as theirs? All at once the decision no longer seemed so difficult but obvious and almost easy. Why had he agonized over it for so long?

He got up, anxious to terminate the conversation, as if afraid that lingering would undermine his new-found resolution.

"We'll talk more about it some other time," he said.

Which was dishonest because it implied that his wife could still influence a decision that he had at last reached with finality.

♦ ◆ ♦

He called Werner the very next day and asked to see him as soon as possible. Werner invited him to come over to his apartment.

"Today? on Sunday?"

"What better day to see friends?" Werner replied amiably. "Besides, my Sundays haven't been Sundays for a long time."

When he arrived at his apartment, Werner opened the door dressed in a stylish dressing gown, a cigarette in his hand, and led him into the living room where a uniformed SS major stood by the desk. The relaxed manner in which Werner introduced the officer indicated how used he had become to wielding power.

"Anything else, *Herr Oberfuehrer*?" the SS major asked in a military manner, winding up their business.

Werner bristled. "Keller, how many times have I told you—" He shrugged and made a dismissing gesture. "No, that's all for today."

The officer made his boot-clicking, *Heil Hitler* departure. Werner threw himself into an armchair, waving the baron into another, and stared for some moments fitfully into the air. It was one of the few times the baron had seen him temporarily out of energy.

"God save me from lackeys," Werner muttered.

Presently he bounded out of the chair.

"How about a drink, Otto?"

He poured out a couple of cognacs.

"So you're an *Oberfuehrer* now," the baron said, impressed against his will. "I had no idea you were so high up in the SS. That's a general, isn't it?"

Werner laughed. "So I've finally impressed you, you blue-blooded stiff-neck you!" he said in his blunt manner. "Actually, not quite. A special SS rank. Creates a lot of confusion. Below a general but above a colonel. Strictly between the two of us, of course. I don't advertise my rank. Keller shouldn't either, but some people can't do without that yes-sir, no-sir stuff." He waved his hand disparagingly. "So what's doing with you, Otto? I'm glad to see you. Really glad. A change of pace. That's what I need: a change of pace."

"I told you you're always welcome at my place. Come for a weekend—a week."

Werner roared with laughter.

"A week! You know how long it's been since I took a vacation? I figured it out the other day—seven *years*! I don't belong to the leisure class like you."

He raised his glass and took a big gulp. Behind the banter, the baron sensed a slightly superior tone, the hallmark of a man used to ordering others about. A subtle change had taken place in Werner since he had last seen him.

"A weekend sounds good, though," Werner continued. "Maybe I can swing that—some time."

"I hope you can. That would be delightful."

The words sounded formal, but the baron meant them. He liked Werner. In fact, he was somewhat awed by him. For in Werner he felt that he was facing the New Germany that was elbowing its way onto the world stage, a New Germany that was raw and vulgar, true, but also powerful and fascinating.

"I appreciate your seeing me so soon," he presently said, aware that Werner was waiting for him to present his "case." He suddenly realized that Werner was no doubt daily confronted with innumerable people pleading their cases. The image of himself among them was distasteful to him. "There is, hm, a little matter..." he began but stopped, aware of the falseness of his words. "You remember, Werner, the last time we met you asked whether there was anything you could do for me. Well, I think now there is something—I don't really know whether you can help, but I thought I'd ask."

"Go ahead."

"May I take a moment to explain the background?"

"Go ahead."

"You probably haven't heard about a certain Freiherr von Wedlingen?"

"No."

"He was a battalion commander in the Great War who had a distinguished service record. In fact, he received the *Ritterkreuz*. He was my father-in-law. I say *was* because unfortunately he was a bit of a blabbermouth and kept shooting off his mouth against Hitler and sundry—maybe he was a bit shellshocked. Anyway, one day he was hauled off to a concentration camp where he evidently didn't keep his mouth shut either, for soon afterwards he was—we're not entirely sure what happened. But it seems he received a severe beating. After which he was released. But he never recovered and, three months later, died abruptly of a cerebral hemorrhage."

The baron paused. Werner too remained silent and betrayed no emotion. The baron sensed a sudden distance between them, as if their apolitical friendship had suddenly been hauled into a political arena where it was split into opposing loyalties.

"Why are you coming to me now?" Werner asked, finally. "I might have been able to do something for him while he was in the camp."

"I wish we had come to you," the baron said, wondering why they hadn't. But it had never occurred to him that Werner had a position powerful enough to effect a man's release from a concentration camp. "The reason I'm coming now is that the government wants to expropriate—under the guise of a special tax—the bulk of his estate, claiming that it belongs to an Enemy of the State."

"Where is the case now?"

"With the Appellate Court. But my lawyer has learned, confidentially, that we're about to lose the appeal."

"Has there been an official verdict yet?"

"No, nothing official."

"Hm."

Werner sat thinking, swirling the cognac about in his glass.

"We don't like to mess with the judiciary, if we can help it," he said pensively after some moments. "But maybe the case could be transferred to a *Sondergericht* since it involves an Enemy of the State."

The *Sondergericht* was a special court, established outside the normal structure of the judiciary, to try cases involving anti-Nazi activities.

"I thought the sentences of the *Sondergericht* are harsher," the baron interjected.

"Generally, yes. But, being *special* courts they're more amenable to—shall we say, direction and control."

"I see. If that's so—whatever you can do will be greatly appreciated, Werner."

"Really?" Werner looked at him with a sly smile. "And how do you propose to show your appreciation?"

The question was launched with such directness that it took the baron aback.

"I'm prepared to join the Party, if that's what you mean."

"Well, that's a change. And a good start. But I have something more than that in mind."

"I see. I'm sure we can arrange something. Maybe a percentage—or a lump sum—depending on the judgment...."

Werner suddenly broke into a loud guffaw, slapping his thigh.

"You think I'm one of those venal hypocrites, eh?" he cried. "If you weren't a good friend I'd really take offense, Otto!"

"I'm sorry," the baron mumbled, confused.

"You underestimate my belief in the New Reich, my belief in Hitler who, I happen to think, is one of the authentic great men of all time. Besides, I don't approve of beating *Ritterkreuzträger* to a pulp."

"I'm sorry," the baron mumbled again, becoming more and more confused. "I didn't mean to insult you... I thought...."

Werner leaned forward.

"I do want something more, Otto. Something more valuable than money."

"I'm not following you."

"I want your heart, Otto. Not just lip service," Werner said intensely. "I want your faith. In the New Germany, the Germany of the future, not your Old Germany that's past and done with and rotting in the grave. I want your loyalty, Otto. I want your *soul!*"

"That can't be given on orders, Werner."

Werner sat back and poured himself another drink.

"I thought you would be pleased that I was willing to join the Party," the baron said. "That's more than I was willing to do until now."

"I am. Of course, I am," Werner said, sipping on his glass. "I take it," he continued, subtly baiting his words, "that you're joining on condition that the appeal is successful."

"I wouldn't put it quite so—crassly."

"How would you put it?"

The baron felt hot and uncomfortable.

"My lawyer suggested several times that I join the Party to sway the judges, and I didn't," he said defensively.

"Maybe because you hoped to win the appeal without it. You *are* doing it to win the appeal, aren't you?"

"Yes," the baron admitted reluctantly.

"Funny, isn't it, Otto. And you thought I was venal. It seems some of us nasty Nazis don't lag behind you blue bloods when it comes to honor."

He took a sip from his glass and rolled it pensively around his tongue.

"All right," he said. "I'll see what I can do."

At the door the baron extended his hand.

"Werner," he said solemnly, and for once it was he who earnestly pumped the other's hand. "I shan't forget your help."

◆ ◆ ◆

The meeting left the baron in an ambivalent mood: at once pleased and troubled. But in the end the feeling won out that it had been a good trade. How could a movement be wicked that elevated a decent, honorable man like Werner to such a position of power? The baron felt a warm glow.

It wasn't until he had almost arrived home that the thought of his wife made him feel uneasy. How would she take it?

He briefly considered keeping the meeting secret but as quickly dropped the idea. His wife had a right to know. It was her estate, after all. Anyhow, joining the Party was his business. He had entered into a bargain and would keep it, being a man of honor. For whom was he doing it anyway?

He invited his wife to his study after the girls had gone to bed, duly kissed good night and patted on the cheeks by their father.

"Do you have a Benedictine, Otto?" the baroness inquired after they had sat down.

"I wish you wouldn't have any more, Olga. I have something of importance to tell you."

It was true that she had drunk rather more than usual at dinner. She felt a flash of anger but restrained herself.

"As you know, I went to see Werner today," the baron began. "I told him exactly what happened to your father. It might interest you to know that he doesn't approve of beating *Ritterkreuzträger* to a pulp. Those are his very words."

"Don't tell me that he offered to bring the offenders to justice," the baroness interjected sarcastically.

"Werner happens to be a very decent fellow, an idealistic fellow. I really don't know why you dislike him so much, Olga. The gist is that he offered to have our case transferred to a *Sondergericht*."

"A *Sondergericht*!" the baroness exclaimed. "So the whole estate can be confiscated?"

"That was my objection too. But his answer was, yes, they're generally harsher but they take orders from outside—meaning, in this case, from the *Gauleiter*—and he's an aide of the *Gauleiter's*. I had no idea he was so far up in the hierarchy. Do you know he's almost a general?"

"In the SS!" she snapped caustically. "He has really impressed you, hasn't he?"

"I wish you'd stop sniping at him."

"You used to be turned off by those people, Otto. And now they impress you."

"I would think you would be impressed, too. The higher he is, the more helpful he can be to us. Don't you see that, Olga?"

"And what's the trade-off?"

She always came straight to the point, the baron thought.

"The trade-off..." he began hesitantly. "You remember what you yourself have said many times, Olga—that you won't let them take away your father's property in addition to his life?"

"But not at the price of joining the killers!"

"Don't start with that again. Just because some sadists are rampant in the concentration camps doesn't mean they're all killers."

"Since when have you become an apologist for the Nazis?" the baroness snapped.

"Curb your voice, will you?" the baron ejaculated under his breath. "The servants don't have to hear all this."

They both fell silent.

"I would think you'd appreciate what I'm doing," the baron said after a while. "Most wives would. I'm not doing it just for me, you know, but for you, for our family, our name, our heritage. We can't help what they did to your father, but at least we can try not to let them get away with stealing his property."

"It's precisely our heritage that's involved—Germany's heritage. Don't you see that, Otto? They've corrupted everything Germany stood for. I don't want to give them a penny either, but joining them gives them something more than money. It gives them your heart and mind. It gives them your soul!"

How like Werner's words, he thought. Everyone wants your heart and soul.

"You're exaggerating, Olga," he said drily. "Joining the Party doesn't mean I'm selling my soul. It merely means writing my name on a piece of paper."

"But that piece of paper means something!" the baroness exclaimed. "It'll be used to convince little people who look up to us and our family—look what the von Hallenbergs are doing; if they join, the Nazis must be all right!"

There was a long pause as each tried to retreat from the confrontation into which they had been hurled with more passion than either had intended. Presently the baroness got up and went to the liquor cabinet and poured herself a drink while the baron watched, resentfully aware that she was trespassing on an unspoken rule that she was a guest in his study.

"You might have asked at least," he murmured, annoyed.

She walked with the drink to the large picture window and stood looking out into the rose garden.

"You used to be a man of integrity when I met you," she said without turning around.

The baron felt a twinge of anger. But it presently gave way to a feeling of uneasiness mixed with admiration for this wife of his who was so sure of her convictions. How was it that he didn't have any strong convictions? All he really wanted was to be left alone with what he was born with. But was that enough? A man like Werner didn't care to defend what he was born with. Of course. Because he was born with so little. But Werner possessed something more valuable—a readiness to do battle, to stand up for his convictions— just like his wife.

He walked to the bar and poured himself a drink, too.

There was little further talk between them that evening.

* ◆ *

The baron's application to join the Nazi Party was speedily approved. The baroness learned of his acceptance from the mailman, a devoted Nazi who innocently tendered his congratulations. But by then the baroness had become so inured to the prospect that she did not even bother to mention her discovery to the baron.

Meanwhile, matters took their course with the appeal. Dr. Metzner was notified that the case was being transferred to the jurisdiction of a *Sondergericht*, which he rightfully took to be dreadful news, seeing in it corroboration of his worst predictions, since the baron did not inform him of the actual state of affairs. The lawyer's surprise was even greater when the *Sondergericht* promptly reversed the judgment of the lower court. But even then the baron did not enlighten the baffled lawyer, although he did tell him that he had joined the Nazi Party.

"Congratulations, my dear Baron," the lawyer said. "A wise decision, a most wise decision. Still," he added, puzzled, "it's most peculiar. *Most* peculiar."

The baron called Werner as soon as he heard the good news and sent him a case of genuine French cognac.

"My heartfelt thanks to you again, Werner," he said. "And of course I went through with my end of the bargain."

"I know," Werner said complacently. "In fact, I'm planning a little surprise for you."

"What kind of a surprise?"

"Ha, ha!" Werner laughed. "I ain't tellin'."

The baroness received the news of the reversal almost wordlessly. The baron made a point of telling her the news with a certain flourish that was meant to convey what he was too refined to voice in so many words: namely, an air of triumph and vindication that he had made the right decision. As far as he was concerned, the mere formality of joining the Nazi Party was a cheap price to pay for what had been achieved!

* ◆ *

Although the baron and the baroness had for some time lived separate lives, nonetheless their marriage had possessed until then an element of friendliness and amiability. Now even this drained away, although, paradoxically, the baroness's fierce opposition, so lacking in her docile acceptance of his mistresses, rekindled some of the respect and admiration the baron had felt for her in the early years of their marriage. The change was most apparent at dinner time, which, though it had never been a lively occasion, now drowned in a miasma of superficial social chatter.

As for the baroness, to her long-standing loneliness now was added a loss of respect for her husband, which further aggravated her loneliness. She tried to relieve it by drinking even more, which further alienated the baron, and by resorting more and more often to a massage, which was at times merely a means of relaxation but at other times had become overtly sexual. One-sided as it was, it was an experience that Marianne seemed to enjoy, perhaps because it put the maid in a superior position to her mistress, while it left the baroness, after a transient illusion of meaningful human contact, more bereft and empty than ever.

Now that the decision to join the Nazi Party had finally been made, the baron experienced, in addition to relief, a certain secret excitement, as if about to partake of forbidden fruit. He was joining a vulgar but all the same carefree rabble, a rabble unencumbered by tradition and restraining moral values. For in a secret corner of his heart, the baron sometimes found his orderly life, so regulated by custom, routine, and repetition, to be a little burdensome, and at such times he would fantasize about breaking out of the cosy strait-jacket of his life. How free it must feel to be a mere Otto-what's-his-name, to break the golden chain that held him fettered!

◆ ◆ ◆

If the baron thought that he could sneak into the Nazi Party through the back door, so to speak, unobserved and unheralded, he was in for a rude surprise. Shortly after becoming a Party member, he received an unctuous letter from the *Kreisleiter** welcoming him into the Party and announcing that he would be the guest of honor at a festivity that the *Kreisleiter* had the pleasure of giving in his honor since his illustrious family had been a mainstay of the *Kreis* since the days of the Thirty Year's War! His decision to join the "dynamic progressive forces of National Socialism" was of the utmost importance, so important that the *Herr Baron* would be pleased to learn that a high-ranking member of the

---

* The Nazi-appointed head of a government unit resembling a county.

Gauleiter's personal staff would attend the festivity, as well as reporters from the leading newspapers.

If the baron needed any proof that this was Werner's handiwork, he received it two days later when he was called by the *Gauleiter's* office and Werner came on the line.

"About that invitation, Otto," Werner said cheerily. "I'd be delighted to take you up on it for a weekend."

And he went on to name the exact weekend when the *Kreisleiter's* festivity was to take place.

"You wouldn't happen to be the *Gauleiter's personal* representative at the initiation festivity the *Kreisleiter* is arranging in my honor, would you?" the baron inquired.

"The what?" Werner replied, tongue-in-cheek.

"And you didn't by any chance *suggest* to the *Kreisleiter* that he arrange this festivity in the first place?"

"Whatever makes you think that," Werner said innocently.

The baron remained silent, struggling with a mixture of admiration and anger.

"Come on, Otto," Werner said, picking up his feeling. "You received your money's worth. Now I want my pound of flesh."

The baron realized instantly the added complications this festivity would bring into his already complicated relationship with his wife. For his wife's reaction was, as he had anticipated, categorical: She would not come to the festivity if Hitler himself attended! But how could he attend a festivity of this sort *without* his wife? Her absence would be tantamount to proclaiming her opposition in public. Werner's presence, both at the festivity and in his home, further complicated a situation for which he could see no acceptable resolution whatever.

In the end, the baroness fell ill the day before Werner's arrival. The baron automatically suspected that the illness was feigned, but when he learned that their family doctor had been summoned, he hastened to her rooms.

He found her in bed looking pale and unkempt, which was unusual for her. Her face had a puffy, suffering expression, and she spoke haltingly. She had awakened, she told him, with sharp abdominal pains.

Their conversation was interrupted by the arrival of the doctor, who examined her while the baron waited outside. On coming out, the doctor said:

"I was afraid it might be appendicitis. Fortunately it isn't."

"What is it then?"

"I don't know. But it bears watching. Abdominal pains always do. Meanwhile, the baroness is to stay in bed. I'll be by again tomorrow."

That the doctor, a strait-laced, conscientious type, was in cahoots with his wife was out of the question. The baron returned to her room.

"Seems the doctor is stymied," he said.

"Yes," the baroness said softly. "If it just wouldn't hurt so."

They left it at that. The baron never found out whether the pain was real or feigned or neither, namely psychological. Nor did he want to know. All in all it was not a bad solution, he thought, certainly better than any he had been able to find.

When Werner arrived next morning, the baron explained his wife's indisposition. Indeed, he amplified it some. Werner made no comment. No particular love had ever been lost between Werner and the baroness even before Werner had joined the Nazis, although their relations had always been coldly cordial.

Thus, the baron found himself sitting alone on the reviewing stand, flanked by the *Kreisleiter* on one side and Werner in civilian clothes on the other, while contingents of Hitler Youth and *Bund Deutscher Mädel* paraded past with a Hitler salute that he returned with a frozen smile, and a band shrilled a strident accompaniment that was mercifully toned down somewhat at the evening dance. But the most painful thing of all were the speeches: Werner's, elegant, intelligent, adroitly taking advantage of the occasion; the *Kreisleiter's*, fawning, gushy, trying to live up to the occasion with embarrassing poetic flights; finally the baron's own speech, which he tried to make as brief and noncommittal as possible without giving offense.

Through it all, the baron squirmed inside and felt intensely uncomfortable.

The Name Change

Once Samuel had given his "blessing" to Paul's transformation into an Aryan, Emilia proceeded with her plan. It was the *Deutsche Rasseamt*, the German Race Office, that she had to petition for a declaratory judgment that Paul was a pure German.

Soon after filing her petition, she received a notice asking her to present herself in person at the Race Office. When she did, she was referred to a man who sat with some self-importance in a small office.

"We have received your petition, Mrs. Silver," he informed her. "In the main it is in order and contains all the necessary information—except for one crucial item."

"And what is that?" Emilia asked apprehensively.

"The identity of the natural father."

"But—I was told that's optional."

"Whoever told you that is absolutely wrong, I assure you," the official said emphatically.

"I can't give the name of the father!" Emilia blurted.

The man looked at her with an insolent smile. "You mean—" he began.

Emilia suddenly understood how he took it.

"No, no," she corrected herself quickly. "I do know the father. But I prefer not to name him."

"Mrs. Silver, let me set you straight," the man now said condescendingly. "It's not a question of what you prefer. That information is absolutely mandatory."

"Couldn't an exception be made? You see—the father doesn't know. . . ."

"Mrs. Silver." The man's tone was a little softer now for he was torn in his loyalties: As a Nazi charged with upholding the purity of the German race, he welcomed women like Emilia as strayed sheep returning to the fold, but as a man he felt contempt and anger at her infidelity. "I assure you, you could go to the director of the *Rasseamt* himself and he would tell you precisely the same thing. However, I can assure you that the matter will be kept in strictest confidence once the man has made his deposition."

"You mean, he has to make a deposition as well?" Emilia exclaimed.

"Of course," the man said and now his tone was not only condescending but plainly annoyed. "Otherwise anyone could come along and make such a claim."

◆ ◆ ◆

As she hurried away from the building, Emilia's thoughts were in turmoil. Would Baron von Hallenberg admit their liaison, let alone his paternity? And even if he did, what then? The possible consequences were too unnerving to contemplate.

Of course she could abandon the whole project. But she very quickly dropped that idea. Not after putting Samuel, and herself too, through all this agony. Moreover, her rehabilitation in God's eyes was not supposed to be easy. She had prayed that this bitter cup would pass from her, but how it would pass was for God to decide. This too was part of God's retribution, that she needed to humiliate herself before the baron.

In the end, her religious need for atonement and punishment once again carried all else before it.

It was not difficult to obtain Baron von Hallenberg's telephone number, but getting through to him personally was more difficult. Finally she was given a time to call back. When she did, a man came on the line.

"This is Baron von Hallenberg."

"I'm—I'm someone you knew a long time ago, Baron von—Otto," Emilia began awkwardly. What did one say to a near stranger with whom one has had, eighteen years earlier, a brief relationship that had become concretized in a human life? "This is Emilia. Emilia Silver. Do you remember me?"

There was a pause, whether because the baron struggled to remember or because he was surprised, Emilia had no way of knowing, but the pause seemed endless to her. Finally he said:

"I do remember you, Emilia, of course I do." The baron's voice hovered between friendliness and distance. "How have you been?"

"Fine, thank you."

Again there was a pause. Finally Emilia said:

"I'd like to—I mean, I must—talk to you, Otto. If I may. Please!"

"What about?"

"It's a personal matter, too personal to discuss on the phone," she said quickly.

This much at least she had prepared in advance, as also a meeting place.

"All right," the baron said. "Where would you like to meet?"

After the arrangements had been made and Emilia hung up, she became aware that she was in a sweat and trembling.

◆ ◆ ◆

The meeting place Emilia had found was a rather unfrequented café in a side street. She came early and positioned herself at a table that afforded a clear view of the door, while partly shielding her. And waited, starting each time the door opened. An excruciating, intolerable wait. Had the baron changed much in eighteen years? And what about herself? She dabbed nervously at her hair but in a moment felt angry at herself for wanting to make a good impression on the baron not only for the sake of her objective, but, well, for her own sake as well.

Once more the door opened. This time a tall, elegantly dressed man entered and stopped by the door, looking around as he pulled off his gloves, and now she was certain that it was the baron and in a moment their eyes met. He approached slowly, a small, tentative smile on his face.

"Emilia," he said pleasantly, extending his hand. "I would have recognized you anywhere. Why, you look as lovely as ever."

She laughed, half-embarrassed, half-pleased, feeling herself engulfed once again in the gracious congeniality that had so attracted her years before.

"I recognized you too at once, " she mumbled.

For a while they chitchatted to bring each other up-to-date while Emilia struggled to launch into the business proper. Finally, the conversation began to lag.

"I'm sure you were surprised to hear from me," she said.

"I must admit I was."

"If it could have been avoided—I would have done anything—as I've avoided it for eighteen years," she said, nervously twisting her wedding ring around her finger.

"That sounds ominous," he said with a slight chuckle.

"Yes, it will come as a shock to you."

"What will, Emilia?"

She took a deep breath.

"It has to do with—then. I never told you that our relationship had some—consequences. I became—I mean I was . . . pregnant," she blurted.

The baron's smile froze but he remained silent. She looked up and met his eyes.

"A boy, Otto."

Still there was no response from the baron, not a negative response and not a positive one, his face remaining rigid and inscrutable as if he had not heard her words. At length he said:

"How do you know it's my son?"

She opened her purse, took out an envelope and removed a handful of pictures, taken over the years, that she had carefully prepared. The baron looked at them thoughtfully, one by one, closely studying especially the most recent ones. Finally he put them down.

"And why are you telling me all this now, suddenly, after all these years?"

"Because my husband is a Jew."

"I knew that."

"It makes Paul a half-Jew. Half-Jews aren't treated like Jews but they're persecuted too. They can't enter any of the higher professions. There's even talk of them having to leave school."

"I've heard of that," the baron murmured.

"He's tall and fair and German-looking—just like you, Otto! Not at all like my husband."

They both fell silent.

"And the fact that I'm a baron and rather wealthy—has nothing to do with it?"

That thought had never even occurred to her! She stared at him, her eyes filling with tears.

"If I had been after that, why would I have waited all these years, Otto?"

Again the baron remained silent.

"I swear before God Almighty that he's your son, Otto! If it hadn't been for the Nazis, you would never have known—but God is punishing me . . . ."

Tears had begun to roll down her cheeks. She pulled out a handkerchief and quietly cried into it. The unpretentious simplicity and honesty of the act touched the baron.

"Please stop crying, Emilia," he said, torn between sympathy and irritation. "I can't talk to you that way."

She dried her tears.

"I'm sorry," she said, forcing her face into an expression of composure. "I've petitioned the *Rasseamt* but they won't consider my petition without your deposition."

"I see."

There was a long pause. Finally the baron said:

"I'm sure you understand this isn't something I can decide on the spur of the moment. It involves my name, my family, my wife—"

"She doesn't have to know," Emilia interrupted quickly. "They assured me at the *Rasseamt* that your name will be handled in strictest confidence."

"I see. I *will* give the matter my most serious consideration, Emilia," the baron said, closing the subject. "That much I promise you."

◆ ◆ ◆

The memory of the young, buxom, dimpled young woman with whom he had had a brief affair years before was one of the cherished memories of the baron's life, a memory he had not forgotten, to his own surprise. But the thought that he had fathered a child with her was something else again.

At first the baron could not help dwelling on certain suspicions. But as he continued to think about it, they began to lose their substance. If she had wanted to blackmail him, she would hardly have waited, as she said, until the boy was almost grown up. That argument alone was irrefutable. But even more irrefutable was the boy's appearance. His figure and features bore an unmistakable likeness to his own. There could be no doubt of it.

This did not mean, of course, that the matter was simple or that he would rush to do Emilia's bidding. For one thing, he needed to be sure that the matter would be treated in strictest confidence. After all, his wife and children were involved, his family name.

To check out the question of confidentiality, he called the *Rasseamt* himself under the guise of calling for a client. The information he obtained confirmed that the name would be kept confidential, as far as the Race Office was concerned, but it was questionable of how much value that was, the man said, because—

"You realize, of course, that the child has to take the father's name."

"You mean, the child would be a—a full-fledged son with—with . . . and take on the father's name?"

"Of course," the man said drily. "A son is a son. Do you think we would permit the son of a pure-blooded Aryan to run around with a Jewish name?"

The baron hung up in high excitement. For the thought had suddenly exploded in his mind—a son! an heir! How come he hadn't thought of it himself at once?

So the answer formed itself effortlessly.

But there were certain conditions.

◆ ◆ ◆

When they met again at the same café a week later, Emilia looked pale and tired. After a brief exchange of small talk, the baron came to the point at once.

"I've given the matter considerable thought, Emilia," he began. "I'm sure you appreciate that it's not an easy decision to make as the boy will have to take my name—"

"Your name?" Emilia interrupted.

"Yes."

"But his name is Silver!" Emilia exclaimed. "He isn't a baron!"

"He is if he's my son," the baron said, somewhat nettled. "I am a baron, you know."

"On the birth certificate perhaps, yes—but that's a mere formality. I mean—in everyday life he'll continue to carry his present name."

"Emilia!" the baron exclaimed, at once amused by her naiveté and annoyed at her ignorance. "He has to be enrolled in school under his legal name. Besides, you want him to be a full-fledged German, don't you? How can he be with a name that's clearly Jewish?"

"But Paul isn't a baron," Emilia stammered, getting more and more confused. "He was brought up in a middle-class Jewish home—he thinks my husband is his father."

"He can't have two fathers. You're asking *me* to be his father."

"You are—his biological father. But my husband is still his—his—*real* father!" she blurted.

She stopped, flustered, suddenly realizing that she was arguing against her own cause. The nitty-gritty details had never clearly presented themselves to her. In her mind she had naively expected that the boy would continue in every way as he was—except that he would have the privileges of a German.

The baron took advantage of her silence.

"Emilia, I've decided to declare my paternity. But you must understand," he added quickly, seeing her grateful reaction, "that this means he must truly be my son."

"What do you mean?"

"I mean that he can't be my son and think that he's your husband's son at the same time."

"Yes. Paul will have to know, of course. I'll talk to him soon. I promise."

"You mean, he doesn't know yet?"

"Not yet."

"I think you still don't quite understand the situation, Emilia. Let me be explicit. It'll have to be more than just telling him I'm his father. I'd like to get to know him. I'd like to have a hand in his education. I don't doubt that you gave him a good upbringing, but I'd like my son to be brought up in a manner befitting his new status. Of course I'll assume all the financial responsibilities."

"I'm not asking you to do that. I'm not asking you to adopt him."

"If he's my son, I don't need to adopt him," the baron said tartly.

"But he can't disown his whole life!" Emilia cried.

"I'm not asking him to. I just want to have a hand in whatever happens to him from now on. I want to have a relationship with him. That's what you're asking me to do, isn't it?" the baron exclaimed, becoming more and more exasperated himself. "You can't have it both ways, Emilia."

They were both silent.

"I'm not willing merely to pretend," the baron said. "Even if it were possible—which it isn't."

"So—just what do you want?"

"I want to meet him so that we can get to know each other and become friends. I want to introduce him to my wife, my children, the estate—the business."

"I see."

Again both were silent.

"Anyway, those are my conditions, Emilia."

"I see," Emilia murmured.

◆ ◆ ◆

All that week Emilia had agonized over the baron's impending decision, afraid that he might refuse to acknowledge his paternity. And now, within an hour, the whole situation had once again changed as the very assent that she had feared the baron might not give had suddenly, by its very extent, become the problem.

Everything in Emilia rebelled against the notion that the baron would usurp her husband's place in Paul's life. Somehow she had always assumed that the change would only affect the boy's status in the world at large without bringing any change into their family life, deteriorated as that life had by now become. But what other options did the baron leave her?

Her most immediate fear centered on the forthcoming meeting with Paul. She had always known that she must one day inform Paul, but she had kept postponing it. How she would have loved Samuel to be present at their meeting, because his presence would have lent legitimacy to her infidelity. But that was asking too much.

She chose an hour when she and Paul were alone in the house. She invited Paul to her room because she felt safer there.

"Sit down, *Junge*," she said tensely.

Paul noticed that she was fidgety and solemn, which she rarely was. She remained standing by the window, as if needing to tower above the boy who was by this time half a head taller than she.

"I have something of great importance to tell you, Paul," she began hesitantly. "Something that will shock you—something that's very difficult for me . . . ." She faltered.

"What is it, mama?" Paul said uneasily.

"One wants one's child to think well of one . . ." Emilia whispered. "What I've done is a sin, and God is punishing me for it . . . ."

She began to speak hesitantly of the wealthy baron she had met many years before when she was only twenty-two and was alone for the summer, how she had been attracted to him and one day had been pushed into a compromising situation—she corrected herself, angry with herself for even yet trying to beautify and excuse her action: until one day she had found herself in an intimate position that she was every bit as guilty in provoking as the man.

"There's no need for all this, *Muttchen*," Paul interrupted. "We all have done things we'd rather forget. I'm only seventeen and already I could tell you a bundle."

Emilia waved aside his words.

"Hear me out, Paul. We can't sin and get away with it, and I have sinned and tried to get away with it, and now God is punishing me for it. So let me be."

She turned away and stared out of the window again while Paul remained silent, not daring to speak up again. Suddenly she turned back to him and said almost fiercely:

"That man is your father, Paul!"

Paul stared at her.

"Your father," Emilia repeated, as if responding to Paul's objection. "He wants to meet you—to get to know you . . . he has three daughters and is happy to have a son . . . ." A pleading note crept into Emilia's voice. "It means you're not a half-Jew anymore, Paul—it means you can get an education and go into any profession you want"—she was becoming fluent as she came to the reason and justification for her action—"you won't be shut out anymore, won't be beaten up anymore, won't be persecuted! It means you'll be able to take your rightful place in this New Germany!"

She stopped, panting a little. Suddenly she buried her face in her hands and her shoulders began to heave. Paul got up distressed and, bending down to her, placed his arm around her shoulder.

"*Muttchen*, please," he said hoarsely. "You wouldn't have had to do all this for me."

"I needed to do it, Paul . . . so God would forgive me . . . ."

♦ ◆ ♦

It was a while before the whole impact of the news really sank in on Paul. He had been unhappy over his ostracism as a half-Jew, wishing desperately that he could join the Hitler Youth, but to be so suddenly catapulted free in this manner was more than he had ever even fantasized. It meant that his whole way of seeing the world had abruptly been changed. It was like someone in a wheelchair suddenly finding out that he can walk or like a midget made tall overnight.

It was an intoxicating change: To be all at once a full-fledged German with all the rights and privileges of full-fledged citizenship and the son of a nobleman to boot! Baron Paul von Hallenberg. How the very name made the world resonate differently!

He would join the Hitler Youth and thumb his nose at all the boys who had avoided and tormented him until now. It was they who would come to him now, asking to be readmitted to his good graces. He spent hours lovingly elaborating the scene as he fantasized how he would return in a burst of glory and everyone would crowd around him and he would be spectacularly rehabilitated!

Before long, however, some other thoughts and feelings began to intrude. His real father wanted to meet him and take a hand in his future. How do you deal with a stranger who suddenly wants to take on the role and prerogatives of a father? How do you even address him? And then there was his—what was he now?—stepfather. How strange and unsettling to think that a man who had raised and nurtured him all his life was suddenly *not* his father! It was one thing to rebel against a father, such a rebellion still unfolded within a basically indissoluble relationship. But with a stepfather the whole frame of reference had changed, the whole framework of one's accountability.

Paul now became even more uneasy and uncomfortable in his stepfather's presence and as a result avoided him more than ever.

The name change itself materialized quickly, so quickly that even Emilia, much as she had lived with this for over a year now, found herself caught somewhat off guard. To suddenly see a registered letter addressed to Baron Paul von Hallenberg and realize that this is your son, to see the new name staring at you from an official document and then to go to the school and transact the name change itself in an unbelievably brief period of time, unbelievably brief considering the massive consequences this simple transposition of a few letters on a page had on a person's life—all that, after the months of agony and struggle, seemed too ludicrously simple and ordinary.

As for the Hitler Youth, Paul joined it within two weeks of his "rehabilitation."

◆ ◆ ◆

During all these events, Samuel had remained largely on the sidelines, mostly by choice but also because his wife had not involved him in order to spare him unnecessary pain. Yet even this choice only deepened his isolation. Events were taking their course. He was not needed. Worst of all: He was the central problem, the cause that had brought all these lives into such violent commotion.

Although Samuel had given his "blessing," he could not have anticipated the teeming complexities and subtle poisons lurking in the folds of this "blessing." But how could he in good conscience have denied Paul the status that was rightfully his? Wasn't it the truth? Yet that, precisely, was the problem: that it was the truth on only one level whereas on another it condoned and strengthened an utter lie!

And now, in addition, this man who had fathered Paul wanted to take an active part in his life! When Emilia had informed him of that, something had snapped in him. For it attacked his status as Paul's father directly for the first time. He could face having his place usurped biologically, but he could not face having it usurped emotionally as well, least of all at a time when he himself was in such dire need of emotional support.

Finally, there were his feelings toward Emilia. Matters had gone far beyond the infidelity as such. Here too what was right on one level was terribly wrong on another, for even while she needed to have done what she did for Paul's sake, she was at the same time by that very act turning her back on her husband. For by turning against him not for anything he had done, she had bought, however unwittingly, into the distorted values of his enemies. How to deal with a country that condemned you not for something you have done but for the mere circumstance and accident of your birth?

The maddening thing, Samuel thought again and again as he wandered about the sanctum sanctorum of his spirit, his library, feeling oppressed now even by his books, which suddenly seemed empty to him—the maddening thing was that there was no way out of all this. She needed to do what she had done, and yet she needed *not* to have done what she did! How square that circle?

Sometimes Samuel thought that the only solution lay in counting himself out altogether.

All these crosscurrents and contradictions gave Samuel the feeling that he was an outcast not only in his own country but in his family as well, which deepened his isolation and made him withdraw even further into himself.

◆ ◆ ◆

Soon after the name change, the baron informed his wife of the state of affairs. Disclosing the love affair as such was not difficult since it had taken place before he had met and married her, but the matter of his paternity was more difficult.

As it turned out, the baroness received the news rather calmly and raised amazingly few objections even when the baron informed her of his intention to introduce Paul into the family as his potential heir. She realized how negatively the lack of a son had affected the marriage. Perhaps Paul's advent would improve the marriage. Besides, the baroness was wise and practical enough to realize that opposing the baron in this matter would run into fierce opposition. As for her daughters' inheritance, there was more than enough to go around, especially since her successful appeal had left her with a sizable inheritance of her own, and she was not a very materialistic person anyway.

"Well, so you finally have a son," she said at the end of their conversation. She had drunk rather heavily which, for once, the baron had welcomed. "Does that make you happy?"

"As a matter of fact, it does."

"Sprung full-grown from the head of Zeus," she added dramatically. "You don't even have to go through the trouble of raising him."

"That depends on your point of view," the baron replied drily. "I would have preferred to raise him."

"Ah, yes," the baroness sighed.

The news and alcohol had put her into a pensive mood. She raised her glass and said crisply:

"A son has been born. Let's drink to that."

She drained her glass without waiting for him to respond. Then she threw him a sideward glance and singsonged:

"So, Otto, are we going to be happy again now?"

The baron shifted uncomfortably. Why did she always have to bring up the same uncomfortable subject? Why couldn't she finally accept their marriage for what it was: limited but not disastrous?

◆ ◆ ◆

The baron was anxious to get his first meeting with Paul behind him and to that end put some pressure on Emilia because she had twice postponed the meeting, mostly on realistic grounds. Not that the baron *really* looked forward to the meeting—encounters involving emotion were difficult for him—but he knew it had to be and so, the sooner the better.

The meeting was finally arranged for a Saturday. The baron sent Schulman to town to fetch Paul—he had insisted on this although Emilia had wanted to send Paul out by train—and waited tensely in his study after instructing Marianne to bring Paul directly to him.

Paul was dressed in his Sunday best, which made him feel uncomfortable. But he was glad he had when the chauffeured limousine drew up in front of the house. The luxurious car sent a thrill through him, but, once inside, he felt uncomfortable again, unsure whether he was supposed to chat with the chauffeur or not. He decided against it, mostly because he didn't know what to say, and sat back and tried to enjoy the ride, but his mind kept racing.

When they drew up in front of the manor, he found it to be both larger and smaller than he had anticipated—larger than any house he had ever been in but smaller than his fantasy had elaborated. Marianne opened the door, neatly attired in her maid's uniform, curtsied briefly, and led him to the baron's study.

The baron was standing by the large fireplace in which a small fire was burning, his tall, slender, still athletic figure amazingly like Paul's.

But even more alike were their features, a likeness even more pronounced than on the photographs so that for a moment both stood still, riveted fast against their will, both lifted briefly out of their respective anxieties by the amazing likeness. Finally the baron approached.

"I'm Otto von Hallenberg," he said, extending his hand.

"I'm Paul Silv . . . Paul."

"Welcome, Paul. I'm glad to welcome you here."

He led Paul to the large sofa in front of the fireplace and motioned him to sit down.

"Did you have a good ride?"

"Yes. Thank you. Very pleasant."

"May I offer you something? Are you thirsty? Hungry?"

Paul shook his head. "No, thank you."

The baron went to pour himself a drink.

"I guess cognac is still a bit early for you," he commented with a forced little chuckle.

"I've tasted it. But I don't much like it."

The baron returned to the fireplace with his glass.

"We'll be having dinner later on. You can stay for dinner, I hope? I'd like you to meet my wife and daughters."

"Yes, thank you."

There was a pause.

"I suppose," the baron finally began uncomfortably, "that your mother informed you of the state of affairs."

"Yes."

"We were both young," the baron said somewhat awkwardly. "Things like that will happen."

He stopped, flustered, realizing that his words stamped Paul as an accident. He *was* an accident, but that was no way to start a relationship. Nor was it how he had meant it.

Paul nodded vaguely, mumbling something. The baron sniffed at the cognac and took another sip from his glass.

"I'd like us to get to know each other, Paul. I hope we can become friends and make up for what we've missed all these years."

"So do I," Paul mumbled politely, wondering inside: Did he really?

"I've wanted a son for many years," the baron continued. "The von Hallenbergs have an illustrious history. I'd like you to feel proud of your new name."

"I'd like to know more about your history."

The baron pounced on his words.

"Would you like me to introduce you to some of your progenitors?" he inquired, gesturing around the walls, which were studded with portraits.

"Yes, I'd like that," Paul mumbled.

The baron began to lead him around the large room, talking with increasing animation as he pointed at portraits of stern-looking men in various formal attires, each portrait carefully labeled and identified with a bronze plaque. It was the baron's favorite occupation. What great good fortune to have come so suddenly into possession of a son, the baron was thinking—and what a fine son he was too, a spitting image of himself! As he talked, he became aware of a desire to impress Paul that surprised him. He rarely felt such a need with anyone.

Paul kept nodding mechanically, now and then making a brief comment but soon no longer really registering what the baron was saying because his head was spinning. Finally the baron himself noticed it.

"Well, that's enough history for one day," he laughed. "Let's go out and I'll show you around the estate."

"I'd love that."

"We breed some fine horses here. Some sheep too, but that's a sideline. Later we'll have dinner, and you'll meet my wife and daughters. But I told you that already, didn't I? My daughters are thirteen, eleven, and eight."

Paul remembered few details about the rest of that day. He was surfeited with new impressions and difficult feelings and could absorb no more. He remembered things mostly as a kaleidoscopic blur that he would, he told himself, sort out later: the estate with its stables and stately old trees and small peasant houses and people stopping to lift their caps with a little bow and a respectful "*Grüss Gott, Herr Baron;*" the baroness, a handsome woman with black hair pulled smoothly back, gracious and yet somewhat distant, looking and behaving like a baroness should; the three girls, giggly, curious but well behaved, decked out in their Sunday finery; and servants, servants everywhere. In Paul's heated and confused imagination they sprang up everywhere, though in reality there were only three.

Evening was falling when Schulman drove Paul back to town, accompanied by the two older girls who had wheedled permission to accompany him from their parents. Fortunately, they amused themselves with things like counting the cars they passed and needed no entertainment. The last impression Paul retained of the day as he reentered his own house was how small and dingy it suddenly seemed.

His parents were still up, sitting in the living room, looking up questioningly when he entered, his stepfather looking wan and depressed. But he quickly excused himself, saying he was tired—which was true, he was exhausted—and climbing to his room, he fell into bed.

It was the first of many visits.

◆ ◆ ◆

Paul's name change caused a stir among his classmates, of course. Some of the boys taunted him, egged on by Herbert who had not forgotten the article he had given Paul and thus had a notion of what had happened. But most of his classmates accepted him back readily enough, as if relieved that they no longer needed to uphold the purity of the Aryan race, all the more so as his status had been so impresssively elevated, for Paul had always been popular and a leader in his class until his artificial fall from grace.

Paul himself gave no explanation for the change, having been unable to find one that was serviceable. He simply countered every friendly or hostile inquiry by banteringly replying: Wouldn't you like to know! The few who didn't leave off, egged on by Herbert, finally did after Paul deliberately picked a fight with one and gave him a resounding thrashing.

Joining the Hitler Youth further cemented his rehabilitation with his peers. Indeed, some fuss was made over him when he joined and, curiously enough, some of the boys who had previously most tormented him now actively sought his friendship.

Paul was pleased with his revived popularity and acceptance. He was delighted to be "one of the boys" again and threw himself with fervor into the activities of the Hitler Youth. Even his studies improved.

The only one who did not accept Paul's rehabilitation was Herbert, whose enmity had in no way lessened. To see Paul suddenly not only rehabilitated but so impressively elevated was more than he could stomach. All at once the tables had been turned completely.

Unable to persecute Paul openly any longer, Herbert now changed his tactics and resorted to furtive, devious attacks, such as scribbling over his homework and bad-mouthing him behind his back whenever he could.

One day when Paul entered the classroom late, though before the teacher had arrived, the class fell strangely silent, a silence broken here and there by a few snickers. When he looked up, he saw written in huge letters on the blackboard:

BARON VON BASTARD!

He was still groping for some appropriate response when the teacher entered and saw the blackboard. He stopped for a moment and then motioned to a boy in the front row to wipe the blackboard clean and began his lecture.

After school that day, Paul waited at an intersection that he knew Herbert would pass on his way home. When Herbert saw Paul he froze and then broke into a limping run. Paul easily gained on him but before he could reach him, Herbert tripped and fell headlong on the pavement. Paul stood over him.

"Get up."

Herbert didn't budge.

"Get up, I said!"

"What do you want from me?"

"Get up before I make you get up."

When Herbert still didn't move, Paul grabbed him by the shirt and yanked him up. Herbert let himself be pulled up without offering any resistance, his eyes full of fear and hatred and yet capitulation too, as if secretly welcoming his punishment.

His abject submission suddenly deflated Paul's anger.

"You're a fuckin' coward, Herbert! A sneaky, slimy coward who can't come out in the open and fight fair! Next time you do anything I'll break your balls!"

With that he let go of Herbert, turned around, and walked away.

◆ ◆ ◆

Paul's changed status fanned Erika's interest anew since it shed a fresh, romantic light on Paul. But for Paul the excitement of his new life and the expanded opportunities it offered began to overshadow his relationship with Erika and made it seem less important. His life had expanded; therefore the relationship, having stood still, had shrunk. Erika suddenly appeared to him somewhat immature and limited so that he spent less time with her and found himself making excuses, honest excuses, for the most part, but excuses nevertheless.

As a result of Herbert's enmity, he no longer visited the Hoffer apartment. Instead, he would meet Erika elsewhere in prearranged places, which gave their meetings a furtive quality that further eroded their relationship.

Erika reacted with feelings of hurt and rejection that in time turned into anger, as she began to run through a gauntlet of accusations.

"You're seeing another girl" was the first thing she accused him of.

"I'm not," he assured her.

After a while she shifted to another accusation.

"I guess now that you're such an important person, I'm not good enough for you anymore."

"Don't be silly, Erika."

He would try to defend himself:

"Erika, I can't spend every minute of the day with you. I've got other things to do too."

"You never used to. You just don't love me anymore."

"I do, I really do," he would remonstrate, though his words made him feel somewhat uncomfortable, and he would take her in his arms and kiss her until she calmed down.

But one day, in anger and exasperation, he cried:

"All right! Maybe I don't love you anymore!"

And though it was said in anger, he didn't retract his words or comfort her back to reassured feelings, knowing in his heart that it was true.

Then finally Erika understood.

After that they continued to see each other sporadically awhile longer, but the vitality and thrill had gone out of their relationship, and after a while their meetings quietly stopped.

◆ ◆ ◆

Much as Samuel tried to tell himself that in the final analysis nothing needed to change in his relationship with Paul, the fact was that everything had changed. At first, upon hearing that he was not Paul's natural father, Samuel had thought that things might now actually improve between them because his ambivalence had found an explanation and could come out into the open, so to speak. But in practice the opposite happened because it concretized their estrangement and made the rift all the more difficult to bridge.

Again and again Samuel reminded himself that he had been Paul's *de facto* father since birth, regardless of whether he was his natural father as well, and that had not changed, could not change, would never change, however many barons suddenly appeared on the scene—but in reality he felt the change and so did Paul.

Over and over again, too, Samuel told himself that Paul had every right to enter into a relationship with the baron—but emotionally he could not stomach it. That Sunday when Paul had been picked up at the house to visit the baron for the first time had been one of the gloomiest days in his life. He who was accustomed to thinking in shades of gray, aware that infinite gradations existed between good and evil, he who had all his life rejected all manner of simplistic either-or extremes now found himself doing just that: Paul was *either* his son *or* the baron's—he could not be both. To put it even more trenchantly: taking up relations with the baron meant by that very fact that Paul was turning against him!

It was a measure of how sadly Samuel's strong personality had become undermined by events.

The only place where Samuel felt at home these days, in a world that was daily slipping more and more out of his grasp, was his store. And yet there too he was no longer in control.

He would sit day after day alone in the store, for he had finally dismissed Leopold, unable to afford him any longer. Actually he could no longer afford the store either, but he felt unable to let go as yet of this last bastion of his identity and self-image.

Here he sat day after day amidst his dwindling selection of jewelry and watches, listening to the footsteps indifferently passing by outside to detect the telltale sound of someone converging on the store. But few gentiles braved the Star of David displayed above the door, and few Jews could still afford his merchandise.

His only steady customer was he himself. Slowly, bit by bit, he cannibalized his inventory, gradually stripping his shelves and display cases bare in order to support his family, his savings having by this time been exhausted. Every time he took another ring or watch or silver goblet to be sold at discount to a wholesaler, he cringed inwardly, experiencing it like a rape. And yet it needed to be done to survive.

How much longer could he hold out? He tried not to think of it.

And yet here, in this cannibalized store, he felt in a strange way most at home because here at least he could be what he was: a human being branded an outcast! Here, for all the world to see, sat the shame of Germany to rouse some wayward conscience that was perhaps struggling still.

It represented, this daily silent vigil, his protest, his outrage, his wordless defiance.

◆ ◆ ◆

Emilia was aware of her husband's withdrawal, if not of all its ramifications and complexities, and it increased her own feelings of guilt. It seemed to her at times that she had merely traded one set of torments and guilt feelings for another, for what she had set right with Paul, she had set wrong with her husband. But whenever she attempted to break through the silence that had settled between them, the attempt miscarried.

One day Emilia said in her anguish:

"Why won't you let me come near you anymore, Samuel?"

Samuel sat staring at the table, mutely tracing designs on the white tablecloth with his index finger. Finally he murmured:

"I don't want pity."

Tears started to Emilia's eyes.

"I don't pity you!" she exclaimed. "I feel for you! That isn't pity!"

"I don't want your pity," he muttered again.

He seemed to want to say something more but fell silent. No, he couldn't offer her her freedom. Depleted as their marriage had become— depleted as he had become—whenever he wanted to offer Emilia her freedom, he drew back.

He could not face life without her.

◆ ◆ ◆

Throughout Paul's metamorphosis into an Aryan, Samuel had clung to the belief that this need not mean that Paul would make common cause with his former persecutors. But his precipitate joining of the Hitler Youth exploded that hope once and for all. Then Samuel told himself that he could not reasonably blame Paul for joining—he was a seventeen-year-old boy, after all, who yearned to belong—but in his heart he could not help blaming him.

Although Paul had enough sensitivity not to advertise his joining, Samuel noticed it, of course. One day he caught sight of Paul slipping up to his room wearing a Hitler Youth uniform. The shock was such that for a moment Samuel thought that his eyes were betraying him. A member of his family wearing a Nazi uniform in his own home!

He saw Paul in uniform only one more time, on an evening in October 1938. Samuel and Emilia had begun to eat dinner without Paul at the usual hour when Paul stormed in late and quickly sat down at the table dressed in his Hitler Youth uniform, which, in his haste, he had forgotten he was wearing.

Samuel froze. Staring at Paul, he slowly put down his knife and fork.

"Don't ever," he began, "don't *ever*, EVER wear that uniform in front of me again!" he shouted, his voice rising to a tormented pitch that was quite unheard of from Samuel, and thus all the more shocking.

Johann

ohann couldn't imagine working in a stuffy office anymore, as he had once done as a clerk in the *Verkehrsamt*, the Motor Vehicle Bureau. To be in the fresh air, to rub shoulders with people, to feel a part of the big world—that was important to Johann who lived with his wife and seven-year-old daughter in a small attic apartment on the top floor of Ingeborg's building. Johann enjoyed circulating on the streetcar all day, issuing and punching tickets. Only during rush hour the job was sometimes trying because people stood jammed in the aisle so that it was hard to get to each and every passenger. But that didn't bother him particularly, as it bothered some of his fellow conductors, who considered every unpaying passenger a personal affront. If he wasn't able to get to them, it was his problem, not theirs.

That day, a Wednesday in the Spring of 1938, the driver muttered an oath as the streetcar suddenly came to an abrupt stop between stations. A cat had been hit by a car and lay sprawled on the tracks. Johann jumped down, picked up the cat and brought it back into the streetcar.

"It's got a broken leg," he said to the driver. "I think that's all. I'll take it home to my daughter. She loves animals."

The driver set the streetcar in motion, muttering something. A high school student offered to hold the animal, which meowed plaintively from time to time, and rode with them to the end of the line where the streetcar went off duty. Johann took back the cat and thanked the student.

"Why don't you get your daughter a nice healthy kitten instead of a stray cat that's on its last legs," the driver commented as they took the streetcar back to the terminal.

"Nursing them back to health is half the fun for her," Johann said. "She's got a whole zoo of sick animals."

Actually Johann liked rescuing too. In fact, it was he who had started his daughter on it. In the summer when they were out on a lake in a rowboat and came across some insect exhausting itself in the water, he would maneuver the boat around until the girl could fish the struggling creature out of the water. Then they would both watch with pleasure as the insect slowly rallied and began to stretch and dry its wings until it finally flew away as if it had never been a hair's breadth from drowning.

"Playing God," his wife Maria called it disdainfully.

Johann knew that bringing home another animal would upset Maria. The girl's room was small and already crowded with a rabbit, two pigeons, a guinea pig, several mice, and two cats, one of which was dying. In theory, an animal was to be let go once it had recuperated, but in practice that seldom happened. Well, one more didn't matter, Johann thought as he climbed the steps to his apartment with a box containing the cat. On the second floor, he ran into Ingeborg who was just leaving her apartment.

"What have you got there?" Ingeborg inquired.

"A cat with a broken leg."

Ingeborg winked at him. "Maria's gonna be mad!"

Johann grinned guiltily. When he entered the apartment his daughter crowded around excitedly, at once suspecting that the box contained an animal.

"What is it? What's in the box, daddy?"

"I swear, if it's another animal!" Maria exclaimed. "Her room is a pigsty already!"

"Only until it mends, Maria," Johann said placatingly. "It's got a broken leg."

"Let me see, daddy, let me see!" Hannelore cried.

"Hush now, Hanne! You'd think your father brought home some treasure."

"Promise you'll let it go once it mends, Lorle?" Johann said.

"Please, mommy! I promise! Please!"

"I've heard that one before," Maria grumbled. "Alone the food all those animals gobble up. As if we had too much money." She disappeared in the kitchen, slamming the door behind her. "Supper will be ready in ten minutes!" she hollered from the kitchen.

Hannelore, delighted with the cat, immediately named it Streaky because of the white streak on its face. She then proceeded to give it a thorough "physical examination," diagnosed a broken leg, abrasions, and a "big, big scare" but pronounced Streaky definitely curable.

"Go wash your hands, Hanne, and sit down," Maria ordered, coming out of the kitchen with the supper tray.

"How's she been today?" Johann inquired while Hannelore was in the bathroom. "Has she been out playing?"

"She don't want to go outside. She ain't been outside for days."

"We have to encourage her. No wonder she's pale."

"What do you want me to do, carry her outside?" Maria said aggressively. "It's you who always tells me to let her have her way."

"Maybe we ought to have Dr. Gartner take a look at her."

"That costs money."

"I'm getting my paycheck tomorrow."

"That's been spoken for a hundred which ways," Maria said resentfully, falling silent as the girl returned and sat down at the table.

◆ ◆ ◆

Hannelore's pallor and lack of energy stood out all the more in contrast to the child she used to be—a wiry, active child, never ready to sleep. Now, she hardly finished eating the little she ate before saying she was tired and wanted to go to bed.

"That's not normal," Johann said to Maria.

"Kids ought to go to bed early," Maria insisted.

In Maria's eyes it all boiled down to a matter of discipline. She could see nothing wrong with the child that a little more discipline wouldn't cure. Hannelore was a picky eater and—lazy, lazy, lazy. She had to be drummed out of bed in the morning to get to school, she fell asleep over her homework and lately had been caught napping in class several times. When the teacher sent a note home, Maria took it as proof positive of the child's laziness.

"Now do you believe me?" she demanded of Johann.

"Any child will sometimes fall asleep in class, Maria," Johann said placatingly.

"I don't see her falling asleep over those scrawny animals you bring home all the time," Maria snapped.

Johann's whole approach was different. Controlling others, even a child, went against his grain and was distasteful to him. As a result, Maria had always been the disciplinarian in the family, though that increased her resentment against what she regarded as Johann's passivity. Where Maria meted out punishments at the drop of a hat, Johann would find a dozen excuses for the child—she hadn't slept well, she had an upset stomach, the subject was boring, etc. Especially when it came to eating he would coax and cajole. "One spoon for mommy—one spoon for daddy," patiently spooning the food into the child's mouth.

"A good whack on the behind, that'd get her to eat fast enough," Maria would grumble.

The matter of physical punishment was an especially sore area. Any kind of violence was repulsive to Johann, especially toward a child, in part because he himself had been beaten as a youngster. The matter had brought on one of the few out-and-out confrontations between them.

"Please don't use violence with her," he had said upon learning that Maria had given the child a sound thrashing.

"I wasn't *violent* with her. I gave her a spanking," Maria had objected defensively.

"I don't want you to beat her—ever!" Johann had said emphatically.

"I didn't *beat* her. I gave her a spanking," Maria had insisted.

But in the end she had backed down. Henceforth she talked about "a good whack on the behind," but she never again laid a finger on the child. Although Maria ran the family in most respects, she backed down when Johann felt strongly about an issue, in part because his forceful reaction pleased her since it was one of her abiding dissatisfactions that she had married what she considered an unassertive, unambitious, passive man. She could not see the difference between tolerance and patience, on the one hand, and passivity, on the other.

Their most severe confrontation had occurred in connection with his clerkship at the Motor Vehicle Bureau. The salary was better at the Bureau and the job offered better chances of advancement, but Johann had felt cooped up and unhappy and had insisted on leaving. Finally, when all her other arguments had failed, Maria had blurted out in exasperation:

"But your job at the *Verkehrsamt* is more respectable! Instead of marching up and down like a moron in a drafty streetcar all day!"

Respectability. Ah, yes. That was one thing that gentle, twenty-nine-year old Johann had no proper sense of: to do things simply because others did them. He was a person who knew his own mind and followed it. It was one of the characteristics that endowed him with such courage when the chips were down.

In time, Hannelore's lethargy became so severe that Johann insisted that Maria take her to Dr. Gartner.

The doctor didn't like the look of the child and, after examining her, diagnosed anemia, prescribing iron pills, plenty of bedrest, and fattening foods.

"But she won't eat, doctor," Maria objected.

"Every child will eat," Dr. Gartner declared categorically. He was an old-fashioned, dogmatic doctor. "It's just a matter of finding foods she likes. I want to see her again in a month."

Maria didn't argue with him. But at home she vented her anger.

"What does the old fogey know about feeding kids anyway."

However, the visit did change her attitude somewhat because the medical diagnosis gave the matter a different slant. She began to cook Hannelore some of her favorite dishes, mixing in extra butter and cream to make them richer, and eased up on her discipline a bit.

♦ ◆ ♦

It was symptomatic that the parents had split their daughter's name, Hannelore, in half, each parent appropriating half the name: Maria called her *Hanne* and Johann *Lore* which he had further changed into the more loving diminutive *Lorle*. It was, furthermore, symbolic of the child's birth. For she was not a shared creation, except in the most rudimentary biological sense, since she was a total accident. Thus, instead of Maria and Johann's liaison being a short-lived affair, as it should have been, it became a marriage.

Johann came from a lower middle-class family that had some pretensions to status and education. Only Johann had "sunk," as his family tirelessly proclaimed, although that was to be expected for he had never amounted to much in school, probably—no, certainly, they claimed—because his intelligence was limited. His family could see no other reason for his indifference to money, advancement, and power, in short to all the things normal people considered important in life, seeing in his lack of ambition not the cause of his underachievement but his excuse to explain it away.

Maria was five years older than Johann. He had met her when he was only twenty, a sexually inexperienced and shy young man, blond and fair-complexioned and of a rather slight, though wiry, build. By contrast, Maria had had a number of affairs. She was somewhat stocky and harsh-featured, though quite pretty, except for a disfiguring scar on her upper lip, the result of a harelip that had been operated on when she was a child.

For all that, Johann had never regretted the marriage, which, by then, had lasted for eight years. In his passionless, rather asexual way, he was devoted to Maria and certainly never considered divorcing her, particularly because of the child with whom he had developed a very special relationship from the start.

♦ ◆ ♦

After Johann and Hannelore left in the morning, Maria would find herself alone in the small apartment, feeling restless, bored, and unhappy. Was this what married life was all about? She was not a devoted *Hausfrau*, although she did like things to be fairly neat and clean. What was there to do in such a small apartment once the dishes and the cleaning and shopping had been done? Especially since Johann paid little attention to neatness or even cared very much about food.

After finishing the dishes on this particular morning, Maria drifted toward the only mirror she tolerated in the apartment. Putting two fingers over her upper lip, she turned coquettishly from side to side as she looked at herself in the mirror. Yes, she was attractive, even lovely until she removed her fingers. How could such a small, coin-sized patch of skin so upset her life? Her whole life had been lived in the shadow of her harelip. She stopped and approached the mirror, scrutinizing her face.

Suddenly she whispered: "Mirror, mirror on the wall...."

As a child and well into adolescence, she had played a game that she had adapted from the fairy tale Snow White. She would position herself in front of the mirror in her room and intone:

"Mirror, mirror on the wall, who is the ugliest of them all?"

And the answer that invariably came back was... ME!

"Mirror, mirror on the wall," she now whispered, "who is the...."

Then she suddenly burst into tears.

What had impressed her so much about Johann was that his gentle affection outlived their sexual encounters—in contrast to her experiences with other men—and gave her the exuberant feeling that for the first time in her life a man truly cared for *her*, harelip and all! It left her glowing with happiness and excitement. But in time Johann's very acceptance—what she called his passivity—became the cause of further pain. For in the perverse court of her disparaging view of herself, his steady, passionless devotion demoted him because she could not believe that any worthwhile person would want her. Thus his very tolerance and devotion in the end aggravated, rather than disarmed, her unhappiness.

It was then that Maria once again attempted to seek reassurance in sex, but this only created further problems. For Johann was not a very sexual or sensuous man and Maria's demands soon brought on episodes of impotence, which upset Maria even more, because they increased the very sense of worthlessness that she was trying to obliterate through sex in the first place.

♦ ♦ ♦

Uneducated, apolitical Johann, circulating on the streetcars of Munich, rubbing shoulders all day long with people from all walks of life, soon came to see what Germany's educated elite, the professionals and industrialists, did not permit themselves to see because their very intellectualism helped so many to rationalize away their doubts about the Nazis and their misgivings and fears.

Johann's first upsetting experience consisted of the book burnings that erupted all over Germany in 1933. Though anything but a bookworm himself, Johann respected books and intuitively grasped that a society that burns books will in time be devoured by its own intolerant flames.

But what truly shocked Johann was the treatment of the Jews. Growing up, Johann had had only a vague idea what a Jew was, precisely because German Jews were so assimilated that few stood out as such.

He remembered a dinner conversation when Hannelore had first entered school.

"What's a Jew?" the girl wanted to know.

Johann thought for a moment.

"They're people who sometimes have a different religion," he said. "Although they can also be Christians."

"They're foreign people who don't belong here," Maria interjected.

"You mean, they speak a foreign language?" Hannelore asked.

"No, they speak German," Johann said.

"Then how are they different?"

"They have different blood in their veins," Maria said.

"You mean, it's a different color?"

"No, Lorle," Johann laughed, "it's just as red as yours and mine and it hurts just as much when it's spilled."

"Then what's different?"

"Hush now and eat your potatoes," Maria said sharply.

"But the teacher said all Jews are bad," Hannelore persisted. "What makes them bad?"

"They're not bad." Johann said. "They're human beings like you and me, Lorle. There are good ones and bad ones among them."

"Don't drum things into the child's head that's going to get her in trouble," Maria interjected, annoyed.

"Do we know any Jews?" Hannelore now wanted to know.

"No," Maria said impatiently, "because they don't belong here."

"Why don't they belong here?"

"Because they're different, I told you."

"But how are they different, mommy?"

"Do hush now and eat!" Maria exploded.

It wasn't easy to explain to a child. How was it that it was so easy to persuade a whole people that the Jews were different and evil?

◆ ◆ ◆

One early afternoon a man dressed in the brown uniform of the Nazi Party boarded Johann's streetcar, which was full except for a few seats in the rear. As the man walked down the aisle, he caught sight of a black-haired youth who looked Jewish. The Nazi stopped in front of him.

"You're a Jew, aren't you?" he said. "Get up!"

The young Jew was about to get up when Johann approached.

"There are seats in back," he said.

"I don't want a seat in back," the Nazi said. "I want this seat."

"It's occupied, as you can see."

The Nazi's eyes narrowed belligerently. "You a Jew-lover or somethin'?"

"I'm in charge of this streetcar," Johann said quietly. "Please move on."

The Nazi turned back to the young Jew who had remained sitting, mostly because the two men were blocking his way.

"Get up, I told you!" he barked. "Are you deaf, pig?"

The young Jew started to get up again, but Johann pushed him down. As he did so, he caught a glimpse of the terror in the young Jew's eyes.

"Please," Johann said, turning back to the Nazi, "don't make any trouble here."

The two men stood facing each other for a moment, the Nazi taller and heavier than Johann.

"*Please*," Johann repeated softly and insistently in an effort to reach through to a core of decency and compassion in the man beneath the rubble of intolerance and hatred.

For a moment longer the Nazi stood staring at him. Then he suddenly moved on to the rear, muttering under his breath.

The incident remained with Johann for days. He could not forget the terror in the young Jew's eyes, nor the hatred in the man's. But most terrifying of all was the realization that all this hatred and conflict was man-made and had no objective reality whatever, not like illness or death or any of the other real calamities afflicting mankind.

◆ ◆ ◆

When he told Maria of the incident, she exclaimed reproachfully:

"Are you crazy? You're going to lose your job before long. Or worse."

"Someone had to help the young man."

"But you didn't have to be the one. There's nothing you can do for Jews."

"If that's true, it's terrible, isn't it."

"What do you mean?" Maria flared. "Jews don't belong here."

If they don't belong here, Johann wondered, who does? If not those who were born and raised here, who speak the same language and work here, who pay taxes and die here?

"It seems to me they belong here as much as anyone, Maria," he said quietly.

"You're going to get into real trouble with opinions like that," Maria snapped. "The block warden is already sniffing around."

It was true that the Nazi block warden had made inquiries about Johann.

It was useless, Johann thought. Maria ran with the crowd, like most Germans. Like himself, for that matter. Was he any different? In what way was he standing up for the Jews? He had prevented a young Jew from being publicly humiliated. What was that against the permanent, lacerating humiliation being inflicted on Jews daily all over the country in the name of the German people?

So there was no use being angry at Maria. If anything, he needed to be angry at himself.

Thereafter, whenever Johann saw a Jew, he could not help experiencing a sense of shame and guilt that made him want to go up to the man or woman or child and reach through the fear, distrust, and resentment that divided them to the bedrock of their joint humanity.

◆ ◆ ◆

Hannelore did not improve, despite iron pills and rich food. On the contrary, she seemed to be getting weaker, and mealtimes, despite Johann's efforts and patience, were becoming more and more of a struggle. Even Maria no longer grumbled and threatened with whacks on the behind, because even she finally realized that something was amiss.

One day Hannelore began to complain of pain in her limbs. They took her back to Dr. Gartner, who examined her again very carefully and ordered a number of tests.

Before Maria could return for the results, Ingeborg came up to tell them that the doctor had called—they themselves had no telephone—and requested to see them both. When they entered his office, he waved them into two chairs facing his desk in a manner less abrupt than usual. After a brief introduction, he said:

"The report has come back. I'm afraid it's not good. Not good at all."

He paused, not for dramatic effect, but because even for crusty Dr. Gartner the disclosure of bad news was painful.

"I'm afraid Hannelore has a serious illness—leukemia."

There followed a stunned silence. They had heard leukemia mentioned as a dread disease but knew almost nothing about it. Dr. Gartner went on to explain briefly what leukemia was: an uncontrolled proliferation of white blood cells.

"And that is bad," he said, "although we have some relief for the symptoms."

"But the—the long-range...?" Johann ventured.

The doctor hesitated.

"We want to know," Johann persisted.

"Don't badger the doctor, Johann," Maria interjected. "He said there's help."

"Is there, Dr. Gartner?"

"To be honest, Herr Stantke—the chances are very slim."

He did not add—though he knew it—that in those days the chances were next to nothing at all.

◆ ◆ ◆

The realization sank in only by degrees. Fatigue is, after all, a common human condition, especially in a child, and for the moment the pain in the limbs subsided with the help of medication. So it was difficult to believe that a life-threatening illness had invaded the child, impossible to believe, not only for Maria, who totally denied it, but even for Johann, who insisted on a second opinion, and it was only when the diagnosis of leukemia was confirmed that he slowly began to confront the unbearable truth that the child would not live and it was only a question of how long she would survive.

Then came anger. Gentle, tolerant Johann who could be so accepting of people and their foibles railed against fate and could not be gentle toward it. He was not a churchgoer, but he did believe in a Higher Power, which he now assailed with the age-old lament: Why a seven-year-old child? What had she done? Why not me? Why, why, why?

Only then did the struggle for acceptance start, an acceptance that seemed at first totally beyond Johann's reach, all the more so as Maria continued to deny the child's illness, which brought on some paradoxical results. For Maria now once again resorted to strict limit setting, on the theory that the child's illness required it more than ever. But the unconscious motivation was that it bolstered her denial because limit setting does imply, after all, a continuity of existence. By contrast, what little discipline Johann had previously mustered now collapsed into utter permissiveness, which led to additional friction between the parents whose pain was further heightened by their inability to face the tragedy together. But then, tragedy pulls a marriage together only when there is a strong underlying bond; otherwise, it merely splinters the marriage further, as each partner struggles to draw on his own resources and thus further depletes what energy is available for the relationship.

In time the child became so weak that she was unable to attend school full-time. Instead, a half-day program was arranged with the school.

"How much longer will she be able to go to school altogether?" Johann inquired of Dr. Gartner.

"I don't know," the doctor said honestly. "Not very long."

Now the explanations to the child became more difficult.

"We've got to build up your blood, Lorle, so that it can become strong again before you can go back to school," Johann explained to her.

He had explained to the child about the illness: about the white and red blood cells—the white and red knights, as he called them—and how they needed to get the two in balance again. In one of his few visits ever, Johann had gone to the library to read up on the illness. What he did not tell the child was that there was no way then known to man to restore the upset balance again. It was a priceless treasure never to be restored.

Johann had some qualms about lying to the child about the seriousness of the illness but had permitted himself to be persuaded by Dr. Gartner.

"There's always hope," the doctor had said, being able to say that much truthfully without resorting to false hopes. "One mustn't take all hope away from the child. Nor from yourself either," he had added.

The child's return home from school affected Maria deeply and finally made her realize the seriousness of Hannelore's condition. For children to move from home to school and out into the world was the way of the world. The reverse process forced Maria to acknowledge at last what she had until then so strenuously denied: that this child's evolution was one of involution, of return home, to bed and finally to darkness, darkness not of the womb but of the grave.

♦ ♦ ♦

Once Maria admitted the fatality of the illness, she became depressed. She no longer snapped at Johann or tried to discipline Hannelore. But that didn't mean that she was able to give the child true emotional support.

Hannelore had never become for Maria, as she had for Johann, the centerpiece of the marriage and the major blessing of her life. She had not wanted the child in the first place and later had felt resentment against her, even some jealousy. But the impending loss was nevertheless more than she could bear and threw her into a state of semi-paralysis.

So the brunt of relating to the child and supporting her emotionally with some cheerfulness and equanimity fell to Johann. It took all his strength to feign both. Where Maria had been unable to face the child's death and had clung with all her might to the child's living, Johann attempted instead to accompany her on every step of her journey, into pain, into fear, into death itself. He threw all the energy of his life into remaining close to his daughter. His defense against her death was to go with her to the very threshold of cessation itself.

The shared experience wrought a curious change in both. It was as if they had drawn around themselves an invisible mantle that enveloped them in a world of their own making, a world of intimacy, of fantasy, and even of good cheer. In their world Johann was "Big Mumu," a powerful giant who could defeat all the little "Evil Mimies" of fate, except for the big fate that "Master Krogan" held in store for his nearest and dearest, namely Lorle. Even pain, which the child was experiencing more and more often now, was given a respected but not an overwhelming place. And so it came to be that the cheerfulness and equanimity that Johann had at first feigned became in time strangely real as father and daughter were enveloped in a world of their own making, a world of great love, intimacy, and understanding.

It was during this time that Johann became a deeply spiritual person.

♦ ◆ ♦

Johann's life now revolved totally around his daughter. He rushed home after work to spend the evening with her and went almost nowhere else while Lorle tried desperately to stay awake until he came.

By now she had stopped going to school altogether, at Dr. Gartner's request, and spent most of the day in bed. For a while Johann tried to continue doing some homework with her, but Maria thought the exercise was ridiculous.

"What's the point?" she said.

"It gives her something to do, something to look forward to, some hope."

"Look forward to what?" Maria said despondently, staring at him. "That's make-believe."

"I don't think so. Whatever we can do to keep her interested is real."

"It's make-believe," Maria insisted.

The effort was short-lived, in any case. Although Lorle had said that she liked the idea, she hardly ever did any of the homework and seemed unenthusiastic even when Johann helped her with it. As a result, the project soon collapsed. It was as if the girl herself recognized that schoolwork was a sham at this point.

However, Lorle did enjoy being read to, though she usually fell asleep. The animals were another source of continuing pleasure. She couldn't do a very good job of cleaning the cages anymore—a job that Maria quietly took over without grumbling—but she still spoke to them and played with them whenever her strength permitted.

Lorle's greatest joy, however, were her fantasy journeys into Master Krogan's powerful realm, which became for her a source of reassurance and pleasure. It was the child's way of asking questions, of verbalizing fears, and binding anxieties that she was unable to express in any other way. In time their fantasy trips became a kind of ritual, pursued with variations in details, but the essential journey was always the same: Under the protection of Big Mumu, who was, of course, Johann, they would journey to Master Krogan's distant realm where Lorle would be safe forever, but on the way their progress would be obstructed by all sorts of Evil Mimies whom they would foil and elude with hair-breadth escapes that left them both jubilant and triumphant.

Master Krogan was God and death all rolled into one. But death made, somehow, tame and acceptable and no longer frightening.

◆ ◆ ◆

Except when he was with Lorle, Johann now became very silent. He had never been a talkative man, but now he pulled silence around himself like a shroud. It was as if he were afraid that if he opened his mouth, out would come a shrill primeval scream, a monstrous wail of sorrow and torment. How could it be that his Lorle, the person he loved above all else in life, was being taken from him?

He felt alive and real only when he was with the child. For him, too, their fantasy trips came to assume a reality more real than his daily life. Punching tickets in the streetcar, walking along the streets or talking to someone, he felt unreal, unsubstantial, absent, phony, going through actions that had lost all meaning and relevance so that he would ask himself at times how it was that he was still living and going through all the motions of daily existence when the most treasured possession of his life was being ripped from him. Then he would hurry back to the child as if really alive only in her presence. And yet, with her too, his torment did not subside. To see the child slowly wasting away and to be powerless to do anything to help her, choked him with a sense of utter despair.

There were other symptoms now, not just weakness. The pain in Lorle's limbs had increased, the glands in her neck had become painfully swollen, and sores and ulcers had appeared in her mouth and throat. But most of all, she complained of severe headaches that the prescribed medication was unable to control.

"Why must there be pain, Daddy?" Lorle would ask time and again. "Why didn't Master Krogan make the world without pain?"

How could Johann explain the scheme of things to a child when adults had difficulty understanding it?

Maria, too, had become taciturn and withdrawn. She went about her household chores without grumbling now and cared attentively for the child. But there was about her an absent air, as if a ghost had come to inhabit her body.

Between Johann and Maria there was almost no communication now except on the most superficial level of daily life. Their pain and sorrow were too immense to talk about in any way. A stranger listening to their conversation would not have gathered that their child was fatally ill.

◆ ◆ ◆

One morning Hannelore woke up with a dry cough, chest pains, and a high fever. Dr. Gartner came in the late afternoon and diagnosed pneumonia.

"When the body is weakened, there is great susceptibility to infection," he explained. "I'll be back tomorrow."

By the following morning, the child's cough had become worse, and her temperature had risen. Silently they watched Dr. Gartner bending over her. Then they all stepped into the living room. There was a brief discussion about taking her to the hospital, but the idea was dropped. Then the conversation died. Johann and Maria were both afraid to ask. Finally Dr. Gartner said:

"It's very often the end."

He solemnly shook their hands without speaking. At the door he turned to them once more.

"It's kinder this way," he said, "because it goes faster."

Then he was gone.

By the following morning, the child's breathing had become shallow and rapid. It dominated the room and seemed to have overpowered even her cough. Johann sat by her bed, holding her hand, feeling each shallow, labored breath going through him like a knife and yet terrified that her breathing would stop. From time to time he bent forward and replaced a wet cloth on the child's burning forehead from a bowl of cold water which Maria constantly replaced, not because it needed renewing but because it gave her a sense of doing something. She couldn't sit still, couldn't even stay in the room, yet the room drew her back irresistibly.

In the afternoon Johann was still able to reach the child when he called her name. But when he tried to talk to her of Master Krogan, she could no longer hear him. By early evening she no longer responded even to her name. Only her hand still showed signs of life. In the middle of the night her breathing became irregular and seemed to struggle up from untold depths.

And then it suddenly stopped.

◆ ◆ ◆

Looking back later, Johann could barely recall the funeral. He felt as if he had been placed in a vacuum chamber in which everything reached him muted and over a great distance. He could admit his loss only by degrees. Had he felt its whole impact at one stroke, he might have fallen unconscious or gone insane.

Maria's parents invited them to stay with them for a few days after the funeral. They lived in a village not far from Munich. But Johann insisted on returning to their apartment after only one day, with the excuse that the animals had to be fed. The real reason was that he felt he couldn't live anywhere but in close proximity to Lorle's abandoned room—although he didn't know how to live there either.

Maria would have liked to stay on with her parents—she wanted nothing so much as to get away from the apartment—but she didn't have the heart to let Johann return alone. It wasn't that she felt a need to be near him. He couldn't comfort her any more than she could comfort him. It was simply the conventional feeling that this was a time when a husband and a wife ought to be together.

They returned to the apartment the day after the funeral. Even as they stood outside the apartment—Johann fumbling for the key, Maria waiting behind him—they could feel the heaviness and fear: fear of the apartment, of the emptiness, of each other, fear even of themselves. The door opened upon the silent, stale-smelling living room in which a cup of coffee still stood on the table, abandoned half-consumed before the funeral. The door to Hannelore's room stood slightly ajar. Both were aware of it but neither looked at it. Johann took off his coat and sat down at the table, staring numbly at the floor, while Maria went into the kitchen, where she moved some dishes about in an idle, unfocussed way, without rhyme or reason.

The two cats came and rubbed against Johann's legs, meowing to be fed, and he could hear the other animals moving restlessly in their cages. He bent down and picked up one of the cats. It was Streaky, the cat with the broken leg. The leg was healed now. Only a slight limp remained. He remembered bringing the cat home, remembered Lorle's excitement, and felt tears pushing up into his eyes. Life had stretched and stretched then with no end in sight. Where did it stretch now? Endless now too—with emptiness. The cat purred on his lap but presently jumped down, wanting to be fed. To think the cat had no sadness and thought only of food. How blessed—and how terrible!

He went to the kitchen for some milk, and the two cats followed him. Maria stopped her idle puttering and watched him bending down to pour the milk.

"What're we going to do with the animals now?" she asked aimlessly.

"I don't know."

He squatted down, stroking the cats as they lapped up the milk. Everything pointed back to Lorle. Everything reminded him of her. Lorle laughing—touching—being alive, not....! That was the thought that couldn't yet be thought. And yet it had to be faced and finally accepted.

He stood up and walked back to the living room and then, without conscious deliberation, on to her room. The bed. The bed in which Lorle had died. He forced himself to look at it. And then at last it came. Leaning against the door so that it closed behind him, he wailed a keening lamentation for the dead. Uncontrollable and primeval. Without thought or shame.

After that, finally, acceptance began.

♦ ◆ ♦

At first Johann was drawn back obsessively to the apartment, to the child's room, and to her animals. He spent hours in her room, caring for them. It was his way of reliving the times they had spent together by staying in touch with what she had loved best.

Maria would come into the room to find him lying on the floor, surrounded by the animals, his head propped up on one elbow. She would stop by the door and watch him while he remained oblivious to her presence, her initial sympathy gradually turning into annoyance and finally reproach. One needed to get on with life, this life that was falling apart around them more and more every day. One couldn't remain fixated on the past. There was a point beyond which grief and pain became self-indulgence, the hallmark not of sensitivity but of an inability to accept the forward movement of life.

"It smells awful in here," she would say.

He would start, as if recalled from far away.

"Yes," he would mumble. "I must open the window."

"You should get rid of the animals."

"Yes," Johann would agree vacantly.

In time Maria began to insist.

"When are you going to get rid of the animals, Johann?"

"One day—soon."

"When?"

"Soon."

"There's such a thing as overdoing it," she would mutter, leaving the room.

And Johann would nod, knowing that she was right but knowing, too, that sometimes pain needed to be extracted by driving it in and through.

♦ ♦ ♦

Then one day Johann began to shun the child's room and seemed unwilling to enter it, or even the apartment. He would walk or ride about town for hours, his coat flopping open, looking into people's faces as if to find some comfort and connectedness there, before finally returning home, numb with fatigue.

Finally one Sunday morning he got up early, carefully collected all the animals in two cages, and set out for the country in a commuter train. The only animal he kept was Streaky.

It was a pleasant, sunny day. In a village about half an hour from Munich, he got off the train and walked out to the meadows surrounding the village until he reached a small stream where his family had picnicked on several occasions. Here he sat down and took the animals out of their cages one by one and set them free. They quickly dispersed. Only the cat remained with him while he continued to sit in the sun, his mind floating free now so that he could not have said whether he was thinking of the child, or of himself, or of nothing at all.

Finally he got up, brushed off his clothes, and returned to the village, followed at a distance by the cat. It was as if the animal understood what was happening. Before entering the railroad station, he looked back once more and saw the cat, walking with its tail held stiffly aloft, the tip waving as if to say good-bye.

When he looked out again the cat was gone.

The Night of the Broken Glass

Such was the state of affairs on the eve of the fateful Ninth of November 1938, the eve of what was later called the *Kristallnacht*, the Night of the Broken Glass, although much more was broken than glass: hearts and minds and bodies were broken.

Paul had joined the Hitler Youth with the enthusiasm of someone finally realizing a long-cherished dream, seeing in joining proof positive that he was at long last a full-fledged citizen. Once his desire for equality had been satisfied, however, his basic independence reasserted itself, and he began to view the Nazis and the Hitler Youth with some objectivity. And what he saw made him uncomfortable.

Paradoxically, it was not until his rehabilitation that he began to question the Nazis. While he had been ostracized, his isolation had been so painful that it had overshadowed everything else. Now questions pertaining to the right and wrong, the justice and injustice of Nazism began to surface, quietly at first, but persistently, and he began to remember how often and how vainly his stepfather had tried to talk with him about these matters.

What offended Paul most about the Hitler Youth was their militaristic, superior attitude and their insistence on unquestioning obedience, made all the more distasteful by a martinet troop leader who disliked him. It was one thing to rehabilitate Germany, he was all for that, but to preach *Deutschland über Alles* (Germany above all) seemed to him unjustified and grandiose.

His experiences when he was ostracized as a Jew had also taught him something that he could not readily forget. Having been rejected not because of anything he was or had done, he now could not help wondering whether his newly won acceptance was any more substantial.

Paul's doubts were further galvanized by an incident that he could not forget. On the way home from a Hitler Youth meeting, Paul and a group of four boys ran into a Jewish boy who had been, until his recent expulsion from school, one of the brightest and most studious pupils in school.

"Hey, there's Cohen the Jew!" one of the boys cried.

"Let's get him!"

They surrounded the frightened boy and began to tease him with questions and insults while the boy kept turning around in a circle to face his tormentors.

Paul tried to intervene.

"Come on, guys, let's go. He's done nothing to us."

But no one paid any attention to him.

As it happened, another group of Hitler Youth boys came along just then, Herbert and Paul's troop leader among them. Seeing what was happening, they joined the first group, and now their taunts quickly turned ugly. They formed a tight circle around the boy and began to kick and punch him, egged on by Herbert and the troop leader, while Paul tried to intervene, tugging at one boy after another.

"Come on, leave him alone, he's done nothing to us . . . let go of him . . . we're so many . . . it's unfair . . . ."

He became more and more frantic as the Jewish boy began to sob, his nose bleeding, his jacket torn, his eyes bloodshot and swelling. But the only one who paid any attention to him was Herbert, who jeered:

"What's the matter, Baron baby? Goin' soft on Jews on account of your sweet step-daddy?"

To punctuate his taunt, Herbert swung with full force at the boy so that blood spurted from his mouth. For a moment the boy gagged. Then he spat out a tooth.

Paul fell back, tears obscuring his vision. And then he suddenly turned on his heels and broke into a run.

The incident affected Paul deeply. Against all his feelings of fairness, Paul had deserted that boy to protect his own hide, and to avoid jeopardizing his own newly won status. It confronted him with something he had not yet faced in his own character: namely, cowardice.

◆ ◆ ◆

The *Kristallnacht* of the Ninth of November was the worst peacetime pogrom in Nazi Germany, a reaction to the fatal shooting of a minor German diplomat in Paris by a teenage German Jewish refugee. The event resulted in beatings and deportations and lootings and the torching of Jewish stores, homes and synagogues, while the police looked idly on and fire trucks stood by merely to protect adjoining non-Jewish properties.

It was a night that should have jolted the conscience of Germany and the world.

But it didn't.

◆ ◆ ◆

That evening Samuel was about to lock up when a group of four men in Nazi uniforms came into the store. He was at once apprehensive, aware that a uniform added a measure of impersonal cruelty to whatever evil already lurked in its wearer; but for the moment the four men seemed to have no ill intentions. The leader of the group was a large, heavy-set man with a paunch who did not look particularly threatening.

"You're a Jew, aren't you?" he said, looking around the store.

"There's a Star of David above the door," Samuel said uneasily.

"So it is," the paunch said pleasantly. Suddenly he barked: "Watches!"

Samuel opened a case and took out a tray of rather cheap watches.

"There are some nice watches here," he mumbled.

The heavy man leaned over the tray of watches and studied them. Suddenly he flipped the tray over, scattering the watches on the floor.

"Cheap stuff," he said. "We want to see your *best* watches."

He winked at his companions, who responded with an appreciative laugh. Then he looked back at Samuel almost benevolently while Samuel hesitated, evaluating what to produce. He knew that he had to produce something of value and yet wondered how valuable it needed to be.

"And none of your dirty Jewish tricks either," the paunch said, as if reading his thoughts. "We want the best!"

Samuel bent down, slid open a case, and took out a beautiful gold watch, not his best but one of the best.

"Ah, that's better," the paunch said. "How much is it?"

"Five hundred seventy-five marks."

"Five hundred seventy-five," the man repeated appreciatively, turning the watch around in his hand. "Hm. Not bad." He turned to his comrades and winked. "Shall we take it?"

The men passed the watch around with approving grunts and exclamations. Were they really buying a watch? Samuel wondered for a moment but at once dismissed the thought as preposterous.

The leader dug into his pocket.

"Tell you what, Jew," he said, producing a coin. "I'll give you half a mark."

He put the coin on the table, lifted the watch, and held it ceremoniously aloft for everyone to see. Then he dropped it on the floor. Samuel made a spontaneous move to pick it up.

"Hold it," the man said and, lifting his foot, brought his boot down on the watch and ground it slowly and carefully into the floor.

"There," he said with satisfaction. "Now let's have another."

"I—I only have the ones I showed you."

The man reached across the counter and grabbed Samuel by both ears, jerking his head forward.

"Now you don't mean to give us a hard time, do you, Jew-boy?"

"No, sir."

"Good. Then get another."

He released Samuel who bent down and brought out another watch.

"Excellent," drawled the paunch with satisfaction. "How much is this one?"

"Three hundred twelve marks."

The man dug into his pocket for another coin before lifting the watch as before, dropping it and grinding it into the floor.

"Another!" he barked.

"Come on, let's get on with it," interposed one of his companions. "This is boring."

"What's your hurry, Willi?" the paunch said gruffly.

"Please," Samuel said, "what is it you want?"

"Shut up, Jew!" the paunch shouted. "We ask the questions here!"

"Why don't we just take him along to the station," suggested another. "They'll ship him off to a concentration camp where he belongs."

"Nah, let's take care of him here," Willi said.

"Okay," the paunch said to reassert his leadership. "Over here, Jew!"

Samuel came slowly around the counter.

"How many teeth have you got, Jew-boy?"

"I—I don't know."

"Well, we'll tell you how many you have left when we get through with you," the paunch said, laughing coarsely.

He pulled his arm back and punched Samuel squarely in the face. Samuel staggered back against the counter.

"Okay, Horst, he's yours," he said, stepping aside.

Horst stepped up and pulled Samuel forward. Samuel raised his arm protectively.

"Put your arm down, Jew!" Horst bellowed. "And stand up straight!"

Samuel hesitantly dropped his arm.

"This one's for all the German customers you've cheated," Horst exclaimed, cocking his arm. His fist landed with a thud on Samuel's face. Samuel fell backwards against the counter, stunned. Blood began to trickle from his mouth and nose.

"All yours, Willi," Horst said, grinning.

Willi stepped forward. He looked at Samuel who kept blinking and shaking his head to clear his vision. The blood was coming faster now, and his left eye was swelling shut.

"Watch this one, fellows," Willi said.

He pulled Samuel forward and positioned him like a bowling pin. Samuel closed his eyes, swaying a little.

"Eyes open, Jew!" Willi barked. "No cheating here!"

Samuel opened his eyes.

"Watch this one, gang," Willi repeated.

He stepped forward and threw a powerful punch at Samuel's stomach with his left fist. Then, as Samuel doubled up, he caught him with an upper hook with his right fist that almost lifted Samuel off his feet. He collapsed with a thud on the floor.

"See whether you can better that one, Klaus," Willi said smugly, stepping aside.

A small crowd had gathered outside the store, watching with curiosity through the windows. The watching faces showed no hatred but no sympathy either. No one spoke. No one stepped forward. Klaus walked over to Samuel who lay on the floor without moving.

"Get up, Jew," he said without much conviction.

Samuel didn't move.

"Up, Jew!" Willi shouted. "Or we'll make you stand up!"

Samuel began to lift himself shakily to his knees.

"He's got no stuffing left in him," Klaus said. "Let's move on."

"What do you mean!" Willi shouted. "He's got half his teeth left!"

He pounced on Samuel and pulled him to his feet. Samuel stood tottering on his legs, half supported against the counter.

"There you go," Willi said to Klaus, stepping aside. "Let 'im have it."

At this moment a man pushed through the crowd of people standing outside, entered the store, and positioned himself in front of Samuel.

"Please, leave him alone," the man said.

"Who are you?" the leader said, taken aback, assuming that the man might have some sort of authority.

"He can't take any more. Please, leave him alone," the man repeated.

"And who are you?" bellowed the leader. "You got some sort of authority here?"

"I'm asking you to leave him alone," the man said once more. "He can't take any more."

"You don't say!" the leader cried. "A Jew-lover! Well, well."

"Let me flatten the guy," Willi exclaimed, trying to elbow the leader aside.

"Let's turn him over to the Gestapo," Horst suggested. "They adore Jew-lovers."

"Come on, Siegfried!" Willi cried impatiently, pulling at the leader. "Let me at him!"

"Lay off, will you?" Siegfried shouted, feeling the situation slipping away from him. "I'm in command here. I'll take care of the guy."

"Then take care of him and don't just stand there and talk about it!" Willi snapped.

"Come on, guys, we're attracting attention," Klaus said with a look at the crowd growing outside the store. "Let's get out of here."

"After I take care of this Jew-lover," the leader growled.

He struck the man full force in the face. The blow threw him against Samuel but he remained standing, only blinking to clear his vision.

"Come on, Siegfried," Klaus said again. "We've got other stores to attend to. The guy isn't worth it."

He moved toward the door, followed by Horst.

"Okay, okay, move on!" Horst shouted, moving out into the crowd. "The show's over!"

The crowd parted to let the two men pass through, followed by the leader and Willi. Then it began to disperse, except for a few curious onlookers. Meanwhile the man had turned to Samuel and was assisting him to a chair. Samuel's face was swollen and blood-smeared and he moved along the counter with difficulty, half doubled over. The man eased him into a chair.

"Thank you," Samuel mumbled.

"We've got to get you to a doctor," the man said. "I'll go and get a taxi."

Samuel had closed his eyes. The man walked to the door. A few people were still standing outside.

"Please, won't you go home?" he said to them.

They began to move away, except for a middle-aged woman who stepped forward.

"Can I help? I do want to help," she said nervously, her lips trembling.

"You can stay with him while I find a taxi."

It was a while before he was able to locate one. By the time he returned, Samuel was so weak that he laid stretched out on the floor. Together they lifted him and half carried and half walked him to the door.

"Please, lock up," Samuel whispered, fumbling for his keys.

By the time the man rejoined them after locking up, Samuel was leaning in the corner of the car, breathing hard. He seemed barely conscious. The man bent close to him.

"Do you have a doctor? Where does he live?"

Samuel didn't respond. The man gave the driver the address of his own doctor, who, luckily, was at home. After hearing about the blow, the doctor hardly examined him.

"He's got to get to a hospital at once," he said.

By the time Samuel could be admitted—hospitals were in great demand that night—it was late, and Emilia had been summoned. When she arrived, accompanied by Paul, the man told them what had happened and introduced himself.

"My name is Johann Stantke," he said.

◆ ◆ ◆

Samuel, bleeding internally, was rushed into surgery. For several days he remained in critical condition but then began to recover. Emilia visited him daily, sometimes accompanied by Paul, who usually remained in the background.

One day, however, Paul came alone, directly after school. He pulled a chair up to the bed and sat down but then didn't know what to say or do and sat awkwardly fidgeting with his hands. Finally he said:

"Papa, I want to tell you—I'm terribly sorry."

The events of the *Kristallnacht* had shocked Paul profoundly. His stepfather's brutal beating and emergency operation had brought home to him what hours of argumentation had not. What had all that to do with the rehabilitation of Germany?

"Thank you," Samuel said in a hoarse voice barely above a whisper. He was still very weak, and his face was bruised and swollen.

"I think what happened is—*terrible!*" Paul blurted.

"I'm glad you feel that way, Paul."

Paul sat kneading his hands.

"I guess—I haven't been what you'd like me to be," Paul plodded on. "But I can't help being—who I am."

"No one's blaming you for being what you are," Samuel said hoarsely.

Both fell silent. Paul sat hunched forward, clasping and unclasping his hands. Samuel closed his eyes.

"I'm so tired all the time now," he murmured. "Forgive me."

"Shall I come back another time?"

Samuel shook his head, opening his eyes.

"Come closer, Paul."

Paul got up and bent close to him.

"Be what you are—but let others be what they are too . . . ." he whispered.

Paul's eyes filled with tears.

"Yes, Papa."

"And do come again . . . it's been such a long time . . . ."

He closed his eyes again and moments later dropped off to sleep.

◆ ◆ ◆

A week later Samuel was sent home, still very weak, but his bed was needed, especially since he was a Jew. Dr. Goldstein, their family doctor for more than fourteen years, now took over. Dr. Goldstein was a portly, indomitable optimist.

"He'll be as good as new in no time," he assured Emilia. "He's lucky to have got to a hospital in time. Others weren't so lucky."

Emilia clung greedily to his optimism.

Dr. Goldstein came almost daily but it was unclear to Emilia just what he did for Samuel. He would take Samuel's pulse and listen to his heart and sometimes suggest an item of food in a diet that Emilia did not have to be told to make as rich and nourishing as possible. But mostly he would just sit for a while and talk to Samuel with cheerful optimism.

Meanwhile the family's economic situation continued to deteriorate. The income from the store had not been much, but even that was now eliminated, while the expensive store rent continued. Emilia did not dare broach the question of giving up the store. Maybe a smaller store, in a more Jewish neighborhood. But what Jew was still thinking of watches and rings and silverware these days?

These and other worries pressed in on Emilia, and there were no answers; there were no answers, and even the questions she hardly dared pose, for Samuel seemed to live, ever since that night, in another dimension, a dimension where there were no rents or grocery bills. Even food hardly interested him anymore.

As for Dr. Goldstein, Emilia finally screwed up her courage, embarrassing as it was, to inquire whether his frequent visits were really still necessary, what with the bills and all . . . .

Dr. Goldstein cut her short.

"Don't worry about the bill!" he exclaimed. "I'll charge you for only one visit a week. After all, we've got to pull together in times like these, don't we?"

Suddenly Emilia understood. Dr. Goldstein needed the visits as much for himself as for his patients. He needed to fill up the long hours of his fading practice and bolster not only his battered self-image but also the shattered concept of a world that was not really the cheerful place Dr. Goldstein was still trying to make it out to be.

♦ ◆ ♦

Another person—Johann—visited the house regularly at this time. He came once or twice a week, bringing with him some small gift, perhaps a few evergreen branches he had picked on the way or a small bottle of heavy cream. Insignificant as the gifts were, they conveyed a warmth and love that made them special. Johann's quiet kindliness and calmness made him an ever welcome guest.

Johann would sit for a while by Samuel's bedside, usually, after an initial inquiry or two, without speaking. But when Samuel felt a need to talk, Johann responded readily enough.

On the whole, however, Samuel felt little need to talk; indeed, he felt increasingly unable to talk. Everyday concerns had lost their interest for him. The things that preoccupied him, that consumed him—how did one talk about those? And even if one were able to talk about them, were there any answers, explanations, solutions? What consumed Samuel now went beyond the mere circumstance of being persecuted as a Jew. What consumed him was the realization that human beings could be wantonly cruel and worse: could *enjoy* being cruel, could enjoy *intentional* cruelty for no other reason than the *pleasure* of tormenting another human being! That was the horror buried deep in the human heart that he had failed to recognize, the catastrophe that transcended the mere phenomenon of Nazism, bad as that was, because it went to the very core of human nature. He could not accept it or grasp it or forgive it, even if there had been someone responsible. But Samuel had become convinced that there could be no God in a lawless world such as this.

It was not the beating itself that was so devastating. It was the slow, sadistic manner of its perpetration.

On one occasion Samuel tried to speak to Johann about this.

"How do you deal with evil, Johann?" he asked, speaking slowly and laboriously because he found it difficult to find words for what was so inexplicable to him. "Do you fight it head-on by taking up arms? Or do you fight it from within the system? Or by joining the victims? Or do you count yourself out altogether . . . ." His voice trailed off.

There it was, the eternal, fundamental question. In the simplest terms Samuel had posed all the possible options.

Johann sat for a long time without answering. Samuel could not know that his question had struck at the very heart of Johann's own struggle.

"I don't know," Johann said finally. "I keep asking myself the same question."

And although Samuel knew that no one could give him a ready answer, Johann's failure to do so left him with the aching conviction that there was no answer and that it was futile even to search for one.

◆ ◆ ◆

When Johann visited, Paul began to engage him in various discussions, anxious to know what had enabled Johann to stand up for his stepfather while he himself had let his comrades beat up a Jewish boy whom he could have protected at far smaller risk.

"Do you know that you could have got hurt and worse?" Paul asked.

"Of course, I knew that," Johann replied.

They were sitting in Paul's room.

"And it didn't faze you? It didn't scare you? Four bullies against you?"

"I was scared," Johann said simply.

"But you went ahead anyway."

"There are always risks."

"But why should you take such risks?" Paul persisted. "Why should you lay yourself on the line for a Jew you didn't even know? You could have wound up in a concentration camp."

"There are certain things we do without thinking, Paul. I just couldn't walk past that store and see someone being savagely beaten up and do nothing."

"But all over Germany people are walking past and doing nothing! You told me yourself that a crowd was standing outside, watching."

"All I know is, I couldn't do it," Johann repeated. "We have to live with ourselves . . . what's the matter, Paul?"

He had suddenly become aware that Paul was on the verge of crying.

"That's what I wasn't willing to do—to put myself on the line . . . I only thought of myself . . ."

"What should you have thought about, Paul? What are you talking about?"

It was then that the story of Paul's Aryanization spilled out for the first time: How he had wanted it and welcomed it, thinking only of himself; how it had slowly begun to turn sour ever since the *Kristallnacht*—no, ever since the beating up of a Jewish boy whom he could have protected instead of running away without lifting a finger. In the same way he had turned away from his stepfather who was going through so much more than he had ever gone through as a half-Jew, this man who had reared him and been good to him, though he wasn't his father—but he *was* his father because he had reared him and been good to him—he loved him . . . .

He was sobbing fiercely now.

Johann went to Paul and put his arm around his shoulders, now and then patting him gently as he emptied himself out. When Paul's tears subsided, Johann said:

"That's what you must tell him."

"What?"

"That you love him."

"What good is that now? The harm is done."

Johann shook his head. "It's never too late to tell someone you love him."

"But I'm ashamed—after the way I treated him and argued with him and avoided him . . . ."

"Paul, it's good to see where you've gone wrong. But don't overdo it. Raking yourself over the coals won't change the past. What matters is, what are you going to do about it now?"

"What can I do?"

"Tell him you love him. *Show* him you love him. I had a daughter who died of leukemia not long ago. That's all I was able to do for her. But it's a lot."

"Johann, I didn't know!" Paul exclaimed. "I'm so sorry!"

"You're showing love to me now."

"But I'm not a loving person, Johann. Not like you."

"You are, Paul. There is a great storehouse of love in all of us."

"How can you say that? Those Nazis would beat up their own mothers if they were Jewish!"

"Even they," Johann said with conviction. "Deep down. That's why they backed down when I confronted them."

Paul shook his head, wiping away his tears. "I don't believe that."

"It's the only thing we can believe in."

"You're an idealist, Johann, a starry-eyed idealist," Paul said.

But he felt very close to Johann.

◆ ◆ ◆

At first Samuel had made some effort to get up, shuffling about with the support of Emilia or Paul. But his efforts proved so tortuous that he soon gave them up despite Emilia's prodding. Thereafter, he rarely left his bed except to go with help to the bathroom. He lay in his bed now, propped up on high pillows that enabled him to look out of his second floor window, sometimes picking up a book, perhaps a volume of his favorite essays or poetry. But even reading proved too strenuous as his thoughts drifted and he dozed off. He slept a great deal now and found concentration difficult. Everything required too much effort. Only sleep did not. Only oblivion beckoned.

Paul had begun to spend a great deal of time in Samuel's room. Sometimes he brought along his homework and sat working in the armchair near the bed. He wanted to be with his stepfather, but he had also begun to take a greater interest in his studies.

Emilia, too, spent long hours in the room. It became an unspoken agreement that she would sit with Samuel in the morning, while Paul was in school, and attend to the household after Paul came home. The life of the entire family had become concentrated on Samuel.

Paul came to love the time he spent alone with his stepfather. They, too, did not talk much, for some things are spoiled rather than consecrated by talk. In any case, Samuel felt too weak for much talk. Paul's presence was enough. The way Paul glanced over at his stepfather to see whether he needed anything, the way he propped Samuel up in bed or helped him to the bathroom—all that attested to the love and respect Paul felt for him again, eloquent testimony to the compassion that he felt at last.

It was during these hours that Paul began to reorient his attitude toward the New Germany that had previously so fired his imagination. For if what they had done to Samuel represented that New Germany, then the question had to be asked: Was it worth a damn?

In these long, quiet hours together lay, finally, their healing and their reconciliation.

◆ ◆ ◆

In the initial enthusiasm of his full-fledged citizenship, Paul had felt an openness toward the baron that had made him very willing to reciprocate the baron's desire for a meaningful father-son relationship. But this willingness waned as he once again drew close to his stepfather. Even the baron's title, lineage, estate, and wealth, which had so impressed, in fact overawed him at first—how could a seventeen-year-old boy help but be overwhelmed by such a fairytale transformation?— began to pale. When he was with the baron and his family now—a family into which he had been warmly welcomed—he could not help feeling disloyal to his stepfather and somewhat guilty.

In an effort not to antagonize the baron, Paul tried to speak to him about his conflict, hoping to enlist the baron's support to reduce his weekly visits. But he expressed himself so awkwardly that the baron became confused.

"I'm trying to understand this correctly, Paul," the baron said. "You say you love to visit—but you want to come less often. It sounds a bit contradictory to me, if you don't mind my saying so."

"I'm trying to explain it to you, Otto." The word father had never so far crossed his lips, nor had it been solicited by the baron. "My stepfather is very ill—he doesn't seem to be recovering from the beating and the operation."

"Most unfortunate, this whole Jewish business," the baron interjected. "I do want you to know that I don't approve of it."

Well meaning as the words were, they grated on Paul. Unfortunate, yes, Paul thought, but what are you *doing* about it? The image of Johann flashed into his mind. How differently Johann spoke about "this whole Jewish business!" Immediately, however, this feeling was overwhelmed by the memory of his own cowardice, and he felt ashamed of his resentful thoughts.

There was an awkward silence.

"You were saying something about your stepfather," the baron finally prompted.

"Yes. I want to stay with him as much as possible while he's so ill."

How much simpler to put it that way, Paul thought. Why had he complicated the issue by trying to talk to him about his feelings of guilt and disloyalty?

"But you were saying something about feeling guilty when you come here?" the baron said.

"Well, my stepfather is a Jew," Paul mumbled, "and you—we—are Aryans."

"Granted, but why does that make you feel guilty?"

"Well, we Aryans are persecuting the Jews, aren't we?" Paul muttered.

"I'm not persecuting them," the baron said somewhat curtly. "In fact, I've had some very good Jewish acquaintances. Still, they are a foreign minority and should get their own country."

"They're trying to."

Again there was an uncomfortable silence as both realized that their conversation had drifted into an area both had assiduously avoided until now. Once again the baron was the first to try to bridge the gap.

"I think we have no real differences, Paul," he said placatingly.

"Anyway, we were talking about your visits."

"Yes. I just want to stay with my stepfather as much as possible. That way I can also help mother. For the time being only," Paul added, "until he gets better."

"All right," the baron said. "I do want to respect your wishes, Paul. But I hope that you will resume your weekly visits as soon as your stepfather gets better. Which I hope will be soon."

The talk left Paul with a vaguely dissatisfied feeling. But for the moment he had achieved what he had wanted, and from then on his visits diminished.

◆ ◆ ◆

As time went on and Samuel failed to recover—indeed, wasted away—Emilia became increasingly agitated. She was beset by financial worries, but her deepest concern centered on her husband's recovery, which had become the only way she felt she could be forgiven and rehabilitated in her own eyes. For Emilia was convinced that it was the emotional injury she had inflicted on Samuel that delayed his improvement. Hadn't Dr. Goldstein said that he would be up and about in no time?

Emilia's guilt-ridden mind looped every issue back to her self-recrimination and guilt.

Time and again she importuned Dr. Goldstein: Why wasn't he mending? Why was he so lethargic? He wasn't even eating properly. Hour after hour he would stare out of the window or sleep as if he would never wake up again. Dr. Goldstein tried to outdo himself with explanations and reassurances. But in time even his optimism wore thin. Finally he said to her one day:

"Maybe he doesn't want to get better. Maybe his will to live is broken."

"That's not true!" Emilia cried. "It can't be true!"

Dr. Goldstein didn't understand the vehemence of her reaction, but his face suddenly clouded over with fear.

"I wonder why any of us still want to live," he murmured.

Coming from optimistic Dr. Goldstein, the pronouncement was shattering, particularly for Emilia who only saw in it confirmation of her own worst self-reproaches.

But if it was she who had broken her husband's will to live, why had God demanded it? And why, if God wanted to punish her, was He in addition punishing her husband, who was blameless?

She hurried to Father Sebastian in the hope that he would help her out of her confusion. But he only said:

"My daughter, the Lord works in wondrous, mysterious ways. It's not for us to question Him. That's blasphemy."

Maybe the Lord works in wondrous ways, Emilia couldn't help thinking, but that was little comfort for her. The only thing that could comfort her now was Samuel's recovery.

Still she did not give up hope and daily pressed him: Do get up, *Männchen*—walk a little—eat some more—you've got to regain your strength . . . ."

"For God's sake, Mama, leave off, will you," Paul would intervene when he was present. For in some ways Paul now understood his stepfather better than his wife did.

Samuel didn't have the heart to tell his wife that he didn't want to regain his strength. Strength for what—to live in a country where he was not wanted? To please her, he would try to swallow another spoonful or two of the food she so solicitously cooked for him every day, and sometimes he would even let her support him as he labored to reach the armchair. But the effort proved too great. One day Emilia was unable to get him up from the armchair and had to wait for Paul to come home from school to help her. Then even she finally no longer pressed him to get up.

As Samuel faded, Emilia became more and more frantic. Life had become an unending circle of torment and pain. Wherever she turned, whether to her husband or to Paul, her guilt was staring her in the face. There was no way out and no one to speak to, not to her husband nor to Paul nor even to her priest. One day her agitation was such that she cried out aloud:

"Samuel, why are you torturing me so?"

And breaking into sobs, she ran out of the room.

A while later she returned and sat down by his bedside, no longer crying, and took his hand in hers, and they remained like that for a long time, quietly, without speaking.

The one she had really cried out against, of course, was God.

◆ ◆ ◆

Christmas passed. One day in late January 1939, Paul entered his stepfather's bedroom with a large paper bag and sat down by the bed. Samuel lay with closed eyes, but Paul could tell that he was not sleeping.

"Papa," he said softly.

Samuel opened his eyes and a faint smile lit up his features.

"I brought something," Paul said.

He opened the bag and took out the khaki shirt and black pants of his Hitler Youth uniform. Then he took out a pair of scissors and proceeded to cut and rip both into shreds, dropping each piece into the bag while Samuel watched silently. When he had finished, Paul said:

"I've left the Hitler Youth, Papa. For good."

Samuel remained silent, but tears slowly began to trickle down his cheeks.

♦ ◆ ♦

Next day Samuel seemed to rally all at once. He sat up in bed, ate more than usual, and responded more alertly when spoken to. Emilia was overjoyed.

"Did you see how alert he's been all day?" she said to Paul at the dinner table.

"Yes," Paul agreed, "but I don't think we should jump to any conclu—"

But his mother didn't want to hear him out. "Maybe he's over the hump," she interrupted him.

The next morning Samuel was already awake when Emilia came into his room. That itself was unusual. She helped him with the morning toilet and then fed him his breakfast. He also ate more than usual.

"I'm so glad you're feeling better, *Männchen*."

Samuel smiled faintly.

"Now you just eat properly and you'll be back on your feet in no time," Emilia bustled on. "Dr. Goldstein says there's no reason in the world why you shouldn't be up and about."

When he was through with breakfast, Samuel asked to be propped up in bed. Emilia happily complied and then sat down beside him on the bed.

"I'm so glad you're feeling better," she said again.

"Millie," he said.

He spoke slowly, but his voice was stronger than it had been for a long time.

"Yes, *Männchen*?"

"I've been thinking. You must give up the store."

Although the store had been one of her principal worries, she was surprised that he brought it up just when he was beginning to feel stronger. He had never spoken of the store during his entire illness.

"I was thinking the same thing," she agreed. "You could open a smaller store in a Jewish neighborhood."

He shook his head but remained silent.

"I've been disposing of a few things," she said hesitantly. "I hope you don't mind. We needed money."

He nodded. "I'm glad something is left."

"We'll manage," Emilia said quickly.

"You know where the documents are."

It was half question, half statement.

"What documents?"

"To the house—the life insurance."

"Yes," she said, beginning to feel uneasy.

"That should help too."

"There's no need to talk about life insurance."

Samuel closed his eyes. He looked all at once drained. When he opened them again there was a look of desperation in his eyes.

"Millie," he whispered. "I'm dying. Why do you make it so difficult?"

If he had struck her in the face, she could not have reacted more violently. Her whole face contorted.

"Don't talk like that!" she cried. "You'll be up and about in no time!"

"You mustn't deny it any longer, Millie," he whispered.

It was hard to die when the person closest to you was so adamantly denying it.

"Don't talk like that!" she cried again in a strangled voice. "You're getting better!"

"It'll be easier for both of you, Millie . . . forgive me . . . ."

A groan escaped from Emilia's lips. She slid from the bed to her knees and burying her face in his hand began to sob convulsively.

"It's me who needs your forgiveness, Samuel."

For some time her sobs were the only sound in the room. When they subsided, he said faintly:

"I forgave you when I gave you my blessing, Millie—Paul has truly become my son now—thank you . . . ."

He closed his eyes, exhausted, and moments later fell into a deep sleep. For some time Emilia remained slumped by the bed, her body quivering now and then as if in a last discharge of pain and grief.

Finally she dried her eyes, and tiptoed silently out of the room.

◆ ◆ ◆

Samuel's rally was brief and the collapse abrupt. Two nights later he seemed so weak that Emilia and Paul spent the night by his bedside, alternately watching over him and dozing fitfully while Samuel lay with closed eyes, breathing heavily, a slight rattle in the back of his throat. If it had not been for a responsive pressure when they took his hand and spoke to him, they would have thought him in a coma.

The wake had started. The soul was slowly releasing its hold. Both were conscious of it. Both were engulfed by the quiet subsiding, the quiet fading away. Pain had brought on the end, but surrender was bringing it to completion. It all possessed a rightness that for the moment lifted his dying even beyond sadness.

Toward morning—it was about five o'clock—his breathing became labored. At one point when Emilia spoke to him, he struggled to open his eyes, but only one eye opened and it was distant and unfocused and soon fell shut.

Another half hour went by. His breathing was shallow now, almost imperceptible. And then it suddenly stopped. No final words. No struggle. No convulsion. They felt the end because suddenly the silence in the room deepened and became complete. They sensed it and knew it and did not move. No tears. No lamentation. For the moment not even pain.

Surrender and acceptance. Do not jar the quiet passage.

Slowly the lamplight faded as the morning entered the room.

Between the dying Jew and his own dead child, there developed, in Johann's heart and mind, a wondrous resonance. Perhaps it was the injustice of both events that tied them together for him, the one man-made, the other divine; or it might have been the loss entailed in both events: the child's death robbing him of the person he held most dear in his own life, while Mr. Silver's death symbolized for him the loss of what he held dear in the country at large.

The *Kristallnacht* had shocked Johann into a full recognition of what was happening in Germany. He remembered the struggle he had experienced when he was drawn to the small crowd in front of Mr. Silver's store and saw what was happening inside. Poor fellow, he had thought, feeling compassion for the Jew; but what could a single, weak man do against four such bullies? Interference would merely turn him into another victim. He had thought of calling upon the other onlookers for assistance, but when he looked at their apathetic, merely curious faces, he knew that was futile.

He was about to move on when the fierce blow to Mr. Silver's stomach made him realize with a sudden searing shock that he was witnessing not just a beating but that here a man might well be slowly being beaten to death while he stood idly by. It was then that he had detached himself from the crowd without further hesitation, propelled forward by a need deeper and more demanding than any act of conscious deliberation, and had confronted the four men.

♦ ◆ ♦

Johann had never been a talkative man, but after Hannelore's death he had become taciturn, toward Maria as well as everyone else. Nor did Maria speak much to him. The child's death had left them with nothing in common. Had a deeper bond existed between them, the loss might have pulled them together. As it was, it merely broke them apart.

The deepening estrangement did not affect Johann, who was something of a loner, as much as it did Maria. She had known for a long time that she was unhappy, but only now did the full extent of her unhappiness come home to her. Besides, what was there to do all day in the small apartment? There was only so much cleaning, shopping, and cooking you could do for two adults. The days now became oppressively long so that she thought about getting a job.

When she presented the idea to Johann, he merely said:

"That's a good idea."

"But how do you feel about it?" she demanded somewhat aggressively.

"It's fine with me."

Maria had been prepared to fight for her decision, and his immediate acquiescence annoyed her. His ready acceptance of things had always grated on her because she saw in it a spineless passivity.

"It'll mean some changes," Maria warned. "Like shopping and cooking."

"Sure," Johann said.

"But at least we'll finally have some money to buy things."

Food and material things had never been particularly important to Johann. He was thin and abstemious, not by design but by nature.

"God!" she blurted. "Don't you ever object to nothin'?"

"What do you want me to object to?" Johann replied with a touch of irritation. "I understand that you feel bored at home now. I hope you find a good job."

Maria pursed her lips, which puckered up her scarred upper lip in a rather ugly way.

"What's the use," she muttered, and pushing back her chair, walked out of the room.

◆ ◆ ◆

One evening the bell rang and the Nazi block warden stood outside. He was a portly, middle-aged man who looked more like an amiable Bavarian burgher than a Nazi. But he had joined the Nazis early on and was a dedicated follower.

"Herr Stantke," he said, "may I have a word with you?"

Johann waved him into the living room but did not ask him to sit down.

"The matter involves attending the funeral of a Jew," the block warden began with a certain solemnity.

"Is there a law against that?"

"No, Herr Stantke. At least not yet. But it shows a certain attitude of friendliness toward Jews. Good Germans don't have Jewish friends—living *or* dead."

"We have no Jewish friends either, you can bet your life on that," Maria interjected quickly.

"I'm not saying you have," the block warden continued pleasantly. "But then again your husband did go to the funeral of a Jew. I assume you didn't go to celebrate his death?"

"I did celebrate his death," Johann said enigmatically.

The block warden cackled.

"That's more like it," he said, misunderstanding. "Anyway, just a little reminder. No harm meant."

He moved to the door, gave a smart Hitler salute, and was gone.

"I told you you're gonna get yourself into a heap of trouble with your Jew-loving," Maria said irritably when the block warden had gone. "What's this Jew to you anyway? I warned you not to keep visiting him."

Johann couldn't help noticing that she no longer said *us* but *you* are going to get into trouble.

"Well, he's dead now," Johann said.

"And good riddance too!" Maria exclaimed.

They both remained silent.

"It's sad, isn't it," Johann said suddenly.

"What is?"

"All this...." Johann said vaguely, leaving the sentence unfinished, and walked away.

It was how most of their exchanges ended these days.

◆ ◆ ◆

The *Kristallnacht* and Mr. Silver's subsequent slow wasting away had triggered a struggle in Johann that came to preoccupy him more and more. It was at Mr. Silver's funeral, in particular, that he had been shocked into a new awareness.

Except for Mrs. Silver and Paul, Johann had been the only non-Jew at the funeral, and though everyone there knew how he had intervened and saved Mr. Silver, he had felt a certain tension and antagonism beneath the mourners' surface cordiality. And then a casual remark had suddenly hit Johann with the force of a new revelation.

"As a German, you just can't know how it feels," someone had said in reference to the persecutions. "After all, you're not affected."

It suddenly made him realize that, Nazi or not, as a German he was automatically a member of the oppressing master race because the persecutions did not touch him. That fact alone made him a silent accomplice and therefore guilty!

◆ ◆ ◆

An exchange with Maria soon afterwards further clarified his feelings. Ironically, when it came to the Nazis, Maria kept urging him to do the very thing that so annoyed her in their marriage, namely, to keep his mouth shut.

"We'd still be swinging in trees if man had kept his mouth shut," Johann replied.

"Better than swingin' at the end of a rope," Maria shot back.

"Did it ever occur to you, Maria, that we become accomplices when we keep our mouth shut?"

"Accomplices?"

"Yes, to the persecution."

"I ain't persecutin' no one. Not even the Jews, though I got no use for them."

"I don't mean personally. I mean we become guilty by doing nothing."

"Make sense, will you?" Maria said, annoyed.

"Suppose there's a fire, Maria," Johann persisted uncharacteristically, "and you stand by doing nothing. Are you guilty of helping to spread that fire or not?"

"What's keeping your mouth shut got to do with a fire?" Maria exclaimed.

"The Nazis are the fire."

"The Nazis are no fire! They're pretty damn good, if you ask me. What they're doing is a damn sight better than breadlines and stuff."

At this point Johann fell silent. Maria was incapable of understanding the issues with which he struggled. But for him things were becoming clearer.

Yes, merely standing on the sidelines made one an unwitting accomplice. But if that was true, didn't one need to do something?

That was the question that now began to prey on Johann's mind. It was a difficult question and one that Johann tried at first to evade. Hadn't he intervened for Mr. Silver and for the young Jew on the streetcar? Wasn't the block warden's warning proof enough that he was not a Nazi? What more could he do?

Then another voice asserted itself. You can't sit on those laurels forever, it said. What are you doing now? What are you doing *now*?

But what *could* he do?

◆ ◆ ◆

One day, standing idly in the streetcar during an afternoon lull, contemplating some advertising posters, the idea suddenly struck him: He could make some posters with anti-Nazi slogans! That would stir up the consciences of people.

The idea excited him. Where could he put up the posters? Inside the streetcars they could easily be removed. What about handbills? Handbills were small and could be scattered secretly all over town. But who could he trust to print them? He needed something he could do himself, something permanent. Paint! Yes, paint! How obvious! Even if letters were painted over, the new paint would remind people that something had been erased and suppressed. Slogans could be painted on walls and buildings all over town, his thoughts raced on. He would become known as the anti-Nazi sloganeer of Munich!

What would be the message? his fantasies ran on. It should be stirring but above all short because it had to be painted on quickly. Splashed on in a flash!

He now began to mull over various slogans. How about: *Germany, Awake!* But awake to what? It was too ambiguous. A Nazi might well take it as exhorting him to further enthusiasm. *Rise Up, Germans!* That sounded good but, again, rise up against what? How about *Resist Evil* with a swastika painted in the middle? No, that was too complicated, requiring two colors to be effective. How about simply *Down With Hitler?*

Yes! DOWN WITH HITLER! Excellent!

As he circulated about Munich on the streetcar, Johann began to scout suitable walls for his slogan. He needed walls secluded enough to afford protection from discovery while he painted, yet visible enough to catch the eyes of passers-by—not an easy combination. But over the course of a week or two, he pinpointed almost a dozen likely sites.

As he thought about his plan, he became more and more excited and determined, although under no illusion about the riskiness of such an undertaking—the KZ's* and the Gestapo, the Secret Police, had long since become dreaded bywords. But at least he would be rid of his guilt.

One day Johann went out and bought the necessary equipment—brushes, paint, paint thinner, etc. In a state of high excitement he hid everything in the wardrobe in Hannelore's room, knowing that Maria

---

* The German abbreviation for the concentration camps, pronounced kah-tset.

never entered the room anymore.

One difficulty remained. How could he walk around with paint and brushes and remain inconspicuous?

After some experimentation, he came upon the idea of using an old musical instrument carrying case. A man with a musical instrument. What could be more innocent?

Maria meanwhile had found a job as a cleaning woman in a hospital. It was night work and even her days off did not coincide with Johann's so that they saw little of each other, leaving Johann free to come and go as he pleased. For he had decided not to take Maria into his confidence, partly because of the risk involved but primarily because he didn't trust her anymore.

◆ ◆ ◆

One night Johann finally ventured out. He had reconnoitered his first target with great care: a statue of a field marshal on a horse in the center of a small square. He traversed the square daily on his streetcar rounds. The base of the monument was high and well visible from all sides.

He arrived at the deserted square at three o'clock in the morning. Crouching behind some bushes, he opened his instrument case and removed the paint and brush and crept to the base of the monument. Approaching vehicles would be visible a long way off by their lights. Not so pedestrians. Only their footsteps would warn him. He crouched and listened again. Certain that the square was deserted, he dipped the brush in the paint and with a dozen quick strokes painted on the slogan. When he finished, he ducked down and listened again. No footsteps. He scampered around to the other side of the monument and crouched down. A pair of car lights was approaching in the distance. And came closer. He felt his heart beating faster. But the car turned off into a side street. He painted the slogan quickly on the other side of the base, dripping paint, which annoyed him. Was he trembling? No, all his senses were sharp, clear, and alert.

He circled back to his case and packed away his equipment and walked quickly across the street and away from the square. A block away he stopped and looked back. The square lay deserted as before, the field marshal sitting in lonely splendor high on his prancing horse. How easy it had been!

Next day, as his streetcar approached the square, he imagined everyone staring at the monument and commenting in hushed exclamations and whispers. But when the streetcar reached the square, hardly anyone looked. And those who did showed no overt reaction. Had they even seen his slogan? The letters were small when viewed from a distance. He must make them larger next time.

When he passed the square next day, the slogan had been painted over. And by the following morning, even the paint had been removed. Only a few smudges remained.

◆ ◆ ◆

Disappointing as the results were, Johann went out again a few nights later and a third time a week after that. But the slogan disappeared as quickly each time, and there was little discernible reaction among the many people who circulated on the streetcar all day.

Returning in the wee hours of the morning after the third trip, he found Maria at home before the end of her shift. She was sitting at the dinner table, hunched unsteadily over a cup of tea, her scar accentuated by the pallor on her face.

"How come you're home?" he exclaimed in surprise.

"Where've you been?" Maria demanded hoarsely.

"I took a walk."

"At three in the morning?"

He set down the case.

"How come you're home?" he asked again.

"I don't feel so good," she said plaintively. "They sent me home."

Her eyes fastened themselves on him. They looked feverish. She sniffed suspiciously.

"What're you doin' out in the middle of the night? You smell of paint."

"I paint slogans on walls."

"What kind of slogans?"

"Anti-Nazi slogans."

Maria's jaw dropped. The enormity took a while to sink in. Finally she said in a jagged tone:

"Are you crazy? You're gonna get the Gestapo down on us."

"You know nothing about it."

"I do now."

"But you're not involved."

"I'm living under the same roof."

She had broken out in a sweat and appeared to be faint. She put her head down on her arms.

"Come on, I'll help you to bed," he said.

He assisted her to the bedroom and helped her undress. She was bathed in sweat but, once in bed, began to shiver. He fetched another blanket and sat down beside her, stroking her hair until she fell into a deep, exhausted sleep.

◆ ◆ ◆

Maria's fear was not unrealistic. Clan responsibility was a favorite Nazi tactic. But it was only one, among several factors, that cemented Maria's decision to leave the marriage.

Maria's primary reason for staying in the marriage, after Hannelore's death, had been her fear that she could not support herself. Another had been her fear of loneliness, of being unable to find another man. But this fear, too, proved groundless because she had met a man at work who was interested in her. Gustav, who was thirteen years her senior, had been deserted by his wife and their two children. He became infatuated with Maria and she, after some initial hesitation, responded readily enough.

All this bolstered Maria's self-confidence and courage and snapped the remaining bonds of her marriage.

Once she decided to leave, Johann's nocturnal activities became academic. What was important was to prepare the ground for her departure.

One evening she asked Johann:

"Are you happy?"

"What about?" The question had taken him by surprise.

"With me—with our marriage."

Johann was silent. Although he wouldn't have raised the question, he wouldn't avoid it either.

"Not very," he said.

"Then why are we keeping it going?"

"We're married."

"But if we're unhappy? You're not against divorce."

"No."

"Then why do we go on?"

"Are you saying, you want out, Maria?"

She hesitated for only a moment.

"Yes."

He remained silent for a long time. Finally he said:

"If you want out, I won't stand in the way."

That was all. What more was there to say?

◆ ◆ ◆

Maria moved out on her day off, while Johann was at work. Gustav, who helped her, had asked her to move in with him and, in fact, had proposed marriage once they both obtained their divorce. The evening before her move, Maria informed Johann of her decision.

"I see" was all he said.

His passive acceptance briefly triggered a wave of anger in Maria. But then it gave way to a feeling of guilt.

"I'm sorry if I'm hurting you," she said.

"You don't have to apologize."

"I don't want to hurt you."

"I believe that."

"It just ain't workin' no more, Johann. Ever since Hanne left."

"I know."

Both were silent.

"Maybe *I* should get another place," Johann said. "That way you wouldn't have to move."

"I have a place."

He started a little.

"Where?"

"Does it matter?"

"I guess not."

"You can keep the furniture for now," she said. "Maybe later I'll want some things."

There was another pause.

"Maria, where are you moving?"

"I'm moving in with someone, Johann."

"I see," he murmured, falling silent.

His calm reaction suddenly angered her.

"You don't much care anyway," she flung at him.

What did she want him to say? Would she stay if he told her he cared?

"Does it still matter whether I care or not?"

"I guess not."

She pushed back her chair and went into the bedroom.

When he returned from work next day, her things were gone. On the table lay her keys.

For a few days Johann felt intensely lonely. But he felt no fear of the future, and soon his basic self-sufficiency reasserted itself. The marriage, such as it had been, had been over with Hannelore's death, for the child had been the only meaningful link that had still existed between them.

After Maria left, Johann threw himself with redoubled energy into his anti-Nazi work.

♦ ♦ ♦

Over a month had passed since Johann had first begun his crusade. He had gone out five or six times, each time with little discernible result. Were people just too scared to talk about it in public? Or was something more dramatic needed?

As he pondered the problem, an idea struck him one day. What if he were to paint his slogan on a moving object, an object circulating all over the city so that thousands of people would see it—for instance, a streetcar?

The idea thrilled him. Why hadn't he thought of it before? People couldn't help noticing the streetcars. And it would be easy for him because he knew every part of the terminal where the streetcars were parked at night. He even knew the approximate rounds of the night watchman and the existence of a hole in the fence where he could slip in unnoticed. And even if he were discovered, he could always explain away his presence since he was an employee.

He set about at once preparing the details.

♦ ♦ ♦

He started out at eleven o'clock one evening, planning to arrive at the terminal after midnight. It was a blustery April night, chosen by Johann on purpose because it was certain to make the watchman less zealous.

Near the terminal, he turned into a side street and circled around to the back. He slipped quickly through the hole in the fence and ran toward the nearest streetcars, where he crouched down to listen. There was no sound, no indication that the watchman was anywhere about.

By now his eyes were accustomed to the darkness and he set to work. He wouldn't attempt to paint the slogan on all the cars, of course. There wasn't enough time for that. He would paint the slogan on a dozen, maybe fifteen scattered cars, on the side away from the doors so the streetcar personnel wouldn't immediately discover the slogans. He felt a thrill of exhilaration, like a field marshal planning an attack. Tomorrow thousands of people would see his words, and hundreds would be moved by them and maybe a few would be motivated to undertake some act of protest or resistance....

He stopped to listen. Not a sound. Where was the night watchman?

Leaving the carrying case behind, he moved on to a second car, working quickly, with practiced smoothness. Picking out a car here and there, he began to move in a wide circle around the terminal. How many cars had he painted?

Suddenly he froze, crouching down. A streetcar door had been slammed shut not far from him. The crews were always admonished to close the doors when they left their cars at night, but many neglected to do so. He listened intently. Yes, now he could hear approaching steps as a second door was slammed shut. He looked around. Across from him, a streetcar door stood open. He dashed over, climbed into the streetcar, and ducked down, his heart pounding. The steps were coming directly toward him now. Presently the beam of the watchman's lantern fingered the ceiling of his car, and the door was banged shut. Then the steps receded. After a while another door was banged shut, more distant now, coming from the direction of the repair shops. Then minutes passed without a sound.

Johann stirred, aware that he was bathed in sweat, feeling suddenly quite exhausted. What time was it? Almost three. He crept to the door and slowly pried it open. He knew all the quirks and eccentricities of these doors, but in the surrounding stillness, the door creaked with deafening loudness.

He slipped out and began to circle back to his carrying case, painting a few more cars on the way. How many had he painted now? Thirteen, maybe fifteen. His hand moved automatically by now despite his chilled, stiff fingers. All at once he felt disoriented as a phalanx of streetcars stared at him indistinguishably from all sides. Where was he? Where had he left his carrying case? What if he couldn't find it? He could feel the cold sweat trickling down his back.

Reaching the fence, he remembered that he could simply follow it around to the hole where he had started. He began to run along the fence, although he was much more exposed there, and finally reached the hole and turned back to the cars and found his carrying case. Thank God! What time was it anyhow?

Four twenty. Soon the first crews would arrive.

He put his gear away, moved quickly toward the fence, and slipped through, and soon found himself back on the main thoroughfare where he finally slowed down. He felt no fatigue now, no numbness. He had done it! In a few hours the city would be buzzing with his message as it circulated all over town!

He entered a café that had just opened. A sprinkling of silent workingmen sat about, sipping their morning coffee. He sat down by one of the large windows. From here he could watch the streetcars going by, fanning out to different points in the city to begin their passenger runs. When the waiter came, he ordered coffee, eggs, rolls, and jam—an extravagant breakfast but he felt like celebrating. Also, he suddenly felt ravenously hungry.

He began to nod off when he was pulled awake by a distant rumble. In a moment he could see a procession of streetcars heaving into sight in the dim morning light. And then he could see one car and then another and after a while a third bearing the bold letters of his slogan:

DOWN WITH HITLER!

He felt a rush of triumph and exuberance.

But then, just as suddenly as it had begun, the procession stopped. Half an hour went by, then an hour before he heard another approaching rumble. He craned his neck. Yes, the procession of streetcars was starting again. But car after car passed by and not a single one carried his slogan!

He leaned back and closed his eyes, feeling suddenly faint and utterly drained. He had not expected the slogans to stay on for long, but he had expected them to circulate at least one day.

All his effort—all the risk—and what had he accomplished?

◆ ◆ ◆

The terminal was abuzz with excitement. While Johann changed into his uniform, his neighbor told him the news. A saboteur had painted a subversive slogan all over the streetcars! They had intercepted most of the cars and were painting them over now, but a few had slipped through and had to be tracked down individually by the police.

"The guy must think the *Führer* can be knocked down with a feather!" the man guffawed in high amusement. "He must be cracked!"

The driver of his streetcar also mentioned it. Since they knew each other better, he was less guarded.

"Takes courage. I'll hand him that. But for what? This ain't a system you can topple with a slogan."

"How can it be toppled?" Johann wondered aloud.

The man shrugged with an air of resignation.

"It can't be."

All day Johann strained to hear some talk about his slogan, hoping that someone had in some way, however minutely, seen or heard about it and been touched. But he heard only two comments, and both were amused and contemptuous.

Before leaving the terminal that evening, he heard some other news: The night watchman and the three crews that had left the terminal with the slogan had been arrested and had been taken away by the Gestapo!

◆ ◆ ◆

Next morning Johann woke up with a fever and pains all over his body, with alternate spells of shivering and sweating. He put on his morning gown, went unsteadily downstairs, and knocked on Ingeborg's apartment door.

"Johann, whatever is the matter?" Ingeborg cried. "You look awful!"

"May I use your phone to call work? I feel sick."

Ingeborg had drawn close to Johann and Maria during Hannelore's illness and their subsequent estrangement. In fact, Maria had confided to Ingeborg that she was involved with someone even before she had informed Johann. It made Ingeborg feel sorry for Johann, for she liked him a great deal.

"Now you get back to bed," she said in a maternally authoritarian manner. "And let me have a key. I'll be up later with some hot food."

"I'm not hungry."

"You've got to eat. How do you expect to get back on your feet?"

Johann spent the next day in bed and another two days at home before returning to work, while Ingeborg came up three or four times a day bearing hot broths and other nourishing goodies and hovered over him until he had eaten.

The chilly night spent crouching outdoors, alternately cold and breaking into a sweat, had brought on the illness. But the deeper cause was a profound physical, emotional, mental, and spiritual exhaustion. Johann had had no starry-eyed fantasies regarding the effectiveness of what he was doing. It was simply his way of shedding his guilt. Still, he had believed that there existed a strain of resistance in the German people that could be aroused. Now he had to admit to himself that this belief had been a naive miscalculation.

But the worst thing was something he had forgotten to include in his calculations altogether: the arrest of the night watchman and the three crews— seven innocent men who might be sent to prison or even to a concentration camp! He had harmed seven human beings for no useful purpose whatever!

The realization precipitated yet another harsh moral crisis in Johann.

♦ ◆ ♦

Johann and Paul had continued to see each other after Samuel's death, drawn together by their respective preoccupations with the Nazis, and a strong bond had developed between them. Different as their ages and personalities were—Paul almost eighteen now, Johann by this time thirty-one; Paul an extroverted, action-oriented materialist, Johann, for all his recent foray into political action, essentially an introvert preoccupied with moral and spiritual questions—different though they were, their meetings and discussions helped to crystallize in each a path that was true to his own nature.

Paul admired, indeed revered, Johann for his commitment and willingness to risk himself for his beliefs, in contrast to what he saw as his own ambivalent, cowardly evaluations of risk versus expected benefit. Nevertheless, in their discussions he never tired of accusing Johann of softheaded, unrealistic, starry-eyed idealism.

"It's quixotic!" Paul cried. He had just read *Don Quixote* and it had greatly impressed him.

"It's what?" Johann asked with a touch of amusement.

"Tilting at windmills. What I'm saying, Johann, is that you're a visionary."

"You don't say. I'm what?" Johann asked, gently teasing Paul for his pride in newly acquired big words.

They both grinned.

Paul was the only one to whom Johann had revealed his secret activity, which Paul considered quixotic indeed. What was needed, Paul maintained, was to plant bombs, not paint slogans. The system itself had elected violence, violence against Jews, violence against whoever opposed it, violence increasingly even against other nations. One could defend the march into the Rhineland, even the *Anschluss* with Austria, but how could the annexation of Czechoslovakia be defended? Paul was more and more convinced that only violence could end it.

"Blow up the *Feldherrnhalle* when all the Nazi bigwigs are assembled there to celebrate their Party Day!" Paul exclaimed. *"That* would be an effective protest, not slogans!"

"Have you forgotten, Paul, that the *Kristallnacht* was the result of *one* Jew killing *one* German, in return for which thousands of Jews were killed and imprisoned and deported?" Johann objected, shaking his head. "No, violence breeds violence."

"And you think slogans are the solution?"

"Maybe not. But that doesn't make violence right," Johann said with conviction.

"You forget that even your slogans bred violence."

Johann remained silent. Paul was sorry he had said that. He knew how Johann agonized over the arrest of the seven men, although the six crew members had meanwhile been released. Only the night watchman hadn't. Rumor had it that he had been sent to a concentration camp.

On another occasion Paul said:

"All action involves violence, at least potentially. How will you ever do anything if you're not prepared to hurt someone?"

"Isn't violence what we condemn the Nazis for?" Johann countered. "When we kill, we lose control over the consequences. We become no better than the killers."

"That doesn't have to follow," Paul replied heatedly. "There's a difference between initiating violence and defending oneself against it. Anyway, how do you propose to end this system? Do you think it'll just fade away? How do you ever oppose violence without using violence?"

"Yes, that's the big, the awful question," Johann agreed, brooding.

Paul was aware of his friend's inner struggle and wanted to be supportive. But Johann's arguments exasperated him more and more as his own thoughts and feelings matured in a different direction.

One day when Paul visited him in his apartment, Johann seemed depressed and unusually restless, pacing about without being able to settle down. Paul had never seen him in such a state.

"Johann, what's the matter?" he inquired solicitously. "Are you all right?"

"The problem," Johann said as if continuing a discussion just inter-rupted—indeed, he seemed to be carrying on a constant internal dialogue with himself these days—"the problem is, how do we get rid of the guilt?"

"I'm not following you," Paul replied.

Johann stopped pacing and faced him.

"Because we're all guilty, Paul. Don't you see? As Aryans we automatically belong to the oppressors!"

His tone was uncharacteristically intense, almost harsh. And when Paul wanted to say something, Johann cut him short.

"I don't want to kill. I don't care how high-minded the cause. Because killing leads to killing leads to killing."

He looked at Paul as if in physical pain and whispered:

"If all action involves us in violence, what are we to do, Paul? How do we escape from the guilt?"

◆ ◆ ◆

Johann had reached a point where Paul could no longer follow him, a point from which he could only struggle on alone.

If even peaceful action entailed violence—and nonaction placed one among the oppressors—what was one to do?

He remembered his conversation with Samuel. How do you deal with evil? Samuel had asked. By taking up arms—or from within—or by counting yourself out? Yes, that's what Samuel had done by committing a species of suicide. Was suicide the solution then?

But he had mentioned a fourth option: Joining the victims. One could join the victims! One could become one of the oppressed! That was one way in which one could continue living without adding to the sum total of evil and injustice in the world, one way in which one could absolve oneself definitively of all guilt!

One could belong to the masters or declare one's solidarity with the victims. There was no middle ground.

◆ ◆ ◆

Johann received the idea in a sudden intuitive flash, but he accepted it at once, as is characteristic of thoughts that bring a long period of internal gestation to fruition. He would not reveal his scheme to anyone, not even to Paul, not because he distrusted Paul, but because he felt Paul would not understand and would try to dissuade him.

Johann now became very busy. He brought his papers in order, gave notice on his apartment, and quit his job, visited his parents, taking with him a suitcase of personal belongings that he asked them to keep for him, and looked up Maria, and met Gustav for the first time. With all, he spoke in a friendly, pleasant manner, giving no indication that anything unusual was under way, feeling like a man who has at long last rid himself of a crippling problem. Finally, he took a week-long walking tour through the Bavarian Alps, a trip that he had long wanted to make and that he had in fact planned to make with Lorle when her illness and death intervened.

When he returned, he shut himself up in his apartment and set to work on two posters on which he printed in large colorful letters:

RESIST THE NAZI EVIL!

He took two days to complete the job to his satisfaction. When he finished, he pasted the two posters on two thin sheets of plywood, which he connected with straps to fit over his shoulders.

One last visit remained. Of all the people in his life, Paul had become the closest. He sat down and wrote him a letter. Facing Paul, he felt an overwhelming desire to tell him what he was about to do, but he suppressed it and they talked amiably for over an hour. When Johann got up to leave, he took the sealed letter from his pocket and handed it to Paul.

"I didn't want to mail this, so it wouldn't fall into the wrong hands," he said. "I'd like you to promise me that you won't open it until Sunday."

Paul laughed. "What's all the mystery about, Johann?"

"You'll see. Promise?"

"Sure," Paul said lightly.

It was then Thursday.

Johann shook hands with him, aching to embrace him. But he only pressed his hand hard. Paul didn't notice anything unusual.

◆ ◆ ◆

The following morning, Friday, Johann slept late. He fixed himself some breakfast with the little food left in the kitchen. Then he sat down and wrote a short letter to Maria, offering her the furniture and asking her to keep some of his clothes. Finally, he brought Streaky, the cat, down to Ingeborg, who had agreed to take him. In the early afternoon he washed and dressed carefully, put on his warmest clothes, certainly warmer than the mild day warranted, and then a coat on top of that. Taking up the posters, he folded them inside out so that the legend wouldn't show, tucked them under his arm, and left the apartment. On the street he placed the apartment key in the letter to Maria and dropped it in the nearest mailbox.

He flagged down a taxi and told the driver to take him to the *Karlsplatz*, a large, busy traffic circle in the heart of Munich. When they reached the circle, it was late afternoon, and the afternoon rush hour was well under way. Cars, bicyclists, and pedestrians were converging from all sides, pushing through the traffic circle pellmell. He set down the posters and for some minutes observed the flow of traffic with a sense of power and elation. No one could take his action from him. No one could stop him.

For a moment he imagined returning to his apartment, his job, his life. It would be nice—for a day, a week. But then the torment would start again. The guilt. The intolerable feeling that something needed to be done without having the means to do it. No, that life no longer attracted him. He was satisfied with his decision. There was no other way, only sadness and regret that he lived in a world that made such decisions necessary.

Finally, as the traffic light changed and the traffic came to a halt on all sides, he picked up the posters and walked rapidly into the center of the large traffic circle, turning the posters inside out and slipping them over his head as he walked so that they hung down in front and in back.

RESIST THE NAZI EVIL!

By the time he reached the center of the circle the light was beginning to change and the traffic was about to move again. He stopped it, spreading his arms wide so that the cars ground to a halt on all sides, which created a small island of empty space in the middle of which he began to circle slowly, as drivers ogled him on all sides and the backed up traffic honked and tooted all around him. Only a few bicyclists flitted through, looking curiously at him as they passed, until even they stopped coming because pedestrians had begun to pack the spaces between the cars to see what was causing the traffic jam.

For some minutes the scene lasted, frozen like a tableau cast in bronze. Despite the honking and commotion all around him, there was a strange quality of stillness in the charmed circle in which Johann perambulated, as though a spell cast over the scene protected him as he slowly circled around, a faint smile on his lips now. And no one stepped forward to stop him or take hold of him or cart him away, as if his life too were cast in bronze, charmed and forever protected.

The spell was broken when two policemen pushed their way through the crowd and one of them began to unsnarl the traffic while the other led Johann away, the poster still over his shoulders, as the crowd parted and closed behind him.

It was not until Sunday, when Paul opened the letter, that he had any inkling of Johann's action, though the letter was brief and did not spell out any details.

"My dear friend Paul," it read.

"By the time you read this I will be somewhere, probably in a concentration camp. Forgive me for not telling you about my plan, but I knew that you would try to argue me out of something I felt I needed to do. I realize it is a futile act, but I can subscribe to no other to declare my opposition to the Nazis and my solidarity with its victims. No doubt my body will suffer in the KZ, but at least my spirit will be free. Perhaps one day we will meet again. I hope so. Then we will talk more about it."

Paul made a concerted effort to find out what had happened, but the police would only tell him that Johann had created a public disturbance and had been turned over to the Gestapo. And at Gestapo Headquarters he was informed that Johann Stantke had been sent to the Dachau Concentration Camp for "re-education." More he could not find out.

The news shocked him profoundly. Though his friendship with Johann had become more and more important in his life, he only now fully realized how strongly Johann's quiet, unpretentious personality had impressed itself on him. Coming on top of his stepfather's death, the loss was hard to bear. Perhaps his act was futile and a waste—Paul understood that it was deliberately meant to be symbolic—but when all had been said, there remained its courage and commitment. *That* was its power and its glory.

Paul's thoughts now revolved almost constantly around Johann and his stepfather, for in his mind the two had become curiously interlinked. How different they had been and yet how similar in their basic character! His stepfather had been an intellectual through and through, every sentence proclaimed it like a trumpet blast, in contrast to Johann who was not an intellectual, yet what he had to say was always imbued with intellect and spirit. Perhaps that was the difference between them, Paul reflected: intellect versus spirit. But why *versus*? Why not intellect *and* spirit? In the past Paul had never been comfortable with the notion of spirit. What was spirit anyway? Something hypothesized and shakily deduced. But now it set him to thinking.

♦ ♦ ♦

After Samuel's death, Emilia and Paul decided to cut expenses by selling the house, which was much too big for them now anyway. They were fortunate to find a buyer almost at once. Few assets remained besides the house. The store had little left on its shelves. A life insurance policy now formed the backbone of Emilia's income, together with the proceeds from the house.

The apartment they moved to was small, but comfortable. All the same, moving required adjustments. What Emilia missed most was her airy room overlooking the garden. But she was glad to be out of the house that contained so many painful memories.

As the summer of 1939 approached, the last summer of peace, Paul decided to help out by finding a summer job. But the baron wouldn't hear of his plan.

"Why don't you come and live here, Paul," he suggested. "I'd like you to become familiar with the estate and you wouldn't have any expenses into the bargain."

"I want to help mother out financially."

"I'll be glad to pay you a stipend as well."

It was a tempting offer. Still, Paul didn't accept at once and asked to have a week to think it over. He was reluctant to leave his mother alone in the city. But the greatest obstacle was his conflict over his new status and his relationship with the baron. Since his stepfather's death, he had been haunted by the feeling that he was being disloyal to his stepfather if he identified too strongly with his Aryan nobleman's status. But how could he be disloyal for being what he was? And to whom was he being disloyal? to his stepfather or to the Jews in general?

He had gone as far as to consider taking back his Jewish name. But Johann had been outspokenly against it.

"It's a fine impulse, Paul," he had said, "but if you want to oppose the Nazis, you can do much more good as an anti-Nazi Aryan than as an anti-Nazi half-Jew. A Jew can't help being against the Nazis but an Aryan can choose. Besides, I don't think you can even do it. After all, it's your mother's affidavit, not yours."

Paul had acceded to his logic with a secret feeling of relief, but this had merely increased his guilt. The truth was that he was caught between

two identities and felt at home in neither. How he would have loved to
talk about all this with Johann!

His loss was all the more painful because there was no one to take
Johann's and his stepfather's place. He no longer tried to discuss his
feelings with the baron, remembering their unsatisfying talk. As for his
mother, everything connected with her husband still tapped so many
guilt feelings that she could not be helpful.

She urged him to accept the baron's offer.

"I'll be fine," she assured him. "Don't worry about me, Paul."

"My little martyr," Paul teased her lovingly, aware of his mother's
predilection to take a back seat to please others. "But I do worry about you."

She ignored his teasing. "It will be a wonderful summer for you, Paul.
And you can come and visit often."

Her urging actually showed him how much she would miss him.

He finally worked out a compromise with the baron. He would spend
half his time with his mother in Munich and the other half on the estate.

It was an arrangement that accurately reflected his feelings and his
conflict but it worked out rather well.

♦ ◆ ♦

In spite of his hesitations, Paul did become involved in a number of
political discussions with the baron.

One of the baron's favorite refrains was "I don't consider myself a
Nazi *but*—" followed by a series of quasi-defenses of and apologies
for the Nazis.

In one such conversation the baron mentioned that he was a member
of the Nazi Party. The revelation shocked Paul. He had considered the
baron a sympathizer but not a Party member.

"I thought you didn't consider yourself a Nazi!" Paul exclaimed.

"I'm not. Joining the Party was a mere formality."

"But why did you join if it meant nothing to you?"

The baron retreated behind a cold, supercilious front.

"One needs to do certain things in life even if one doesn't believe in
them, Paul."

"Needs—for whom? for what?" Paul pressed the issue.

The baron was silent for a moment, using the silence both as a shield
and a spear.

"You have to understand something, Paul," he said presently. "The
reason I asked you to become acquainted with the estate—with our

far-flung affairs—is so you can appreciate the ramifications and complexities of what you will be asked to carry on one day. We have holdings
all over the country. Why do you think I travel around so much? Ours
is an ancient lineage and what we have has grown through the dedicated
work of many generations who labored ceaselessly to uphold the
common weal—at times," the baron added with emphasis, "at the
expense of their own comfort and wishes."

Paul had the uncomfortable feeling that he was listening to a lecture,
sincere as the baron was. How many times had he said all this? he
wondered. The baron's whole life had become overshadowed by his
tradition and lineage. Where were his own thoughts and feelings? Paul
asked himself. And from these thoughts flowed yet another reflection
that was even more disturbing: Was the life the baron was grooming
him for really the life he wanted to live?

Slowly Paul began to realize that, despite all the baron's fine words
about honor and service, his interest in the world at large was quite
limited and that he seemed willing to sacrifice the very honor he touted
in the guise of upholding his tradition and lineage.

In time, their political conversations upset them both so much that
they avoided further talks on the subject. It was ironic that Paul's anti-Nazi
views now upset his natural father as much as his previous pro-Nazi
opinions had upset his stepfather. He had railed against his stepfather's
humanistic world of reason and learning without realizing how much he
had been shaped by it after all.

◆ ◆ ◆

Throughout that summer of 1939 the hope for peace faded increasingly
into the certainty of war, throwing Paul's life into renewed turmoil. For
Paul was about to turn eighteen and graduate from high school,
whereupon he would be subject to the draft, first into the *Arbeitsdienst*,
the Labor Service, and then into the *Wehrmacht*, the Armed Forces.
Service was the price of Aryanhood, but what made his army service
such a new and fearful proposition was the likelihood of war.

How could Paul, with his newly acquired beliefs, become a soldier
in an aggressive, Nazi-launched war?

The threat of war thus became a personal and utterly pressing issue
for Paul, one that made him follow the daily news with avid interest. On
the outbreak of war, there hinged a basic, momentous decision for Paul.

◆ ◆ ◆

The baron, too, had begun to worry about the outbreak of war, fearful of losing the standard-bearer he had only so recently acquired. He could not prevent Paul's induction into the Armed Forces, but perhaps something could be done to get him into a safe and challenging job in the Service.

Once again the baron thought of Werner Strapp. He had not seen him since his festive initiation into the Party. Surely Werner, high-ranking SS officer on the *Gauleiter's* staff that he was, would be able to pull some strings for Paul.

Werner greeted him heartily on the phone, but when the baron asked to see him, he let out a sigh.

"Otto, I don't know where my head stands as it is. Maybe you can tell me over the phone."

"I'm afraid it's a bit—delicate."

Werner emitted his old, brawling laugh.

"Well, tell you what," he said. "If you can come to my office tomorrow, we'll manage to squeeze in some minutes together."

Werner's office was in an imposing building with spit-and-polish SS soldiers guarding the entrance and each floor. The baron felt as if he were invading a fortress. A soldier accompanied him to a pleasantly furnished vestibule where an SS officer sat behind a desk.

"The *Herr Brigadeführer* will be with you shortly," he said to the baron.

The baron made note of the higher rank, the equivalent of a Brigadier General. Presently a bell buzzed, a padded double door opened and a bemedaled army officer emerged. When the baron entered the large, elegantly furnished office, Werner jumped up to shake hands.

"Otto, how are you?" he exclaimed. "Sit down, sit down."

"An impressive office," the baron said, genuinely impressed, as he sat down. "And congratulations on your promotion."

Werner guffawed. "I'm not sure working twenty hours a day is a promotion. I'm being fattened for Berlin: transfer to Headquarters. And what can I do for you, Otto?"

"I'm coming on account of my son."

"I thought you had no son."

"Well, that's a long story," the baron said evasively.

"Okay, okay, another time."

"My son is going to be eighteen in November. I was thinking that it might be possible to get him into some—well, specialized branch of the Service where his talents can be used more effectively. He's a very bright, gifted boy."

"I get'cha," Werner exclaimed briskly. "How's he physically? strong, healthy?"

"Strong, athletic, and healthy as a bull."

"No problem then, no problem. I can get him into SS Officer's Training School overnight and from there . . . ." Werner waved his arm meaningfully.

The baron looked embarrassed.

"Werner," he began hesitantly. "I hope you'll take this in the right spirit, but I—I don't think the boy will want to join the SS."

"Hm. He's either a fool or a genius or subversive." Werner guffawed brightly. "Just kidding. Well, let's see. What's the boy interested in?"

"I don't rightly know. I guess it depends on what is available."

"Tell you what. Discuss it with him and then get back to me—but soon. I'm leaving for Berlin in a couple of weeks. Meanwhile I'll give it some thought." Werner glanced at the clock across the room and shoved back his chair. "Sorry to throw you out like this, Otto, but—" He made a vague, restless gesture, getting up and pressing a button with his left hand while extending his right hand. "Good to see you, Otto, good to see you. Let me hear from you soon."

◆ ◆ ◆

To Paul, the baron put the matter rather differently. He prided himself on being something of a diplomat.

"Paul," he began, "as you know, you'll be drafted soon. Have you given any thought to what you'd like to do in the Armed Forces?"

"I can't say I have," Paul answered truthfully.

Paul had given no thought to what to do in the Service precisely because his thinking focussed on whether to serve at all.

"Well, do you have some interests, ideas? I mean, being in a fighting unit might not be the kind of thing you want to do in view of your—hm, opinions. Though we have our disagreements, I do respect your feelings. There are all kinds of specialties in the Armed Forces, you know."

"The specialty I like best is being a civilian," Paul grinned.

The baron chuckled. "I'm afraid that's one specialty they don't have."

The conversation seesawed back and forth for a while without producing any results so that the baron finally said somewhat gruffly:

"For all the interest you seem to have in the subject, one would think I was the one being drafted."

"I still have time, Otto. First I have to graduate. Why do you press the issue already?"

"Because we're on the brink of war and such things have to be tackled ahead of time. They can't be arranged at the last minute."

"Arranged? Arrange what?"

"I have some highly placed contacts," the baron said, not wanting to mention Werner Strapp because he felt that Paul wouldn't take kindly to an SS general intervening on his behalf. "They could do a lot for you."

"Maybe they could keep me out altogether?" Paul hazarded.

"That's beyond their purview," the baron replied coldly.

To take advantage of one's connections and station in life was one thing, but to shirk military duty altogether was quite another. The von Hallenbergs had always served their country illustriously!

Both fell silent. Finally the baron said:

"Give the matter some thought, Paul. Serious thought. Because time is of the essence."

◆ ◆ ◆

The outbreak of war on September 1st brought matters to a head for Paul, and Poland's rapid defeat within a month made it even more pressing. Paul's dilemma now shifted from *whether* to avoid being drafted to *how* to avoid it.

He could, like Johann, count himself out. The idea briefly crossed his mind, but he discarded it at once as a futile, ineffective, merely symbolic gesture which he could admire and respect but not adopt as his own. The world was run on the principle of an eye for an eye. Compromise, conciliation, concessions—all these were merely exploited by men like Hitler as foolish signs of weakness. Force, brute force of arms, was the only thing Hitler understood.

The plan that now began to take shape in Paul's mind was rigorously simple in its logic. If he wanted to fight the Nazis, the thing to do was to join those who were fighting them, i.e. the British or the French.

But how could he to get to one of those countries?

To get out of Germany legally was no longer possible. But to get to France directly was impossible on account of the Maginot and Siegfried Lines, two heavy strings of fortifications facing each other across the common border. The only other way was via a neutral country like Switzerland or Belgium.

Paul began to spend considerable time in the library, researching the geography of the border regions. After much deliberation, he decided that the easiest way to get to France was by way of Belgium in the area of Monschau-Malmédy, the very area where Germany had broken through in World War I. It was a relatively unpopulated, forested area of low mountains.

He now set about planning his escape in earnest. He had to be able to walk long distances, sleeping in the fields if necessary. It was vital to plan everything meticulously, paying attention to the smallest detail. For if he were caught, there was no doubt in his mind that he would be imprisoned or shot as a deserter.

◆ ◆ ◆

Once he made up his mind to escape, he faced the necessity of telling his mother. He would have loved to spare her the pain, but leaving secretly would only have increased it.

He raised the subject one evening after supper.

"Mama," he began, "there is something I must tell you."

"What is it, *Junge?*"

"I've decided that I can't fight for Nazi Germany."

Emilia didn't at once register what he meant. Instead she said plaintively:

"Who would have thought there'd be another war? Hasn't the world suffered enough in the First War?"

Her plaintive tone was symptomatic of Emilia's depressed state since Samuel's death. Valiantly as she tried to lift herself out of it, she seemed unable to do so.

"No use talking about that," Paul said. "The question is, what can I do to avoid the draft?"

"What can you do?" Emilia lamented. "Once you graduate you'll be called up."

"I know. But what if I'm not around?"

"What do you mean? Where will you be?" Emilia asked naively.

"I hope—in France."

Emilia's eyes widened.

"*Junge,*" she breathed.

"I've planned everything very carefully, Mama. I'm going to make my way through Belgium to France. It should be easy to slip over the border on a dark night."

"But what are you going to do in France?"

"Join the French Army."

Tears suddenly started to Emilia's eyes.

"Mama, you must understand. I'll be in the war in any case. It's only a question on which side. I can't fight for Hitler—papa wouldn't want me to. I want to declare my solidarity with the victims too—but in my way." He used Johann's phrase that had very much impressed him.

"It's all so dreadful, so dreadful."

For a moment tears threatened to overwhelm Emilia, but she pulled herself together.

"I guess you have to do what you have to do," she murmured, dabbing at her eyes. "Are you planning to leave soon?"

"As soon as I can get everything ready."

"And when is that?"

"In two or three weeks, I hope."

◆ ◆ ◆

After her husband's death, Emilia had become more and more depressed. Paul's impending departure was merely the last straw, the final blow. Valiantly she tried to bolster her sagging spirits by telling herself that she was about to lose Paul *anyway*. It was only a question of which army, as Paul had said. Besides, Samuel would have been pleased to know that Paul was fighting against the Jew-haters and Jew-killers. Except—he wouldn't have had to fight in any army if she hadn't . . . .

To think she had done all she had done only to see the boy drafted, a draft that would have by-passed him as a half-Jew and that might now kill him!

It was more than Emilia could bear. There had been too many losses in her life lately: her husband, her self-respect, her religion . . . .

For Emilia had lost her religion. It wasn't a deliberate act, a clearly thought out decision, but came about through a slow process of erosion.

She had gradually gone to church less often and, in particular, had avoided stern Father Sebastian, the priest who had made such exacting demands. She needed a breather, she told herself, a break. She would return later. She had done her penance and deserved a rest.

But what kind of a God was this who exacted such penance? A penance that had destroyed her family and had deeply wounded her husband and finally had contributed to his death? A penance that was now bringing about this final, infamous flight from a draft that could have been avoided . . . .

Emilia did not dare raise outright such angry, blasphemous questions, but they were there all the same. And her struggle to suppress them only drove her deeper into her depression.

◆ ◆ ◆

One problem remained: money. Paul needed money to get to the border and across Belgium to France and then to hold out there for a while until he could get into the French Armed Forces.

He had saved some money from his summer earnings with the baron, but that was far from enough and to ask his mother to draw on her limited resources was out of the question. So the only one who remained was the baron. He briefly considered taking him into his confidence but quickly discarded the idea. The baron would never sanction his undertaking and might even actively sabotage it. The only thing left was to ask him for a loan—on trust—or, if all else failed, to take some money from the safe in his study, which the baron was in the habit of leaving open while they worked. He would repay it some day.

He chose a day when they were working together in the baron's study. It was, in their superficially friendly but rather formal relationship, the time when both felt most relaxed and on occasion even swapped stories and laughed.

"I wonder, Otto," Paul began casually. The request was too crucially important for him to launch right into it. "Do you trust me?"

The baron looked up in surprise and with a hint of amusement. It was the frame of mind Paul had wanted him to be in.

"What prompts you to ask such a question?"

"No, really," Paul insisted. "Do you?"

"I would hardly be introducing you to all my business affairs if I didn't, would I? But why do you ask?"

"Because I have a big favor to ask of you. A favor that involves trust."

"Really."

"I want you to say Yes to something I'm going to ask you to do without insisting that you know what it's all about."

"I'm afraid you're speaking in riddles, Paul."

"I'd like you to give me a loan."

"For what?"

"No, no," Paul said jocosely. "That's what you're forbidden to ask."

"Pardon me," the baron replied in a like vein.

"I could make up some cock-and-bull story but I'd rather not," Paul continued. "That's why I'm asking you to trust me."

"Why can't you tell me the real reason?"

"Because I can't."

"That shows a lack of trust on your part, doesn't it?" the baron said, smiling.

"Otto, please," Paul said, growing serious. "I'm asking you to trust me this once. It's very important to me and I'll repay you—one day. I promise."

"How much do you have in mind?"

"A thousand marks."

The baron whistled softly. "Not exactly peanuts."

"I know."

The baron's face was impassive as he sat considering.

"Well," he said finally. "To show you my good will and trust—when do you need the money?"

His ready assent gave Paul a twinge of guilt. He was, in a way, betraying him. It would almost have been better to steal the money, for in a curious way that would have been a more honest act. But these feelings were quickly swallowed by his elation, which made him say unthinkingly the one thing that was an outright lie:

"Thank you, Otto, thank you very much. You won't regret it."

◆ ◆ ◆

The baron gave him the money the following Saturday when Paul came out to work with him. He planned to spend the following week with his mother and start out on his journey early the following Monday morning. As for the baron, he wrote him a brief letter and asked his mother to deliver it in person.

"Dear Otto," it read in part. "Forgive me for taking advantage of your trust and generosity, but I saw no other way. I need to do what I'm doing but do not want to implicate you. I'll repay the money one day. Thank you for everything—and for making this possible!"

With his mother he worked out a simple letter code so that he could let her know roughly where he was and what he was doing. Emilia had an old school friend in Switzerland to whom Paul would write, and she would relay his simple, coded messages to Emilia. Writing directly to his mother from abroad would expose her to too much danger.

They spent a good week together. On Monday Paul got up at dawn to catch a train to Koblenz and from there to the border. He packed a few remaining belongings into his knapsack and carried it to the front door. When he entered the kitchen, his mother was in her morning gown, preparing breakfast. Her eyes looked red and swollen, and she moved about mechanically as if some part of her were missing. Over breakfast each groped intermittently for something to say.

"Will you write often?"

"Yes, Mama. Did you put the code in a safe spot?"

"I hid it in the flour jar in the kitchen."

They fell silent.

"You're taking your warm jacket?"

"Of course."

"And warm underwear?"

He had to smile. "Yes, Mama."

Finally they gave up and sought refuge in silence.

At length Paul got up. Standing behind his mother, he placed his hands on her shoulders and remained like that for some moments. Neither moved or spoke, although Paul saw that his mother's lips were moving. Finally he bent down and kissed her on the cheek.

"Good-bye, *Muttchen*."

He stepped back to avoid coming into her field of vision, nor did she turn around, only her lips continued to move in silent prayer, each avoiding further contact as if afraid that it would break down what little self-control they still possessed. He moved to the door and lifted the knapsack to his shoulders. Then the door closed behind him with a dull, metallic thud.

◆ ◆ ◆

Paul spent the night in Koblenz and next day went on to Stadtkyll, a small town near the Belgian border. His plan was to find accommodations as close to the border as possible and from there reconnoiter the countryside before attempting the crossing. As a cover, he bought a large sketch pad and crayons so that he could pose as an art student making landscape sketches, for which he had a certain facility.

As he walked on toward the border, he ran across a number of border patrols with police dogs. There seemed to be more than he had anticipated. One of them stopped him and demanded to see his identification papers.

"See you in uniform soon, *Herr Baron*," one of the soldiers teased him good-naturedly as the patrol passed on.

A small village near the border seemed perfect for his purposes. But when he asked for a room at the only *Gasthaus*, he was told that no rooms were available because a detachment of soldiers was billeted at the inn. Instead, the owner referred him to a farmhouse a few miles down the road where he might be able to rent a room.

The farmhouse was set back from the road and overlooked a broad

valley that separated Germany from Belgium. There was no answer
when Paul knocked on the front door, but he could hear someone
working in a shed in back of the house. When he rounded the house,
he saw a man of about fifty with a lined, rugged face feeding some pigs.

"A room?" the man said in response to his inquiry. "Sure. For how long?"

"A few days. Maybe a week."

"With meals?"

"Breakfast and supper, if that's possible. I won't need lunch because
I'll be sketching outside."

The man scrutinized him curiously for a moment.

"Sketchin', eh? And you don't get hungry sketchin'?" he said with a
touch of mockery, but his eyes were kindly.

He quoted a price that seemed very low to Paul, compared with city
prices, and led the way back to the house. The room was an attic room
with slanting ceilings, an old-fashioned iron bedstead, a large wooden
wardrobe, and a dresser with a pitcher of water and a washing bowl.

"Ain't fancy. Though the toilet's real cute—outside," the man said
with a straight face.

Paul chuckled and pulled out his wallet.

"Let me pay you for three nights."

The man left. He seemed friendly despite his bluntness. There was
an open, solid quality about him that Paul liked. If he knew what this
man knew, he would no doubt be able to amble across the border without
the least mishap. He picked up his sketch pad and crayons.

There were a couple of hours left before darkness. Outside he passed
the man.

"I understand the border is close by," he hazarded. "Can you tell me
where it is so I won't stumble—accidentally . . . ." He faltered.

The man eyed him with an appraising look.

"There's a little stream at the bottom of the valley. If you fall into it,
you're in Belgium—half in Belgium," he corrected himself with a chuckle.
"But I'd stay away from it," he added. "The border patrols got orders
to shoot on sight."

"Thanks for letting me know," Paul said, trying to be casual, and left.

By the time he returned for supper, he had a sense of the valley,
although he had not ventured near the stream. How ridiculously close
and peaceful the border was, totally imaginary and of man's making,
and yet how deadly! When he entered the kitchen, a young woman was
standing at the stove. She was about twenty, with long brown hair,
strong features, and frank, open eyes. Paul was startled.

"Supper'll be ready in ten minutes," she said matter-of-factly without introducing herself.

While he waited, Paul tried to make some conversation, feeling ill at ease, but the young woman didn't respond. Presently the man came in.

"You two met?" he asked. "My daughter Margaret—what's your name?"

"Paul."

"We met," the girl said briefly. "Sit down, Father. Supper's ready."

She brought on the soup. Throughout the meal neither spoke. But after the meal the man once more became talkative.

"Well, you done your sketchin'?" he inquired.

"There wasn't enough time. But I will tomorrow."

"Funny thing to be doin' while the world's at war. Where you from?"

"Koblenz," Paul lied.

"How old are you?"

"Seventeen."

"Then they'll get you too soon. I bet you're just rarin' to go."

"I suppose so," Paul said evasively.

The man laughed coldly.

"I have three boys myself."

"Really?" Paul said politely. "Where are they?"

"In the Hitler Army."

He said the words with a touch of anger and contempt. Paul expected him to say something more, but instead he fell silent. The girl had been sitting by silently.

"More potatoes anyone?" she asked.

"No, thank you," Paul said.

She got up while the man moved to the only armchair in the room, lit a pipe, and fiddled with the radio. Paul offered to help with the dishes and Margaret let him. By now he felt relaxed with her and with her father too. In fact, he felt curiously at home with both, as if he had known them for a long time. When they finished with the dishes, they sat down again at the table. At nine o'clock the man said good night and went upstairs, while Paul and Margaret continued to sit at the table, at first talking intermittently but becoming more and more awkward and self-absorbed as the evening progressed. The girl had a quality that aroused and excited him on a level that Erika had never touched. Suddenly he leaned forward and kissed her. She did not turn her head away, but her lips remained noncommittal.

"I feel such a strong pull toward you," Paul said. "It's as if I've known you all my life."

"I like you too, Paul."

"I've never felt like this before."

He bent forward again and this time Margaret's lips responded as Paul began to tremble as if he were slowly being stretched too tightly. Suddenly he leaned back and let out an exuberant laugh.

"What is it?" she asked, startled.

"I can't believe it. To think that a few hours ago we didn't even know each other!"

"It's crazy, isn't it."

"No, it's beautiful."

They fell silent again as they kissed and embraced.

"It feels almost as if I'm in love with you," he whispered.

"You just want me."

"No, it's much more than that," he protested earnestly. "Such strong feelings can't . . . really."

"My little serious philosopher," she said gently.

They continued kissing and embracing. Suddenly Margaret pulled away.

"What's the matter?" he asked.

"What's the use, Paul. You're leaving in a few days."

He remained silent. At that moment it was hard to remember that he was to leave.

"There's not much future," Margaret murmured.

"Is there ever in war?"

"I guess not."

He leaned forward and kissed her again.

"And meanwhile?" he said insistently. "What do we do meanwhile?"

"Yes—meanwhile," she muttered.

"I wish there were a future," he whispered.

They sat for a long while embracing and fondling with growing feelings. Finally he said:

"Will you come upstairs, Margaret?"

She shook her head.

"Why not?"

"You're leaving, Paul."

They continued embracing and caressing. After a while Paul said again:

"Please, Margaret."

"No, Paul."

It was late when they finally separated and Paul went upstairs and undressed in his cold room. The valley stretched below in the dark night. He could see the opposite ridge looming on the Belgian side. Borders, he thought—between nations, between human beings. How desperately one wanted to break them down and yet couldn't. He suddenly felt lonely and intensely sad. Was Margaret feeling the same loneliness and longing?

He jumped into the frosty bed, his teeth chattering, he wasn't sure whether he shook from the cold or from the tension of his feelings. Slowly his body warmed up and he lay still, listening. Perhaps she would still come? The old farmhouse creaked now and then and seemed to hum in the stillness. He lay like that for a long time, listening, until he fell asleep.

He awoke abruptly, instantly awake, his heart pounding as he felt her slipping into the bed beside him, the whole length of her body pressing against his.

"I tried, Paulchen," she whispered. "I really did."

◆ ◆ ◆

The next days went by very quickly. Margaret's father saw what had happened because Paul followed his daughter about like a lovesick dog, doing very little drawing. But he did nothing to stop Paul, only teasing him good-naturedly now and then.

As the days went by, Paul forgot for hours at a stretch why he was there, so involved was he with Margaret. Then he would suddenly remember and feel a sharp twinge of guilt and shame. He had told Margaret about his plan to escape, without going into the details of his background, trusting her implicitly by now and recognizing also that she could be of inestimable help to him in making the crossing. But much as he liked her father, he did not feel ready to confide in him. In police states it was safer to involve as few people as possible.

One evening four days later, the talk came around to the war. Suddenly, her father turned to Paul.

"Why does every generation have to reinvent war?" he exclaimed. "Like my boys. Couldn't wait until they got to the front. If you kids had any sense, you'd take off across that border and run off to the South Seas."

It was then that Paul said impulsively:

"That's what I'm planning to do."

A smile spread on the man's rugged face.

"Only not to the South Seas."

"I suspected as much the moment I laid eyes on you," the father said, slapping the table with satisfaction. "Good boy."

His exclamation pleased Paul, pleased him irrationally, in fact, because he liked the man very much. He possessed a solidity, a rugged, knowing warmth and honesty that made Paul feel grounded and safe—just like his stepfather and Johann. He felt a sharp jolt of guilt. Here he was pleasuring his time away when he ought to be moving on!

His face had clouded over.

"You look like you've swallowed a heap of heavy thoughts," her father remarked.

"Paulchen, what's the matter?" Margaret asked solicitously.

Paul sat staring at the table.

"Nothing," he muttered. But in a moment he said: "I think I ought to be getting on."

◆ ◆ ◆

After her father had left, Margaret said:

"Must you, Paul?"

"Must I what?" he said, not understanding.

"Couldn't you stay awhile?"

The question pushed the issue into the forefront of his mind. Until then he had been vaguely aware of his desire to stay but had elbowed the thought aside. Now it began to sear his mind. How dearly he would love to sit out the war in this quiet, forgotten valley, away from the turmoil and problems of war, of Nazis and Jews—what had he to do with all that? Here he would stay, helping to run the farm. He would more than earn his keep, and if they picked up his trail later, he could still escape, and by then he would know every inch of the border . . . . Yes, here he would spend his life, forgiven and forgotten, impervious to guilt and war, with Margaret lying protectively by his side, forever and forever, amen!

So he rationalized and fantasized. But at the end of all his dreams, there always stood the image of his stepfather and the memory of the long hours in his sickroom, and he remembered the silent rage that had ripened in him then against the vicious system that had unjustly attacked this good man and cut him down, and he knew that not love and not even his fear of the great unknown beyond the border could stop him from keeping the silent promise he had made then that he would have nothing further to do with this system and fight it as best he could. The memory of Johann too pursued him insistently. Where was Johann now? Was he even still alive? He ought to do something, as Johann had done, was doing, sacrificing his very life . . . .

There followed days of vacillation and torment. Defensively he would explain to Margaret why he needed to leave, why he couldn't stay and keep his self-respect, and Margaret would nod and understand even while her eyes clouded over and her face became sad. Finally one evening Paul said:

"Margaret, why don't *you* come with *me*?"

Her eyes widened. It was a thought that had not occurred to her before.

"I would just be a burden to you," she said.

"No, you wouldn't."

She turned her head and looked past him out of the window as if something there had suddenly caught her attention. But it was merely the chaos of her thoughts and feelings racing around inside her.

"How can I leave Father," she said finally.

He waited, anticipating her next words, afraid of her refusal. But she only said:

"I'll talk to Father about it."

When they met next day, Margaret avoided his eyes and seemed abstracted, and her father, too, was more taciturn than usual. After he went to bed, there was a heavy silence.

"I went to see him," she said presently. "The minute I approached he turned to me as if expecting me, as if he already knew why I came. He was staring at me—there was fear, panic in his eyes—like I'd seen him look only once before—the night mother died . . . I couldn't say anything . . . ."

She suddenly began to cry.

"I can't do it to him, Paul . . . he lost everyone—his wife, then his sons . . . he needs me . . . ."

Paul wanted to cry out: But I need you too! I love you and am afraid to venture out alone into the world! Yet though his heart felt twisted with pain and fear, he didn't say it. Because there was also that in him which understood and knew that in the end it was better for them both if he went on alone.

◆ ◆ ◆

Next evening, when her father got up from the table and bade them good night, Paul placed his hand on his arm.

"I'm leaving tonight," he said.

The man stopped and for a moment stared abstractedly into Paul's young, confident face.

"God be with you," he murmured.

He left, strafing his daughter with his eyes. She sat close to Paul, holding his hand in hers, hunched forward, staring at the floor.

◆ ◆ ◆

Margaret insisted on leading Paul to the border stream herself, although by this time he knew the area fairly well himself.

"I won't let you go alone," she insisted. "I know every stone. I've gone down there hundreds of times."

"But I can't let you run the risk."

"It's no risk for me. It's a risk without me."

Finally he consented.

They planned to start at two in the morning. That evening Paul packed his knapsack while Margaret watched silently from the bed. Paul didn't want to sleep but Margaret urged him to.

"You've got a long day ahead of you."

Finally he dozed off fitfully while Margaret counted the striking of the hours. At two, she roused him.

"Paulchen, it's time."

He drew her close to him. Not too much tenderness now. Not too much love.

"Paulchen, please. We've got to start."

She was now the pillar of strength. He pulled his limbs out of bed and quickly slipped on his clothes to shield himself against the cold night. The knapsack stood by the door, pregnant with flight. Margaret helped to hoist it on his back.

She was standing in the dim light, bundled into a heavy coat, tumescent with warmth, temptation. A last embrace. And yet another.

Then the silent house. The creaking door. The dewy meadows dropping down to the dark valley. Patches of trees here and there. The night not starry, which was good. He walked behind her, numb, yet all his senses alert. Finally there was a soft murmur of water, which they followed until she stopped by the trunk of a fallen tree.

"You can cross here," she whispered.

"This is it?"

"Climb up. I'll steady you."

A last embrace, truncated by the presence of danger.

"One day," he murmured.

"Yes," she whispered back. "One day . . . ."

He climbed up, balancing himself on the trunk, and walked quickly across the stream. On the other side he turned around once more and waved. She was a mere dark patch now, almost indistinguishable from the surrounding darkness. Was she waving to him?

Then he began to walk. When he turned around once more, he couldn't see her anymore. Was she still waving?

II

1943 - 1945

KZ Buchenwald[*]

The shrill morning whistle nagged at the fringe of Johann's consciousness, distantly heard yet rejected. On one side, Vladimir stirred, on the other, David began to move. He could feel their bones against his body, could hear the intimate moans and noises of the barracks' awakening. He moved his numb arm to stimulate the circulation that had been squeezed out of it by the hard boards. Eight to ten men slept jackknifed against each other, with two or three blankets to share, in a space in which three or four might have been comfortable. Suddenly the lights glared down at him, pulling him awake even through closed eyelids, and the noises of the camp broke like assassins into his consciousness as the concentration camp came alive with shouts and curses and the dull thud of clubs and rifle butts on human flesh.

Johann found it the most difficult time of day, this brief, fierce struggle to wake up or, more accurately, not to wake up: these precious seconds of as yet detached consciousness before the tortured weight of the day reasserted itself, dragging in its wake the reality of this utterly appalling existence.

Dazed, the prisoners tumbled out of their bunks, knowing that any hesitation would attract the attention of the barracks orderly, himself a prisoner, who was coming along the aisles brandishing a club to help the tardy to their feet.

"Snap to! Act sharp!" he yelled.

Johann could hear the orderly's club going to work down the aisle as each prisoner groped blindly to pull his mud-caked, dilapidated boots over bare, swollen feet, twisting the wires together that in most cases held the boots in place instead of shoelaces.

As the prisoners shuffled out to the muddy parade ground, greeted by

---

* The described conditions in the concentration camp are historically accurate and true. However, the names and personalities of all SS personnel are invented.

the harsh glare of floodlights, dawn had not yet broken. And now began the interminable roll call that was conducted with ferocious exactness as if it mattered one whit whether this or that prisoner were still present and accounted for, since that same prisoner might be killed that day for no particular reason, killed between an SS guard's bored drags on a cigarette.

Finally, the SS officers arrived, sleepy and in ill humor, to take the final count, as dawn at last began to break and the sun rose. It was one of the few moments in the desolate day that brought a brief moment's cheer into the prisoners' lives before they were marched off to their harrowing labor.

Another day had started in the Buchenwald Concentration Camp.

◆ ◆ ◆

Johann had spent most of the intervening years in Dachau, a concentration camp not far from Munich. In the spring of 1942 he had been transferred, for no apparent reason, to Buchenwald, an even more dreaded concentration camp in the heart of Germany, five miles from Weimar, a pleasant town famed as the residence of Goethe, Germany's greatest poet. The camp itself was located on a wooded mountain, the Ettersberg, which overlooked the rolling Thuringian countryside, dotted here and there with village church spires, while in the distance loomed the hazy outlines of the Harz mountains.

Like all KZ prisoners, Johann had gone through changes that had made him unrecognizable. He was emaciated, weighing barely one hundred pounds, his hair shorn to control the lice and other vermin that infested the prisoners, his striped uniform torn and threadbare, his movements slow and lethargic, a lethargy due not only to malnutrition and exhaustion but to the everpresent knowledge that there was absolutely no place to go. Only his eyes were still alive and alert, looking huge in his sunken face, imparting to his body a weird lopsidedness, as if the life of the whole man had retreated into his eyes.

Like all prisoners, too, he had been stripped of his identity, not only of his outward identity but stripped right down to the very marrow of his status as a human being. It was a relentless process experienced by all prisoners who survived for any length of time. The superficial earmarks of being human—one's hair, personal possessions, clothes—were the first to go. Then the more important identities: the roles of husband, father, profession, along with one's hopes, expectations, and dreams. Finally the most important human earmark of all: one's sensitivity, empathy, compassion . . . .

So the prisoner stood stripped bare, at first physically, as the body, deprived of fat, began to cannibalize itself by devouring its own muscle and then stripped by slow degrees emotionally, morally, and spiritually as well. Eventually the prisoner succumbed to a numbing apathy to protect himself from a reality that cannibalized not only his body but his soul as the faculties of love and compassion and common human decency were ground up in the daily inhuman struggle for survival. All that remained was indifference, ruthlessness, cruelty, and greed.

In a KZ, a human being had to become inured to pain and suffering—first and foremost his own. Man's emotions could not live at such an intensity of horror. The sight of beatings, cruelty, torture, and death was too unremitting to permit a prisoner to marshal any feeling, let alone empathy. He needed to disengage, to look the other way, and after a while he didn't even do that anymore as he stared with dulled eyes and deadened senses past the hideous, the indescribable, the utterly incomprehensible.

That was the inhuman challenge that the concentration camps flung down for victim and oppressor alike: How to remain human in an environment that was totally inhuman and depraved—how to remain human when everything in one wanted to shut down, go numb, block, deny, escape.

◆ ◆ ◆

Johann differed from the other prisoners in one crucial respect: He had chosen to be there! The others had not and had, at first, even denied being there, nurturing vain illusions of reprieve. For Johann alone there was no reprieve. Returning to civilian life—the unattainable dream of all the other prisoners—would only have redoubled his torment. For now he knew just how horrible conditions were for the oppressed with whom he had needed to declare his solidarity.

Thus, whenever feelings of despair threatened to overwhelm him, Johann reminded himself that there was no other place for him to go: Here he had to make his stand, here suffer willingly through his agony. But at least here he could say: I don't belong to the oppressors, neither directly, nor indirectly. Here I need feel no guilt or shame.

That was the blessing he could find nowhere else—although soon even that comfort was to be taken from him.

◆ ◆ ◆

Although Johann had always been an abstemious man who had lived his life on a level of basic need, he was not prepared for life in a concentration camp. Here existence was screwed down to a level where even the most basic of basic needs was considered a luxury: a daily hunk of dry bread, watery soup with a few pieces of vegetable or, rarely, a sliver of meat; clothes utterly inadequate for the weather and the labor; dilapidated, leaking, mostly sockless shoes. A shoelace was a rarity, a piece of rope to hold up one's pants a joyous blessing, gloves—utterly unattainable.

In retrospect, Johann realized that his act had been based on the assumption that there was, even in the concentration camps, some sort of order, if not of legality, at least of human values, however distorted; that there were limits to the suffering one human being was willing to inflict on another, boundaries beyond which civilized men would not go—assumptions that were totally exploded in this fiendish world that operated on a belief system which considered whole categories of people—Jews, Slavs, gypsies—not only inferior but altogether subhuman. The fact that the inmates came to look so like non-humans in their filthy, vermin-ridden emaciation and with their greedy, animalistic obsession with food and sleep made it difficult to relate to them as human beings—which excused further inhuman treatment. Thus, a ghastly cycle was set up that fed brutally on itself in this moral vacuum where any guard could take life with impunity, where any brutality, however heinous, could be practiced without punishment or shame.

But even this wanton cruelty paled in the face of the ultimate horror: the slow extermination, introduced and upheld by the Nazi State itself, by starvation, overwork, sickness, or simply freezing to death. The entire population of a camp was sometimes left to stand all night in threadbare clothes in subfreezing temperatures for some minor infraction by a single individual. For here the official, stated goal was not to sustain life, even a hard life, but to squeeze it relentlessly to death.

Knowingly, purposely, and without apology, the Nazi system had deprived itself of all humanity, of all the rejuvenating human juices that could have cleansed it of its shame.

How could prisoners survive in such a system?

An even more terrible question: How could the guards survive?

For they had a choice. The prisoners had none.

◆ ◆ ◆

Johann had been sent to work in the quarry. It was one of the worst labor assignments in the camp, both because of the very hard labor and because of the particularly sadistic SS guards.

One of the worst guards was an SS corporal nicknamed by the prisoners, with grim gallows humor, Skippy, which derived from the game ducks and drakes—skipping flat stones over a surface of water.

Skippy was a heavyset, lazy man in his twenties who had, over the years, developed such an uncanny marksmanship with stones that he could hit a prisoner with unerring accuracy over astounding distances. He always held a couple of stones in his hands that he rotated lovingly between his fingers before hurling them at some prisoner who seemed to him to be shirking work, not working hard enough or, if no adequate reason presented itself, for the sheer joy of showing off his marksmanship. The size of the stones as well as their intended target were telling indications of Skippy's frame of mind because, as his displeasure mounted, so did the size of the stones as well as the vulnerability of the body part at which they were aimed.

Skippy's constant presence, without moving very much from his spot, unnerved the prisoners and kept them in a state of terror, of which Skippy was boastfully aware. For a prisoner never knew when, or usually even why, a stone would hit him, nor was there any way of avoiding them, because stepping aside tripled Skippy's fury since it foiled the excellence of his marksmanship. Prisoners had even on occasion been known to step *into* the path of a hurtling stone. Nor was this merely an unnerving, otherwise harmless game, for Skippy's mortality rate was high: twenty-seven men, to be exact—as he was proud of informing the prisoners—not counting the innumerable injuries that often led to death because a maimed prisoner lost what little reason for existence he possessed in a concentration camp.

Johann himself had on several occasions become Skippy's target. Once he had been struck so painfully in the crotch—one of Skippy's favorite "playful" areas when not bent on blood—that he had doubled up, straightening only, despite the severe pain, because he knew that if he didn't, another missile, larger and even more painful, would come his way.

Johann realized that the dilemma Skippy posed for the prisoners was insoluble, except by withdrawing into oneself. He had learned early in his imprisonment that ordinary consciousness, directed outward as it is in pursuit of everyday gratification and avoidance of pain, was sheer torture in the fearsome world of the KZ, where no gratification existed and pain was unremitting so that there was but one possible escape: to withdraw into a place deep inside oneself where one could tap into a more profound source of identity and strength.

Johann marshalled this ability to withdraw into himself as he struggled with his fear of Skippy. Out of a sense of desperation, he began to plunge deeper and deeper into the only world still open to him or to anyone else in a KZ: his inner world. And as he did so, he began to perceive that even here, in this hellish place that robbed human beings of every conceivable dignity and freedom, one final freedom still remained: the freedom to choose one's attitude.

He couldn't change being at Skippy's mercy. He couldn't change being hungry and cold. He couldn't change much of anything really. But he could change and choose his attitude!

◆ ◆ ◆

At this time a young Jew, Benjamin, barely twenty years old, came to sleep next to Johann.

Benjamin had until then managed to hide out in the countryside, protected by a farmer for whom he worked. As a result he looked tan and healthy, a rare sight in a concentration camp. When it became too dangerous to shelter Jews, the farmer had suddenly turned him in and he had been shipped straight to Buchenwald, where he stood out among the emaciated prisoners like an ox among sheep (Rule # 1 on any list of camp survival imperatives: *Don't be conspicuous!*). In addition, Benjamin had about him a vague air of complaint, nothing outspokenly rebellious, but, in a concentration camp, dangerously misplaced because there was absolutely no one to complain to and no one who cared, which this newcomer, who was altogether still in a state of disbelieving shock over his unexpected betrayal by his erstwhile protector, had not yet understood.

Johann saw Benjamin's combination of conspicuousness, ignorance, innocence, and vague complaint as dangerous and tried to warn him that he was bound to attract all the sadistic impulses rampant in the camp. (Others realized it too but said nothing. Rule # 2: *Mind your own business, don't get involved or attached.*)

"Benjamin," he said. "Lie low. Shut up. Don't be conspicuous. You stand out too much already. It's dangerous."

"What do you want me to do? stop breathing?" Benjamin complained, unaware of the bitter irony of his words.

Johann could see that Benjamin didn't really understand. Not that he disbelieved or mistrusted Johann. On the contrary, he liked and trusted Johann, who felt protective toward him. But only harsh experience could convince Benjamin of the gulf between the world "out there" and the world "in here."

About a month after his arrival, Benjamin woke Johann up in the middle of the night.

"Johann," he whispered, shaking him gently by the shoulder.

He was lying jackknifed behind Johann.

Johann roused himself from his sleep, the deep sleep of an exhausted, drained body which, deprived of replenishment from without, was attempting to recharge itself from within.

"What is it, Benjamin?"

"I've had a bad dream. A nightmare."

Is that all? Johann wanted to shout. Isn't our whole life a nightmare?

"What about?" he muttered.

"I was in this deep pit, all dark and slimy, trying to get out. My mother was sitting on a ledge above me, motioning me to come up, and I was trying to reach her but every time I got up a little way, the wall collapsed, and I slid down again. Finally my mother cried, 'I've had enough of this,' and stomped off."

Benjamin was silent. So was Johann.

"What do you make of it?" Benjamin whispered.

Still Johann was silent. What was there to say? It was all so obvious.

"It's rough, Benjamin," he finally whispered gently. "I know. I've been through it all myself."

He became aware that Benjamin was crying. He reached out and touched him, trying to send through his hand what he couldn't convey in words: that he understood the boy's loneliness and utter sense of abandonment. All at once Johann felt an overwhelming sense of kinship not only to Benjamin but to all the other men who slept as if knocked unconscious in all the desolate barracks of this and every other camp. How terrible if there had been no one at all with whom to share their plight!

"We're all in this together, Benjamin," he whispered.

"You think the world cares? You think they even know?"

"I'm sure they do."

"I hope so," Benjamin mumbled.

He grasped Johann's hand and in this way they went back to sleep, the human touch acting as a bridge between them.

Benjamin attached himself to Johann. His loneliness and terror drove him to turn to a man whose strength was so palpably greater than his own, so that Johann became both a father figure for him and a lover. Lying in their clothes, jackknifed tightly against each other, Johann could at times feel the young man's erection, which Benjamin tried awkwardly to hide. Only once did Benjamin press close to him, breathing sharply as he ejaculated and moaned, followed by an urgently whispered "forgive me, forgive me," to which Johann did not react, feigning sleep. He felt no stirring of anger, repulsion or sexuality, only compassion—and detachment. Sexual need was a problem for very few inmates, even those who had been imprisoned for their homosexuality. One had no energy left for such luxuries.

It was the only time it happened and neither spoke of it afterwards.

Benjamin had also been assigned to the quarry where he worked close to Johann whenever he could, surreptitiously assuming some of his work, which Johann appreciated, although fearful that it would attract Skippy's attention. At first, Skippy seemed not to notice, which surprised Johann, but eventually it was picked up by Skippy's watchful eye, and a number of stones came hurtling their way.

Henceforth, Benjamin was more careful.

◆ ◆ ◆

Among the SS personnel who tormented and terrorized the prisoners, one of the most brutal was the camp's Third Officer-in-Charge, *Untersturmführer* (Second Lieutenant) Herbert Hoffer, the brother of Erika, Paul's first love.

Hoffer, who had at one time sneered at the Hitler Youth, had become a rabid Nazi once admitted to their ranks. As soon as he had come of military age, he had rushed to volunteer for the SS and had been accepted, after minor surgery corrected his limp. In the SS, he had volunteered for the *Totenkopfverband* (the Death Head Units), which operated the concentration camps, motivated both by visions of power and considerations of personal safety, since Hitler had by then invaded Russia and most of the available manpower was being sent there. His zeal had taken him rapidly through the ranks to become an officer. He was sent to Buchenwald in 1942, where, after acquiring a reputation as one of the most cruel members of the SS establishment, he became Third Officer-in-Charge of the camp.

Hoffer loved to roam about the camp, showing up in unexpected places. Wherever he appeared, there was a visible tensing, not only among the prisoners but among the SS guards as well, for he enjoyed throwing his weight about even with them. His specialty was whipping, not the official whippings administered on a *Bock*, a contraption over which prisoners were strapped, kneeling and often stripped of their pants. Rather, his whippings were extracurricular "bonuses," although he was not averse to more lethal approaches when the occasion demanded.

To indulge his specialty, Hoffer carried a whip he had had made expressly for him. It had a short handle with a loop, through which he slid his right hand while a cat-o'-nine-tails dangled from the other end, though it had only three knotted cords, quite enough to slash the skin open with deep gashes. With this whip Hoffer strutted about imperiously, ominously striking his highly polished boots which produced a clacking sound that had earned him the nickname, "Clackerack."

About two months after Benjamin's arrival, Hoffer appeared at the quarry in a foul mood. Prisoners developed very keen perceptions along these lines, although with Clackerack that was hardly necessary since his whip was always an unerring barometer of his moods. That day, he set to work with it at once.

As bad luck would have it, Benjamin slipped and fell just then on the steep incline where he was working, sending his pick clattering noisily down the slope, which attracted Hoffer's attention.

"You!" he bellowed, waving to Benjamin. "On the double!" Then, as Benjamin began to trot toward him: "Faster, swine!"

Benjamin accelerated his pace and arrived fearfully in front of Hoffer, who eyed him wrathfully, feeling for some reason challenged, although Benjamin had done or said absolutely nothing to challenge him.

"How long you been here, Jew-swine?"

Benjamin's religion was obvious as prisoners wore triangles of different colors to identify them as Jews, political prisoners, convicts, homosexuals, or Gypsies.

"Two months."

"Two months, what?"

Benjamin, not understanding, remained silent, which Hoffer interpreted as evidence of further insubordination.

"Two months, *what*?" he bellowed, bringing his whip down on Benjamin and then kicking the nearest prisoner for the answer Benjamin didn't know how to give.

"*Herr Untersturmführer!*" sang out the kicked prisoner.

"Got that?"

"Yes, *Herr Untersturmführer*," Benjamin exclaimed briskly now, though Johann could sense while bending over his work that he still had no serious inkling of who this *Untersturmführer* really was, not yet knowing his murderous disposition.

Hoffer eyed him silently, this prisoner-what's-his-name, No. 101537, this Jew who was still full of muscle and nerve, this riffraff prisoner still full of vibrant juices, his anger fanned now the more intimidated and compliant Prisoner No. 101537 became.

"What's all that fat on you?" he barked, poking him with his whip. "You think this is a resort, eh? Shirking work, eh? Stand at attention when I speak to you!" he shouted.

Prisoner 101537 ludicrously snapping to attention now as he imagined a soldier would or should, even saluting in his confusion while Clackerack puffed up with anger as if to gather strength for the grand assault he was about to undertake against this human being.

A deep silence had settled over the quarry as the prisoners' attention was drawn to Hoffer and his victim, even though each prisoner continued to tend diligently to his work in order to avoid drawing attention to himself. And now, as Prisoner 101537 stood in front of Clackerack and looked into those ice cold, steely eyes, even he began to have an inkling that he was not standing before an ordinary man—a human being facing a human being—but before a man who cared less about his life than he would about a stray dog.

"Pick up that rock, Jew-swine!" Hoffer yelled, pointing at a boulder weighing some one hundred pounds.

Obediently, Prisoner 101537 bent down, anxious to please now in order to escape whatever it was the *Untersturmführer* had in mind, but, finding the boulder too hard to lift, he glanced at Hoffer, as much as to say, That is more than I can lift, more than any human being can lift, it not yet having dawned on Prisoner 101537 that the impossible was precisely what was being demanded of him. Receiving no response, he strained to lift the heavy rock and did lift it finally, holding it in his arms with a look at once imploring and servile as he stood, pregnant and incongruous, as if presenting Clackerack with a present.

"Up the hill!" Hoffer commanded.

Prisoner 101537 turned slowly with the rock straining in his arms and then set one foot forward and then another and another, it going well thus far, with no mishaps and even his muscles were settling into their job, so that it looked as if the impossible could be negotiated—yes, why not. Up above, beyond that steep incline, there would be respite, there would be peace.

A sharp swish, heard as if in slow motion, followed by the sharp crack of a whip to signal that Prisoner 101537's tottering pace was unacceptable.

"Faster, *Schweinehund!*"

Another lash, harder than the first—or was it merely that the pain of the first had lingered and was reinforced by the second?—so that the boulder, managed until now in trembling arms, began to slide through his arms and dropped to the ground, followed by his body, which collapsed over the rock as if to suck strength and solace from its ancient, enduring veins, strength to get up again and straighten, to lift the rock once more into his straining arms in order to continue upwards, upwards toward a goal that was becoming increasingly elusive and unreachable. And now at last Prisoner 101537 began to understand that this was not to be an ordinary walk but a walk beyond a human being's capacity and comprehension, a walk beyond empathy and compassion, a walk until one reached one's end.

Again the lash, the fall, the struggle to get up, the incline steep and steeper, as unattainable as heaven. *Baruch Adonai*, thou holiest of holies, I can go no farther . . . .

For three hours Prisoner 101537 labored, managing finally to get the boulder up the steep ravine, only to be sent down again for boulder No. 2. And then No. 3. But by then Clackerack had long since tired of the game and had left, commanding others to carry on to teach Prisoner 101537 a lesson, though no one knew what the lesson was. For three hours the prisoner labored, collapsing more and more often but lashed on again and again, the sport now of a group of boisterous, laughing guards who grew increasingly high on their work, whipping him on more and more mercilessly while the silence among the prisoners deepened, as in a wake, until finally the clothes and skin of Prisoner 101537 hung in tatters and he collapsed and could go no farther.

He was taken back to camp unconscious. By daybreak he was dead.

♦ ◆ ♦

Commonplace as death and killings were in the camp, Benjamin's death had a profound effect on Johann.

When his death first began to prey on Johann's mind, he reacted with annoyance and tried to dismiss it. He would have needed ten hands to count on his fingers the number of deaths he had witnessed, many just as brutal. As a new prisoner, he had reacted to such incidents, as all new prisoners did, with horror and pity. But in time these emotions became blunted. The struggle to remain human did not, could not, include even the remotest rescue fantasy. Those who fell prey to the SS and the prisoner-foremen, who were often as cruel as their SS overlords, could not be rescued. They were like people sucked irretrievably into a maelstrom. One needed to let go of them as surely as one needed to let go of anyone whom death gathers unto itself. Never mind that here death was unjustified and abhorrent, that was the murderers' responsibility, not the prisoners'.

So the thought of intervening for Benjamin had not even occurred to Johann at the time. The very idea was ridiculous. The only result would have been that two victims would have labored up that steep ravine instead of one. That was a certainty and it wouldn't have taken Clackerack and his cohorts three hours to finish him off either. If he wanted to commit suicide, he could do it more easily by running into the high voltage barbed wire fence surrounding the camp, as some prisoners did.

Then why did Benjamin's death now suddenly precipitate such guilty conflict and shame?

It was unreasonable, illogical, insane. But had his intervention for Mr. Silver been logical? Had dying for one's beliefs and personal integrity ever been reasonable? Had the actions of the Jesuses and Gandhis of this world ever been a matter of logic and reason?

He had thought that joining the victims was all that was necessary to escape from guilt, that the only self-sacrifice demanded of him was to suffer passively alongside the victims, in mute and silent surrender. But that suddenly seemed inadequate as the momentous question arose in his mind: Perhaps he had merely taken the first step and now needed to take a second step to move beyond mere passive solidarity toward becoming truly his brother's keeper?

But where would that end, that responsibility?

Johann knew that he was facing a life and death question in the most literal sense—but then, what was his life still worth anyway?

◆ ◆ ◆

As the quarry contingent returned to the camp one day, *Untersturmführer* Hoffer stood near the parade ground talking to a man who was fashionably dressed in an expensive gray overcoat, with hat, silk scarf, and leather gloves to match, while an elegant Mercedes Benz stood close by. Hoffer was talking to the man with an air of respect, pointing around the camp now and then, to which the man responded with slight nods of the head. As Johann's column shuffled past, the civilian leaned toward Hoffer and said something, whereupon Hoffer shouted:

"You there! The blond one! Yeah, you! Come here! On the double!"

Johann stepped out of the column and trotted toward the two men.

"He's a political prisoner, *Herr Direktor*," Hoffer said, seeing Johann's red patch, apparently in response to a question the civilian had asked. He was about to say something more when the civilian said:

"Would you mind if I ask the man a few questions?"

The word *man* had a strange ring that Johann hadn't heard for a long time. Hoffer's face twitched a little, expressing distaste, but he said readily enough:

"Certainly, *Herr Direktor.*"

The civilian took a few steps toward Johann, an unheard of act in the camp. Prisoners were always commanded to step closer. Nevertheless, Johann remained wary. Despite his unthreatening manner, this elegant civilian who had access to a concentration camp and was being shown around respectfully by the Third Officer-in-Charge must surely be an unsavory character, probably a high official from the SS Main Administrative and Economic Office, the headquarters administering the concentration camps.

"How long have you been in Buchenwald?" the civilian inquired.

"Eight months."

(Rule # 3: *Give the barest minimum of information and never volunteer any.*)

"And before that?"

"Dachau."

"And how long were you at Dachau?"

"Three and a half years."

The man was silent for a moment, nodding pensively. He seemed to be digesting the information, although he expressed no overt reaction.

"Where do you work?"

"In the quarry."

"How is the work?"

The question took Johann aback because it revealed the man's ignorance, not only because the question itself was ridiculous, but because of the proximity of the SS officer.

"It's work," he replied noncommittally.

"Hard work?" the man persisted, lowering his voice.

"Yes."

"What did you do in civilian life?"

"I was a streetcar conductor."

"Any other skills?"

"No."

Again the civilian nodded, somewhat absent-mindedly now. He seemed ready to terminate the conversation.

"Thank you," he said and in a moment turned away from Johann and rejoined Hoffer who waved Johann on.

It wasn't until some time later that Johann found out that the civilian was Martin Hammerschmidt, the wealthy shoe manufacturer from nearby Erfurt.

His name was soon to become legendary among the Buchenwald prisoners.

◆ ◆ ◆

Before Johann was able to resolve the moral and spiritual conflict precipitated by Benjamin's death, an event supervened that changed everything. In a concentration camp life and death were lived from day to day and hour to hour, unpredictably.

Johann did not know why he ran afoul of Skippy that day. Skippy had not taken any particular dislike to Johann, nor did he indulge in personal vendettas or power struggles for the simple reason that to do so would have implied a measure of equality that Skippy did not for a moment acknowledge in his ruthless fixation that he alone was boss.

The first sign Johann had that Skippy had his eye on him came in the forenoon when a stone hit him in the leg. It was painful but not serious. Johann quickened his pace and, for a while, Skippy seemed pacified. But around midday, as he stretched for a moment, another stone hit him in the chest. It knocked the wind out of him and almost knocked him over, sending him the unmistakable message that he was in Skippy's bad graces.

Johann quickened his pace again, but by afternoon was so exhausted that his pace not only slackened but actually dropped below its usual norm. So small was the prisoners' reservoir of strength that even a temporary increase in demand drained their reserves completely.

It was then that it happened. A stone, not large but well-aimed, hit Johann's head with such force that he blacked out instantly and did not regain consciousness even by the time he reached the camp hospital.

When he heard what had happened, Dr. Birnbaum, the chief prisoner-doctor, merely shook his head. Ordering him placed on a bunk in a far corner of the receiving room, he did not expect him to survive the night.

Direktor Martin Hammerschmidt

artin Hammerschmidt sank into one of the plush armchairs that stood in clusters about the large, lavishly furnished living room of his spacious villa after the last of the company had left. It was almost two o'clock in the morning of an October day in 1943. The affair had been one of the biggest social events the Hammerschmidts had ever given, with about fifty highly placed officials and officers in attendance.

Helen, Martin's wife, sat down next to him on the armrest and put her arm around his shoulders.

"Did you have a good time, *Liebchen*?" she asked.

"Yes," he replied, not entirely truthfully.

Although Martin enjoyed people, he found large social affairs rather tiresome. It was his wife who promoted and enjoyed them.

"Do you think it was a success?" she asked solicitously.

"A smashing success," he said generously.

He turned to his wife and placed his hand on her lap. The moment he did so he felt a stirring of desire, which both pleased and annoyed him. The anticipation of making love was pleasurable, but he felt annoyed, too, for the attraction. To think that at forty-eight sex was still so vitally important! But at least his desire only focused on his wife. There was something about her cool beauty that endlessly excited him. It was like drinking sea water, quenching your thirst for the moment, only to make you thirstier. Was it her very elegance, with its vague air of haughtiness, that forever challenged him to pierce through to the essence within?

"Thank God tomorrow is Sunday," he said, pursuing his own thoughts. He pressed his hand lightly against her thigh, smiling up at her. But Helen was still preoccupied with the party.

"You seemed bored at times," she said.

"Ah, my little spy was keeping an eye on me," he said teasingly.

"Be serious, Martin."

"I think you did a superb job," he said solemnly. "Everything without a hitch, and a good time was had by all. What more can you ask for?"

She smiled, pleased.

"I wish I didn't keep getting the feeling that you're bored. Like when you were standing in the circle surrounding General Kessel, I saw your eyes roaming around the room."

"Was it that obvious?" he chuckled. "But he is a bore, you know, with his endless, pompous stories."

Helen laughed.

"And did you see fat Hubert maneuvering what's-her-name around the dance floor?" she exclaimed gaily.

It always gave her a little thrill of satisfaction to hear her husband speak with easy, disparaging familiarity about some highly placed person. Though she had been raised in an affluent home, highly placed people still secretly frightened her and made her feel like a little girl, perhaps because she associated power with the strictness of her lawyer father. There was a streak of insecurity and timidity in Helen that was quite belied by her self-possessed exterior.

Martin suddenly turned serious.

"Do you ever get a funny feeling, hobnobbing with all these bigwigs?" he said.

"I think we're lucky to know them."

"Yes, with us they're all genial and smiles. But I sometimes wonder how they behave with people over whom they have power."

"Why should they behave any differently?" she said naively.

"Because when people have power they turn ugly," he said somewhat tartly. "Especially the Nazis."

His wife's inability to see things against the broader backdrop of what was happening in the country and the world at large often annoyed him.

"Let's go to bed," he said. "It's late."

Helen didn't move.

"I know you think I have no interest in anything but you and the children," she said. "But why should I be interested in this war? No one ever asks us little people. That's why one needs influential friends."

"Little Helen's Instant Survival Kit," he said. But even as he said it he realized that he was being patronizing and regretted it.

"One does need influential people, Martin." Her voice had assumed a pouting, girlish tone that masked a layer of underlying anger. "Take the trouble we had recently with our ration cards, for instance. One phone call to Franz and the matter was cleared up. It would have taken us days to straighten out on our own."

"Come, love. It's late. I'm sorry if I've been short."

He got up.

"Are you tired?" she asked.

"That depends on how you mean it," he said, bending down and kissing her.

"I'll be with you in a minute," she said, understanding. "I'll just turn out the lights."

◆ ◆ ◆

Martin Hammerschmidt was a wealthy man, a very wealthy man, and he was by no means averse to enjoying his wealth: imported cigars, fine vintage wines and brandies, elegant clothes, luxury cars, a large villa, a summer house by the seashore—there was little he didn't have. He had accumulated his wealth through hard work and saw no reason to underutilize it.

Martin was the director and sole owner of the *Hammerschmidt Schuhwerke, A.G.*, which had been established by his father at the turn of the century. But it was Martin who had developed it into one of Europe's larger shoe manufacturing concerns, employing almost a thousand people in a modern factory on the outskirts of Erfurt. Martin attributed his success to a simple business philosophy: Focus on making an excellent product, and sales will take care of themselves. Quality and durability had been the original success formula, and quality he continued to pursue uncompromisingly, as epitomized by the company's advertising slogan, which he himself had coined: Hammerschmidt Shoes . . . As Tough As Nails!

Martin prided himself on being a pragmatic, hardheaded businessman, but human considerations often got in his way. Hardly a week went by that some cause or person did not receive a donation. Nor did a week go by that he was not seen on the factory floors, talking with foremen and individual workers, sometimes working a machine himself when there was a problem, for he prided himself on knowing every facet of the business that he ran with paternalistic benevolence. Shoes stood high on his list of priorities—but human beings stood higher. Anyone who had a complaint or a problem was sure to gain his ear. As a result, Martin inspired a high degree of loyalty among his workers and employees, to whom he was known simply as the *Herr Direktor*, affectionately so by most, respectfully by all. For Martin had an innate gift to inspire confidence and trust because he combined in his person a rare combination of charm, accommodating geniality, spontaneous generosity, and an unbending integrity of character. Despite his genial

manner and seemingly gregarious disposition, he remained an individu-
alist not given to running with the herd.

Even before the outbreak of war, Martin could tell what was happening from the growing number of orders that he received from the Armed
Forces. Once war broke out, he was swamped with so many orders that
he could hardly keep up. Now, almost all his production went to the
military. Had shoe production not merited the highest priority in raw
materials and workers, second only to armaments production itself, he
would have had to close his factory.

Financially, Direktor Hammerschmidt had no reason to complain
about this state of affairs. But, although awash in money, there was less
and less to spend it on, or rather: Everything was still available, but at
steep black market prices. The Hammerschmidts' latest social affair was
an example. It lacked nothing in way of fancy foods and drinks, but the
tab was horrendous.

Martin derived a certain pleasure from having such highly placed officers
and officials eating and drinking his black market provisions and thus
having them beholden to him, though he harbored reservations about them.
He enjoyed his self-image as a wheeler-dealer of influence. Also, Helen
enjoyed these social affairs and considered them important. But the main
reason for cultivating influential contacts was that labor and raw material
bottlenecks multiplied as the war began to turn against Germany, so that
it was increasingly necessary to know the right people to keep production
flowing with the help of gifts, of course, and often downright bribes.

In spite of hobnobbing with influential Nazis, Martin himself had never
joined the Nazi Party. He had too many reservations about the Nazis,
reservations that had become more and more insistent as the war
progressed. The exacting, high-minded shoe manufacturer in him continued to insist on manufacturing the best possible product—if civilians
deserved the best quality, how much more so did soldiers whose very life
could depend on being warmly shod!—but more and more doubts had
lately begun to plague him, waking him up at night. Yes, soldiers needed
boots more than civilians—but for what? To wage war, to conquer, to bring
a New Order—a New Order Martin did not believe in. But what had he
to do with the New Order? he would argue with himself. He wasn't
manufacturing guns. He wasn't even a politician or soldier. Shoes—what
could be more innocent than that? But then another voice intruded that
said: How come you are prospering so mightily from this New Order if
you have nothing to do with it? How come your factory has the highest
priority in materials and labor in an economy where everything is by now

strictly rationed? In short, how can you claim that shoes are peaceful civilian products when soldiers can't do without them?

Yes, of late Direktor Hammerschmidt woke up more and more often at night and had trouble getting back to sleep.

◆ ◆ ◆

When Martin first met Ernst Siebert, he liked the looks of the man at once and felt drawn to him by the kind of visceral attraction that operates outside the realm of intellectual analysis. There was nothing particularly noteworthy about Siebert's looks, except possibly his height, which made him tower above most people. The man who introduced Siebert to him at a social affair did so with a certain air of mystery, but he did not identify Siebert's position and Martin did not ask. He met important people all the time and was not easily impressed.

Not long afterwards Martin ran into Siebert again, this time at the opera house at a new production of *The Magic Flute*. They exchanged a few polite words and passed on, but after the performance, Martin joined a group of acquaintances at a nearby café and there met Siebert again. In fact, he came to sit right next to him. When the discussion focussed on the opera, it turned out that Siebert knew a good deal about music which interested Martin because music was his own primary hobby. Siebert, it emerged, played the viola, although, he said regretfully, he had little opportunity to practice at present.

"What a coincidence," Martin exclaimed. "I play in a chamber music group and we're in all likelihood soon going to lose our violist. Maybe you'd be interested in taking his place."

Before parting company, Martin gave Siebert his card and invited him to be in touch with him about the group. He did notice that the man volunteered almost no information about himself but gave that no further thought.

After Martin's devotion to his wife, his business, and his two children —a girl studying at the University of Vienna and a boy who had a safe desk job in the Navy, thank God—Martin loved nothing so much as classical music in general and playing his instrument, the violin, in particular. He had organized a chamber music group, which met in different homes twice a month. He rarely missed one of these sessions. In addition, he owned the best phonograph collection money could buy. Music was his pride and joy, his relaxation, entertainment, and replenishment.

One day soon after the opera performance, Martin ran into an old business acquaintance, Kurt Boeck, who owned a textile factory that, like Martin's, worked primarily for the Armed Forces. They had known each other for many years and were comfortable with each other, though not intimate. Boeck and his wife had also been at the *The Magic Flute* performance as well as at the subsequent discussion in the café.

"Well," Boeck remarked as they were walking to their cars, "I see you and Siebert hit it off well together."

"Yes, he's a likable fellow. You know me, Kurt, music is my passion. He might join my chamber music group."

"Really?" There was a hesitant intonation in Boeck's voice. "You know, of course, who he is."

"As a matter of fact, I don't. He didn't talk much about himself."

"No wonder."

"Why? What does he do?"

"He's an SS officer. A *Hauptsturmführer*, I believe."

"You're kidding!" Martin exclaimed. "Since when are SS officers music lovers?"

"This one is. What is more—you really should know this, Martin, if you don't." Boeck lowered his voice conspiratorially. "He's the Assistant Commandant of Buchenwald."

Martin stopped so abruptly that Boeck, who was walking slightly behind him, ran into him.

"You're not serious!" Martin exclaimed.

He was facing Boeck, who had stopped too, with an utterly nonplussed expression.

"I am. I assure you, I am," Boeck laughed. "What did you expect? a man with horns?"

"No, but—how can he love music!" Martin blurted. "I mean, it just doesn't . . . ." He was groping for words.

"I had a similar reaction when I first met him. Maybe it goes to show that things aren't as bad in the camp as rumors would have it."

But already Martin was walking on, silently now, very silent, and, as silently, shook hands with Boeck once they reached their cars.

◆ ◆ ◆

The information made a strong impression on Martin. Siebert just didn't fit into his conception of a man running a concentration camp. Maybe Boeck was right when he said that things weren't so bad in the camp. The rumors one heard were so horrible as to be, in fact, plainly unbelievable.

It forced Martin to realize that he had relegated everyone connected with the concentration camps to a sort of different species—yes, with horns or some figurative approximation thereof—convinced that the men running these camps must be a breed apart, easily recognizable, instantly identifiable as evil. It was the comfortable thing to do and many Germans did it to perfection. How much easier if evil presented itself not in the guise of ordinary people but in clearly defined form!

So Martin had to face the uncomfortable fact that the different breed looked human, acted human, spoke human. What was more—and this was even more unsettling—that these men could appreciate the "higher" things in life, like music, art, and literature (did not Hitler himself love music?), which only "cultured" people with "refined" tastes and sensibilities were supposed to be capable of appreciating. Suddenly every value he had believed in as elevating man had to be put in quotes and questioned for its validity. And with that, the whole uncritical structure of his assumptions and rationalizations began to topple. If Assistant Commandant Siebert seemed no different from himself, then it was clear that he had to deal with what he stood for and could no longer simply dismiss him as belonging to an alien species!

This insight marked a change in Martin's complacent attitude toward the Nazis. For the truth was that, though not a Nazi himself, he had placidly accepted them.

These thoughts and feelings did not crystallize overnight. His first reaction was to fall back upon schemes of avoidance: He would forget his invitation to Siebert to audition for the music group. It wasn't yet sure anyway that the violist was leaving. But then the violist did leave and still Martin struggled to find excuses: Siebert might not play well enough or, conversely, be too advanced for the group. Anyway, it wasn't up to him but to the whole group, and so forth.

One day, however, Siebert called up to inquire whether the violist had left, and he expressed such a strong interest in joining the group that Martin saw no way around letting him audition. He could always use his influence in the group to vote him down. He was also helped by the thought that perhaps he *ought* to have some dealings with the man. What better way was there to learn about this ugly side of Nazism and determine what was really going on in the camps? Perhaps one could even bring some beneficial influence to bear on the man.

◆ ◆ ◆

When *Hauptsturmführer* (Captain) Siebert auditioned for the sextet, his playing skills were found to fit in so well with the group that the members voted to invite him in despite Martin's opposition. What was more, Siebert soon made himself well liked, for he was easygoing, excelled at telling stories, and usually brought along some wine or even brandy, precious commodities by this time. The drinks added to the liveliness of the proceedings (if not always to the quality of the music) and raised Siebert's popularity among the members. Siebert's "occupation" was not discussed, although Martin had revealed it to the group. Assistant Commandant Siebert could have been a kindergarten teacher for all the notice his rank and position elicited.

But in Martin the knowledge continued to fester. At first he continued to lie in wait, hoping to find something different in Siebert that would establish a firm distinction between them. But instead he found himself drawn time and again into the circle of their similarities and common interests so that he finally had to admit to himself that it was the knowledge of Siebert's position, not the actuality of his behavior, that stood between them.

Then Martin fell back once more upon rationalizations. What did he really know about Buchenwald? Whispered references, furtive confidences, oblique snatches of conversation that described events that were plainly improbable—in short, rumors, rumors, rumors! He had never yet come across any hard evidence that could be tracked down. Maybe it was all a vast, unjustified exaggeration. Granted that the Nazis were a rough and occasionally brutal lot, but, by God, they were human, after all.

Thus did Martin try to compartmentalize good and evil in order to keep his doubts at bay.

◆ ◆ ◆

Martin tried to draw Siebert out about conditions in the camp. But whether he approached the subject on a personal level by showing an interest in Siebert's work or from a more abstract political-philosophical angle or by talking about "enemies of the Reich" and how they deserved to be behind barbed wire, Siebert wouldn't rise to the bait and remained tight-lipped and did not respond except with the barest of unrevealing banalities.

Only once did Siebert reveal a glimpse into himself after Martin had managed to get him thoroughly drunk, for Siebert turned out to be a heavy drinker.

"It's a bad business, Martin," Siebert kept repeating drunkenly. "A bad business. Just stay out of it."

"What is a bad business?" Martin asked, feigning ignorance.

"I should have stayed out of it myself," Siebert continued drunkenly without listening to Martin. "'Cause now I'm damned—damned, damned, *damn!*"

"How did you get into it?"

"Ba-a-ah!" Siebert cried with sudden ferocity, making a wide sweep with his arm. "Stupidity! Idiocy! Ignorance!"

"Of what?"

"The whole mess!" Siebert cried.

"What mess?"

"The whole fuckin' mess, Martin!" Siebert repeated drunkenly. "Just stay out of it, I tell you. Stay out."

So it went, round and round.

After that, Martin Hammerschmidt and *Hauptsturmführer* Siebert retreated back to their comfortable bridge—music—across which they could communicate without distress.

◆ ◆ ◆

One morning Martin's secretary announced that Vogel, the night watchman, wanted to see him. Vogel was a man in his late sixties who had been in his father's employ since the earliest days of the company—he was the second oldest employee and, as such, the trust and loyalty on both sides ran deep. He would long ago have been given a more comfortable job, but Vogel, who was something of a loner since the death of his wife, liked the quietness and solitude of circulating by himself at night.

Nevertheless, although the *Herr Direktor's* door was always open, especially for an old employee like Vogel, it was highly unusual for anyone to come directly to him instead of through their supervisor.

"Ask him in," Martin said.

When Vogel entered, Martin rose from his chair and warmly extended his hand. No question here of a Nazi salute.

"How are you, Vogel? I haven't seen you in a long time."

"That's right, *Herr Direktor*, and I beg pardon to call on you directly, but it's a matter you need to hear about personally, I think."

"You're always welcome," Martin said cordially.

He waved Vogel into one of the comfortable armchairs, but the watchman picked up a straight-backed chair that stood along the wall.

"Beg pardon," he said, bringing the chair quite close to Martin's desk.

In Nazi Germany such behavior was immediately understood. Walls have ears, was a favorite saying. Martin waited patiently until Vogel had seated himself. There was a slowness and tranquillity about the man that stemmed, one sensed, from a sense of inner peace.

"You know the small shed at the end of the lot near the back fence, *Herr Direktor*?" Vogel began.

"Yes."

"It hasn't been used for a long time. Two nights ago I smelled a funny smell when I passed by, but I didn't think nothin' of it. Well, last night the smell was so awful that I decided to look inside. I found a man, *Herr Direktor*, a man who was—who was . . . ." Vogel stared out of the window. "I can't describe it—no flesh, just bones, delirious . . . ." He fell silent for some moments. "I gave him some bread—and other food—but he couldn't keep nothin' down—only some hot broth." He looked at Martin in distress. "I don't know what to do, *Herr Direktor*. That's why I came to you."

A dozen thoughts crowded through Martin's mind simultaneously: Could the man stay in the shed?—he should call a doctor—or could he take him into his house?—but the danger—and the servants couldn't be trusted—and how would Helen feel?—and the man might die anyway . . . .

"Could the man stay in the shed, Vogel?" he asked finally. The watchman shook his head.

"There's no water. And people see you go in and out."

"If we could find someone to take him in," Martin mused.

"That's what I was thinking, *Herr Direktor*."

"Yes, but who?"

"Me."

"You, Vogel?"

"I've given it a lot of thought, *Herr Direktor*. I live alone. And I have an empty room."

Martin felt a sense of relief. He sat considering.

"But do you know what you're getting into, Vogel? You know what helping an escaped KZ prisoner means if he's discovered?"

"I do, *Herr Direktor*."

"And you have no qualms?"

Vogel shook his head.

"No doubts?"

"What worries me is getting him into my apartment."

Martin had propped his elbows on the desk and now buried his face in his hands, aware that he and Vogel were facing one of the most serious and dangerous decisions of their lives. Yet this simple man had no qualms, while he was vacillating . . . but he had more to lose! he had a family, a factory, he was an important member of . . . but life was what any man had to lose, rich or poor, family or no family . . . .

Yet even as he was still considering the pros and cons of the matter, he knew that it was already settled, settled on a deeper level than reason and analysis or even risk and danger, because he intuited that he couldn't live with any other decision. Martin was, despite his hardheaded business sense, an impulsive man who trusted his intuition.

"When is the best time to get him to your place?" he asked, reverting to his customary decisiveness.

"Between three and four in the morning, I'd say, *Herr Direktor*."

"I'll be at the shed at three."

◆ ◆ ◆

When Martin arrived at the shed at three o'clock, Vogel was already there. It was an overcast night, which was helpful, though it made movement more difficult since they couldn't use flashlights. Martin had obtained the use of an old company car because his Mercedes would have been too conspicuous, and he had brought along some old blankets to protect the vehicle from telltale odors.

When they entered the shed, the stench was overwhelming. Martin remained close to the door to get used to the smell and accustom his eyes to the darkness while Vogel bent down to a dark shape on the floor.

"It's me—Vogel," he whispered. "I've brought someone along to move you to my place, Alfred."

There was no answer.

"Can you hear me?" Vogel whispered tensely. "We've come to move you. You'll be safe in my place."

There followed a guttural sound that Martin couldn't make out. It could have been a Yes or a No or just a groan. Vogel turned to him.

"Grab his legs, *Herr Direktor*."

Martin stepped forward and groped for the man's legs. They were matchstick-thin and felt bony and fleshless.

"Ready?" Vogel whispered.

Martin tightened his muscles and gave a heave, expecting the weight of a man. But the man's body was as light as a child's. He walked backwards toward the door while Vogel supported the man under the arms. Once outside they spread out the blankets and wrapped the man in them. When Vogel picked him up in his arms, there was a whimper from the blanket.

"We'll be there soon, Alfred," he whispered.

Martin had parked the car as close as he could, some fifty yards away. He opened the rear door for Vogel and slipped quickly behind the wheel and started the car. The grinding of the starter sounded excruciatingly loud in the stillness. Finally the engine turned over.

The streets were dark and silent. The hum of the engine was for long minutes the only sound. It had a soothing, almost lulling effect. Now and then Vogel gave him a brief direction, but no sound or movement came from the huddled figure in the blanket whom Martin could barely make out in the mirror. There was a peacefulness and unreality about the scene that stood in stark contrast to its latent danger.

Vogel's apartment was located on an upper floor in a long two-story building. Vogel picked up the wrapped figure and carried him upstairs while Martin followed. In front of the apartment Vogel whispered:

"Get my keys, *Herr Direktor*. In my right pocket. The long key."

Martin groped for the keys and unlocked the door. Vogel switched on the hall light, which blinded them for a moment. There was a whimper from the blankets. Vogel carried the man into a small room to the left of the entrance and put him down on the floor. Martin could see the shaven head now, the cavernous eyes, the high cheekbones from which the stubbly skin hung without flesh or roundness or color, the thin, fragile neck that looked too frail to support anything. But the eyes seemed clear now, looking out at them both with a terrible stillness.

Vogel bent down to him.

"We're in my place, Alfred. How do you feel?"

"Fine."

The incongruity of the word, which was breathed in clear, unaccented German, struck Martin, coming as it did from a head more wasted than anything he had ever seen in his life.

Vogel straightened.

"I'll have to clean him up first," he said in a half-whisper, though there was no reason to whisper anymore.

"Can I help?"

Martin suddenly became aware of the fact that he no longer noticed the stench.

"I can manage now. And—thank you, *Herr Direktor*."

"Why do you thank me? I could as well thank you."

"I would have done it in any case."

Again Martin felt a rush of admiration for this simple, solid man who never wavered for a moment. He held out his hand.

"You're a decent man, Vogel. And a brave one."

Vogel grasped his hand.

"So are you, *Herr Direktor.*"

They stood looking each other in the eyes for a moment, each nurtured by the other's warmth and trust.

"I'll try to get a doctor," Martin said. "And Vogel: All expenses are on me, of course."

"Thank you, *Herr Direktor.*"

"And I hope you won't mind that I'll be back to visit."

♦ ◆ ♦

Martin managed to get Dr. Ziegelmaier to visit the very same afternoon without explaining any details. He did it after wrestling with himself for over an hour, for the risks were obvious. He did not really know Dr. Ziegelmaier very well because he and Helen had only recently begun to consult the elderly physician after their own long-time doctor had been drafted. In the end, it had been the memory of the night watchman's unwavering courage and integrity that had shamed him into calling the doctor.

While Dr. Ziegelmaier examined the man, Vogel was busy in the kitchen. Martin stood by the window of the small living room and looked down on a neat row of truck gardens that faced an identical two-story apartment building on the other side. From time to time he left the window and made a quick, restless turn around the room to relieve his anxiety. Vogel had cleaned up the man, he had disposed of his clothes and had done yeoman's service. But there was no mistaking who the man was. He would have had to be blown up like a balloon to twice his size to acquire anything like human proportions.

Suddenly Martin was overcome by panic. He went to the slightly ajar door of the living room and listened intently. There wasn't a sound to be heard from the room. Had the doctor left surreptitiously and was even now contacting the Gestapo who would drive up at any moment to arrest them?

He chased the fantasy away and returned to the window. Finally Dr. Ziegelmaier came out. Martin motioned him into the living room and called Vogel from the kitchen. The doctor spoke for some moments. Martin picked up phrases like "nothing much to be done— lots of rest and good food—not too rich . . . ." But there was a rushed quality in the doctor's words that suggested that the gist of what he had to say was yet to come.

"Will he pull through, Dr. Ziegelmaier?" Martin asked when the doctor had finished.

The doctor shrugged. "He's far gone. But there seems to be a lot of stamina in these concentration camp prisoners."

A dead silence fell in the room. Presently the doctor said:

"Needless to say, Herr Hammerschmidt, I won't come again."

"What about your oath to help, doctor?"

The doctor's eyes retreated behind a cold curtain.

"May I remind you, Herr Hammerschmidt, that we're at war and that these are supposed to be our enemies. Besides, the Hippocratic oath doesn't demand suicide. To help an escaped KZ inmate is, I believe, punishable by death. Anyway, there isn't much I can do for the man."

He turned to go.

"I hope you'll respect that not everyone shares your views, Dr. Ziegelmaier," Martin said.

The doctor had reached the door and turned around.

"I do," he said. He lingered for a moment. "I can't say I'm very comfortable even with this, Herr Hammerschmidt, but I'll act as if I'd never seen the man."

"Thank you, *Herr Doktor*."

♦ ◆ ♦

For several days Alfred hovered between life and death. But on the fourth day, for the first time, he was able to retain some semi-solid food without at once throwing up. Vogel welcomed Martin with the news, which both quietly celebrated.

It marked the beginning of Alfred's recovery.

Alfred now began to eat a little more each day and started to gain some weight. Within a week he was able to walk by himself to the bathroom for the first time, another event that Vogel and Martin, and this time Alfred too, quietly celebrated.

Martin was amazed by the gentleness with which Vogel, this aging, solitary man, nursed Alfred back to health. It was like a father nursing his son, and, indeed, Alfred, who was in his thirties, could well have been his son. And maybe there was more truth in this than Vogel himself realized, because the core sadness of his life had always been that he had had no children.

As Alfred gained strength and began to sustain a conversation, Martin's visits became more protracted, and he obtained a key from Vogel so that he could visit the apartment in the evening, when Vogel was at work.

Alfred was an Austrian Jew, a journalist, and a socialist to boot, which was enough to send him twice over to a concentration camp. He was arrested immediately after the annexation of Austria in March 1938 and after three years in Mauthausen, an Austrian camp near Linz, was shipped to Buchenwald. Both were infamous camps, although not quite as deadly as Auschwitz, the extermination camp. Until six months before his escape, he had worked in the Orderly Room in a relatively safe job but he fell out of favor with a newly arrived SS officer who assigned him to the latrine detail, one of the deadliest in camp.

As Alfred regained his strength, Martin began to ply him with questions, which Alfred soon answered freely, as he discovered that talking about his experiences proved therapeutic. Martin came away from these conversations deeply upset. Alfred's stories were just too lurid, too ghastly, to be believed: prisoners forced to climb trees until the top branches gave way and hurtled them to their death; prisoners pushed into the latrine trench to suffocate in the excrement while the SS guards stood by laughing; prisoners shut up for weeks in a sealed, dark barrack until they went crazy; not to mention infamous installations like the "Bunker," the camp prison, where heinous crimes were committed, or "Detail 99," the code name for a stable outside the compound proper where prisoners were systematically mowed down with machine guns. But perhaps the worst infamy were instances of prisoners being buried alive —

"Come on, Alfred," Martin interrupted. "It's bad enough without embroidering."

"Embroidering!" Alfred looked at him with a mixture of sadness and anger. "I wish I were embroidering. Let me tell you about an incident I witnessed myself. One day a son stood up for his father who was being severely beaten. They made the son lie down in a trench and buried him alive—right in front of his father . . . the father died anyway from the beating a few days later."

Martin would sit and listen, unbelieving and yet hypnotized, feeling his chest reverberating from the loud, painful thump of his heart as if he himself were being tortured. At first he had refused to believe the more shocking stories. Harsh conditions, yes—official indifference to suffering, yes—even wanton killings . . . but personal, unmotivated, unremitting torture and sadism—that was too much! He went so far as to wonder at times whether Alfred's imprisonment had affected his sanity. Could he be a paranoid psychotic, understandably so but psychotic nevertheless? He would question Alfred about details, would lay subtle traps to test his memory to see whether he was confabulating or at least exaggerating, would dispute lurid details—but always the stories remained the same, the details did not change, everything was so and did not deviate. Nor did Alfred's manner bear out Martin's suspicions, because his bearing was subdued, his voice quiet, his words restrained and factual. For all the horror of his experiences, there were no ringing condemnations, no vengeful fanaticism, no fervor of delivery even. Instead his voice dropped almost to a monotone with each build-up of horror—which made it all sound even more horrible!

"I can't believe that human beings can do such things to other human beings, Alfred!" Martin would exclaim again and again.

He found it impossible to believe because it rocked his understanding of human nature, his whole perception of what man was capable of.

"How can human beings do such things, Alfred?"

Again and again he would pose, urge, that question upon Alfred. It became a deeply personal question, almost an obsession: For how could one say with assurance that one was immune to such deeds when many of the prisoner foremen and orderlies were just as cruel as the SS? One couldn't point the finger at the SS without at the same time pointing the finger at oneself!

"How do you explain such things, Alfred?"

You who have gone through these horrors, who have been in this hell and have taken the measure of yourself and of your ability, or inability, to remain human.

"What did you do when the chips were down, Alfred?"

♦ ◆ ♦

Alfred's recovery proceeded apace, hastened by Martin's need to understand, which actually helped Alfred work through his own experiences. The two men soon became fast friends.

As Alfred once again began to take an interest in his surroundings, he became restless. In civilian life he had been a journalist, a man of energy and drive, which made his confinement in the apartment painful despite its obvious blessings. Martin brought along newspapers and books, but Alfred found it hard to concentrate.

"If I could just get out of the country," he said again and again. Martin tried to dissuade him. Such an attempt was too unlikely to succeed, even though Alfred was beginning to look like a normal human being again. His cheeks were rounding out and his hair was growing. One day Martin suggested:

"Why don't you write about your experiences, Alfred. Write a book. That would give you something to do."

Martin had given the matter some thought, so the suggestion was neither offhand nor unpremeditated. But Alfred reacted negatively.

"What would I want to write a book for?" he exclaimed. "Who would read it?"

The thought struck Alfred as ludicrous, aeons removed from the realities of life, because he had spent more than five years living at the level of the most basic of basic needs. Writing was a civilized, a human activity.

"I'm not joking, Alfred," Martin said earnestly. "Who but someone like you can write about the concentration camps? And you're a journalist to boot."

"Who would want to read such a book?" Alred repeated.

"A lot of people. The world needs to know."

"The world," Alfred said bitterly. "Because the world cared so much when Hitler began to kill Jews."

"We can learn from it at least in retrospect."

Alfred got up and stood staring out of the window of the tiny room.

"God, how I'd love to walk across a meadow again! to sniff flowers, grass, pine trees!" he exclaimed under his breath.

But when Martin visited next time, Alfred himself returned to the subject.

"I can't go back to all those experiences, Martin. The mere thought . . . ." He shook himself. "It's all still too close."

"You told me about them."

"Talk. Yes. But when you write—when it stares back at you . . . ."

"I understand."

"Anyway, once the war is over, people will want to forget about all this—just as we forgot about World War I."

But it was clear that something had begun to work in Alfred.

A week later Martin found him writing when he arrived in the apartment. Alfred set his pad aside somewhat shamefacedly.

"What are you doing?" Martin inquired.

"As you can see—writing," Alfred said evasively.

"May I ask what?"

"Making some notes," Alfred replied briefly, falling silent, as if explaining further would admit something he was not yet ready to admit. Martin did not press him further.

◆ ◆ ◆

Martin's increasingly long absences in the evening —arriving late for dinner or leaving again after dinner—did not go unnoticed by Helen, of course. For a while, the usual umbrella excuse of business satisfied her, used as she was to Martin's long, and at times erratic, hours, but in time this explanation wore thin because Martin displayed a degree of preoccupation that was unusual for him. He was not a man given to carrying his work home.

Martin had not told Helen about Alfred. Not that he didn't trust her. No, she would have stood by him if he had believed in the devil, he was sure of that. But she felt anxious enough about the war and the Nazis without adding further to her anxiety. On the other hand, not involving her had the disadvantage of embroiling him in false excuses, stoking her suspicions. One evening Helen finally blurted out:

"What is keeping you away so much, Martin? Is it another woman?"

He burst out laughing. "Helen!" he cried. "Have I ever been unfaithful to you?"

"There's always a first time. They say men in their fifties start running after—what do you call them?—chicks."

"I'm only forty-eight. And I hate chicken," he joked. "Give me veal every time."

But Helen was in no mood for jokes.

"Making light of it only strengthens my suspicion," she said, pouting.

"Come, love," he said solemnly, drawing her down to his lap, knowing that pouting was her way of asking for reassurance. "I'm really entirely happy with you. I couldn't be any happier."

Such categorical assurances calmed her down for a time, but the constant need to reassure her was tiresome. Love required spontaneity, not forced pledges. But when he considered taking her into his confidence, the thought of her agitated reaction was enough to reseal his lips.

However, he did reduce the frequency and length of his absences, especially after dinner, which helped to placate Helen. And by this time, Alfred was so deeply absorbed in his writing that he failed to notice Martin's reduced visits.

◆ ◆ ◆

As Martin came to see Nazism for what it was, the issue of doing something concrete moved into the forefront of his preoccupation. What good was it to have come into possession of all this knowledge if it remained hidden and led to no action?

Martin was a doer, an activist. Mere ideas and speculation had never greatly interested him. Both as a businessman and as a human being, he had always been driven to translate ideas into practice. The bottom line was always: What could be done about it?

But what could be done about Nazism? What could one do about this camp that was festering practically on one's doorstep? What could be done about such unutterable evil?

♦ ◆ ♦

One day Martin ran into Kurt Boeck, his manufacturer-acquaintance who had revealed *Hauptsturmführer* Siebert's identity to him. Boeck was sitting in a café and asked Martin to join him for a drink.

The two men were on friendly terms, although Boeck's feelings toward Martin were somewhat ambivalent. On the one hand, he was envious of Martin; on the other, he admired him, for he saw in Martin the kind of successful, worldly, self-assured entrepreneur that he himself aspired to be.

Boeck employed about eight hundred people in his textile factory, which was engaged in high-priority manufacture of cloth for uniforms and other apparel for the Armed Forces, whereas Martin employed over a thousand people. A bantering sort of rivalry had developed between the two men over the size of their respective factories.

Today Martin noticed an unaccustomed air of smugness about Boeck. "Well, Martin," he said, lifting his glass, "it looks like I'm finally overtaking you."

"Over my dead body," Martin joked.

"I'm getting two hundred fifty new workers."

Martin whistled softly. "My, you must be manufacturing robots," he bantered with a touch of envy, for he was constantly looking for workers himself. In those days of labor shortages, Boeck's proclamation was tantamount to announcing that he had found a cache of diamonds in the street.

Boeck leaned back, enjoying Martin's discomfiture.

"I don't suppose you'd care to tell me how you did it?" Martin asked.

"That depends on how much it's worth to you," Boeck grinned teasingly.

Martin was unsure whether Boeck was serious or joking. Boeck had always impressed him as somewhat venal and greedy but his unabashed bluntness took him by surprise.

"Well, you'll find out anyway," Boeck said. "So I'll tell you—for a brandy." He leaned forward and lowered his voice confidentially. "I'm getting prisoners from Buchenwald. At seven and a half marks a head a day! Can you beat that?"

Martin's jaw dropped. He had heard of satellite concentration camps being established in factories but somehow had always connected those with huge enterprises like I.G. Farben and Krupp.

"Yep," Boeck said smugly, leaning back again.

"Skilled workers?"

"They're supposed to be skilled. But I figure any kind of worker is better than none at that price."

Martin was silent, struggling with whether to say anything or not. He suddenly felt an intense distaste for Boeck.

"Do you know what goes on in a place like Buchenwald, Kurt?" he said.

Boeck shrugged. "I suppose it's no picnic. But at least they'll have decent working conditions in my place. Can you beat that?" he gloated. "Seven and a half marks a head."

Martin was barely able to conceal his disgust. He signaled to the waiter.

"A double brandy for the gentleman, please."

"Aren't you having another?"

"No, I've got to get back to the factory."

The idea of having another drink with Boeck just then was utterly repugnant to him.

◆ ◆ ◆

Martin came away from the meeting feeling rather sick. Boeck's smug, self-satisfied greed nauseated him in the light of what he now knew about the concentration camps. Didn't the man realize that he was profiting from a brutally exploitative system? Didn't he realize how hugely he would profit from the labor of these grossly abused human beings?

Martin was so worked up about the news that he decided to visit Alfred on his way home in order to vent his feelings. But to his surprise Alfred became more and more quiet as he talked. Finally Martin stopped.

"You don't seem upset, Alfred. How come?"

Instead of answering, Alfred began to ask him a series of questions. What kind of a man was Boeck? What kind of a building would the prisoners work in? be quartered in? etc.

"How should I know?" Martin exclaimed irritably, not seeing the connection. "Why do you want to know anyway?"

"Because those are the important things, Martin," Alfred said quietly. "Not how much profit the guy is going to make off the prisoners."

"How can you say that?" Martin exclaimed, feeling hurt and angry to be abandoned by the one ally he felt sure he could count on.

"You don't seem to understand, Martin. I wish prisoners *were* properly exploited in the camps because that would mean they'd at least get fed and clothed. Have you ever heard of a farmer starving his animals to death?"

Martin was silent.

"You're looking at it from the wrong point of view, Martin," Alfred continued. "Look at it from the point of view of the prisoners. They want to live. They want to eat. They want to be clothed properly. They want to *survive*. They're way beyond caring about money and profits. Sure, the man uses slave labor and you can say that's immoral. But to hell with that as long as it helps the prisoners *survive*."

"But the SS will still be running the show," Martin objected.

"Sure. But the factory owner can do a lot. He can soften things, improve the living quarters, issue work clothes. He can even supplement the food rations if he has a mind to use some of his profits for the welfare of the prisoners. There are good and bad satellite camps. What's the matter, Martin?"

Martin's eyes had suddenly widened. He stared at Alfred.

"I just had an idea."

"What?"

"Couldn't—*I* start a camp then?"

Now it was Alfred who stared at him.

"You . . . ?"

For some moments both were silent as the thought sank in with all its ramifications. Then Martin got up and began to pace about the room in his excitement.

"If Boeck managed to swing it, I certainly can. I've got connections aplenty. And there's Siebert!" he suddenly cried, stopping. "I was thinking of cutting off all contact with the man, but he can come in handy now, can't he? By God, Alfred!" Martin veritably shouted, hitting his fist into his other hand in his enthusiasm. "If Boeck can do it, so can I!"

"You bet your life you can!" Alfred cried, infected too now by Martin's enthusiasm.

◆   ◆   ◆

The idea opened up entirely new possibilities. Suddenly Martin saw that something more could be done than merely piously wringing one's hands and flinging impotent curses at the Nazis: One could subvert the system from within!

He set to work at once with characteristic energy and enthusiasm.

His first step was to arrange another meeting with Boeck who could give him valuable information on how to proceed. Despite their rivalry, Boeck felt flattered and vindicated that Martin wanted to follow in his footsteps. He was pleased to help him, even offering to introduce him to an officer of the SS Main Administrative and Economic Office in Oranienburg near Berlin who had been pivotal in approving his own application and shepherding it through the bureaucratic maze of other agencies, since machinery had to be procured, additional raw materials had to be allocated, etc.—"all this for a consideration, of course, a sizable consideration. For that matter, Martin," Boeck added, winking slyly, "this might cost you a little more than just a double brandy with me, too."

"Why, of course, Kurt," Martin said genially with never so much as a disapproving twitch in his accommodating smile. "No problem."

Boeck laughed. "You're easy to do business with, Martin. I admire that."

◆ ◆ ◆

It was late in 1943 when Martin set the necessary machinery in motion, and by February 1944 his application had been approved "in principle," but "in practice" nothing yet had happened. Martin discovered that to translate "in principle" to "in practice" usually meant further red tape or a bribe—usually both. For a decisive man like Martin, who had little patience with bureaucratic shufflings and intrigue, the whole process was distasteful and trying, although he actually preferred to deal with bribable officials because at least he had a handle on them.

After making the necessary application, Boeck's "pivotal" official—an SS *Obersturmbannführer* (Lieutenant Colonel)—personally came down from SS Headquarters in Oranienburg to inspect the *Hammerschmidt Schuhwerke* to see whether it lent itself to the establishment of an *Aussenlager*, a satellite camp, because this required a separate factory building, or at least a wing that could be sealed off, surrounded by a tall barbed wire fence as well as watchtowers, since these accouterments of concentration camps could not, of course, be dispensed with.

Martin had given these matters much thought, but the solution had actually been quite simple. His factory consisted of two buildings, an old one, the original factory, and a modern, much larger one. It was thus not difficult to consolidate the civilian workforce in the modern building, a process that had been happening more or less anyway. To cordon off the old building with a barbed wire fence was a simple matter, to be financed, of course, as the *Obersturmbannführer* smilingly informed Martin, by the factory owner, though the SS would supply the specifications since the height of the fence and the intervals between watchtowers were all set down in the regulations. By contrast, the officer never so much as inspected the sleeping and bathroom facilities, which were in short supply, although he did briefly walk through the mess hall.

"Excellent setup, Herr Hammerschmidt, excellent setup," he kept repeating. "I assure you, your application will sail through in no time. I'll give it my highest recommendation."

"I'm much obliged, *Herr Obersturmbannführer*. I promise you that you and the SS won't regret it," Martin replied with just the right combination of finely-shaded meanings, from the promise of succulent bribes to patriotic breast beating in the service of the *Vaterland*.

The *Obersturmbannführer* understood—on both counts.

The problem that now preoccupied Martin involved the number of prisoners that he should requisition. Here Martin was caught in a bind. On the one hand, he wanted to help as many prisoners as possible; on the other hand, if he squeezed in too many, he would violate the very reason why he was getting them in the first place, namely, to create humane living and working conditions. How to arrive at a happy medium?

The question distressed him, as indeed the whole notion of numbers. Martin was used to working with numbers that represented objects: shoes, machinery, money—all of which were in the end expendable. But here he was working with lives, lives that in all likelihood would be lost if he did not include them. How could he say *three hundred*, for example, when there was surely room for one more—and one more after that. And once you opened the door, why not ten more—a hundred more?

The whole process was unnerving.

When he brought up the subject with Boeck, Boeck shrugged and advised:

"Apply for as many as you can, Martin. These people aren't fussy and if there are too many, you just send them back. But you can't get more without a lot of bother and red tape."

It was with Alfred's help once again that Martin finally arrived at a figure. He had been reluctant to approach Alfred in this matter because he assumed automatically that Alfred would press for the highest, and thus ultimately for an unrealistic, number. To his surprise, Alfred was more hardheaded and unsentimental about it than he himself. When he mentioned this to him Alfred said:

"Because I've been in the camps and you haven't, Martin. One thing you learn there is to think of the people you *can* help, never of all the people you *can't* help. If you think of those, you go crazy and can't help anyone."

The number Martin finally requested was three hundred twenty-five, a number immediately accepted by the *Obersturmbannführer*.

Martin saw much of Boeck during these days, not only to obtain his help but also because Boeck had meanwhile received his complement of prisoners, and Martin saw here a chance to exert some beneficial influence since Boeck wasn't really a bad person once allowances were made for his vanity and greed. Martin learned that the best approach was to appeal to Boeck's business acumen.

"You know how workers are, Kurt," he would say with an air of complicity. "If you squeeze them too hard they only take it out on your product. As far as I'm concerned, it's just plain good business to treat workers properly, prisoners or no prisoners."

That was language Boeck could understand.

It was valuable training for Martin because he learned to pitch everything toward the imperatives of production and profits. As long as he had tried to talk about protecting the prisoners for their own sake, Boeck had listened with polite indifference. But profits and production—those pulled weight.

◆ ◆ ◆

Martin's relationship with Siebert meanwhile underwent some changes. After Alfred's rescue, Martin had again wanted to sever all relations with him, for he was one of the architects of this fiendish system, even if Alfred had not implicated him as much as many others. But that was in the end academic, akin to saying that a rapist had raped only one woman instead of five. Even if he had never lifted a finger against a prisoner—and he most certainly had—he was still one of the people in charge and could have ameliorated, if not entirely prevented, the random killings and wanton brutalities that daily occurred in the camp. He was guilty, there could be no doubt of that.

To sever their ties meant, first of all, to expel him from the music group. But when Martin felt out the other members, he ran into unexpected opposition because Siebert had by this time ingratiated himself with the group. Above all, he kept the group in liquor. The alternative was for Martin himself to resign, but there—Martin was ashamed to admit it—he balked. He had organized the group; why should he leave it? It provided one of the few pleasures still capable of relaxing him.

Martin was still struggling with this issue when the decision to establish a satellite camp made him backpedal without moral scruples, for it was clear that Siebert could be of inestimable value to him, if for no other reason than that the actual slate of workers, once his request was approved by SS Headquarters, would be put together in the camp itself.

Martin now began to ingratiate himself unostentatiously with Siebert. The best way to do so was through liquor, brandy in particular, which Siebert consumed in prodigious quantities. Quite often now Martin, too, would bring along a bottle to the rehearsals, casually leaving what was left in the bottle to Siebert.

Then one day Martin invited him to dinner, along with Boeck and his wife and a young woman. Boeck was delighted to establish a more personal relationship with Siebert, since satellite camps (Buchenwald had more than fifty such satellite camps) were under the overall command of the camp and thus of Siebert.

"Didn't know you got that close to him," Boeck said admiringly to Martin.

"So how much is the invitation worth to you?" Martin joked.

Boeck laughed loudly, appreciating both the dig and Martin's wit. Yes, he admired many things about Direktor Hammerschmidt.

The woman was a pretty young woman of casual acquaintance. This was admittedly a long shot because Martin had no knowledge of Siebert's tastes beyond knowing that he had an eye for women. As it turned out, the two hit it off rather well, and a passing comment made by Siebert three weeks later indicated that they were continuing to see each other.

Martin did not immediately tell Siebert about his efforts to establish a satellite camp because he first wanted to further cement his relationship with him so that Siebert wouldn't jump to the conclusion that he was merely cultivating him for selfish purposes. He had discussed this with Alfred, as he now discussed almost every move with him, finding Alfred's knowledge and advice invaluable, and they had both agreed that this was the best approach. When Martin did finally break the news to him, Siebert reacted with pleased surprise.

"A wise move, Martin, a very wise, profitable move," he congratulated him. "I wasn't sure how you felt about such matters or I would have proposed it myself."

"Goes to show how wrong you can be about a man," Martin said platitudinously, with a pleasant smile that somehow wrought it into a statement of significance.

"When your application is approved, I'll get you the best workers in the camp," Siebert said.

"Thank you, I appreciate that, Ernst. What I need are experienced, skilled workers."

"You'll get the very best I have," Siebert promised grandly.

It was hard to believe that this man, who could be so cordial and accommodating, was the assistant commander of a death camp. Again and again Martin had to remind himself of that fact. The paradox gave him a distressing jolt every time, though no one would have guessed it looking at his smiling, imperturbably genial face.

Yes, Direktor Hammerschmidt was learning to be quite an actor!

◆ ◆ ◆

Once Martin had informed Siebert, their relationship underwent a further change. Martin had been afraid that the news would give Siebert license to feel in charge, with consequent arrogations of superiority and power. But quite the opposite happened. Siebert saw in Martin's efforts to establish a satellite camp a legitimization of his own position, a certification that they were now brothers-in-arms, with the result that he began to treat him with a certain familiarity and even confidentiality, as befitting partners and colleagues, dropping some of the reserve and secrecy that he had hitherto maintained in matters pertaining to the camp.

It was at this time that Martin expressed a desire to visit the camp. He didn't press the matter, doubting that Siebert would allow it, but to his surprise Siebert readily consented, which showed Martin to what extent Siebert now considered him a partner from whom things no longer needed to be hidden.

For Martin the experience was a wrenching one. He had thought that Alfred's stories had prepared him for the realities of the camp. But that column of silent, skeletal men trudging by apathetically in utter exhaustion, supporting wounded comrades and followed by a cart on which were piled the dead—that silent, hopeless procession was shattering and continued to haunt Martin.

He had entered the camp with a desire to help. He came away from it with an unbreakable determination to do everything in his power to aid these brutalized human beings, be the price in risk and money ever so high.

♦ ◆ ♦

Although Martin had not told Helen about Alfred, there was no way of keeping the *Aussenlager* project secret. He therefore decided to initiate her slowly, before the project actually materialized.

The first difficulty cropped up when he wanted to invite Siebert for dinner.

"You told me he's the Assistant Commandant of Buchenwald," Helen objected. "Why would you want to associate so closely with a man like that? Isn't it enough that he's in your music group?"

"I have my reasons, Helen. Will you bear with me, please?"

"Why can't you tell me your reasons?"

"I will—in time. I promise, love."

So Helen had acquiesced gracefully enough; certainly Siebert never picked up any antagonism because Helen, unsophisticated as she was in certain respects, was gracious and sophisticated in social matters.

But when Martin tried to speak to her about conditions in the camp, Helen cut him short.

"Don't talk about such things, Martin. It's too horrible. Besides, I don't believe that it can be true."

"I assure you it's true, Helen. In fact, it's worse."

"Then I don't want to hear it."

"Please, Helen," he finally said to her one day. "I need to talk about these things. I know it upsets you, but I must have someone to talk to."

He knew that if he put it in this personal way of needing her help, she was more likely to respond.

"But they only upset you too, *Liebchen*," she replied. "Why talk about such horrible things?"

"Because something needs to be done."

"Done," she said nonplussed. "There's nothing you can do."

He dropped the subject then. Only to take it up again another day.

"I've been thinking, Helen. Maybe something can be done."

"Something subversive, Martin?" Helen asked apprehensively.

He laughed. "No. It has the blessing of SS chief Himmler himself!"

"It has?" she said suspiciously. "What is it?"

"I can have some KZ prisoners assigned to my factory as workers."

"But then you—you run a concentration camp yourself!" she exclaimed. "How do you help by doing that?"

"I wouldn't run it like a concentration camp. That's precisely the point."

"I don't understand."

He explained it briefly. Then the subject was dropped. But next day Helen herself came back to it.

"Have you already done anything to establish this—this camp, Martin?"

Then finally he took the plunge.

"Yes, Helen."

She remained silent. He could see that she was hurt and struggling with emotions.

"I haven't told you until now because I didn't want to upset you," he said.

"So that's why you've been making up to Siebert," she mumbled.

"Yes."

He leaned toward her.

"Love," he said insistently. "I realize you're upset about this—and might spend some sleepless nights—as I will too—but what I've learned about these camps is so ghastly that I'd despise myself for the rest of my life if I didn't try to do what I can for these people." He took her hand in his. "Ordinarily there isn't anything I wouldn't do for you—you know that—but in this case, please don't ask me to change my mind."

Helen sat silently for a long time, biting her lips as she struggled with her feelings. Finally she said under her breath:

"All right, I won't ask you to change your mind, Martin. But will you promise me something?"

"I'll try."

"Let me know what you do in the future. I'd rather know. Don't keep me in the dark again."

"All right, I promise. Thank you, love."

◆ ◆ ◆

Spring came and still Martin's application was lost somewhere in the bureaucratic maze, with no prisoners in sight, though the old factory building had been cleared of civilian workers and the barbed wire fence had been installed, complete with watchtowers at every corner, which silently dominated the scene.

As it turned out, the pivotal *Obersturmbannführer* was less pivotal than he had made himself out to be for the sake of extracting the greatest possible bribe. After remonstrating with him again and again, Martin finally decided to take matters into his own hands by using his own contacts. Through them he found out that his application had successfully cleared almost all the necessary agencies but had got stuck in an office of the SS that had nothing directly to do with the concentration camps but worked in conjunction with the High Command of the Armed Forces to ensure an uninterrupted flow of war production. Martin was advised that the best approach would be to request a personal interview with the SS general in charge, a certain SS *Gruppenführer* (Major General) Werner Strapp, an appointment Martin was able to get in short order through another contact.

It was a pleasant day in late April when Martin set out for Berlin. In the past he had loved the capital and had spent much leisure time there before his marriage in the company of a woman he had almost married. But for many years now, the city no longer held much attraction for him, least of all now, with its gutted buildings and depressed air. Martin was surprised at the extent of the bomb damage, which the official news always steeply minimized. The devastation was enormous.

He had to wait awhile before *Gruppenführer* Strapp was ready to see him. When he was finally admitted, he was surprised by the robust virility of the man whom he had expected, for some reason, to be much older. Strapp received him coolly, with a perfunctory Heil Hitler salute, and waved him to a chair in a manner suggesting that introductory small talk was neither necessary nor appreciated. In his countless dealings with all manner of officials, Martin had developed a very fine sixth sense for things of this sort so that he came straight to the point.

"I have come to see you, *Herr Gruppenführer*, about my application to establish a satellite camp in my factory, the *Hammerschmidt Schuhwerke*."

He paused briefly to evaluate whatever response Strapp might make but detected none, though he found Strapp's eyes to be open and straightforward, so that he continued:

"I'm told that the application has been approved by"—here he rattled off a number of agencies, more to impress Strapp than because it was essential, careful to throw no blame on Strapp's own office —"a process that has taken some time, as you can imagine, so the *Gruppenführer* will appreciate that I'm anxious to bring the matter to a successful conclusion as I'm under daily pressure to increase my production for the Armed Forces. I was therefore advised to take the matter up directly with the *Herr Gruppenführer*, because he's no doubt unaware that my application has for some reason not cleared his office." Martin smiled ingratiatingly.

"I'm perfectly aware of it, Herr Hammerschmidt," Strapp replied bluntly.

"I see," Martin muttered, taken aback.

"In fact," Strapp continued, opening a lower drawer and taking out a neat folder, which he dropped on the desk, "it's been sitting right here in my desk."

The man's directness momentarily threw Martin off balance. Finally he said: "May I ask why?"

"Yes. Because I'm not convinced of the merits of the application."

"Once again, may I ask why?" Martin asked politely. The man's straightforwardness was beginning to relax him. He was used to the delicate, circuitous maneuverings of bureaucrats but found straightforward people actually much easier to deal with. "Does the *Herr Gruppenführer* doubt my credentials or my ability to turn out a high-quality product?"

"Not at all," Strapp said matter-of-factly. " I merely doubt that you can turn out a high-quality product with the kind of labor you're requesting."

It was amazing. The man appeared to be questioning the very forced labor system that he, as an SS general, would have been expected to uphold.

"I'm sure the SS Main Administrative and Economic Office wouldn't offer the labor if it couldn't perform adequately," Martin hazarded. "It is supposed to be skilled labor."

"I'm here to pass on the product, Herr Hammerschmidt, not the labor. I know the gentlemen at the Main Administrative and Economic Office believe in the quality of their labor."

Martin was silent. The man was obviously powerful enough, and independent enough, to countermand the Main Administrative and Economic Office. Another approach was needed.

"*Herr Gruppenführer*, as a manufacturer I would say the product depends on how one treats one's labor," Martin said straightforwardly.

"Precisely," Strapp agreed with unexpected emphasis. "Even skilled labor needs the right environment."

"That's something one can create."

Strapp leaned back. Martin sensed that those critical eyes were evaluating him.

"And what kind of an environment are you planning to create, Herr Hammerschmidt?"

"An environment conducive to good production, *Herr Gruppenführer*," Martin said carefully. Was the man trying to trap him?

"Just so, Herr Hammerschmidt. But what does that mean?"

"Appropriate working conditions."

"Meaning—?"

"Well," Martin hazarded. "I haven't yet managed to get good work out of empty stomachs."

"Or out of mistreated people . . . !?"

Strapp's tone hovered between a statement and a question. Martin wasn't sure.

"Or mistreated people," he agreed.

Both men fell silent. Strapp's objection seemed to center on the one thing Martin hadn't expected, namely, that good quality products couldn't be turned out by a devastated labor force. He suddenly had a wild fantasy that Strapp was objecting to the whole way concentration camp labor was being utilized and treated.

Suddenly Strapp let out a laugh. It was a loud, disarming guffaw that instantly broke through the charged atmosphere in the room.

"If I didn't know how lucrative this sort of thing is for you industrialists," he exclaimed, "I'd almost think you were requesting these prisoners to fatten up the wretches!"

"God forbid!" Martin replied in the same light vein. "My sole concern, like the *Gruppenführer's*, is a good product!"

Again Strapp laughed. The atmosphere in the room had suddenly become transformed from one of confrontation to almost one of joviality. An outsider would have thought that the two men had known each other for some time, so relaxed did both suddenly seem in each other's company. Strapp opened the folder and studied the application for some moments.

"Three hundred twenty-five, eh?" he murmured.

"Yes, *Herr Gruppenführer*."

He sat considering the application for a while. Then he took up a pen and scrawled his signature with a large hand on the top page and affixed a stamp under the signature.

"There you are, Herr Hammerschmidt," he said, handing Martin the application. "Good luck with your KZ labor. I look forward to seeing your vaunted product."

"You won't be disappointed, *Herr Gruppenführer*. Thank you."

Martin got up with a Hitler salute, which Strapp cursorily returned.

"And if you run into any trouble, give a holler," Strapp said as Martin opened the door to leave.

Martin's heart was singing. Not only had he obtained his coveted signature but he had acquired an ally of sorts, though he wasn't sure just how much of an ally. What a strange interview it had been, he reflected on his way home on the train. Behind their harmless, unimpeachable words another conversation had taken place—the real conversation! Had Strapp really objected to the whole concentration camp system or was he merely complaining about the shoddy products that system turned out for the war? Still—the man was likable. He seemed straightforward, almost trustworthy. What was such a man doing in an SS general's uniform? The deeper one penetrated, the more confusing and paradoxical human nature became. The saint was forever lurking in the shadow of the beast . . . .

One stamp was still needed to secure final approval but that turned out to be a mere formality. Within a week, in early May 1944, Martin finally had his concentration camp!

◆ ◆ ◆

Matters now shifted back to the local level, as the actual process of obtaining the workers got under way. But if Martin had thought that three hundred twenty-five skilled workers would materialize on the morning after he obtained his final approval, he was grossly mistaken. Nor was Siebert's involvement quite what he had expected it to be.

"I'm trying to get you the best workers, Martin," Siebert said to excuse the delay. "That takes a little time. You want the best, don't you?"

When Martin discussed the matter with Alfred, Alfred said:

"Martin, I think you ought to be prepared for a surprise."

"What kind of a surprise?"

"That you won't get all the skilled workers you want."

"What do you mean?" Martin exclaimed. "I'm paying the SS for skilled labor."

Alfred had himself worked in the Orderly Room assembling slates of prisoners scheduled for shipment elsewhere. So he was well acquainted with the process that he now explained to Martin.

"You see, Martin, whenever a slate of prisoners has to be put together, an enormous amount of jockeying begins, for everyone wants to get on a good list and off a death list. As I told you before, there is a prisoner infrastructure in the camp, composed of prisoners occupying powerful positions, like work foremen, block chiefs, hospital orderlies, and the like. It's those powerful prisoners who start putting pressure on the Orderly Room clerks who are putting the list together. So in a way it's those powerful prisoners who actually put the list together—and they go by considerations that have nothing to do with experience on machines and the like. The SS Labor Officer *thinks* he's putting the list together, and Siebert *thinks* he's getting you the most skilled workers, but in reality—do you see how it works? Within limits, of course. The Labor Officer and Siebert can, if they wish, add or delete any name they want."

As so often, Martin was struck by Alfred's matter-of-fact analysis. It was as if he were dissecting some impersonal company organization.

"I understand," Martin said, "but why would a hospital orderly, for instance, want to get someone on my list?"

Alfred let out a soft sigh.

"Martin, everyone has friends or enemies or favors to repay or favors to bank for the future! Just because it's a death camp do you think human interactions stop? On the contrary. Because it's a question literally of life and death—you have no idea how much jockeying and intrigue goes on! I wish I could add some names myself," he added after a moment.

"Give me their names," Martin exclaimed impulsively. "I'll try to . . . ."

But he stopped in midsentence as he realized the impossibility of what he was saying.

It was a strange, deadly world!

Actually, it was Martin's impatience that made the wait seem so long, because in reality it took only two and a half weeks before he received his labor contingent. But after the arduous five month wait, it seemed almost the longest wait of all.

◆ ◆ ◆

Martin and Alfred spent much time discussing how to receive the prisoners. Martin harbored fantasies of welcoming them with a little speech. Yes, they would be expected to work here, he would say to them, but their persons would be respected; there would be no brutalities, no harsh, unjust punishments; they would be fed and clothed well, he would see to that.

Alfred sank into an unbelieving silence.

"Martin," he groaned with quiet exasperation when Martin had finished. "You can't mean it."

"Of course I mean it. I mean every word of it."

"I know you do. But don't *say* it! You think KZ prisoners still listen to speeches? Do you know what it says over the main gate when you enter Dachau? LABOR MAKES FREE! And at Buchenwald: RIGHT OR WRONG—MY COUNTRY! KZ prisoners are way beyond words. Only actions count with them. But you know who will listen? The SS will listen. You're laying out your whole plan and tipping them off. A good general doesn't do that. Do you think they'll let do-gooder Direktor Hammer-schmidt undermine their whole system? Just because your *Aussenlager* was approved doesn't mean it can't be taken away from you. Don't destroy the whole thing before you've even got started, Martin. You've got to ease into it slowly. You've got to seem to be playing ball with the SS. You've got to educate the guards gradually or you'll blow the whole thing."

In the end, as usual, Martin deferred to Alfred's superior judgment and agreed to give merely a brief, blunt speech, designed only to introduce himself. That much he insisted on.

◆ ◆ ◆

The prisoners arrived in the early morning hours of a Thursday, an hour Martin had specifically requested so that the arrival would not be witnessed by the bulk of his civilian workforce, although his workers had been informed of the project, of course. The news had occasioned some raised eyebrows and some surreptitious questions, but Martin's reputation was so good among his workers that few seriously questioned what he was doing. "The *Herr Direktor* must know" was the general consensus. He enjoyed that much trust.

The prisoners arrived in six trucks into which they had been herded so tightly that they had trouble breathing, let alone moving. A few had simply been thrown on top of the others for lack of space and lay uneasily on the heads and shoulders of their fellow prisoners. For Martin, who watched the whole scene from an upper window of the factory, it was a harrowing sight, this immovable cargo of hollow-eyed men with shaven heads in striped uniforms who stood squashed together without motion, only their eyes alive with misery and fear. It looked like some hideous, frozen tableau that etched itself deeply into his memory, this moment of stillness, frozen and yet vibrating, immobile and yet immeasurably alive.

Then the stillness was broken by the whistles and shrill shouts of the SS guards who swarmed around the trucks as the prisoners tumbled to the ground, urged on by curses, kicks, and blows until they were lined up in four long rows for roll call, faced by the contingent of SS guards who surrounded them with guns at the ready as if they were mutinous criminals, while four SS men, one to each row, began to read off the long list of names.

Martin watched it all, standing by the window, pale and agitated, feeling an urge to run down to intervene but knowing that that was the last thing he could do, his heart beating tensely as he realized that as of this moment he was assuming responsibility for three hundred twenty-five lives.

◆ ◆ ◆

Alfred was right: Within days Martin discovered that in his vaunted contingent of skilled workmen, there were at best four dozen who had any experience at all on any kind of machine!

The shock was a rude one for Martin, for at this point he was still focused on production. He wanted to help, yes, but the help was to take place within the framework of decent production—production, not profits. He relished profits, of course, but profits were, in the end, by-products of decent, honorable, durable, high-quality production, not the other way around. He had never put high-quality production in second place to anything, and he wasn't about to do so now.

When he discovered the true state of affairs, his first impulse was to confront Siebert and demand that the unskilled men be returned in exchange for skilled workers. He had a right to skilled workers! He was paying for them!

As usual, he discussed the problem with Alfred.

"You can do that," Alfred agreed. "You can go to Siebert and he'll take back those men—maybe. But I don't think you'll get much better ones."

"But I can't turn out decent boots with unskilled labor!" Martin exclaimed. "Not to mention that I'm paying the SS for skilled, not unskilled labor."

"Martin," Alfred said softly, "what you are paying for and what you are likely to get are two entirely—repeat: entirely—different things."

"What do you mean?"

"How many skilled shoe factory workers do you think there are in the whole of Buchenwald?"

"They don't have to be skilled in shoe manufacture. Just some experience working with machines."

Alfred shook his head. "You're not getting the point, Martin. They're skilled *because* they're on that list—not the other way around."

"I don't get your point."

"If I had all the skills I claimed I had . . . . In the end, Martin, you'll have to decide between production—and saving lives."

"I thought the two could go hand in hand," Martin muttered.

Martin struggled with it awhile longer, but in the end decided not to contest the selection. Decisive was Alfred's point that the prisoners he was likely to get in exchange would probably be no more skilled than the ones he had, but some of his credit with Siebert would be exhausted, and he needed Siebert for other occasions.

Instead, being a man of action, Martin decided to embark on a training program for the prisoners, using both the few skilled prisoners on hand

and civilian workers that he transferred from his factory. He was happy to see that the prisoners were eager and picked up fast, no doubt driven by fear that they would be returned to the main camp. For even by then they had begun to realize that this was a desirable *Aussenlager* where a prisoner had a chance to survive.

◆ ◆ ◆

Soon trouble of another kind surfaced, trouble that threatened the very core of Martin's whole venture.

The SS men who had arrived with the prisoners guarded the compound around the clock, of course, mostly from the watchtowers outside and from a guard house by the main gate. But some SS men were also stationed on the two floors inside the factory.

This took Martin completely by surprise, for he had expected sole authority over the prisoners inside the factory. The SS guards, on the contrary, took it for granted that they were solely in charge both inside and outside the factory, meaning that they could at any time push aside the foremen who were actually in charge of the work.

When Martin learned of this arrangement, he expected trouble at once. It was not long in coming. The first incident happened the very day after the prisoners' arrival when a prisoner, intent on listening to a foreman's instructions, unwittingly blocked an aisle down which an SS man was sauntering, whereupon the guard placed his boot against the backside of the prisoner and gave him such a violent shove against a machine, bellowing, *"Platz machen, Judenschwein!"* (Out of the way, Jewish pig!), that the man's face was gashed and bleeding and two front teeth were knocked out. This not being enough, the SS man ordered the prisoner to stand for three hours at attention facing the wall.

"I tried to tell him that he was making us lose three hours of work, *Herr Direktor*," the civilian foreman reported to Martin, "but he just laughed in my face and walked away."

Soon other foremen came with similar complaints. What was more, such incidents multiplied and were getting more and more out of hand as the SS men settled into their new surroundings. Clearly the guards considered the factory their hunting ground, just as they had back in camp, so that something needed to be done.

The logical first step was to take the matter up with the officer-in-charge. This was an *Untersturmführer* (Second Lieutenant) by the name of Haber, a red-haired, freckled young man who wore a perpetual slight sneer on his face that seemed to Martin to have eclipsed all his other facial expressions.

Martin presented the case to him, as he had learned to do, not in the name of any humanitarian motive but solely from the point of view that such treatment of the prisoners interfered with production and thus with the war effort. The beauty of this approach was that it camouflaged his own feelings completely, for it enabled him to harangue the most fanatical Nazi about the need to speed up production for the sake of the patriotic war effort in order to bring the New Order sooner into its power and glory. Heil Hitler!

To his surprise, Haber brushed this argument aside as if it didn't interest him in the least.

"The *Herr Direktor* seems to worry a lot about the welfare of Jews and Commies," he drawled with an insolent smile.

"I'm worried about production, Haber."

"*Untersturmführer* Haber," the officer corrected him. "That's very admirable, *Herr Direktor*," Haber went on, "but it's Jews and Commies who're doing the producing, isn't it?"

"I don't see what Jews and Commies have to do with it," Martin said curtly. "I'm worried about war production."

"G-o-o-d," Haber drawled with an insolent smile, "because that's what I'm here for, *Herr Direktor*, to see that war production proceeds efficiently."

"It will proceed efficiently if you keep your men from interfering."

"I wouldn't call it interfering, *Herr Direktor*. I'd call it helping it along. You don't know this scum as I do. If you don't prod these swine, they won't lift a finger."

"The swine happen to be human beings!" Martin snapped.

But he regretted it at once because Haber's smile deepened into a triumphant leer.

"So the *Herr Direktor is* worried about the Jews and Commies."

"*Herr Untersturmführer*, I'm a manufacturer engaged in high-priority war production. I won't tolerate interference with production. Nor will Assistant Commandant Siebert, I'm sure."

He got up and walked to the door.

"No need to get upset, *Herr Direktor*," Haber drawled after him. "We're both good Germans trying to do our best for the *Vaterland*, aren't we?"

Martin had spoken forcefully but to his own ears his words had sounded curiously hollow and impotent. Adept and self-assured as Martin was, men like Haber were difficult for him to deal with because they possessed a spurious, destructive kind of intelligence that was bent not on promoting meaningful communication but on obstructing and confusing it.

As usual, Martin discussed the matter with Alfred, but while they were still debating the pros and cons of confrontation versus further patience, an incident occurred that brought the issue to a head.

For some minor infraction—or possibly none at all, Martin wasn't sure—an SS guard tied a prisoner's hands behind his back and hoisted him up by his wrists on the crane of a machine. It was, as he later learned from Alfred, a favorite SS punishment that dislocated arms and shoulders and brought on excruciating pains. By the time Martin learned of it—he had been in town on business—the man had been hanging suspended for almost two hours, moaning and every now and then letting out a piercing scream, to the amusement of the SS men in the building as well as their comrades outside who came in from time to time to see "the Jew croaking."

On learning of it, Martin at once proceeded to Haber and demanded that the man be put down. Haber acted as if he didn't know about it but clearly did, and, after alluding disparagingly to Jew- and Commie-lovers, without naming Martin directly, refused point blank to intervene, whereupon Martin went to the factory and, without further ado, personally lowered the man to the floor where he collapsed with limp arms that looked broken.

By evening there wasn't a prisoner in that factory who didn't know what the *Herr Direktor* had done.

◆ ◆ ◆

Next morning, without further consulting Alfred, the first time Martin proceeded completely on his own because he felt that here his whole project was hanging in the balance—he had spent a good part of the night restlessly considering it—he phoned Siebert and requested a meeting at once, preferably in his, Martin's, office. Siebert readily consented, happy as always to get away from the camp.

It was past four o'clock by the time Siebert arrived in Martin's spacious, elegantly appointed office. Martin took out a bottle of brandy along with a fine assortment of cheeses and crackers (by then a rarity in Germany), poured Siebert and himself a strong drink, and jovially clinked glasses but himself took only a sip. After spending some time exchanging pleasantries to permit the brandy to settle in, he came to the point.

"I've requested this meeting, Ernst, because we must settle a funda-mental question."

"Oh?" Siebert said, taking a long sip as he munched on a cracker and cheese.

Martin had carefully planned his approach in such a way as to minimize Siebert's ability to give anything but the "right" answers.

"Let me ask you a question, Ernst. Who is in charge of production?"

"You are, of course."

"If I'm in charge of production—which I was sure you would agree I am—then it must follow that I must have authority in the factory to order the prisoners about as I see fit. Right?"

"Are the prisoners giving you any trouble?" Siebert asked solicitously.

"Would you agree with that?" Martin persisted, brushing aside Siebert's question.

"Of course, you have the authority," Siebert said with a touch of impatience. "You just let my men know who is giving you trouble and they'll take care of it."

"It's not the prisoners who are giving me trouble, Ernst," Martin now said with slow deliberation. "It's your men who are interfering with production."

Siebert was silent while Martin refilled his glass, which he had almost drained. His ready outrage at the prisoners collapsed, and he became suspicious instead.

"My men are interfering with production?" he repeated. "How?"

"In many ways. Prisoners have been made to stand facing the wall for hours, they've been made to run up and down the aisles or ordered to do knee-bends, they've been beaten and knocked around and even punched unconscious. I can't count the number of times the guards have seriously interfered with production."

"I'll speak to Haber about it," Siebert said evasively.

"But yesterday knocked the bottom out of the barrel," Martin continued. "A prisoner was strung up by his arms for over two hours, severely dislocating his arms and shoulders. I'll be lucky if I can get work out of the man in a month!" Martin's voice waxed louder with righteous indignation. "What am I paying the SS good money for, Ernst? To have a bunch of cripples on my hands? Not to mention that you sent me a bunch of unskilled workers when I specifically requested, and am paying for, skilled labor?" He paused to let his words sink in. "Did I go through six months of waiting and getting approval upon approval—" and here he rattled off all the sundry high officials and offices his application had traversed—"only to have a bunch of unpatriotic morons sabotage the war effort by interfering with my production for the Armed Forces?" he exclaimed with well-acted outrage. "If this continues, I'll have to take it up with Oranienburg!"

Siebert looked sheepish. "Hold it, hold it, Martin," he said uneasily. "No one is sabotaging the war effort. Why do you think I came at once to straighten matters out?"

"I'm glad to hear that," Martin said, calming down as if pacified.

Siebert was clearly uncomfortable and was casting about for a way out.

"Have you taken the matter up with Haber?" he inquired.

"Have I ever!" Martin exclaimed with renewed vigor as if he had only been waiting for the question (which he had). "He wouldn't lift a finger!"

"He wouldn't?"

"He accused me of being a Jew- and Commie-lover and laughed in my face. Can you imagine? The insolence! He's the worst of the bunch, Ernst."

Siebert fell silent, seeing that avenue of escape blocked. He looked Martin in the eye with an appraising, suspicious look.

"What do you want, Martin?"

"Give me an officer I can work with."

"Meaning what?"

"Meaning that he respects the factory as my responsibility and doesn't interfere with production."

"And who's going to keep lazy prisoners in line?"

"It's me who suffers if they don't work. I'll take care of them."

Siebert sat considering.

"All right, Martin," he said finally. "We'll replace Haber."

"Thank you, Ernst. When?"

A slight smile came to Siebert's lips.

"Is tomorrow soon enough?"

"Excellent."

Martin hadn't expected it to be that easy. He was tempted to take advantage of the moment to request that guards be withdrawn altogether from inside the factory building but then decided to leave well enough alone. That could be tackled another time.

"Well, now that that's taken care of," Siebert said with obvious relief, "how about another drink?"

"By all means," Martin said, generously refilling his glass.

Siebert took a big gulp.

"You sure have good stuff," he commented, rolling the brandy appreciatively around his tongue. "You're sure you're manufacturing shoes and not brandy?" he said with a twinkle in his eyes.

"Wouldn't you like to know!" Martin laughed. "But there's plenty more where that came from," he said meaningfully.

He got up, went to a cupboard, and returned with a bottle.

"Here's one for the road."

Siebert's face lit up.

"Now you're talkin', Martin. That's better than hassling over a bunch of filthy Jews and Commies, isn't it?"

"Isn't it ever!" Martin laughed, clinking glasses.

♦ ◆ ♦

Siebert was true to his word. Haber disappeared without a trace next day, although it was three days before his replacement arrived, a boyish-looking *Untersturmführer* by the name of Julius Ritter. From the moment Martin laid eyes on him, he felt that he could work with Ritter, presumably on orders from Siebert as well. His impression was further reinforced when Ritter came to introduce himself, which Haber would never have done.

Auspicious as this was, Martin had nevertheless decided to proceed differently this time. He had learned something from Haber and wasn't going to take any more chances. He would groom Ritter so that he could deal with him directly in day to day matters, using a carrot-and-stick approach.

He chose a trifling, easily resolvable incident as an opportunity to invite Ritter to his office, choosing a late afternoon hour to further facilitate matters. When Ritter arrived, respectful and obviously awed by Martin's spacious, elegant office, Martin broke out his most affable and gracious manner, along with his ubiquitous bottle of brandy and his assortment of cheeses, all of which further impressed and flattered the young officer.

The difficulty was quickly resolved, as Martin had expected—Martin purposely yielding a little more than would have been necessary to make Ritter feel important—after which Martin smoothly embroiled the young man in a discussion of his life, where he came from, his career in the SS, etc. Ritter happily obliged, sped on his way by the unaccustomed liquor and the interested, august audience, obviously flattered to have gained the *Herr Direktor's* personal attention.

Finally Martin worked the conversation around to the issues that had made him arrange the meeting. The carrot was simple: Life can be soft here, where this comes from—"have another piece of cheese, Julius, and another drink"—there is lots more, you leave me alone and I'll leave you alone and that goes for all your men, too—they can do what they want as long as they stay outside the factory. I'm interested in production and profits, Julius (he winked at the *Untersturmführer*). We've got a war to win, haven't we? How can these noble purposes be achieved if your men are hell-bent on breaking my workers?

The stick was even simpler: I'll have you transferred out of here if you don't play ball! Remember Haber? The trick was to say that clearly and yet gently enough not to get Ritter's dander up. But the *Herr Direktor* was a past master at this sort of thing.

Are you following me, Julius? Have you got it?

The *Untersturmführer* got it, of that Martin was sure. He would see to it that his men withdrew from the factory and did not interfere with production. Of course, if there was ever any trouble with the trash —

"The trash?" Martin repeated, bemused, wondering how garbage had suddenly crept into their conversation.

"The prisoners, *Herr Direktor*."

"Ah, yes, of course."

Perhaps the *Herr Direktor* hadn't yet come to know the prisoners as he had for two years now, in Treblinka before coming to Buchenwald and in Bergen-Belsen before that, if ever there was any trouble, one holler and his men would come rushing in to help—

"Ah, that's comforting to know," Martin sighed with well-acted relief.

Yes, the *Untersturmführer* got it. He wasn't a dumb kid, just impressionable and gullible. Educable, in Alfred's words.

After accompanying him to the door, where *Untersturmführer* Ritter came to a smart, heartfelt Hitler salute, Martin sank exhausted into one of his leather armchairs, staring for a long time out of the window.

Yes, Martin was beginning to learn. He was learning to become tricky and devious, something he had never before been in his life. It wasn't easy, but then it was in the service of a greater cause.

◆ ◆ ◆

Untersturmführer Ritter withdrew his guards from both factory floors the very next day, stationing only one guard inside the building by the main entrance while another guard was posted just outside the entrance. In this fashion, Ritter proudly explained, if there was ever any trouble, the man inside would become immediately available to help the *Herr Direktor* while the outside man would call for help from the guards outside.

"Well thought out," the *Herr Direktor* said admiringly. "A strategy worthy of a general."

Ritter laughed, pleased.

It was at this point—informing Alfred but not asking him for his approval—that Martin called the prisoners together for a little speech. It was the welcoming speech he had wanted to give and hadn't given, telling the prisoners that their persons would be respected here, that there would be no further brutalities if he could help it, that they would be fed and clothed and would have a chance to come out alive in return for their work.

It was a brief speech, heartfelt yet unsentimental because Martin was not a sentimental man. And of course, though no SS men were present—the ground floor prisoners had been called up to the second floor—he had to be somewhat circumspect all the same.

But the prisoners understood. Now they listened and understood. What is more—now they believed him.

The Showdown

Johann did not regain consciousness until the following day. He had been placed in a dark corner of the receiving room where he was almost forgotten, although Dr. Birnbaum, the chief prisoner-doctor, did pass by once or twice that day, mostly just to see whether Johann was still breathing. Everything depended on whether blood vessels had been ruptured in the head, resulting in internal bleeding.

The truth was that little could have been done for Johann even in a well-equipped hospital. In the camp hospital where there was hardly any equipment and barely any medication except aspirins (and even these were in pitifully short supply and were doled out to those most likely to survive), almost nothing could be done except to wait.

When Johann regained consciousness, he was dazed and confused and showed some slurring of speech and other stroke symptoms. Above all, he complained of an agonizing headache.

"Those are all symptoms from the blow on your head," Dr. Birnbaum assured him. "They'll probably pass."

Dr. Birnbaum did not tell him that it was far too early to tell whether or not any permanent damage had been done. For the moment, he promoted Johann to the aspirin list, which meant that Johann received two and sometimes three aspirins a day, which hardly touched his headache.

Johann himself was amnesic. He could remember nothing about the blow on his head or the week or two preceding it. What Johann remembered mostly were snatches of hallucination that Dr. Birnbaum ascribed to the traumatic shock to his head. But Johann saw in them deeper meanings, though he could not clearly piece them together or explain them. Only their spirit remained with him, a peaceful spirit resonating with an air of transcendent serenity that was at odd variance with the reality of his situation.

Despite his symptoms, despite his weakened condition, despite even his headaches—or was it because of all of these?—Johann now experienced some days of profound peace. Merely to be allowed to lie undisturbed all day in his dark corner, to be able to sink into the vast

silent space of his inner world where all the turbulence of his surroundings and of his own body reached him distantly like the far-off flappings
of impersonal wings—what a luxury! what a blessing!

As the days wore on and Johann's memory began to return, he
remembered Benjamin's death and his subsequent guilt for not having
intervened. Why had he struggled so? Lying here in this lucid, peaceful
darkness everything seemed suddenly so clear. Yes, he was his brother's
keeper! He was because all men were interconnected fragments of a
greater whole, a greater consciousness. It wasn't a matter of choice. It
was a fact that one ignored only at one's emotional and spiritual peril.
Life wasn't worth living if one trampled one's impulse toward love
underfoot and violated one's desire to help others.

Everything seemed suddenly so clear. Even death. Death was not
hard. Having just brushed against it, it seemed to Johann more like a
trusted friend, a reliable accomplice, an infallible ally of last resort to
whom he could always turn and be welcome, the final boon that no one
could take from him. What mattered wasn't death or the fear of death,
but living—and helping. It wasn't enough merely to be a victim, to suffer
with and *alongside*, as he had imagined. One needed to stand up and be
counted. Stripped down to apathy and indifference as the concentration
camp world was, it yet presented for that very reason countless
opportunities for service to others because even the smallest acts of
kindness loomed large in this shriveled, shrunken, brutal world.

Yes, Johann suddenly saw it all so clearly. To choose one's attitude!
That was the great liberating insight that he had achieved. They said
that hope sustained man. But when one penetrated further, it turned
out that hope also shackled man to his expectations and thus to his fears,
to his fear of death, in particular. What was needed was acceptance and
surrender. Living as he did in a totally unpredictable world, there was
nothing to do but to let go, to surrender, to give up any semblance of
trying to control this unstable, chaotic world. And when he reflected
further on this, he realized that this was really not so very different from
the overall human condition: For man was forever trying to control the
great mystery of life and death that was carrying him along, instead of
surrendering into it.

Acceptance and surrender. These were the final inalienable freedoms
of man. To accept and surrender with faith—or at least with grace—or,
if need be, even rebelliously. But to accept and surrender—to one's fears
and hunger, one's weakness and compassion, one's humanity . . . .

Thus it was that Johann achieved in this pit of human degradation and moral collapse—in the very midst of hell—a deep faith and an uncommon degree of spiritualization.

◆ ◆ ◆

A hospital in a concentration camp! The whole idea was an insult, a vicious anachronism, to provide a place for the care and cure of lives in an environment where a prisoner's life could daily be snuffed out in countless casual ways without anyone being accountable or paying the slightest attention, not to mention the lack of proper equipment, sanitary facilities and even simple medicines and bandages. Yet even extermination camps like Auschwitz, where thousands of healthy people were daily being gassed to death, maintained a hospital and even a quarantine camp to keep prisoners with infectious diseases segregated.

These were the maddening contradictions in the Nazi system, with its pretense of legality. Just as physical punishments were supposed to receive prior approval from headquarters in Berlin-Oranienburg, and each concentration camp kept a *Totenbuch*, a death register, where deaths were duly recorded, if not their true cause.

The location of the hospital barracks, which was set somewhat apart from the rest of the camp, was symptomatic of the whole charade. There was only one gravel walkway, which was reserved for SS personnel, while the prisoners had to wade at times through ankle-deep mud and over fallen branches and logs to get to the hospital. Once there, they had to stand outside in long queues until admitted to the building proper where they had to remove their clothes and shoes and wait in the unheated, drafty hallways, often for hours, before finally being seen by the prisoner medical staff who might in turn refer them to the SS Medical Officer in charge. The whole procedure was a trying gauntlet designed to discourage prisoners from going on sick call at all.

In fact, many knowledgeable prisoners refused to go on sick call for any reason whatever because there was always the danger, unknown to most prisoners, that the very SS medical personnel they were turning to for help might greet them with a poisoned syringe and dispatch them forthwith. It was a method resorted to unpredictably, like most things in the camps, when it was felt that too many prisoners were shirking labor and/or that the hospital was in need of empty "beds" (bunks with straw mattresses). Within the hospital itself, moreover, there was a room—Room # 7, containing ten beds—where patients were kept who were to be liquidated before they were transferred to the operating room where they met their death. This room was often "restocked" several times a week. Yet another hazard was to be singled out for one of the medical experiments that were being conducted in another barracks, experiments of an often agonizing nature from which few prisoners emerged alive.

A final anachronism: a TB ward where prisoners with TB were segregated from the rest. It was a ward that was at times used as a place of hiding from the SS—there was a species of underground even in the camp—for it was one place SS personnel shunned for fear of infection. On the other hand, this ward was a favorite target for liquidation so that a hiding prisoner was at the same time in danger of being liquidated precisely because he was there.

Such was the complex, unrelenting world of the Buchenwald "hospital," where the tangled crosscurrents of good and evil were distilled into their purest form: a place where men fought for their lives supported with one hand while the other hand pushed them under.

◆ ◆ ◆

As Johann's headaches and other symptoms subsided and he began to recuperate, he was slowly drawn into the life of the hospital that was dominated, on the prisoner side, by two men: Dr. Birnbaum, the prisoner-doctor who was medically more or less in charge because Dr. Bauer, the SS Chief Medical Officer, was as often as not absent since he loathed his work, not because of any humanitarian motive but because he considered his position an affront to his status as a doctor; and Mondusi, the hospital prisoner-orderly who was, in effect, the hospital administrator because Dr. Bauer was disinterested in administrative matters and left the day-to-day operation of the hospital almost entirely in Mondusi's hands, making him one of the most powerful prisoners in the camp.

Always there were these two powerful hierarchies in the camps: that of the SS and, under it, the hierarchy of the prisoner orderlies and foremen, the Capos, who often wielded as much power as the SS and many of whom were as feared as the SS for their cruelty. For if a prisoner foreman was not zealous enough in performing the SS's dirty work, he could lose not only his job and privileges—a room of his own, enough to eat, and sometimes even a liquor ration—but his very life. It was sufficient motivation to keep most orderlies and Capos in blood-thirsty trim, though there were notable exceptions, such as Mondusi.

Dr. Birnbaum was a middle-aged Jew from Frankfurt who had been a fashionable gynecologist and therefore did not know too much about the rest of the human anatomy, although he dispatched his medical duties conscientiously enough and often complained about the lack of equipment and medication.

"How is one to practice medicine here?" he would exclaim, throwing up his hands.

Dr. Birnbaum prided himself on being a man of learning who loved poetry and peppered his speech with Latin words. Above all, he loved to talk. It was a visceral need, as if he would become dehydrated if he didn't produce a certain amount of verbiage daily. Only in the presence of the SS did he become a monosyllabic, docile yes-man, though he did not go so far as to inform on his fellow prisoners. He had been an ordinary prisoner until his medical qualifications had been recognized as useful. As such his nearly fatal encounters with the SS had left him with the abiding insight that even the lowliest SS man was more powerful than he, *ergo* could rob him of his position and life, *ergo* deserved unquestioning obedience.

"My hands are tied," he would fret defensively. "One murmur of protest and the SS will throw me in with the rest of the prisoners—and who will treat the prisoners then?"

As Johann recuperated, Dr. Birnbaum began to visit him, lingering for a while, although he could not have said exactly why—perhaps it was Johann's calmness that made one come away rejuvenated. He was like a calm island in a turbulent sea, an oasis in the desert—Dr. Birnbaum reached for such similes, waxing poetic. On occasion he even wrote some poetry himself.

One day Dr. Birnbaum was carrying on about his hands being tied, when Mondusi, a man as laconic as Dr. Birnbaum was verbose, said tersely:

"Are your legs tied too, Birnbaum?"

"What do you mean?" Dr. Birnbaum bristled.

"You could stand up on your feet sometime."

The relationship between Mondusi and Dr. Birnbaum was strained. Mondusi was a strong-willed, self-confident, stocky ethnic German from Transylvania who had been a carpenter in civilian life and had come to Austria to work and there had run afoul of the Nazis when he beat up a local Nazi bigwig for pestering his girl friend. He was a natural born leader who would have stood out anywhere but did so especially in this humiliating environment where prisoners slinked about, shrunk in self-esteem as well as physical stature.

Mondusi was a man of great, if practical integrity, at once opportunistic and self-sacrificing in his ruthless commitment to save as many lives as possible, which made him somewhat unpredictable. He probably owed his astounding longevity in the camp to his uncanny ability to balance what was morally right against what was possible. Everything depended on what was good for the greatest number. If administering a poisoned syringe to one prisoner would save the lives of others, he might be seen holding down such a prisoner, giving the SS the impression that he was a docile tool. At other times, he would go to great lengths, at considerable personal risk, to save even a single man.

Mondusi made no secret of the fact that he had no great liking or respect for Dr. Birnbaum, while Dr. Birnbaum, on his side, felt ambivalent toward Mondusi: On one level he looked down on him as a man of limited education, if not intelligence, on another level his deference for the SS had rubbed off on Mondusi in view of his powerful position so that he bowed to his leadership and authority. Thus the polarities of Dr. Birnbaum's character—arrogance versus servility—came into painful conflict over Mondusi, reducing him at times to a rather stalemated position.

◆ ◆ ◆

As Johann began to leave the luxurious tranquillity and security of his bunk, he found himself more and more often helping out with some of the other patients, if only to comfort them. The "nursing staff" consisted of prisoners, almost none of whom had any professional nursing experience. Nor did that matter much since their ministrations were confined mostly to helping patients to the bathroom, washing them, or simply talking to them.

It was at this latter function that Johann excelled. Not that he talked much, for he had never been a talkative man even in civilian life and now spoke even less, but he was able to listen, and the few words he spoke were always full of comfort and encouragement. He was like a calm, receptive pool in which people saw themselves reflected as they wished to be beyond the harsh encrustations of their daily lives.

Mondusi liked Johann and could see how well the sick prisoners responded to him, asking for him and groping for his hand as if the bodily contact transferred some mysterious elixir to them. So the idea came to him one day to keep Johann on the nursing staff, an idea subsequently supported by Dr. Birnbaum. The transfer itself was arranged by Mondusi without difficulty through the Orderly Room.

Johann was now quartered in a small room with two other nursing orderlies. It was a tiny room with narrow bunks and a small window, but Johann had not had a bunk to himself for almost five years, let alone a room shared with only two people. From his bunk he could see a corner of the sky and the tip of some trees. The first night he slept there, he lay awake for hours just looking out of the window.

Johann now threw himself energetically into his new work, aided by rations that for the first time in years alleviated his ever-gnawing hunger and fatigue and slowly returned some strength to his emaciated body as well as some semblance of human appearance.

Thus the summer of 1944 came and went. The Allied invasion of Normandy in June had been successful while the attempt on Hitler's life in July had failed. In July, the American Forces broke out of Normandy and began to race across France, liberating Paris in August. But very little of all that reached the prisoners, and what they heard was grossly distorted by grandiose hopes, on the one hand, and despair on the other, as the news circulated secretly from person to person.

◆ ◆ ◆

When SS *Untersturmführer* Hoffer came into the hospital barracks that morning, his ever present whip dangling by his side, his slim figure looking quite dashing with his polished boots and jaunty cap, certainly in contrast to the patients who looked in their horrible emaciation like a different species altogether—Dr. Bauer, the SS Chief Medical Officer was, as usual, absent.

Although Dr. Bauer made no bones of the fact that he loathed his job —which translated, as far as the prisoners were concerned, into impatience, indifference, and sadism—he obstinately defended his turf and brooked no outside interference in the hospital's affairs, seeing in such interference a further insult to his dignity. As far as Hoffer in particular was concerned, he considered Clackerack a crude, uneducated upstart who should never have been appointed Third Officer-in-Charge, which he let the commandant of Buchenwald know in no uncertain terms when a jurisdictional dispute broke out between them as to whether Hoffer's jurisdiction extended to the hospital. The commandant solved the quarrel by ruling that in principle the hospital was part of the camp compound and thus under Hoffer's overall jurisdiction, but in practice it was to be respected as Dr. Bauer's domain, which both men considered a victory for their position, but which in the end satisfied neither.

The upshot of the dispute was that Hoffer, while not abandoning his forays into the hospital, took pains to choose times when Dr. Bauer was absent, which was not difficult. When he did put in an appearance, he was usually in a foul and belligerent mood, the secret target of his wrath being not so much the patients as to demonstrate to Dr. Bauer that he, Hoffer, was a man of consequence who would not be trifled with, least of all by an arrogant pill-pusher who thought that his university education put him a notch higher than everyone else, for Hoffer's self-esteem, despite his elevation to power, was still at bottom shaky and highly sensitive to arrogations of superiority.

In addition to his whip, from which Hoffer was inseparable, he delighted in a little game that would have been considered childish but for its painful consequences. It consisted of ordering a prisoner to repeat after him, as follows:

Hoffer: Say, I love the *Führer*.

Prisoner: (some reluctantly, most mechanically) I love the *Führer*.

Hoffer: Good! Now say, I love *Untersturmführer* Hoffer.

Prisoner: I love *Untersturmführer* Hoffer.

Hoffer: I love being whipped.

Prisoner: (hesitantly) I love being whipped.

Hoffer: (whipping the prisoner as he roars with coarse laughter) Happy to oblige!

This was the variation when he was in a "happy" mood. When in a foul mood, however, which he was most of the time, he would instead set upon the prisoner with severe lashings, cursing and yelling:

"So you love being whipped! Liar! Filthy swine!"

On one occasion a prisoner tried to get out of the dilemma by denying that he loved being whipped. But this so infuriated Hoffer that he gave the man an especially vicious beating.

No, there was no way out of the dilemma, which was as Hoffer intended it to be.

No one suspected that there was for Hoffer a chord of deadly, if unconscious, seriousness in the game that explained the zest and perseverance with which he played it. For whenever a prisoner repeated *I love Untersturmführer Hoffer*, untruthful and forced as the phrase was, Hoffer experienced a quite irrational sensation of warmth around his heart, sometimes even a disconcerting rush of moisture to his eyes, which certainly no one noticed or could imagine.

The fact was that the drastic change in Hoffer's external status and power, though it gave him an illusion of worth and importance, had not erased his secret sense of inferiority and self-hatred, traceable to the limp that had for years dogged his life. It had merely been driven further underground. Feeding cancerously on itself, it required ever greater excesses of power to reassure Hoffer that he was indeed a man of consequence. No wonder *Untersturmführer* Hoffer had an evil reputation in the camp! Yet for all his unlimited power—much as a man can die of thirst floating on immensities of ocean water—the love and approval that Hoffer so desperately craved became ever more elusive and unobtainable in this environment in which love was the last thing the prisoners would or could ever give.

So when Hoffer appeared in the hospital barracks that morning he was, as usual, in a foul and pugnacious mood. Dr. Birnbaum clicked his heels in military fashion and reported unasked in as military a manner as he could muster:

"Three doctors—nine nursing orderlies—all present and accounted for, *Herr Untersturmführer.*"

Reporting unasked because once, not having been asked, he got a whipping for not having reported. But today Hoffer neither asked for nor was pleased by the doctor's spontaneous report.

"Who asked you, Jewish pig!" he growled.

He then began to saunter slowly along the aisles between the bunks, clacking his whip against his boot as he walked, while Dr. Birnbaum trailed nervously behind him.

Clack—clack.

Silence in the ward. Had it not been too late, all but the unconscious would have marshalled their last strength to escape.

Clack—clack—clack.

Johann stood by a double bunk, staring straight ahead, a bowl of soup in his hands from which he had just been feeding a patient. Hoffer stopped in front of him and peered for a moment into his face as if trying to recollect where he had seen him before. Then he snarled:

"You a Jew? Where's your patch?"

"No, *Herr Untersturmführer.* Political."

Hoffer was silent for a moment.

"Then you hate Jews, right?"

"I don't hate anyone, *Herr Untersturmführer.*"

Hoffer raised his eyebrows. "You don't hate Jews?"

"I don't hate anyone, *Herr Untersturmführer,*" Johann repeated mechanically.

"Then you love them?"

"I don't hate, *Herr Untersturmführer,*" Johann said again.

"Do you *love* them, I asked!" Hoffer shouted.

Johann tensed, expecting a blow.

"I try to love all people, *Herr Untersturmführer.*"

Hoffer suddenly stepped closer.

"You love me then?" he asked under his breath.

It seemed the beginning of his usual game.

"I love *Untersturmführer* Hoffer," Johann said mechanically.

For a moment Hoffer peered into his face as if trying to decide whether he meant it or not. Then he stepped back.

"Ah, you lie, swine," he snarled. "Like all the rest."

He raised his whip and slashed it across Johann's face. Johann staggered back, spilling soup over his uniform, but stepped forward again without raising his arm, knowing that any sort of defense or retreat would only infuriate Hoffer further.

But Hoffer had already turned and was walking away.

◆ ◆ ◆

Perhaps there was something in the encounter with Johann that caught Hoffer's attention or perhaps it was mere chance, in any event Hoffer reappeared in the hospital barracks a mere three days later. As usual, Dr. Bauer had not yet put in an appearance. Johann was tending to a patient with whom he was so involved that he did not become aware of Hoffer striding down the aisle until Hoffer was almost on top of him. When he noticed him, he stepped back from the patient and stood aside at attention to make room for Hoffer. Hoffer stopped and looked briefly at him but then turned to the patient Johann had been washing. This was a man in his fifties who was sitting stripped to the waist, his pitifully ravaged body slumped forward, yet, despite his emaciation and sickness, his face still retained a certain dignity and refinement. He had, in fact, been a university professor—the kind of man Hoffer particularly detested.

"What's the idea, bothering with a wreck like this?" Hoffer barked. "What's the matter with him?"

"Dehydration, dysentery, and abdominal cramps, *Herr Untersturm-führer*," Johann reported in military fashion. "But he'll be back to work in no time."

The trick was not to make a man out to be so sick that he would be slated for immediate liquidation but not to make him out to be so well either that he could be accused of shirking work, resulting in immediate discharge.

Hoffer turned back to the patient and scrutinized him.

"So he'll be back to work in no time, eh?" he snapped. "We'll see about that. Get up!"

The man obediently lifted his thin, dirty blanket and swung his legs over the side of the bunk. Standing up uncertainly, he wavered for a moment on his feet.

"Knee bends!"

"*Herr Untersturmführer, gehorsamst,*"* Johann said. "The man is too weak to do knee bends."

"Who asked you?" Hoffer shouted. "Keep your trap shut."

He turned back to the man who began to lower himself slowly, stopping half way down and then straining up again, his knees trembling. The second time down he stopped even shorter.

"All the way down!" Hoffer barked.

The man went down a little further, hovering suspended, struggling to marshal enough strength to reverse direction.

"I can't . . . please, *Herr Untersturmführer,*" he pleaded.

"What, and you're supposed to be fit for work?" Hoffer snapped. "All the way down with you."

The man went down a little ways. Suddenly his legs gave way under him and he crumpled to the floor.

"Up with you!" Hoffer yelled, bringing his whip down on the man.

The man tried to struggle to his feet.

"Faster. Or I'll send you packing up a chimney!"

"*Gehorsamst, Herr Untersturmführer,*" Johann said again, stepping forward. "The man can't do any more knee bends. It'll kill him."

"I told you to keep your trap shut!" Hoffer yelled. "Up with you, swine!"

"*Herr Untersturmführer,*" Johann persisted. "I'll do the knee bends for him."

The magnitude of Johann's proposition arrested Hoffer and robbed him for a moment of a reply. In all his years in the camps, he had often seen prisoners do violence to other prisoners both on command and spontaneously, but never had a prisoner *volunteered* to take another's punishment! He straightened and a smile came to his lips.

"So you wanna do knee bends for this scarecrow," he drawled incredulously. "Why, I think that can be arranged."

He pointed his whip in the direction of the door.

"Outside!"

Johann turned, followed by Hoffer. In the hall they passed Mondusi who was just coming in. There was a puzzled, questioning expression

---

* Most obediently—a military usage.

on Mondusi's face, but neither he nor Johann said a word as they passed each other. Once outside, Hoffer took the lead and walked around to the side of the barracks where he stopped.

"So you wanna do knee bends for the man," Hoffer said again in a slight singsong, lighting a cigarette. His manner was leisurely, the manner of a man who has a lot of time to devote to something he relishes. "Knee bends—or do you wanna do geography? Or maybe a bit of both," Hoffer suggested almost amiably before Johann was able to respond, sounding for all the world like someone urging on a guest a combination of choice dishes.

"Doing geography" was what the prisoners called, with grim gallows humor, doing pushups, which, together with knee bends, were the favorite minor punishments in the camp, the day-to-day work horses, so to speak, ordered at times for the mere amusement of the SS men, although for the weakened prisoners they often led to grave consequences even without the whippings, blows, and kicks that usually accompanied them.

When Johann hesitated, Hoffer said:

"Let's start with knee bends."

Johann began as slowly as he dared, not going all the way down, while Hoffer leaned against a nearby tree, puffing on his cigarette and clacking his whip lazily against his boot as he watched Johann, now and then sweeping the approaches to the hospital with his eyes to see whether Dr. Bauer was coming. After several knee bends, he suddenly straightened, threw away his cigarette, and snapped:

"What d'you think this is, a kindergarten?" He lashed out at the nearest tree with his whip. "Let's see some action!"

Johann accelerated. For the moment it was still tolerable. As he went down and up, he felt the tensing and relaxing of his muscles and tried to lengthen the brief moments of relaxation at the top and bottom to gain strength, but he knew that it was only a matter of time before his strength would give out and the whippings would start. He closed his eyes. It was easier that way, easier too not to see his tormentor.

"Eyes open!" Hoffer snapped.

Johann felt the sting of his whip through his thin clothes and knew that it would keep him awake that night and prevent him from lying on his back. When he opened his eyes, he could see Hoffer looking off toward the entrance of the hospital barracks where something was attracting his attention. Suddenly he yelled:

"You, there! Come here!"

Two prisoners approached. One of them was hopping along on

his right leg while his other leg dangled limply. The other prisoner was supporting him.

"Who gave you permission to leave work?" Hoffer demanded.

"The foreman, *Herr Untersturmführer*," the supporting man said. "His leg is broken."

The man with the broken leg had sat down, holding his leg, obviously in much pain, though he didn't utter a sound.

"Roll up your pants," Hoffer commanded.

The man pushed up his tattered trouser leg, revealing a bruised, twisted leg. Hoffer looked at it without bending down.

"That doesn't look broken."

He turned to Johann who had stopped doing knee bends.

"Come here. And you, get back to work!" he snapped at the second prisoner. "We'll take care of him."

The man left hurriedly. Johann approached.

"Straighten his leg," Hoffer ordered.

Johann bent down to the leg and touched it gently. The man winced. The leg was crooked and obviously broken.

"It's broken, *Herr Untersturmführer*. He needs to see the doctor."

"It's just sprained, I tell you," Hoffer barked. "Straighten it!"

He bent down and gave the man's leg a jerk. The man let out an agonized scream.

"Like that!" Hoffer snapped. "Except properly."

"I can't do that, *Herr Untersturmführer*," Johann pleaded. "That'll do more harm than good."

Hoffer's face discolored.

"Are you disobeying a direct order?" he snarled, his eyes narrowing.

At that moment Dr. Bauer appeared around the corner of the barracks, followed by a nursing orderly.

"Hoffer, what is the meaning of this?" he demanded.

"The meaning of what?" Hoffer replied coldly.

"First, you take away one of my nursing orderlies and then you take it upon yourself to interfere with a prisoner seeking medical help."

"I know when a prisoner is goldbricking," Hoffer said sullenly. "Anyway, we were about to take him in," he lied.

"A full report will be made of this to the commandant," Dr. Bauer said with satisfaction.

Hoffer's lips curled into a sneer, but he remained silent and in a moment turned around and stalked away.

"The nerve," Dr. Bauer muttered to himself. He turned to Johann and the other orderly and said:

"Bring him in."

They lifted the man and moved rapidly toward the hospital entrance, preceded by Dr. Bauer.

◆ ◆ ◆

It was Mondusi who had summoned Dr. Bauer. Seeing Johann being marched off by Hoffer and witnessing the beginning of the scene through a window, he needed no great powers of imagination to know how it would end. Although Dr. Bauer had not yet come in, Mondusi had a fair idea where he could find him and rushed out to get him. In view of the antagonism existing between Dr. Bauer and Hoffer, it required no persuasion to get the doctor to hurry back at once.

While Dr. Bauer's intervention had saved Johann, it was clear that it did not end the danger. On the contrary. Hoffer was livid at having Johann and the other prisoner snatched from him, in front of other prisoners no less so that the story would be all over camp in no time. As for Dr. Bauer, since his intervention was not motivated by any personal concern for Johann and was merely a by-product of his power struggle with Hoffer, his protection could obviously not be counted on. Both Johann and Mondusi, who had a keen, if pessimistic, appreciation of human nature, were aware of the danger, nor did either underestimate Hoffer's capacity for revenge. It was not ever healthy for prisoners to be caught in a power struggle between what for them were leviathans, for they were all too likely the ones to be crushed in the process. Prisoners were never more than pawns.

"We better get you away for a while," Mondusi said.

He proposed that Johann submerge temporarily in the TB ward, the danger of infection being for the moment the lesser of two evils. Johann agreed and moved the very same afternoon, with Dr. Birnbaum's knowledge but not Dr. Bauer's who was never initiated into such matters since he was himself one of the evil forces that made the hospital what it was.

Almost a week passed and Hoffer did not reappear, raising Johann's hopes that he had forgotten about him. Dr. Bauer had made a formal complaint about Hoffer to the commandant of the camp but what came of it Mondusi was unable to find out. For Johann the enforced idleness was painful, now that his need for rest and food had been satisfied. He was about to ask Mondusi to return him to his nursing duties when

Hoffer reappeared one morning long before Dr. Bauer's customary appearance. Dr. Birnbaum came running up anxiously.

"Where's that orderly?" Hoffer demanded.

"What orderly, *Herr Untersturmführer*?" Dr. Birnbaum pretended.

"You know the one," Hoffer snarled. "With the knee bends."

"He's not here anymore, *Herr Untersturmführer*," Dr. Birnbaum lied. "He's been transferred for liquidation."

This was a ruse that sometimes deflected searches. But it only infuriated Hoffer.

"Liquidation!" he yelled. "I'll do whatever liquidating is to be done here! I didn't see no transfer papers!" He slashed his whip across Dr. Birnbaum's face. "*I'm* going to transfer him! Understand?"

"Y-yes," Dr. Birnbaum stammered. "But Dr. B-Bauer must authorize transfers, *Herr Untersturmführer*."

Hoffer's eyes narrowed with rage. Coming close to Dr. Birnbaum, he raised his whip again.

"Do you want to go curling up a chimney, Jew-swine?"

"N-no, *Herr Untersturmführer*."

"Then get him!" Hoffer yelled.

When Dr. Birnbaum faced Johann he could barely look into his eyes.

"I'm sorry, Johann," he mumbled. "I tried to put Hoffer off. I really tried."

Johann grasped the situation at once. He patted the doctor on the arm, cutting his apologies short, and preceded him out of the room. When Hoffer saw him, his expression brightened with satisfaction, and he gestured to Johann to follow him. Together they left the barracks.

Later, Mondusi reproached Dr. Birnbaum for not insisting that Dr. Bauer must approve the transfer. But as it turned out, the transfer was approved by none other than the camp commander himself who called Hoffer in, in response to Dr. Bauer's complaint. But Hoffer had stood his ground.

"The prisoner showed crass insubordination, *Herr Kommandant*," he had insisted. "If a prisoner can get away with that in front of other prisoners, the discipline of the whole camp will break down."

In the end, the camp commander had thrown him Johann as a sop in return for strict orders—to placate Dr. Bauer—that Hoffer was not to go into the hospital barracks in future without express authorization.

◆ ◆ ◆

Johann realized that his life was now as good as forfeited. To be singled out by an SS officer was tantamount to a death sentence. The only question was: How would Hoffer do him in and how long would he take to do it?

To his surprise, however, he was for the time being assigned to a relatively easy work detail inside the main camp compound, perhaps because Hoffer wanted to have him at his beck and call.

It soon became apparent, moreover, that Hoffer was in no hurry: He would torment Johann at his own leisurely pace. Johann became known in short order as "Hoffer's Jew," the only advantage in that being that it kept the other sadists in the camp at bay. Even the form of the torment became predictable. Hoffer would call on Johann to inflict some punishment on a fellow-prisoner—flogging, for instance—and when Johann refused, he would receive the same punishment and worse.

Beyond that, Hoffer delighted in humiliating Johann whenever he could. Once, for example, after ordering Johann to do pushups, he had him lie face up on the ground and ordered two prisoners to urinate in his face. Another time he had Johann crawl to him and ordered him to lick his boots. These indignities Johann suffered without resistance. Only when called upon to inflict punishment on others did he refuse.

The reaction of the other prisoners to Johann's stubborn resistance was mixed. Most of them deeply admired and respected him, even if some thought his behavior foolish because he was never able to save anyone from punishment—he merely offered himself up as an additional sacrificial lamb. Yet even for these prisoners, Johann's courage and integrity became a beacon and a symbol: foolish perhaps, an ideal impossible to live up to, but giving every prisoner strength to endure and go on.

Although Hoffer seemed in no hurry, it was clear that the situation could not go on for long because Johann's regained strength quickly evaporated under Hoffer's obsessive persecution. More important still, Hoffer's inability to break Johann and make him into a docile handmaiden of his own depravity infuriated Hoffer and led him to ever greater excesses.

Johann's spirit might not break. But his body surely would.

◆ ◆ ◆

Had Hoffer been asked to explain why he was pursuing Johann with such single-minded, relentless vengeance, he would have talked about insubordination, the need to make an example of him, etc. But this, while true, would merely have scratched the surface because a far deeper issue was involved, though Hoffer was only dimly aware of it. It was Hoffer's deep-seated sense of inferiority that needed to

humiliate and break the will of a man who possessed something
Hoffer didn't have—integrity and strength of character—something,
moreover, that a prisoner, mere vermin and scum of the earth, wasn't
supposed to have, and yet had, had what Hoffer didn't have and
would never have.

In the end, Hoffer assured himself, Johann would break like all the
rest. He would grovel and plead for his life. Supermen couldn't be
prisoners. Only inferior men were.

♦ ♦ ♦

At roll call one morning, Hoffer ordered a prisoner who had been
caught stealing a loaf of bread to lie down in a ditch. Telling Johann to
pick up a shovel, he ordered him to bury the prisoner.

Johann caught his breath but did not move. Total silence fell over the
parade ground.

"Did you hear what I said?" Hoffer said without raising his voice.

"Yes, *Herr Untersturmführer.*"

"Then get to work," Hoffer said, still without raising his voice, as
though speaking of the most ordinary thing imaginable.

By this time Hoffer no longer yelled at Johann or barked out his orders,
as if in implicit recognition that they would not be obeyed anyway. It was
as if some sort of twisted bond had sprung up between the two men.

Johann shook his head with a slow, ponderous movement as the
enormity of the request and the enormity of what he was even then
beginning to understand would be the consequence sank in on him.

"All right," Hoffer said, nodding imperceptibly almost before Johann
had even refused. "Then *you* lie down."

He turned to the prisoner who was lying trembling in the ditch and
snapped:

"Get up!"

The man jumped up and began to dash toward the formation of
prisoners standing silently and immovably on the parade ground.

"No! Come back!" Hoffer shouted.

The prisoner slowly returned.

"Pick up that shovel and bury him."

"I—I can't, *Herr Untersturmführer,*" the man stammered. "Please."

"Bury him!" Hoffer yelled, bringing his whip down on the man. "Or
do you want it to be a double funeral?"

Trembling, the man picked up the shovel, dug it into the ground, and threw half a shovelful on Johann's feet. Hoffer brought his whip down on him again.

"Move! We don't have all day!" he shouted.

The man now accelerated his work while Hoffer peered at Johann. He was lying quite still, with closed eyes, breathing deeply. What was this man made of that he wouldn't budge or break or plead for his life even now? Slowly the soil crept up on his chest. Still no pleading, no movement. Furiously Hoffer tore the shovel out of the prisoner's hands, dug it deeply into the dirt, and flung a shovelful at Johann's head, half covering his face. Still the deep, slow, imperturbable breathing.

All at once Hoffer stopped, turned to the guards and foremen, and yelled:

"Move the prisoners out!"

The prisoners began to move out in long formations. Hoffer flung the shovel at the prisoner who had buried Johann and ordered:

"Dig him up!"

When Johann had been uncovered, Hoffer dismissed the prisoner and ordered Johann to pick up the shovel and follow him. There was a single-minded, frenzied intensity in him now as he began to move through the rows of barracks, followed by Johann, pale and silent, carrying the shovel on his shoulder. Presently they came to an open area that had no structures. Now and then Hoffer stopped to dig his heel into the dirt but each time walked on. Finally he found a spot that satisfied him and turned to Johann.

"Dig a hole five feet deep and three feet across. Understand? I'll be back in two hours."

Slowly Johann set to work. Not far from him he could see the tall electrified fence that surrounded the camp with its regularly spaced watchtowers. From the nearest tower the guards were watching him curiously, leaning idly on their machine gun. His head felt clear and he was aware of every detail, and yet he felt strangely removed, as if watching himself dig a hole from a great distance. The thought occurred to him that he could end everything instantly by running into the high-voltage fence: The guards would mow him down even before he reached the fence because they had orders to shoot anyone approaching it. He was aware of thinking the thought, even picturing the scene, but did not move toward the fence. It was like a scene in a movie: One was involved, yet separated from it.

When Hoffer returned almost three hours later, Johann was sitting next to the hole he had dug. He heard Hoffer approaching but did not get up. Nor did Hoffer order him to. It was as if both recognized that they had reached a point far beyond such niceties of obedience. Hoffer was accompanied by two prisoners, one of whom carried a second shovel. He looked at the hole and jumped into it to measure its depth.

"All right," he said, climbing out. "Get in."

Johann did not get up.

"Get in," Hoffer said again.

Johann got up and slid into the hole. It reached to just under his armpits.

"Kneel down."

Slowly Johann knelt down. The rim of the hole was now well above his head.

"Shovel in the dirt," Hoffer ordered the prisoners.

Johann could feel the soil striking his body as the two prisoners set to work. As the earth rose around him, he tried to breathe deeply, but time and again a sense of utter panic threatened to overwhelm him. The thought occurred to him that he could still jump up and run toward the electrified fence so that Hoffer would have to shoot him down. But when he flexed his leg muscles to rise, he could no longer move them and then even the impulse passed. Death was on its way. Why force it at the last moment? It would come as was best for him in the end. For all things were imbued with purpose. Even this, hard as it was to comprehend.

He felt his body becoming more and more tightly compacted as the soil rose around his chest, finally covering his shoulders to his neck. Then he heard Hoffer's voice.

"Stop."

He felt a jolt as Hoffer jumped into the hole and began to trample the earth down all around him. He could see Hoffer's finely polished boots inches from his face. Then the boots left and he heard Hoffer's voice again.

"More dirt."

More soil began to fall around him. He closed his eyes.

"Enough."

Once again the earth stopped falling and he could hear Hoffer ordering the prisoners to leave. When he opened his eyes, he saw Hoffer squatting above him on the rim of the hole, looking down at him. His face was flushed, and there was a wild look in his eyes. The thought occurred to him that Hoffer had gone mad. But people like Hoffer didn't go mad. They took out their craziness on others.

"How does it feel?" Hoffer said. "You going to plead for your life now?"

Johann tried to say something but his throat felt constricted and he could only get out a rasping sound.

"Take your time—take your time . . ." Hoffer whispered. "You got lots of time to think it over."

Then he could hear his steps receding and he was left alone.

♦ ◆ ♦

The sunny September day gave way to a chilly night. Johann could see the cloudless sky slowly sinking away into the night and the camp's floodlights taking over, illuminating the ground around him, though he himself remained in darkness. He could move his head, could tilt it back to look at the sky where stars were glowing faintly. Up there they talked in terms of light years, he thought, while down here on earth everything was so puny, so cramped, mere minutes were enough to snuff out a person's life . . . .

Slowly the pain began to fan out from his knees to the rest of his body until he thought that he could stand it no longer. But what could he do but stand it? Then came numbness, following in the wake of the pain like a trusty camp follower, spreading through his body with a healing hand.

By four in the morning Johann could no longer feel his body. Only his head felt enormous, as if it occupied the whole universe, as he kept slipping in and out of a world of hallucinatory images.

All at once he saw Hoffer, looming darkly above him. He didn't know how long he had been there. He tried to focus his eyes, but Hoffer's face kept splitting into multiple images.

"Stantke—" Hoffer said hoarsely, calling him by his name for the first time. His voice trembled a little. "Can you hear me?"

Johann opened his lips. His mouth felt dry and caked and seemed incapable of speech. He felt himself slipping away again but in a moment snapped back as if time had doubled up on itself. Then he heard Hoffer's voice again.

"Plead for your life, Stantke," Hoffer whispered intensely. "You want to live, don't you?"

"Y-e-s."

"Then plead, damn you! That's not betraying anyone."

"I—want—to—live."

"Louder."

"I want to live."

"*Please!*"

"Please."

"You see!" Hoffer exclaimed, exploding into a triumphant little laugh that sounded weird in the stillness. "That wasn't so hard, was it?"

Again Johann felt himself slipping away and closed his eyes. Then he heard Hoffer's voice again.

"Stantke? Can you hear me?"

He pulled his eyes open. Hoffer had bent close to him. He tried to focus his eyes on his dimly lit features. It was as if a mysterious bond now connected the two men, deeper than words, deeper even than hate.

"You once said you love everyone. Remember?"

"Yes."

"Do - you - love - me - then?" Hoffer whispered slowly.

Johann's body felt numb and disembodied except for his head, which felt supernaturally clear.

"I can't love you as you are, Hoffer . . . . But I can love what you could become . . . ."

Hoffer' eyes became moist. And in a moment the moisture coagulated into tears, much as he struggled to suppress them, and then the tears began to trickle slowly down his cheeks . . . .

Half an hour later, as dawn was breaking, Hoffer returned with two prisoners and ordered them to dig Johann out, staying with them to supervise the work. Johann's body was lifeless when they extracted it and he was delirious. Hoffer ordered the prisoners to carry him to the hospital and stood by while Dr. Birnbaum examined him.

"Will he live, Dr. Birnbaum?" he finally demanded.

"I think so, *Herr Untersturmführer*."

◆ ◆ ◆

Next day Hoffer formally requested a transfer to the Russian Front. It was the only honorable way (in Nazi eyes) that anyone could get out of concentration camp duty without coming under suspicion. He asked that the transfer be expedited, and he himself initiated the necessary papers.

Two days later he did one other thing: He called Direktor Hammerschmidt, whom he had escorted when he had visited Buchenwald, because *Aussenlager Hammerschmidt* was the one place, as even the SS knew by this time, where a prisoner was certain to survive. He came to the point at once.

"I'm calling to send you another prisoner, Herr Hammerschmidt."

"Is he a skilled worker?"

"I don't know about that."

"I'm sorry, Herr Hoffer, I would like to accommodate you but I'm already way over capacity now."

"One more surely won't matter."

Martin let out a sigh. "One more—always one more . . . . But why this man?" he asked, suddenly curious.

"Because he's a—a very special man, Herr Hammerschmidt."

Martin sat considering. It wasn't every day that an SS officer called a KZ prisoner special.

"All right," he said finally, resigned. "Send him over."

Within two days Johann was transferred to Martin's satellite camp.

Hoffer's transfer came through a month later. Three months later, on the 19th of January 1945, *Untersturmführer* Hoffer was killed in action near Lodz on the Eastern Front.

The Plot Against Hitler

The war had brought many changes into Baron von Hallenberg's life. He escaped being drafted, being past draft age, but the servants and other estate personnel were not as fortunate, and those who were not drafted were attracted by the higher wages of war production work. Schulman, the chauffeur, was somewhere in North Africa; Marianne, the baroness's maid, was working in a factory in Stuttgart. The only ones left were Bertha, the ancient cook who had been with the von Hallenbergs ever since anyone could remember, and a new maid who had a physical handicap. Thus, much of the work had to be taken over by the baroness herself as well as by the girls who were pressed into reluctant service.

On the estate, too, the help had shrunk to skeletal crews, placing more work directly on the baron's shoulders. Breeding horses was not exactly a war priority, as it had been in World War I when horses were still used. But the baron clung stubbornly to his horses because horse breeding had been a staple of the Hallenberg way of life for generations.

The baron did not escape war duty altogether, however. He half volunteered and half was drafted into a part-time administrative job with the Rationing Board. It was not a glamorous job, but it did have the advantage of getting him extra ration coupons in an economy in which practically everything had become rationed.

One of the baron's most painful renunciations had been his trips to Munich and other places in his beloved, softly purring Mercedes Benz. He could still drive the car to the railroad station—he now drove the car himself—but that was just about all.

To go to town by train, jostled by the multitude, on occasion unable even to find a seat, and then disembarking in the vast hall of Munich's steamy, acrid-smelling railroad station in order to squeeze finally into a crowded streetcar—all that was most painful for the baron. To rub shoulders with ordinary folk and endure their increasingly evil-smelling intimacy (soap having become yet another precious rationed commodity) merely confirmed the baron in his elitist attitudes. Never had he breathed country air with more relish and appreciation than when he now returned home after a day in the city!

Munich, too, was no longer what it used to be. The many uniforms, the preponderance of women, the reduced motor vehicle traffic all stamped an austere, warlike atmosphere on the city. People walked about with a glum, preoccupied air. Smiles had become rare; lighthearted chatter threatened to become extinct. Life was no longer joyous, let alone playful. An air of sadness hung over the city even before the Allied bombings began. Once they did, the city sank into palpable gloom.

The baron's relationship with Ingeborg had also gradually ended. Ingeborg had finally grown tired of their part-time relationship and had decided to look for a full-time mate. The baron had accepted the breakup graciously enough for the simple reason that he didn't really care very much. The absence of his trusted car had something to do with that too. To wind his way on foot with Ingeborg on his arm in order to thrust his way into some crowded, ill-staffed, ill-stocked restaurant and then to return home late at night exhausted on the train— all that had robbed their liaison of its romantic glitter and had reduced it to a burdensome chore that made the termination more painful to his self-image than it was in actuality. For the baron's view of himself had always been that of a man-of-the-world-with-a-mistress.

For a while after the termination, the baron had drifted through a few casual relationships which were plentifully available in view of the shortage of men, searching for a permanent casual relationship to fill the vacuum. But in the end, the women he encountered bored him. The truth was that he was getting tired of his Don Juan wanderings-about-town, which in turn had something to do with his improved marriage.

In his own way, the baron had always been fond of his wife, even during the years of their alienation. Compared to other women, she had always stood for him in a class by herself. When all was said and done, he knew and trusted her. It was a peaceful, secure relationship. He trusted her like a sister, and yet more than a sister, because lately he had rediscovered his interest in her as a woman as well.

Thus, the baron had altogether become more home- and estate-bound. His estate and study had become a refuge, a fortress against a changing and unsettling world. As the war progressed, the baron moved further and further away from his vaguely pro-Nazi views, which brought him closer to his wife, who had given up drinking almost completely, which also pleased him. What had he really in common with this Nazi rabble and its loud-mouthed *Führer* who was riding the country ever deeper into a disastrous war. Rulers came and went, but the land endured, the nation and its people endured (the baron revered "the people," much as he found them individually jolting)—above all, his lineage must endure!

Such was the baron's state of affairs in the spring of 1944.

◆ ◆ ◆

Paul's flight had been a major shock and disappointment to the baron. Ambivalent as he was about Nazism, it would never have occurred to him to leave the country. One might not subscribe to the motto "my country right or wrong" but to actually turn one's back on one's country, no, that was a treasonous, a dastardly act!

But the most painful fact was that he had counted on Paul to carry on his name. His flight brought home to him how intimately he had incorporated him into all his hopes and plans—and then, too, he had grown fond of Paul, truly fond.

That was why the betrayal of trust was so painful. It wasn't the money as such. It was the abuse of his trust that hurt most. Paul knew that he would never have given him a penny to escape from the country. It was nothing short of extortion under false pretenses! And then to have the nerve to say: You won't regret it—that was too much!

It was that phrase, which Paul himself had recognized, too late, to be an ugly lie, that particularly rankled the baron. And yet in calmer moments he had to admit to himself that it was precisely because he would never have given him the money that Paul had been forced to be dishonest with him. Keen as the baron's initial outrage had been, in time he came to understand Paul and even grudgingly admired his determination and courage.

Actually the issue of Paul being his heir was not a lost cause—at least, not yet. In 1939-1940, when Germany seemed to be winning the war, it had looked as if that would be the end of it since a German victory would obviously preclude Paul from ever returning to Germany. But when the war began to turn against Germany, the baron's hopes revived.

Paul's letter to the baron was ambiguous. The line that struck the baron most, and to which he returned again and again in his thoughts, was this:

"Though I am not a Jew, I keep thinking that the only way I can expiate what I did to my stepfather, when I thought he was my father, is by becoming a Jew." The underlining was Paul's.

What did he mean by that? Was he thinking of taking back his Jewish name? The thought tormented the baron, for with that simple act he would with one stroke foreclose any possibility of being the baron's heir.

Repeatedly he discussed the matter with Emilia, but she was unable to throw any light on it.

"Paul never discussed a name change with me or even mentioned it" was all she could tell him. "All he said is that he wanted to declare his solidarity with the Jews by fighting against the Nazis."

Besides, from Emilia's point of view, Paul was what he was, whatever his name. She had never been entirely comfortable with his sudden name change and peerage anyway.

As the war turned increasingly against Germany, the baron consoled himself with the thought that the whole Jewish problem might well lose its urgency for Paul once the Nazis—who were, after all, the persecutors of the Jews—were defeated.

For now there was nothing to do but wait. If Paul had changed his name abroad, then that was that, and there was nothing he could do about it. All he could do presently was to change his will accordingly: namely, that a Paul von Hallenberg would be his heir—a Paul Silver would not.

Meanwhile, he waited anxiously, along with Emilia, for every sign of life from Paul.

♦ ♦ ♦

The signs were sparse indeed. Even telegrams would have told more. They conveyed no more than the barest skeleton of Paul's fate, i.e. that he had made it safely across the border, was alive and well, and had managed to get to America! That was at first all they knew.

Emilia received the messages every few months by way of Switzerland, innocuous messages buried in her friend's letters, which she would decode with the help of the primitive code hidden in the flour jar in her kitchen that she and Paul had worked out before his departure. Whenever a letter arrived, she would contact the baron, and they would sit down together in her apartment and decode it with barely concealed excitement.

It was not the only time Emilia and the baron met, however. After hand-delivering Paul's letter to the baron, as Paul had requested, they had continued to meet, drawn together by their common bond, in time developing a fondness for each other based not so much on what they had once meant to each other, which was in the end not very much, but on what each now became to the other. For the baron it represented the first non-sexual intimacy that he had ever had with a woman, while for Emilia, who now lived a rather lonely, isolated life, the relationship meant companionship and a chance to get out. They would meet once or twice a month for a lunch that the baron took pains to make lavish, meetings that the baroness was aware of and accepted. For the fact was that though their erstwhile intimacy spiced their friendship, both realized that any attempt to resurrect it would only destroy what they presently had.

It was at one of these luncheons that the baron discovered that Emilia was struggling to make ends meet.

"I had no idea, Emilia!" he exclaimed. "Why didn't you tell me?"

Wealthy himself, the baron had trouble realizing that there were people who did not have enough.

When they met again, the baron broached the subject with some embarrassment.

"I hope you won't misunderstand this, Emilia, but you are, after all, the mother of my son: I'd like to help you financially. It would give me great pleasure, and it won't take a thing from my family, I assure you."

Emilia accepted graciously enough. In money matters she was uncomplicated. Her guilt ran in other directions. Henceforth the baron sent her a monthly check, although she would accept only half of what he had generously offered because that was all she felt she needed. On that score she was adamant.

◆ ◆ ◆

After Paul's flight, Emilia had wallowed in a pit of self-blame. It was as if in the making of Emilia the recipe had read: "Mix all ingredients well and add an abundant helping of guilt," so ensnared did Emilia become in her guilt feelings.

What had she done? In her obsessive pursuit of penance, she had brought pain and misfortune to everyone she loved. Her action had fragmented her family, had contributed toward the death of her husband, and, as for Paul, her penance had merely returned him to the very Jewness from which she had felt obliged to rescue him. But the most ironic, the most terrible thing of all was that she had forced Paul to escape from a draft that would have passed him by as a half-Jew—a draft that might now kill him! She should have seen that God does not want one to do penance on the back of others. It was her pride, her unspeakable hubris, etc. etc.

It was a difficult time for Emilia. No wonder that she lost weight and sank into a depression that made her wish at times that she were dead.

Gradually, however, her self-recrimination began to take on a rebellious tinge. Yes, it might have been her hubris, but who made her do what she did? If God didn't want the penance to which she had submitted in good faith, why had He lashed her on through His chosen priest? Why had He let her push on blindly in His name, bringing misfortune on everyone?

It was then that the erosion of her faith broke out into the open so that she stopped going to church altogether and even refused to see Father Sebastian, though he sent word to her twice that he would like to see her.

Yet for a while her rebellion brought little relief because in some ways she now felt more abandoned than ever. When she had raged against herself, she had at least still felt that God loved her. Who would love her now?

Then one day Emilia was struck by an entirely new thought which set a different constellation of feelings in motion. What if her interpretations of what God wanted had been simplistic? What if He worked in more complex ways? Was it not presumptious of her to think that *she* could know what God wanted? God was God precisely because He worked in inscrutable ways beyond the comprehension of man.

These thoughts were seminal and finally brought on a truce that enabled her at last to grant herself a measure of absolution and peace. What comfort to know that she no longer needed to carry the whole burden of deciding what was ultimately right and true. That was God's worry. His shoulders were broad enough to carry such a load!

She never returned to the Church as a regular church-goer after that, but she would often go into some church along her way in order to pray after her own fashion. She had found her own path to God at last, which enabled Emilia finally to achieve some measure of tranquillity and self-forgiveness.

◆ ◆ ◆

Paul did make his way to America—but not without a string of adventures.

He managed to get through Belgium to France without mishap, crossing the undefended and lightly patrolled Belgian-French border at night almost as easily as if he were taking a stroll in a park. Arriving in Paris two days later, on a Friday, he was exhausted but felt elated and excited. He would be welcomed with open arms and feted as a hero! All his past shortcomings and cowardices were for the moment forgotten. He had rehabilitated himself completely in his own eyes!

That weekend he strolled about Paris in an exalted state, taking in the sights. But when he presented himself early Monday morning at an army recruiting station, the sergeant in charge explained to him that only French citizens could volunteer for the French Army. When Paul persisted, the sergeant finally made some phone calls and returned with an address where Paul was to present himself next day. What Paul did not know was that the address he was given was that of the *Sureté Nationale*—the French FBI!

He was now questioned, at first politely, but in time with mounting impatience and disbelief, until the proceedings clearly turned into an interrogation. His story was just too fantastic and unbelievable: An eighteen-year-old aristocrat raised as a half-Jew making his way alone from Germany to fight his own country. He must be a spy! Or fabricating! Or maybe crazy!

It didn't occur to his interrogators that the very intricacy and unlikelihood of his story was the best proof of its authenticity.

Finally he was detained outright as an enemy alien and a week later was shipped off to a detention camp near Tours, 130 miles southwest of Paris, where he joined several hundred other "enemy" aliens—mostly German Jews! It would have been hilarious had it not been so tragic!

In June 1940, after France was overrun by German troops and capitulated, the French commander of the camp, more humane and intelligent than the system of which he was a part, ordered the camp gates thrown open so that the "enemy" detainees could escape, since most would otherwise have wound up in German concentration camps. Together with two German Jews whom he had befriended, Paul now made his way to Marseilles where a Jewish rescue committee, prodded by his two Jewish friends who vouched for him, closed an eye and shipped him off with other Jews to America.

Paul was crestfallen! He wanted to fight Hitler, and here he was sitting in America, which, at the time, was not yet in the war and stood aloof in splendid isolation. There now followed a harsh, lonely period in New York City eking out a bare living as a manual laborer while going to night school to learn English. The enormous city overwhelmed him. He had no friends, hardly knew anyone, and was too depressed and preoccupied with the war to befriend anyone. But the hardest thing of all was his enforced idleness. The Nazis were marching from triumph to triumph in Europe, and, instead of fighting them, he was languishing in a miserable furnished room in the lower reaches of Manhattan keeping alive on hot dogs and hamburgers! At night he devoured the newspapers and listened to the radio, his only consolation being the hope that one day America too would enter the war.

All that changed abruptly with Pearl Harbor in December 1941. Paul was one of the first in line when the Army Recruiting Station opened on Monday. After basic training he was shipped to North Africa and from North Africa on to Italy. But with the Allied invasion of France in June 1944 he was transferred to France, by now a second lieutenant, on the strength of his knowledge of German and French, and placed in command of a five-man intelligence team interviewing French and, when Germany was reached, German civilians.

Thus, by early 1945, Paul found himself back on German soil in an American officer's uniform.

♦ ◆ ♦

One day in early May, 1944, a man who identified himself as Count von Rath contacted Baroness von Hallenberg on the phone. The name rang a faint bell but she was unable to place him until he told her that he had been a good acquaintance of her father's. He asked whether he could see her, to which the baroness readily consented.

He came to visit on a Tuesday, a day when the baron worked in town, a fact to which the baroness ascribed no importance at the time. Count von Rath was a well-groomed man in his early forties who wore the uniform of an Air Corps colonel. For a while they chatted pleasantly about the baroness's father whom the count held in high esteem. The baroness was beginning to wonder why he had come, when he said:

"I wish we had all opened our eyes a littler sooner—like your father."

The baroness had just then been looking through a window at a tree that was about to break into leaf and for a moment was silent, unsure how to take the count's words. When she looked back at the count she noticed that there was a watchful expression on his face.

"Yes," she replied noncommittally, not wishing to show her feelings too openly. "He was a man who didn't mince words."

"Which is more than most of us are willing—or courageous enough— to do these days," the count rejoined. "Don't you think?" Again the baroness was aware of a watchful, waiting attitude. What did the count want? she wondered again.

"We do what we can," she said blandly, wishing neither to withdraw from the count's statement nor to draw him on. "They say all things pass."

"That's true," the count said with a pleasant smile. "The question is whether one is willing to help things pass more quickly."

If the baroness had had any doubt, it was clear now that the count had not come to chitchat about her father. "A risky undertaking," she said, looking straight at the count. The count was silent for some moments, as if deliberating. Then he said slowly and with emphasis:

"Granted, Baroness. But there are other ways of dying for one's country than in the service of Hitler."

"One of them being indiscretion in speaking out against him to the wrong people."

The count smiled. His smile was all of a sudden the open smile of a man admiring an attractive, intelligent woman.

"Ah, but I don't think I'm speaking to the wrong people," he said straightforwardly. "Actually, Baroness, the person we would like to talk to is your husband."

"Then why are you speaking to me?"

"Because we know where you stand, Baroness. We aren't so sure about your husband."

"You say 'we'."

"To indicate to you that I'm here not just on my own recognizance—though I hope you won't insist on knowing further particulars. Let me just say that 'we' includes highly placed people. Very highly placed people."

"I see," the baroness said. "And what do you want from my husband?"

The count was silent for a moment. Then he said:

"We need a courier, Baroness. Someone not in uniform who is free to move inconspicuously about the country and has some motivation to do so—as your husband has since you have holdings all over the country."

"I see you're well informed. But I'm sure my husband will want to know something about your ultimate objective."

"To end the war as soon as possible."

"How?"

"By eliminating Hitler."

The baroness was silent. Presently the count said:

"May I ask you some questions, Baroness?"

The baroness inclined her head.

"We know that your husband joined the Party. That can even be useful. But is his heart still in it?"

"I'm not sure his heart was ever in it."

"Are you saying you think he'll be willing to become involved?"

"I didn't say that."

"Do you think there is enough of a chance to make it worth approaching him?"

"To tell you the truth—I don't know."

The count was silent, obviously disappointed.

"If we do approach him and he turns us down, do you think we can count on his absolute discretion?"

"If you ask for his word of honor beforehand and he gives it, you can count on his word."

Both were silent again.

"Would you be willing to sound him out, Baroness?"

She sat considering.

"All right," she agreed. "I'll try."

"Thank you, Baroness. I knew we could count on you. May I be in touch with you in a few days?"

The baroness nodded. After chatting awhile longer the count left.

◆ ◆ ◆

Two days later the baroness brought the matter up conversationally with the baron in as hypothetical a manner as she could. Unfortunately, it made the baron's answer rather hypothetical too. Yes, he said, he would consider helping, but, no, it really didn't make any sense to jeopardize everything when the war was coming to an end anyway. But why did she ask?

The baroness reported as much to the count when he called her. The phone conversation was brief and cryptic. One never knew who was listening.

"Would you recommend that we proceed further?" the count asked.

"You have to decide."

"What are the chances?"

"I'd say, fifty-fifty."

The line was silent for some moments. Then the count said: "Can you arrange a meeting?"

"How do you want me to present it?"

"As a get-acquainted meeting. Nothing more."

When the count called back, the baroness told him that the baron was willing to meet with him if it was understood that there was absolutely no commitment.

"I understand," the count said.

They agreed on a time, the following day. The count seemed to be in a hurry.

"Do you want me to be present?" the baroness asked before hanging up.

"No need, Baroness. You've been most helpful. I can't tell you how helpful. We thank you."

◆ ◆ ◆

The meeting took place as scheduled and lasted for almost two hours. The count revealed little more than he had revealed to the baroness, but he and the baron became involved in a philosophical discussion, which the baron fueled, while the count, who felt some distaste for such armchair cogitations, went along in the hope of winning the baron over. But in the end, the baron made no commitment beyond promising to think it over.

There now followed several discussions between the baron and his wife, discussions reminiscent of his struggle over joining the Nazi Party. In contrast to then, however, Olga did not try to influence him in any way. She was willing to deliberate with him, she was even willing to play devil's advocate, but she resolutely resisted persuading him in any way.

"It must be your decision, Otto," she insisted when he pressed her for an opinion.

"But you must have some preference."

"My preference doesn't matter."

"Why? I'm asking you to share your feelings with me. I know it's my decision."

"Otto, if I tell you my feelings, I'm voicing a preference. And if I'm voicing a preference, I'm influencing you. Don't you understand?" she exclaimed. "We're dealing with a life-and-death issue! I can't take upon myself the responsibility of influencing you!"

"Then is whatever I decide all right with you?" he asked after a while.

"Yes, Otto," she said gravely. "I will live with whatever you decide."

In the end, his decision was based on a few simple and, in the main, self-serving considerations, though he didn't put it that way to himself. What could a few individuals achieve? he reasoned. This mighty war machine that had come close to conquering the world couldn't be stopped by a few individuals. Anyway, the war was coming to an end. Why jeopardize one's life at the last moment? Why risk losing everything one possessed? All along he had stayed aloof from the Nazis and their whole parvenue, megalo-maniac world. Why mix with them at the last moment? What mattered now, the baron rationalized, was to batten down and ride out the storm so that one could be of service in future.

So in the end his decision was: No.

When he told Olga his decision one Sunday morning not a muscle moved in her face. She had promised herself to accept wholeheartedly whatever decision he came to, aware of her own painful ambivalence. For while a part of her wanted to hang on to her husband—her newly discovered husband—another part wanted him to make this commitment to a larger cause. So when he told her, the wife in her was happy even while that other part cried.

"No reaction at all?" he asked, somewhat peeved that she showed no emotion even now.

But all she said was:

"I told you, Otto, I will live with whatever you decide."

◆ ◆ ◆

In June 1944, shortly after the Allied landings in France, the baron received a phone call from *Gruppenführer Strapp*.

"Does that invitation of yours still stand, Otto?" Werner wanted to know.

"Why, of course. Stay as long as you wish."

"I wish I could," Werner replied. He sounded tired. "But I'm afraid a weekend is all I can manage. I'm on an inspection trip."

Werner arrived late Friday evening with a case of wine, which they didn't touch that evening, for Werner was visibly exhausted and excused himself almost at once.

The baron had not seen his friend since his transfer to Berlin in 1939 and was taken aback by the change he saw in him. He had not only aged. But what was more, his hearty energy and gusto, Werner's trademarks, had become subdued and had acquired an overlay of gloomy seriousness that was formerly rarely in evidence.

Werner slept late next morning and, after lunch, proposed a walk. They took a long walk through the countryside during which Werner made little effort to keep up a conversation, a reticence that stood out all the more against his former loquaciousness. Now and then he noisily blew out his breath as if to get rid of some toxicity. When they reached the bank of a stream, he threw himself down in the grass and stretched out with a loud exhalation of contentment.

"You don't know what it means to me, Otto, to breathe fresh country air! to see trees that aren't splintered! houses that aren't hanging in shreds! My God!" he cried. "There's still a world out here! a world that has endured and will continue to endure when all this is over!"

He began to speak of the destruction of Berlin, of the beautiful city slowly turning into a heap of rubble. And yet the people were living on, digging themselves out day after day, carrying on with their daily lives.

"Why are they still doing it? What keeps them going? Faith in our cause? stoicism? stupidity? Do they really still believe that we can win this war?" Suddenly he cried: "We're being paid back a hundredfold what we did to Rotterdam and London!"

That evening Werner drank heavily, although showing little effect from the alcohol as they sat talking in front of the fireplace in the baron's study, Olga having retired early. By next morning some of Werner's old exuberance had returned, and he looked well rested for the first time. He wanted to go on another walk.

"You must think me a little crazy, Otto," he exclaimed, "but I can't tell you what it means to me after Berlin just to take a walk in the country. In fact, you can't imagine what a pleasure this weekend is for me altogether. It's like finding myself again."

"I'm glad you're enjoying it," the baron said, pleased.

They ranged even farther this time. It was a beautiful, clear day, with the Alps looming hazily in the distance.

"To think that a simple walk in the country can be such a luxury," Werner exclaimed again.

But in the afternoon he sank back into his somber mood.

"You seem a bit gloomy these days, Werner," the baron commented.

Werner nodded. "There's more than enough to be gloomy about."

Then it began to pour out. What had they done? It was a dream gone totally wrong, a lofty vision that had picked up so much dirty ballast that it had finally sunk under its own weight like a lead balloon!

The baron was surprised by the vehemence of Werner's sudden outburst and didn't know what to say.

"It's a good thing no one can hear you," he said, trying to pass it off lightly. "You sound almost subversive."

But Werner was in no mood for banter.

"Subversive," he muttered gloomily. "How can I be? When I've worked my ass off day and night for sixteen years to bring this system into being—sacrificing everything—my whole private life—my career...." He shook his head morosely.

They walked on silently for a while.

"I wish I *were* subversive!" Werner exclaimed suddenly. "Instead, I'm still functioning as loyal, efficient SS *Gruppenführer* Werner Strapp, most humble and obedient servant and ass-licker of the *Führer*! Still doing my bit for our crumbling *Vaterland*! Why, Otto? Why? Do I still believe we can win—do I still even *want* us to win? What is it about us Germans that can't let go once we've set our mind on something? Is it loyalty, strength—or cowardice and stupidity that elevates good qualities like efficiency and idealism into gods that finally devour us? This lovely Germany that we have so degraded—so raped...."

He stopped, suddenly overcome by emotion, and turned away. The baron was taken aback by the passion, the pain, as well as the honesty of Werner's outburst. He suddenly felt ashamed and guilty. What belief did he have to equal this passionate involvement? It made him feel strangely deficient.

Maybe he should have offered his services to Count von Rath, after all.

Next morning Werner was gone.

◆ ◆ ◆

The baron thought back fondly to the weekend. What a change had taken place in his friend! And how painful it must be to have one's beliefs shattered! He didn't understand the deeper tragedy that Werner had some understanding of: that for all his doubts and aversions, Werner was still loyally serving a cause he no longer believed in.

Even the baroness had picked up Werner's ambivalence.

"Is he still the old rabid Nazi?" she asked.

"If everyone were as rabid a Nazi as Werner there wouldn't be any Nazis left," the baron said.

"Then why is he still in that uniform?"

"Because he'd be shot as a traitor if he'd take it off," the baron replied somewhat tartly. "Besides, he's made a commitment and he's standing by it. That's what all of us have to do."

"You stand by a commitment as long as you believe in it," the baroness said. "To stand by a commitment you no longer believe in is worse than having no commitment at all."

"How simple the world is in your eyes," the baron said patronizingly, for lack of anything better to say.

But he changed the subject.

As for the guilt feelings about Count von Rath that had briefly stirred in him, he once more reviewed his position. But he came to the same decision as before, namely that it would be foolhardy to jeopardize his life and possessions at this late date when even a committed, high-ranking officer like Werner clearly believed that the war would soon be over.

All that remained was a vague regret that he was not a man of action and commitment like Werner.

◆ ◆ ◆

On the morning of August 4, 1944, some two weeks after the failed attempt on Hitler's life, a black car drove up to the manor of the baron's estate and two civilians stepped out with the air of men who are in charge rather than visitors. When the maid opened the door, they demanded to see Baron von Hallenberg and brusquely brushed aside her inquiry as to whom to announce. She bade them wait in a small anteroom and went to fetch the baron.

"What can I do for you, gentlemen?" the baron asked politely when he entered.

"*Gestapo*," said the taller of the two men, who seemed to be in charge. "You're under arrest." And he rattled off a paragraph number from a pertinent law.

"You—you must be mistaken," the baron said.

"Not likely," the Gestapoman said tersely. "You have twenty minutes to pack a small suitcase. Horst," he said to the other man, "accompany the baron."

The baron informed his wife, who helped him pack a few belongings.

"Clearly a mix-up," he said to reassure her as well as himself. "I'll be back tonight or at the latest tomorrow."

"Shouldn't I call the lawyer?" Olga asked anxiously.

"Hold off until you hear from me. I'll call you as soon as possible."

On the trip to town the baron tried to sort things out. A brush with the Secret Police was never desirable, of course, but he had done nothing that the Gestapo could hold against him. It was clearly a mistake that would be straightened out in no time. He would receive an apology and would be sent home—should he insist on being driven back? or maybe even lodge a complaint? With these and similar thoughts, the trip to Munich passed quickly. At Gestapo headquarters he was led into a large hall with simple wooden benches and was told to wait. About a dozen people were sitting about. Now and then a door opened and a man called out a name and someone would rise and silently follow him. Over an hour passed. The baron decided that the next time the man came out, he would ask how much longer he would have to wait. Did they think his time was worthless? When the door opened again, he got up and approached the man.

"I am Baron von Hallenberg. May I ask how much longer I have to wait?"

"Until you're called," the man said, without looking at him. Then he called out a name and the door closed behind him again.

By the time the baron was finally called in the early afternoon, the wait had begun to unsettle him. But instead of confronting someone who could shed light on his arrest even now, he faced a clerk who merely took down a long list of personal data. When the baron demanded to know why he had been arrested, the clerk said without looking up:

"You'll find out in due course."

It never was to be that day. Nor was he even allowed to call home. In the late afternoon he was taken to a small cell where he found a tray of cold food waiting for him. When he realized that he was not to see anyone that day, his nerves gave way and he exploded:

"But you can't just lock a man up for the night without telling him what he's being held for!"

"You'd be amazed what we can do," the guard replied laconically without looking at him.

It was as if they were dealing with a non-person. It had an extraordinarily unnerving effect.

It was then that the baron finally realized that something serious was amiss. He didn't sleep much that night.

♦ ◆ ♦

Next morning the baron was led into a small room where a man sat waiting for him behind a table that was empty except for a pad and pen.

"Hallenberg," the man began tersely without introducing himself. In all his years the baron could not remember having been addressed without his title or at least the aristocratic "von." "We can both save ourselves a lot of trouble if you come right to the point. For come to it you will, I assure you."

The man looked squarely at him, indeed penetratingly, which had an unsettling effect after the previous day's impersonal treatment. He pushed the pad and pen toward the baron.

"So just write out a full confession. It'll stand you in much better stead than lying and dragging your feet."

"What am I supposed to confess?" the baron exploded. "I don't even know the charges against me. This is ridiculous."

The man looked at him with knitted brows.

"You want to play innocent, eh?" he rasped. "I told you: knowing things around here stands you in much better stead."

The baron could see that coming on strong here wouldn't help matters.

"I'm not playing innocent, *Herr Inspektor*," he said, changing his tone. "I really have no idea why I'm here. I'm a Party member in good standing. My family, whose name you are no doubt familiar with, has served our fatherland honorably for generations. I'm not a black marketeer. On the contrary, I work for the Rationing Board. So I'm truly at a loss, *Herr Inspektor*."

"I'm not an *Inspektor*!"

"Then how may I address you?"

"You don't have to address me at all. Just make a full confession."

"I told you, I have nothing to confess."

The man let out a weary sigh, as if the baron's recalcitrance meant he would be home late and wouldn't get to see his wife and children.

"All right," he said matter-of-factly, "you've heard of Count von Stauffenberg?"

"No."

Another weary sigh. "What have you heard?" he shouted suddenly. "You have heard of the attempt on the *Führer's* life, I take it?"

"Yes, of course—on the radio."

The man was silent, as if regretting his outburst. He looked squarely at the baron.

"What do you know about Count von Rath?" he shot at him.

The baron was silent. It was the only connection he himself had been able to figure out during his sleepless night, so he wasn't entirely unprepared.

"I met him once."

"When?"

"A few weeks ago."

"For what purpose?"

"No purpose. A social call."

"Who introduced you?"

"Freiherr von Wedlingen, my father-in-law," the baron lied. "Years ago."

"You just said you only met him once a few weeks ago."

"When I was introduced to him, it was at a large party and we hardly exchanged a word. So I wouldn't call that 'meeting' him."

"And that was years ago?"

"Yes."

"And now all of a sudden von Rath pops up in your life for a social chat. How chummy. Why?"

"I told you, no reason at all. A social call."

"One blue blood chitchatting with another about the weather," the man said sarcastically.

"Among other things."

"What other things?"

"Nothing in particular. You know, social talk. The war. Rationing. The sort of thing one talks about."

"What sort of thing does one talk about?"

"We did talk about rationing, as I recall. It interested him that I was working for the Rationing Board."

"No doubt he wanted to know all about how rationing works."

"It's not classified information, is it?"

"Or maybe he wanted some extra ration coupons for himself and von Stauffenberg."

"No."

"It's no big deal, Baron. A few ration coupons under the table. Happens every day. Why make such a big fuss over it?"

So that was what they were accusing him of! The baron felt a keen sense of relief.

"I'm not making a fuss over it," he said with a touch of disdain, regaining his composure. "It just happens to be untrue."

"Did you know that von Rath was working with the Stauffenberg gang to assassinate the *Führer*?"

"No."

"You're lying!"

"I'm not, *Herr In*—, I assure you. Absolutely not."

"Do you know that von Rath is in our custody?"

"No, I never saw him again after that one time."

The man was silent. Suddenly he said:

"I wonder why you insist on defending a man who has confessed everything."

"If he has confessed everything, why do you need my confession— even if I had anything to confess."

"I'll tell you why, Baron," the man said, suddenly assuming an almost convivial air. "Because we like everyone to stand up *personally* for their actions. It makes a better impression on the *Volksgericht*. You've heard of the *Volksgericht*?"

The *Volksgericht* or People's Court was the dreaded Nazi court designated by Hitler himself to handle, with the utmost severity, anyone connected with the July 20th attempt on his life and the subsequent short-lived Army revolt. The presiding judge, Freisler, was known for his uncommonly bloodthirsty severity.

"I've heard of the *Volksgericht*," the baron said, trying to suppress the effect the news had on him. "But I've done nothing, I assure you. My conscience is clear. I've never sold a single ration coupon or even so much as taken a single one for myself."

The man began to laugh.

"Do you really think that's what you're here for?"

"It's what you accused me of," the baron said, taken aback.

The man shook his head, an amused smile lingering on his lips. Suddenly he turned serious.

"Hallenberg, let's drop the pretense. You've been in on the conspiracy to kill the *Führer*. Why not confess it and save us all a lot of trouble?"

"I've never lifted a finger against the *Führer* or the *Vaterland*!" the baron exclaimed. "And I never would!"

"Very pious, Hallenberg. But von Rath lifted a finger—in fact, a whole hand—and he enlisted you for his little finger exercise."

"He didn't, I tell you."

"But he tried to."

"He didn't."

"*He tried to!*" the man yelled. "We know it from Klausmann. And Götz broke down too after a little 'persuasion.'"

"I don't know any of those gentlemen."

"Cut the gentlemen crap! They're not gentlemen! They're criminals!"

The Gestapoman was silent. There was a long pause.

"You're making it very difficult for yourself, Hallenberg. *Very* difficult," he finally said quietly, almost gently. "We know von Rath approached you to join the conspiracy. We know that from two sources. It's all you have to admit. Don't you want to save your hide? Why not confess it? For confess it you will, I promise you, my dear Baron. It's only a matter of time and how much 'persuasion' it'll take."

He pushed the pad and pen toward the baron again.

"I'll give you two hours. How is that? That ought to be enough time to compose a few lines?"

He moved back his chair and got up.

"Two hours, my dear Baron," he repeated. "Make good use of them."

◆ ◆ ◆

The baron sat staring at the pad, his mind a blank. It was a while before he was able to rally his thoughts.

It was clear that they knew what had happened. If he refused to admit that von Rath had approached him, they would simply take the word of the men the interrogator had mentioned and send him to the dreaded People's Court on the strength of their confessions. He needed to speak up for himself. But how could he do so if he refused to admit that he had been approached by von Rath? It was only by admitting that von Rath had tried to draw him into the conspiracy that he could prove his innocence.

As the baron sat in the isolated room, staring at the bare table with its pad and pen, his course of action slowly became clear to him. Yes, he would need to tell the truth. There was nothing dishonorable or cowardly about that since he wasn't giving away anyone they didn't already have in their custody. He was simply stating what had happened. Once he did that, they would see that he had refused to join the conspiracy and would let him go.

By the time the baron finally roused himself from his cogitations, resolved to make a clean breast of it, over an hour had passed. He drew his chair up to the table, picked up the pen, and began to write:

"Count von Rath (I don't know his first name)"— that should show them how little he really knew him—"approached me in May, I believe it was around May 7th, and requested to see me. I remembered him only vaguely from years past when I had been introduced to him at a party by Freiherr von Wedlingen, my father-in-law...."

He stopped. What was the sense of going into all these details? They added nothing to the basic point. He tore off the page, crumpled it, and put it in his pocket. Then he wrote: "Count von Rath approached me about May 7th and asked me to join in some activity against the *Führer* which he didn't spell out, but I turned him down out of hand as a loyal German and steadfast member of the Nazi Party."

The baron stared at the lines in front of him, sinking into daydreams.

At length the door opened and the Gestapoman returned and sat down at the table.

"I see you've been busy," he said approvingly, seeing the writing.

He picked up the pad and read it.

"Very good," he said, pocketing the paper with satisfaction. "Now that wasn't so hard, was it?"

He prepared to get up.

"May I go now?" the baron inquired.

"Go?" the Gestapoman said with a show of surprise.

The man knitted his forehead.

"Go?" he repeated coldly. "What makes you think we release traitors?"

"But I refused to join them!" the baron exclaimed. "You read my statement!"

"So you did," the man said complacently. "But did you come and—report it to us?"

"Report it to you?"

"Yes, report it to us. Instead of letting the criminal Stauffenberg and his gang come within an inch of killing our beloved *Führer*."

"But I—I didn't join them," the baron stammered. "I turned them down."

"I see you have trouble grasping the essential point, Hallenberg," the Gestapoman said patronizingly.

He pushed back his chair and got up.

"Well, you'll have lots of time to grasp it."

And with that he was gone.

♦ ♦ ♦

The baron remained in Munich until October. Throughout, he did not give up hope. When the baroness visited him, as she was allowed to do twice, he pressed her: Had she contacted Metzner? What did the lawyer say? Had she petitioned the Gestapo for release? Was the Rationing Board willing to get involved? Above all, had she been able to get hold of Werner? Surely he, an all-powerful SS general, would be able to get him out by vouching for his loyalty. Couldn't they see that he was innocent, that he had clearly refused to become involved in any plot against Hitler? How right he had been! How miserably, how despicably the plot had failed! He would have laid down his life for nothing . . . .

But all these avenues of approach proved fruitless. Dr. Metzner in particular refused outright to have anything to do with his case, claiming that it was beyond his competence and that the baron would receive a court-appointed lawyer when the time came.

As for Werner, he assured the baroness that he would do what he could. But the baroness did not tell her husband that he held out little hope.

"Everyone connected with the conspiracy is handled directly by the *Volksgericht* and no one else has access to their cases," he told the baroness. "That's on the *Führer's* personal orders."

The baroness found herself torn between her love for her husband, which made her want to sustain his hopes, and the reality of the situation, which she knew better than he not only because she had never forgotten what they had done to her father but because of the daily vituperation against the conspirators to which she was exposed on the radio and in the newspapers.

◆ ◆ ◆

In early October the baron was transferred to the Gestapo prison on the Prinz Albrechtstrasse in Berlin. Once transferred to Berlin, his wife's visits stopped and his hopes collapsed completely. It was as if layers of obstructing veils were suddenly ripped from his eyes. Until now he had banked on a remnant of legality and fairness on the part of the Nazis that they simply did not have. Now he was finally able to see the situation for what it was.

The brutal atmosphere in the prison contributed to his awakening. Being small fry and on the sidelines of the plot, he seemed at first to have been forgotten as others had their day in court or, rather, their minutes in court, considering the frenetic pace of the proceedings. Morning after morning he could hear the names of the men who were to go on trial that day being called out—high officials, generals, even field marshals—could hear the silent shuffling of their feet as they lined up outside his cell and then the melancholy reverberation of their boots echoing along the bare corridors as they were marched off to court—never to return. Why should he be spared? Who was Baron von Hallenberg to them? Who cared that he was the current bearer of an ancient, distinguished lineage that had served the *Vaterland* illustriously over many generations? Who even cared that he was innocent? Many men he talked to among the constantly arriving and departing prisoners were no more implicated than he—and still they disappeared.

The baron's whole life was now being lived in the shadow of the gallows as he watched each dawn lighting up the sky through the small prison window, wondering whether this was to be his last day.

◆ ◆ ◆

The *Volksgericht* remained in session in Berlin throughout the summer, fall and winter of 1944-1945, day after day summarily churning out death sentences that were almost always carried out at once, mostly by hanging.

The thoroughness of Hitler's vengeance was best exemplified by the fate of Father Hermann Vehrle, an army chaplain who was not in any way involved in the plot. Father Vehrle was asked by one of the conspirators whether the Catholic Church condoned tyrannicide. He replied that it did not. But for not reporting the man, he was promptly executed all the same.

The principal conspirators had been among the first to die, hanged in a calculatedly brutal and humiliating manner: They were hoisted up on piano wires strung over butcher hooks which resulted in slow and painful strangulation. It was said that their hanging was filmed and that Hitler viewed their death throes with great satisfaction.

It was a conspiracy that might have succeeded but for the vacillation and downright bungling of some of the principal participants.

◆ ◆ ◆

The baron received only one visit during his incarceration in Berlin: from Werner Strapp. As it happened, his two cellmates had been taken away that morning and had not been replaced so that he and Werner had the small cell to themselves.

While still in Munich, the baron had often carried on lengthy mental discussions with Werner as if Werner were the judge who held his fate in his hands. But by the time the visit came, most of these mental dialogues had stopped. Still the baron couldn't help plying him with questions: Could he get the charges against him dropped? or at least softened? or at least postponed?

Werner let the questions wash over him. Finally he said:

"Otto, no one 'softens' the *Volksgericht*. Freisler got his marching orders directly from Hitler. I tried to but I'm not exactly in favor anymore myself. But even if I were...." He shrugged and shook his head. "I can't help you anymore, Otto. Even getting permission to visit you was hard. It's all I could manage."

They were both silent as they sat astride a narrow wooden bench in the middle of the cell, facing each other intimately at close range, speaking in undertones.

"To be executed for refusing to become involved," the baron murmured. "It just doesn't make sense."

Suddenly Werner said:

"Maybe that's your real crime, Otto: that you *didn't* become involved in anything, that you've stood on the sidelines all your life, tending your own garden."

He was silent. Then he whispered:

"At least I *believed*. I became *involved* ...."

Again they lapsed into silence. After a while Werner looked up and said:

"So we've come to the end of the road, old friend. Not exactly in lock step—but not so far apart either.... I might not be all that far behind," he murmured enigmatically.

He got up and began to extend his hand but instead both suddenly moved toward each other and embraced.

Then the door closed behind him.

♦ ♦ ♦

Werner's words affected him deeply.

"*Maybe that's your real crime: that you didn't become involved, that you've stood on the sidelines all your life....* "

Werner's words reverberated in him and hit home.

In the shadow of his death, the baron now began to reassess his life and realized what he had not been able to realize until then: that he had avoided making a commitment to anything but his own heritage and in the end had not served even it very well; that all his life he had counted himself out with the convenient excuse that the Nazis were a distasteful rabble, which reduced him in the end to being a coward and an opportunist.

The world he had despised was now seeking him out and shaking him by the neck—literally. How much better it would have been had he at least done something to merit this death that was now coming to him in such a meaningless way.

What an irony! What a waste!

◆ ◆ ◆

October waned and still the baron waited. Morning after morning the names of the condemned droned on. He didn't exactly wish that his name would be called at last, but he no longer dreaded it either. He regretted dying but accepted the end. In the only letter he was permitted to write to his wife, he tried to express some of his new thoughts and feelings.

On November 4th, three months to the day after his arrest, his name was at last called. The generals and high officials had long since been dispatched. His "trial" lasted for all of twelve minutes. The presiding judge looked at his confession and asked:

"Did the criminal von Rath ask you to join a conspiracy against the life of the *Führer*?"

"Yes."

"Did you join the conspiracy?"

"No."

"Did you report the conspiracy and the criminal von Rath to the proper authorities?"

"No."

The judge flipped his head sideways to indicate a group of men who had already been sentenced.

"Hanging."

Somewhere there hovered a defense lawyer who was supposed to defend him, but as far as the baron could tell, he never opened his mouth.

◆ ◆ ◆

He was seventh in line. The men before him and behind him waited silently. No one spoke. Only one of them suddenly began to cry—a youth standing ahead of him in line. He could have been no more than seventeen. He reminded the baron of Paul. He felt a sudden wave of grief and compassion—for the boy, for Paul, for his wife and for the rest of the condemned men, and for himself, for his self-seeking, self-centered life. He silently put his hand on the boy's shoulder and with this feeling of compassion and forgiveness still strong upon him, he felt the noose being placed around his neck and entered upon his final, brief death struggle.

The War Ends

Martin had requested and received three hundred twenty-five Buchenwald prisoners, determining that to be the highest number he could appropriately accommodate, but the number soon swelled to three hundred eighty as his reputation spread among the prisoners, and he was besieged by pleas to take in yet "one more."

Sometimes these requests were made officially (Johann being an example), but more often they came from prisoners already in the factory who wanted to save someone still in the camp. Martin often merely condoned, rather than expressly approved, such transfers. The efficient, business-minded manufacturer in Martin knew that additional prisoners failed to add to production, indeed actually impaired it through overcrowding, but Martin the man, whenever he reminded himself that he was dealing with a human life, simply never found it in his heart to send a prisoner back. One day, he reasoned vaguely, there just would be absolutely no room left so that even his prisoners would finally have to stop importuning him. He forgot that the amenities he offered, substandard as they appeared to him, were still incomparably superior to the camp. He could have doubled and tripled the number of prisoners and still his factory would have been ten times more desirable than the camp, if only because his prisoners weren't maltreated or in danger of losing their lives.

Actually, Martin had given up within months any allegiance he still had had to mere business and profit considerations. Although humanitarian principles had been his primary motive, he had also thought that the venture might further his business or at least do it no harm. But all these self-serving considerations were soon swallowed up by the larger purpose that clashed almost daily with his own narrow self-interest.

There were other problems. For one thing, as the war turned against Germany, it became increasingly difficult to get the necessary raw materials and parts to keep the factory going. But even this difficulty paled compared to the problem of simply feeding the prisoners. Raw materials could still be requisitioned legally, after all, with officially sanctioned high-priority-in-the-interest-of-the-war-effort bluster. But how to throw your weight about in the interest of feeding a ragged bunch of concentration camp inmates whose lives had long since been crossed off as expendable?

This had come as a rude awakening for Martin, despite his by now considerable expertise in concentration camp affairs. According to his contract with the SS, food rations, clothes and all the other daily needs of the prisoners were to be supplied by the SS. But what he was actually getting was far below what he was supposed to get even according to the bare subsistence standards of the SS.

In the beginning Martin thought that the shortage was due to some bureaucratic bungling and tried to straighten it out on that level—to no avail whatever. When he spoke to Alfred about it, Alfred shook his head.

"Martin, Martin, when are you going to learn? You're still such a babe in the woods when it comes to the SS and the KZ's."

"Cut out this babe-in-the-woods stuff," Martin said, annoyed. "Who wants to be an expert in all this anyway? Somebody must be stealing the stuff. I'm going to inform Siebert. He'll be glad to know about it."

"Su-re," Alfred said sarcastically.

When Alfred was sarcastic, Martin had learned, he knew what he was talking about.

"Why the sarcasm?" he inquired.

"Has it occurred to you, Martin, that Siebert might be in on the heist?"

"What heist?"

"The food and other supplies! Don't you understand? *Everyone* is in on the heist! Even some Capos. But one of the biggest paws, I happen to know, belongs to Siebert. Just for looking the other way."

"I can't believe it!" Martin bellowed.

But in a moment he fell silent and became thoughtful.

"So what should I do? Stand by and do nothing?"

"Hm, that's a difficult question," Alfred replied pensively. "If you can afford it, I'd say—do nothing."

"I'm not following you."

"I realize that the supplies have to be augmented somehow—"

"But how? That's the question," Martin cut in.

"Out of your own pocket."

"You're out of your mind! That would be an outrageous expense!"

"That's why I said: *If* you can afford it."

"But it's not only a matter of money. The only way to get extra supplies is on the black market."

"Did you think I thought those fine cigarettes you smoke or the booze you bring along come from the corner grocery store?" Alfred said, amused.

But Martin was in no mood for levity.

"What if I do complain to Siebert?" he said.

Alfred pursed his lips, shrugging his shoulders.

"Then be aware that you're stepping directly on his toes. This isn't like withdrawing Haber and giving you another officer, Martin. This affects his pocketbook, his life style. He won't like it one damn bit."

"Yeah, and the way it is it affects *my* pocketbook!" Martin exclaimed. "But quite aside from the money, Alfred: What about the risk? It's one thing to buy some smokes and liquor for myself and another to feed close to four hundred people. It's going to attract attention. I won't help the prisoners any by landing in a KZ myself!"

"It's not as bad as all that, Martin. You do get some rations, after all. But I agree, it's a big undertaking, an enormous undertaking and responsibility."

Again the businessman in Martin resisted. But even more difficult to handle was the moralist in him. There was something so gallingly immoral about stealing food from prisoners, who were already teetering on the brink of starvation, that the very idea of remaining silent revolted him. Since when did the end justify the means? The whole thing was just too much! And to think that he was hobnobbing and playing music with a man who had his greedy finger in such a dirty pie!

But in the end the moralist, too, yielded to the human being. Yes, he could withdraw in a moral huff and break off all contact with the Sieberts of this undertaking; he could withdraw from all the shadiness and call it quits. But who would suffer? The prisoners. He would be asking them to pay the price of his rectitude. It would be moral cowardice in the name of moral righteousness. He couldn't do it.

So Martin once again realized—hard as it was to stomach—that if he wanted to be effective in helping the prisoners, he had to do everything in his power to seem to be making common cause with their oppressors.

♦ ♦ ♦

What Martin finally did was to stake out a course that snaked artfully between the extremes of confrontation and compliance. For he decided that to do nothing would signal a degree of acceptance that he would ultimately have trouble sustaining even financially because the bite taken out of the prisoners' supplies would become ever more rapacious. He needed to let them know that he was wise to their game and would tolerate it, *provided* that the bite would be reduced and held in check. That would be his ploy.

It was the sort of delicate, pragmatic maneuver at which Martin excelled.
What was important was to bring up the matter in such a tactful way
that Siebert would not feel personally accused or even directly implicated.

"I'm turning to you for help, Ernst" was how Martin now put it to Siebert.
"I tried to straighten the matter out myself without involving you but I
couldn't: Just too many of the prisoners' supplies are disappearing. Listen,
Ernst," he said, waxing confidential, "do you think I'm in this for my health?
We all want to get something out of this. How much work do you think I can
squeeze out of skeletons? If I've got to dip too deeply into my own pockets,
the game just won't be worth the candle and I'm going to chuck the whole
thing. And that isn't going to leave anything for anybody."

Siebert understood. One greedy palm needed to grease the other. He
wasn't voracious. And this Direktor Hammerschmidt was really such a
likable, congenial fellow with whom it was easy to do business. Anyway,
one didn't kill the goose that lays the golden eggs.

Henceforth the supplies that were delivered to the factory showed
a marked increase, though still short, of course. And that was far short
of normal human standards.

The difference now began to be made up by Martin out of his own pocket.
But while his means were considerable, blackmarket prices were such that
money alone was not enough. The only means was barter: exchanging one
highly priced blackmarket item against another, reducing both back to a
manageable equation. But what did he have to trade—except shoes?

Here Martin had to hurdle another moral obstacle. True, now and then
he looked the other way when employees appropriated a pair of shoes.
But on the whole he had always insisted on, and had taken pride in, strict
honesty. Self-respect can't be built on dishonesty, he maintained. In this
Martin was quite old-fashioned and unyielding, much as his genial manner and accommodating style projected a personality that seemed to blow
easily with the wind, so that sidetracking a portion of his production into
the black market violated something he very deeply believed in.

But here too the larger purpose prevailed in the end. Curiously
enough, the risk that he was runningfor blackmarketeering was by
then punishable by imprisonment in a concentration camp or even
death—did not figure very prominently in his deliberations.

Food for the prisoners was not the only blackmarket item involved. For
by this time Martin was slipping liquor and cigarettes not only to Siebert but,
quite regularly, to *Untersturmführer* Ritter and his men as well in order to
increase their investment in remaining assigned to his factory and leaving the
prisoners alone, though the chance for mistreatment had been drasti-

cally reduced since the guards had been withdrawn from inside the factory.

The implementation and management of the blackmarket operation now came to occupy a good deal of Martin's time. The shoes destined for the black market came from the prisoner production so that the civilian labor force knew nothing about it. However, some non-prisoners had to be involved, of course. Fortunately, Martin had at his disposal a number of long-time employees whom he trusted implicitly and it was to one of them, a man by the name of Müller who had been with him and his father for twenty-five years, that he now entrusted the full-time supervision of the blackmarket operation.

Each employee whom he approached—actually only three—was told exactly what was at stake. Martin was proud that all three decided to go ahead despite the risks involved.

♦ ♦ ♦

With nearly four hundred prisoners, it soon became apparent that some sort of infirmary was essential, especially since few prisoners were in the best of health after years of abuse and deprivation. At first Martin tried to organize a daily sick call to the hospital in the main camp but he found that not a soul made use of it. This puzzled him until he learned about the hospital's evil reputation, whereupon he set aside a room in the factory, furnished it with a couple of cots, and assembled a rudimentary medicine chest containing aspirin and the like. But this too remained unused so that it became quite obvious that something was holding the prisoners back. One day Martin discovered the reason.

Walking through the factory one morning, he came upon a prisoner who was literally tottering on his feet. His face was flushed and perspiring and his eyes were glazed and feverish. Martin spoke briefly with the prisoner and then asked a fellow worker to take him to the infirmary. Suddenly the man began to wail and carry on quite pitifully, pleading with the kind *Herr Direktor* not to send him back to the camp.

"Who is trying to send you back to camp?" Martin shouted, trying to make himself heard above the prisoner's obsessed wailing.

Amidst the fearful silence that always descended on the prisoners when one of their number was being dealt with in one way or another, Martin ordered the man to be taken to the infirmary.

But he had understood.

When the prisoners could see for themselves that the man was not returned to camp (on the contrary, Martin had a doctor come to the factory), though he remained delirious for two days and did not return to work until a week later, the infirmary suddenly became the most popular room in the factory, so much so that it soon required a full-time "nurse"and established the need for a doctor.

It took a good deal of charm, all-for-the-sake-of-improved-production-for-the-war-effort persuasion, not to mention two bottles of brandy and a box of fine cigars, to warm Siebert to the idea of sending a prisoner-doctor to Martin's *Aussenlager*.

"You're not pampering the prisoners, are you, Martin?" Siebert asked.

Martin laughed in his face.

"You ought to know me better than that by now, Ernst. It's not the prisoners I care about. It's production I'm after. How can I get work out of physical wrecks?"

It was always a foolproof argument. Only a saboteur of the glorious war that the Führer was conducting with such magnificent, single-minded devotion for the greater glory of the *Vaterland* despite mounting difficulties could find fault with it. Certainly *Hauptsturmführer* Siebert could not. The brandy and cigars further helped to settle the argument.

After the arrival of a doctor in September—a Jewish prisoner by the name of Weiss—a larger room was set aside for the infirmary. For a while it now seemed as if Martin had himself effectively administered the *coup de grâce* to his whole undertaking because there were days when there seemed to be more prisoners lining up outside the infirmary than working. The whole factory seemed at times at a semi-standstill. Martin felt rather dejected about the whole thing and had trouble warding off the growing feeling that his benevolence was being taken advantage of, much as his reason kept telling him that the prisoners were not shirking work but were indeed sick from years of starvation and brutal mistreatment. But where would all this end? Even his means had limits and without production to offset his expenses, his resources would ultimately be exhausted and the whole venture would collapse. In the end this was a factory; it needed to be a factory to continue to exist; if there was no factory, there would be no prisoners to protect.

It was at this point that Martin decided, in consultation with Alfred, to lay the problem directly and quite bluntly at the feet of the prisoners themselves. He called together the entire labor force and addressed them. He knew they were sick, he told them. He knew they weren't just shirking work. At the same time, the work needed to be done. They were running a factory together and the factory was their livelihood and more: their very life! He could do without it. Could they?

He paused to let the point sink in without elaborating further.

After that production picked up miraculously.

It was at this time that a new spirit entered the factory, a spirit of loyalty and even pride in being a "Hammerschmidt KZ'ler." It was helped along by a prisoner Executive Council which Martin helped to organize to administer the internal operation of the factory-camp. It consisted of a factory elder, a tall Sudeten German by the name of Helmuth Konrad who had been an engineer in civilian life and thus was one of the few highly skilled prisoners in the factory, and two assistants, as well as various foremen for the messroom, the sleeping quarters, etc.

The titles were carried proudly, with an armband to identify the wearer, just as in the main camp. The crucial difference was that none of the foremen carried bludgeons and, when one of the foremen tried to abuse his position, he was summarily demoted.

Being a "Hammerschmidt KZ'ler" was more than a badge of honor: It was a badge of survival!

◆ ◆ ◆

Johann was transferred to the Hammerschmidt factory in early October 1944. Since he had no usable skills for factory production work but had worked as a nursing orderly, it was logical to put him to work in the infirmary.

Johann's reputation had not yet reached the factory at this point since its prisoners had left the main camp before his running confrontation with Hoffer. But Hoffer's statement that Johann was "a special man" had been enough to arouse Martin's curiosity so that he made a point of stopping in at the infirmary. What could make an SS officer, one known for his brutality, as even Martin by this time knew, give such an accolade to a prisoner?

Martin chatted for a while with Doctor Weiss before inquiring about the new nurse.

"You mean Johann? He's over there, talking to a patient."

"How is he working out?"

"He's not a professional nurse, of course, but as a comforter, consoler, counselor—I don't know what to call him—he's marvelous."

"I'd like to meet him."

Martin followed Dr. Weiss.

"Johann," Dr. Weiss said. "This is Direktor Hammerschmidt."

Johann got up while the doctor excused himself and left. Martin held out his hand.

"You look familiar," Martin said.

"We met when you visited the camp. You were standing with Hoffer. He called me over and you asked me some questions."

"Yes, I remember now."

"You referred to me as a man."

"You have a good memory."

"It's a word we didn't often hear in the camp."

"It's what you are, isn't it?" Martin said with a smile.

"Yes, but the SS work hard to make us forget it."

"Hoffer thinks you're a special man."

"Really?"

The exchange was ordinary enough, yet it wove a subtle bond between the two men as each recognized a quality of integrity and directness in the other that drew them together. Martin had the feeling that every word this man uttered was whole: not filed down, not slanted, not tampered with in any way. Or was it his eyes that gave him such force? They were limpid eyes that seemed to penetrate what he was looking at, at once warmly personal and yet as impersonal as a spring of water that gives itself amply to all who would drink of it.

Both had fallen silent, a silence as natural as the preceding simple words.

"Well," Martin said finally. "Welcome to *Aussenlager Hammerschmidt*. I'm glad you're here, Johann."

"Thank you," Johann returned simply. "So am I."

◆ ◆ ◆

As news of Johann's confrontation with Hoffer reached the factory, an aura of respect and veneration began to surround him. To defy a bloodthirsty SS officer, to wrestle him to the ground and live to tell about it—that was an incomparable, a miraculous feat! Such a man must have a special power. The concentration camps were full of dead martyrs but few living saints, as someone had observed. Yet Johann had proven that one could stand up for decency and humanity and wrestle the brute in man to the ground.

The prisoners were drawn to Johann not so much for anything he said, although a quiet wisdom always emanated from his simple words, but because of what he had done and proven in his own person. The ordeal he had gone through had purified not only him but gave renewed strength and hope to all who came in contact with him.

Johann thus began to assume a unique position in the camp as his function gradually expanded from nurse to counselor and father confessor and finally to spiritual mentor of the Hammerschmidt prisoners, comforting them in illness, strengthening them when they felt weak and depressed, and helping them overcome differences when they were at odds. Through it all Johann remained sparing of speech and unassuming, almost diffident in his manner, refusing to take personal credit for the energy that was coming through him.

It was in this atmosphere that something unique spontaneously evolved. It began one Sunday, a day of rest, when a group of prisoners lingered around Johann in the messhall after breakfast, talking about their concerns, pitching in with opinions, and sometimes calling upon Johann for a comment. Finally, as pauses developed in the conversation, a deep silence settled over the messhall as many prisoners closed their eyes and turned inward. And then before long prisoner after prisoner spoke up about some personal or universal concern, but always something lifted above the humdrum of daily life, punctuated by deep drafts of silence which the prisoners drank in greedily, robbed as they had been for years of introspection and privacy.

In time it became a regular Sunday morning event to which most of the prisoners looked forward all week, a kind of church service, although no one called it that.

♦ ♦ ♦

In January 1945, Lange, the truck driver who handled the blackmarket pickups and deliveries, was stopped and searched and, when his truck was found to be full of flour, potatoes, and other provisions that he had just picked up for the prisoners, he was summarily arrested for blackmarketeering and handed over to the Gestapo.

Martin was notified when the truck was three hours overdue but counseled patience—the truck might have had a flat tire or broken down, there might have been any number of unforeseen difficulties. When the day wore on, however, and still there was no sign of Lange, he knew that something drastic had gone wrong and set to work to find out what had happened. Through a contact at the police, he quickly learned that Lange had been arrested.

Martin had often anticipated just such an event and had tried to prepare himself for it. If Lange had been arrested, it was clear to him that his own arrest could not be far behind. He put on a calm front—so well that even his wife suspected nothing—but all that night struggled with the thought of escaping. The Allied Armies stood at the borders of Germany so that it could only be a matter of weeks or months now before the war was over. He could sit out the war with Helen under an assumed name in some remote village. He had done his share. He deserved a rest, even a vacation. True, he was abandoning ship but what choice did he have? Of what value was he in a Gestapo prison or in a concentration camp or dead?

But even as these logical arguments agitated him through a sleepless night, he knew that he would not escape. It might be logical but he wasn't dealing with a neat, rational equation. If he had, he would never have embarked on this mad enterprise in the first place. There were values beyond the rational, the sensible, even the wise. The image of Johann kept flashing into his mind. What Johann had done wasn't rational either and yet he had triumphed. What would Johann do in his place? he wondered. He wouldn't abandon ship, that much was sure. As he tossed and turned he felt tempted to go and talk to him, or at least to Alfred, but he knew that in the end he had to work this out by himself.

At length he began to think of ways to deal with the threat. In his mind he went over the various prominent officers and officials he knew but to his shock discovered that the list had drastically shrunk, what with transfers to the front, deaths, and neglect on his part because he had been too busy with the *Aussenlager*. Then all at once he remembered *SS Gruppenführer* Strapp and his parting comment: "If you run into any trouble, give a holler." Yes, he was the man to see. If anyone, an SS general could pass his blackmarketeering off as a necessary, even a patriotic duty for the sake of the war effort.

He set off for Berlin the very next morning. There was no time to get an appointment because the Gestapo might be knocking on his door at any moment. He arrived in Berlin around midday and made his way on foot to Strapp's office, asking people for directions because many streets were unrecognizable, with street signs down and whole blocks in rubble. The devastation was much worse than last time and quite disoriented him. The stately façade of Strapp's office building was pockmarked and most of its windows had been blown out and were boarded up, giving the building a curiously blind expression, as if it were wearing eye patches. He got past the guard, who seemed to be new because he had never heard of *Gruppenführer* Strapp, and walked up to the third floor, the elevator being out of commission. In the waiting room of Strapp's office, which seemed rather threadbare now, a non-commissioned officer sat behind a desk, reading a paper.

"What do you want?" he asked in an unfriendly tone.

"I'd like to see *Gruppenführer* Strapp."

"*Gruppenführer* Strapp is no longer here."

"Where is he? Has he been transferred to the front?" Martin exclaimed.

"You might say he's been transferred," the soldier said sardonically. "But not to the front."

"Where to then? Do you know where I can find him?"

"He's been transferred to heaven," the soldier drawled laconically. "At least let's hope so."

"What do you mean?" Martin cried.

"He put a bullet in his brain. Right here in the office. They found him at his desk in the morning."

Martin stared at the soldier.

"But why?" he whispered.

The soldier shrugged.

"Who knows?" he said indifferently and went back to his paper.

Martin's first reaction was one of panic. What could he do now? He tried to think of some other people who might help him and made some phone calls but in vain. All of Berlin seemed in disarray. It wasn't until he was on the train back to Erfurt that he got hold of himself, and by the time he arrived home, late and exhausted, he had come to a decision.

He would take the bull by the horns, which was what Martin was usually most comfortable doing anyway.

As for Strapp, he wondered what had made him kill himself. Revolutions, he reflected, had a way of devouring their own children.

♦ ◆ ♦

It wasn't easy to get through to the Erfurt Gestapo chief but Martin finally managed to see him a day later. The fact that he had not yet been arrested seemed to him a good omen.

"I must say you're persistent, Herr Hammerschmidt. What can I do for you?" the Gestapo chief said, waving him to a chair.

The words were spoken with polite curtness, as if the man had not yet made up his mind whether to be polite or rude.

"I've come to inquire about my driver who was arrested three days ago. He's an old, loyal employee. I'd like to know why he was arrested."

"Loyal!" the Gestapo chief snorted. "You call blackmarketeering behind your back, using your vehicle for his illegal purposes—loyal? He took you for a ride, Herr Hammerschmidt—or rather, your truck!" The

Gestapo chief emitted a brief, self-satisfied cackle.

"Why that's—that's . . . unbelievable!" Martin stammered.

"Happens all the time," the Gestapo chief said patronizingly, taking Martin's surprise to be discomfiture over his revelation. "Don't let it get you down."

Martin was frantically rearranging his thoughts. With one stroke the whole situation had changed as he realized that Lange had taken the whole blame on himself by claiming to have run a blackmarket operation behind his back. Brave, loyal Lange!

"What is going to happen to the man now?" Martin inquired.

"Well, we can hang him or we can send him to a concentration camp," the Gestapo chief said airily. "Which would you prefer?"

Martin hesitated. Suddenly the whole scenario flashed into his mind.

"I think a concentration camp would teach him a good lesson."

The Gestapo chief stared out of the window.

"Well, we'll take it into consideration," he said.

He seemed ready to terminate the interview.

Martin sat forward in his chair. A cool deliberateness had taken hold of him.

"In fact," he said slowly and with emphasis, "I would be obliged if you could *assure* me that the man will be sent to a concentration camp. It would be worth quite a bit to me."

He had raised his right hand, on which he wore a large diamond ring, and was ostentatiously turning it around on his finger to make sure that the Gestapo chief understood his meaning.

"I see," the Gestapo chief said, his eyes resting on the ring.

"With one additional stipulation, if I may be so bold?" Martin continued politely.

"Go ahead."

"That he be sent to Buchenwald."

Again the Gestapo chief stared off into space, this time with a somewhat puzzled expression, as if trying to understand why this Direktor Hammerschmidt was willing to offer such a bribe for a man who had misused him. Then he made a dismissing gesture.

"Buchenwald, Dachau, Auschwitz—it's all the same to us as long as he gets his punishment."

"I'm much obliged," Martin said, getting up.

He stepped up to the desk, slipped off his ring, and placed it on the desk.

"One more thing, if I may," Martin said. "Could a visit be arranged with the man before he is sent away?"

"Why not," the Gestapo chief said indifferently without reaching for or even looking at the ring.

◆ ◆ ◆

The visit was arranged for the following day. By then Martin had sorted through his thoughts and feelings. Was it right that he was letting Lange bear the whole brunt of it? But could he have saved him by shouldering the blame himself? He would merely have gotten himself arrested too. Turn it as he may, he always arrived at the same conclusion, namely that he had acted correctly and honorably—which didn't change the fact that he was deeply indebted to Lange.

Martin took along half a dozen packages of cigarettes, knowing that Lange was an avid smoker. At the prison he was ushered into a bare waiting room. After ten minutes Lange was brought into the room and they were left alone.

"*Herr Direktor!*" Lange exclaimed, overjoyed to see him, moving toward him to shake hands.

"How are you?" Martin said coldly, backing away.

It hurt him to act this way when he wanted to embrace Lange, but it wouldn't do to speak openly here. Thank God Lange showed no evidence of mistreatment.

Lange stopped, his face expressing puzzlement and hurt.

"I've been to see your wife and kids," Martin continued evenly. "They're fine, though worried, of course."

"Thank you."

Martin was searching for the right words.

"I've come to tell you, Lange," he began sternly, "that I'm truly disappointed that a long-time employee whom I've always trusted would run a blackmarket operation behind my back, misappropriating a company truck for his own shady purposes. It could have brought us all into severe difficulties. You have the good fortune to be in the hands of an understanding Gestapo chief who assured me that he won't invoke the death penalty but will instead ship you off to a concentration camp—to Buchenwald, to be exact. I think you're very fortunate," Martin said, emphasizing each word. "Do you understand?"

Lange's face had changed imperceptibly. Martin could see that he had begun to understand.

"I understand, *Herr Direktor,*" he said under his breath. "Thank you."

"I did bring you some cigarettes—with the Gestapo chief's kind

permission," Martin continued, handing them to him. "And I do want
you to know that I won't punish your innocent wife and children for
your crime. They will be taken care of."

"Thank you, *Herr Direktor.*"

After twenty minutes a guard stepped into the room and terminated
the visit. Firmly pressing Lange's hand, Martin tried in this way to convey
his gratitude. He could feel Lange's responsive squeeze.

♦ ◆ ♦

The Gestapo chief lived up to the bargain. Lange was sent to Buchenwald and from there it was not difficult to have him transferred back to
Martin's factory. By this time such "routine" requests, which did not really
affect Siebert one way or another, were almost automatically honored by
Siebert—for a small consideration, of course. But these considerations were
always handled by Martin with such finesse and joviality that they had
become like a transaction between friends, painless and unembarrassing
and not at all sordid—indeed bringing them, from Siebert's point of view,
closer together! Perceptiveness was not Siebert's strong point.

The day Lange returned to the factory, Martin threw a little "party" for
him in the mess hall. Each prisoner received an extra treat, consisting of a
slice of white bread with margarine and marmalade, and Martin brought
along two bottles of wine, which he shared with Lange and the members
of the Executive Council of which Johann too had become a member, at
the insistence of the prisoners. Together they toasted Lange while a small
music ensemble that the prisoners had organized fiddled and fluted away,
assisted by the *Herr Direktor* on the violin. It was a veritable homecoming.

If any further idolization of Martin was possible, Lange's rescue
accomplished it. He was the ultimate Good Samaritan—the uncanonized
saint of Buchenwald—the man who had brought them here, who
maintained them here, and whose disappearance would cast them back
into the fiendish hell of the camp!

♦ ◆ ♦

As Germany sank into the death throes of final defeat, Martin became
obsessed with the safety of his prisoners, fearful that the demoralization
that was sweeping across Germany might ignite a bloodbath in a last-minute, irrational Armageddon of SS terror and brutality. He lay awake nights
tormented by visions of a roving SS unit drawing up in front of the factory
compound, ordering all the prisoners out, and mowing them down. That

such last-minute exterminations were rumored to have taken place in some other camps—whether fact or fiction—only stoked his fears. The prisoners were like a family to him by this time—more than a family because their very lives depended on him.

He tried to find out from Siebert what their orders were, if any. Were they to defend the main camp? Was any last-minute action planned against the prisoners? And what about the satellite camps?

Siebert answered his questions irritably. How should he know? He wasn't the *Kommandant* of the camp. There were rumors of large-scale shipments to other camps, and some were under way, but that was all. The goddam *Bonzen* (big shots) were only thinking of saving their own hides. They had no time for little guys like him . . . .

Martin saw only two possible defenses. One was to enlist Ritter's SS contingent to protect the prisoners if any outside unit attempted an action against them. But when he broached the subject with Ritter over a glass of brandy, Ritter looked frankly puzzled.

"Now, *Herr Direktor*, that doesn't make sense. To shed Aryan blood to save a bunch of—of . . . ." He stuttered, leaving the sentence unfinished, having by this time more than an inkling of Martin's true feelings toward the prisoners. "Besides, what if they outnumber us?"

The other countermeasure, and the one he proceeded to implement in consultation with the prisoner Executive Council, was to procure some guns which were distributed clandestinely to those prisoners who had some experience using them.

Thus April 1945 arrived.

◆ ◆ ◆

One morning in early April a prisoner came running into the mess hall where everyone was eating breakfast. The man was screaming and seemed in hysterics, jumping about and flailing his arms, alternately laughing and crying, so that it was a while before the prisoners could make out what he was screaming:

"They're gone—they're gone—the SS are gone!"

The prisoners rushed to the windows where the first morning light was just lighting up the sky. The guard towers stood silhouetted against the dawn, their unmanned machine guns pointing eerily into the sky, while the front gate stood slightly ajar, swinging gently in the wind.

The SS guards were gone! As they stared out of the windows, a profound silence settled over the prisoners. It was hard, it was impossible, to believe that this everpresent evil had at last been lifted from their lives. Then bedlam broke loose as the prisoners began to shout and dance and weep and embrace in a delirium of joy.

Martin, informed while still in bed, hurried to the factory. He was greeted with shouts, acclamations, and embraces, was hoisted on the shoulders of the prisoners, and was marched around the mess hall while everyone clapped and whistled and cheered.

At length Martin raised his arms and silence fell on the hall.

"I don't want to be a spoilsport but we must remain on guard. The SS may have disappeared here but the danger isn't over until the Americans have arrived."

He sat down with the Executive Council to decide how they could best protect themselves. It was agreed that the prisoners themselves would man the guard towers and machine guns, dressed in civilian clothes that Martin would supply, while the rest of the prisoners would remain indoors and out of sight. Only Lange was allowed to slip away to rejoin his family.

The precaution was taken none too soon. The same afternoon an alert spread through the factory: A small SS motorized contingent was approaching, spearheaded by a tank. The tank swung around in front of the gate, training its gun on the empty windows of the factory from which all faces had disappeared, while two trucks with SS soldiers pulled up behind the tank. An SS officer jumped out of the tank.

"Who are you guys?" he yelled up at the nearest guard tower, puzzled by the fact that civilians were manning machine guns.

"*Volkssturm!*"* came back the reply.

"What are you defending?"

"A factory. There's been a lot of looting around here."

Still the SS officer hesitated. Just then another officer leaned out of one of the trucks and yelled impatiently.

"Gottfried, let's stop farting around here! The Americans are on our tail. Ask him how we can get to Buchenwald."

After obtaining (false) directions, the officer climbed back into the tank.

"Heil Hitler," he yelled.

Then the tank swung around and rumbled off, followed by the two trucks.

---

* Military units hastily slapped together by Hitler during the panicky closing months of the war, composed of older men past draft age and young boys, some as young as twelve and thirteen.

There followed an anxious night. In the morning a light American artillery reconnaissance plane appeared above the town, followed by a brief artillery barrage. Then another silence settled over the town which lasted well into the afternoon.

Around four o'clock another alert raced through the factory and the prisoners crouched down on the floor under the windows as a rumble was heard in the distance which became louder and louder. Finally the rumble burst upon the compound as a row of tanks swung around the corner and came to rest in front of the gate.

For a minute the silence was profound. Then all at once a shout was heard, followed by shrill laughter, followed by more shouts. And now the prisoners could make out the words:

"Americans! They're Americans! Come out! They're Americans!"

The doors and windows of the silent factory building now flew open and out burst a striped mass of shouting, weeping, arm-flailing, delirious humanity that precipitated itself on the soldiers, pulling and pushing, laughing, shouting, and weeping.

At length the armored unit moved on and silence settled once more over the factory. But now it was a silence of release and joy as the prisoners walked contemplatively about the factory compound alone or in couples or in small groups, some even venturing timidly outside the main gate which stood open now, each prisoner savoring his new-found freedom in his own way—a freedom at once marvelous and frightening that needed to be digested slowly and carefully, much as a starving man must return to food bite by bite.

◆ ◆ ◆

For Martin freedom brought, ironically, a new and quite unexpected danger. It emerged out of a conversation that a group of prisoners had the morning after their liberation.

The prisoners were talking about the future, speculating about what would happen next. Everyone agreed that the Allied military authorities would run the country for a while and would assume responsibility for the prisoners. But what would they do to the Nazis and especially the SS guards?

The conversation became very lively as everyone pitched in with their opinions.

"The Russians are just going to string 'em all up," said one prisoner.

"They don't piss around," agreed another.

"Because they've suffered the most."

"Everyone's suffered. You think the British and French haven't?"

"Not like the Russians."

"I don't think they'll string everyone up," a prisoner disagreed. "Only the big shots."

"And the SS."

"The SS for sure!"

"Every damn one of 'em!"

"And no questions asked."

"And some of the Capos too."

"They're gonna make short shrift of every damn last one who had anything at all to do with the KZ's."

The prisoners were silent as each tasted his own feelings of rage and revenge.

Suddenly someone said:

"What about Direktor Hammerschmidt?"

"What about him?"

"He ran a concentration camp too, didn't he?"

"Are you crazy? He saved our lives!"

"You don't have to tell me! But how will the Americans and Russians know that?"

Suddenly everyone fell silent as the thought sank in.

"By God, he's right. They'll think he ran a satellite camp for his own profit."

They had been so busy revering Direktor Hammerschmidt that it had never occurred to them that anyone might see him in a different light.

Two of the men went off to find Konrad, the factory elder, and presented the problem to him. Konrad grasped the situation at once.

"Call the Council together," he said.

The Executive Council did not need long to deliberate. A two-man delegation was dispatched to find Martin and bring him back.

As Martin listened to them, it slowly began to dawn on him that they had a point: Maybe he was running a risk of being arrested. He let out a weary sigh.

"Will it never end?" he murmured.

The prisoners had worked out a plan which Konrad now presented to Martin. Martin was to move into the factory for a while so that the prisoners could protect him until the matter could be cleared up with the American military authorities. They would be his living shield, his living testimonials and witnesses. He was not to go anywhere without at least two prisoners accompanying him.

"A sort of bodyguard, eh?" Martin said, at once touched and annoyed by the proposal.

He sat considering.

"I have a better idea," he said finally. "How about my 'bodyguards' moving into my house? That way we'll all be more comfortable."

The council took the matter under advisement at once and in the end Martin's offer was accepted.

♦ ◆ ♦

There now followed some days when nothing at all seemed to be happening. It was as if the "Hammerschmidt KZ'lers" had been forgotten. Production was limping along in the civilian factory, using up such raw materials as were still on hand because all raw material shipments had stopped, but the prison factory stood idle, waiting. Waiting for what? Waiting for the future to begin. But for the moment the future seemed delayed, bogged down, caught in a hiatus of eating, sleeping, walking and talking. Not that the liberated prisoners were particularly impatient. Time had become an almost meaningless concept for them. It could not overnight be reinstated in all its old, enslaving glory.

The main Buchenwald camp had been taken over by American military authorities. While prisoners continued to die in droves from malnutrition and various illnesses despite intense medical efforts to save them, a team of investigators began to gather material for later war crimes prosecution and to arrest anyone accused of a crime who was still around—not many because Siebert and almost all the SS personnel had vanished overnight.

Konrad, Dr. Weiss, Johann, and Alfred (who had joined the factory prisoners after the liberation) had moved into Martin's house and took turns in pairs watching over him. Martin joked with a pretense of annoyance that he couldn't even go to the bathroom alone, but as arrests of known Nazis began, including his fellow industrialist Kurt Boeck, he had become convinced that the precaution was indeed necessary.

It was during this time of waiting that one of the members of the Executive Council had a genial idea. If living testimonials were of help, what about a written one? After all, the prisoners wouldn't always be around to protect their beloved *Herr Direktor*. One day soon now they hoped to be leaving. Who would speak up for him then?

A testimonial was therefore drawn up and there now followed innumerable revisions accompanied by heated debates which were conducted with great solemnity and gusto as the prisoners found profound pleasure in being able at last to reciprocate and do something for their beloved *Herr Direktor*. At length the following statement emerged:

"This is to certify that Martin Hammerschmidt, director of the *Hammerschmidt Schuhwerke, A.G.*, saved the lives of three hundred ninety-one Buchenwald prisoners by establishing an *Aussenlager* in his factory where he labored ceaselessly, at great personal risk to his own life and with unstinting sacrifice of his own money and property, to better the lot of the prisoners and ensure their survival.

"In solemn testimony whereof the eternally grateful prisoners have affixed their signatures below."

And then followed page on page of signatures.

It was an act of love, all that the prisoners could give this revered man who had risked his life to save theirs—they, the lowly, despised prisoners whose lives until a few days ago hadn't been worth a penny but who were now suddenly in a position to save their idol.

◆ ◆ ◆

The prisoners' foresight and vigilance was soon put to the test.

A few days later a jeep drew up in the early morning hours in front of Martin's villa and out jumped a Military Police sergeant with two men, who promptly tried to arrest Martin, who had been dressing and was still in his morning gown. As soon as Konrad, Alfred, Johann, and Dr. Weiss became aware of what was happening, they rushed to Martin's side and posted themselves between Martin and the American soldiers.

There now followed a rather comic scene as the soldiers attempted to arrest Martin and take him along, while the four prisoners in their striped uniforms kept interposing themselves and pulling Martin away. Simultaneously, everyone was gesticulating and shouting while Helen, Martin's wife, stood in a corner, trembling like a frightened child. Finally the melee died down with a standoff and everyone stood eyeing one another.

"I've got my orders," the sergeant insisted plaintively, wishing someone with more authority were around to assume charge and take these obstreperous concentration camp prisoners, whom one certainly couldn't arrest, off his hands.

Dr. Weiss, who spoke the most fluent English, now assumed the role of spokesman.

"Captain," he said (if one didn't know someone's rank, captain was always the safest bet). "Captain, we are stubborn to stand for this man to the death. He is not bad SS man. He is good man who saved three hundred ninety-one lives and—and . . . . Where is that statement?" he cried nervously in German, turning to Martin who promptly produced it from a drawer. "Here!" Dr. Weiss cried, triumphantly turning the pages in front of the sergeant's face. "Three hundred ninety-one names! You believe now? You believe?"

"Look, it's not that I don't believe you," the sergeant remonstrated placatingly. "But orders are orders." He suddenly had an idea. "Tell you what: You come along—you all come along—and explain it to the captain."

"No," Dr. Weiss pronounced with indubitable assurance. "Direktor Hammerschmidt stay here. You tell captain to come here."

The sergeant heaved a loud, reproachful sigh, looking unhappy. Then he had another idea.

"I'll tell you what I'll do. If Himmerschnatt here—" he pointed at Martin, "is willing to be locked up in a cellar or closet, I'll leave my two men with you and try to get the captain to come here."

"Did you understand what he proposed?" Dr. Weiss asked, turning to everyone.

"I think so," Martin said. He spoke a little English. "It's all right with me."

"I want to stay with you, *Liebchen*," Helen said, coming out of her corner. "Please, can I stay with you?"

"Can wife stay?" Martin said in broken English to the sergeant.

"Why not," the sergeant said with the air of a man who has made so many concessions that one more no longer matters.

With that the negotiation came to an end for the moment. Martin led the soldiers to a section of the hallway that could be closed off on either side where Martin and Helen sat down on comfortable armchairs moved in for the purpose, with enough magazines to last them for a week, while outside the front and rear doors an MP took up sentry duty, watched over in turn by Dr. Weiss and Konrad in front and Johann and Alfred in back. Then everyone settled down and waited.

While they waited, Konrad hit on the idea that the factory prisoners should also be mobilized. Using an old bicycle of Martin's, he pedaled furiously to the factory, getting there in less than half an hour.

When the prisoners heard what had happened, they started out for Martin's villa at once, led by Konrad.

♦ ◆ ♦

Two officers rode up in a jeep about two hours later, followed in another jeep by the MP sergeant and three additional men. By that time a crowd of prisoners had already arrived on the spacious front lawn and more were arriving by the minute. As the two jeeps pulled up, the crowd parted silently to let them pass.

"What the hell!" one of the officers muttered, astonished, as he got out and surveyed the crowd. "What's going on here?"

"All they lack are banners to make them look like a protest demonstration," commented the other officer.

They entered the villa on the side where Dr. Weiss and Konrad were standing guard and approached them.

"Is there a room where we can talk?" the officer who seemed to be in charge asked.

Dr. Weiss, after checking back with Martin, led them to Martin's study, a comfortable room overlooking the rear garden where they sat down while Konrad went to fetch Johann and Alfred.

"What are all the people doing out front?" the officer asked Dr. Weiss.

"They're here to speak for Direktor Hammerschmidt."

Dr. Weiss produced the statement with the signatures. While the officers studied it, Johann and Konrad silently joined the group and sat down.

"Incredible!" the officer exclaimed. "Incredible!" he repeated, waving his hand speechlessly through the air.

The silence was broken by Johann.

"You're right, Paul. The man shouldn't be arrested."

The officer swung around.

"How come you know my—?"

He peered closely at Johann. It was like seeing an object on the bottom of a stream: One moment it was there, next moment it was gone. The face looked familiar, yet strange. Where had he seen it before? Suddenly he recognized him.

"Johann!" he yelled, jumping up.

He ran to Johann and embraced him impetuously.

"I thought you were dead! I can't believe it! My God, I can't believe it, Johann!"

◆ ◆ ◆

Paul made an exhaustive report after this encounter, requesting authorization to issue Martin an Affidavit of Protection that would call upon all military and civilian authorities to grant Martin aid and protection as a recognized enemy of the Nazi regime.

The authorization was presently granted. Together with the prisoners' signed testimonial, it was deemed sufficient protection for Martin against any possible future arrest and prosecution.

◆ ◆ ◆

Paul had had no news from his mother for several months and felt quite anxious about her fate since Munich had been bombed heavily on several occasions. He therefore took the first opportunity after the liberation of Munich in late April to obtain a three-day emergency weekend pass and drove down to Munich in his jeep.

Although the devastation was less severe than Paul had seen in some cities, the emotional impact on him was strong since it was the city of his birth and childhood. There were almost no civilian vehicles to be seen, only bicycles and pedestrians, and the people looked depressed and ill at ease and hurried along like ghosts.

On his way to his mother's apartment, he made a short detour to look at the house where they had lived and where his stepfather had died. The house itself stood unhurt, despite the damage sustained by the surrounding buildings, but it looked shabby and run down and the tree behind the house, which had been his mother's pride and joy, was splintered and its crown was broken. The sight plunged Paul into a gloomy mood which was deepened by the anxiety he felt over his mother.

When he swung into the street where his mother lived, his heart sank. The entire block was bombed out and was lined with empty, gutted houses. Pulling up in front of her building, he could see that only the ground floor apartments were still inhabited while his mother's apartment had been on the third floor. He ran up the few steps and impetuously rang the bells of both ground floor apartments. Only one door opened a crack.

"What do you want?" a woman said in a broad Bavarian dialect, eyeing his American uniform suspiciously.

"Mrs. Silver—on the third floor—do you know what happened to her?"

"Bombed out," the woman said curtly. "American bombs. Can't you see?"

"Was she hurt? Please. I'm her son."

The woman's face changed.

"Nah, our cellar is solid. She was all right."

"Where is she now?"

"Evacuated to the country."

"Where to?"

"I don't know. Around Starnberg somewhere—said she knew some-one—a baroness. Lucky woman."

Paul thanked her and sped off. Presently he reached Solln, a suburb of Munich, and gained the open road to Starnberg. An intense excitement had taken hold of him. Six years! It had been almost six years since they had last seen each other! Had she aged? Of course she had aged—hadn't he? But his aging was different. His life was only now really beginning while hers was over in a way, buried with her Jewish husband, buried in the rubble of Germany. How deep the wounds of war reached, he reflected as he drove. How much deeper than the mere statistics of the dead and wounded. He suddenly felt an intense sadness.

He drew up in front of the manor on the baron's estate and ran up the broad stairs. A maid he did not know opened the door. His uniform frightened her. While he was still trying to identify himself, the door was suddenly pulled wide open and the baroness stood in front of him.

"Paul!" she exclaimed. "Come in, come in! Emilia! Emilia!" she shouted over her shoulder. "Paul is here!"

She stepped forward and embraced Paul with genuine warmth. And then in another moment he felt himself pulled sideways and saw his mother's face, felt her short compact body against his and her arms around his neck as she broke into happy sobs.

♦ ♦ ♦

The weekend flew by with incredible speed. How can one compress six years into words? Events and facts could be reduced to words—the baron's death, the apartment going up in flames last December with all of his mother's possessions, the baroness's generous invitation to move in with her—but how express the thousand shades of feelings, anxieties, and joys that one has grappled with during six long, uncertain years?

His mother remained by his side all weekend, but the baroness, too, spent much time with them. At first her constant presence annoyed Paul but he soon came to accept it, seeing the trusting, relaxed relationship that had developed between the two women, a genuine friendship. Perhaps it was the loss that both had suffered at the hands of the Nazis that drew them so close together.

Nevertheless, as the weekend progressed, Paul began to feel somewhat uncomfortable and constricted as he noticed a certain proprietariness in the baroness's behavior toward him. It emerged in such comments as "a man is needed around here" and "when do you expect to be discharged, Paul?"—remarks that moved ever closer to expressing explicit expectations, much as Paul tried to avoid them with evasive answers.

Next day, a Saturday afternoon, an argument developed between him and the baroness as the three took a walk around the estate. The discussion started when the baroness remarked how good it was that "the nightmare is finally over."

"Yes," Paul agreed bitterly. "But for many it will never be over."

He was thinking of Buchenwald. His work at the camp had affected him profoundly and was constantly on his mind.

"I know," the baroness replied softly. "But at least we can start rebuilding now. We can begin to forget the nightmare."

"Why didn't the German people think it was a nightmare as long as Hitler was winning?" Paul exclaimed aggressively.

"There were good people in this country too, Paul. Not all Germans were Nazis," the baroness said gently.

"But too many were! Too many turned their backs!"

Olga remained silent and they walked on without speaking for quite a while.

That evening—Paul had to leave next day—their unspoken feelings and expectations at last came out into the open. They retired to the baron's study after dinner and the baroness opened one of the last remaining bottles of wine in honor of the occasion. Paul was sitting with his mother on the sofa facing the fireplace while the baroness sat in one of the armchairs. A large brown envelope rested on her lap.

"Paul," the baroness presently began. "I have the baron's will here. I would like to tell you what is in it."

It was interesting that in front of Paul both women always referred to him as "the baron" rather than as "your father," as if to avoid the painful ramifications of the latter.

"As you know," the baroness continued, "he was pleased to have you as a son and he was happy that you became a part of the family—"

"Olga," Paul cut in gently to head off what he felt was coming, "I know how proud he was of his family lineage but—"

"He wanted you very much to carry it on," the baroness interrupted.

"I know. But I'm afraid I'm not the right person to do that."

"Oh, but you are, Paul, you are!" the baroness exclaimed. "Very much so. He wanted you to. It's right here." She tapped the envelope.

"Olga, you must understand that it takes two to agree to such a proposition," Paul said softly.

"What do you mean?"

"I—I don't want to live in Germany anymore."

"But this is your country. You were born and raised here."

"I'm an American citizen now."

"But your mother lives here. You have a future here."

"I'm going to send for mother as soon as I get out of the Army. We've already discussed it. I'm going to college, Olga. The government pays for that sort of thing for veterans over there."

"Money is no problem, Paul. You can go to the university here. The baron expected you to."

"But I don't want to be clamped into the life of a baron, Olga!" Paul blurted, expressing his feelings at last. "I want to live my own life and I can't do that in Germany anymore!"

A long silence followed.

"I see," the baroness said finally. "Have you thought this through, Paul? Is this really your considered decision?"

"Yes, Olga. I've thought it through very carefully. I'm sorry."

His mother tried to say something in order to smooth things over and comfort her friend but the baroness fended her off.

"No, No, Emilia. Paul has a right to his life. It's just . . . ." She bit her lips, fighting back a rush of tears. "I'll be all right in the morning. Will you excuse me?"

Next morning the baroness appeared outwardly calm but she was pale and very silent. When Paul left she embraced him.

"I do understand, Paul," she said. "I wish you the very best. And I want you to know that you'll always be welcome in this house."

So it had never even come to the point of telling the baroness that when Paul had become an American citizen he had changed his name back to Silver, making himself ineligible in any case, according to the baron's will, to inherit the estate.

◆ ◆ ◆

Slowly the "Hammerschmidt KZ'lers" began to disperse. At first they had continued to cluster together, held together by bonds of common experience as well as fear, as they tried to exercise their weakened muscles of independence in order to prepare themselves for a life of normalcy most had not known for years. But then, slowly, the dispersal began.

The feeding and supervision of the *Aussenlager* had been taken over by the American Military Government which also supervised the screen-ings that were daily taking place to begin the laborious process of shipping the prisoners back home or to new homelands or to various refugee camps, their status now being that of DP's, Displaced Persons.

It would be years before all the Displaced Persons of Europe were shuffled back to their homes or to new homes. And some unfortunate ones never found a new home at all.

One after another Martin's "family" left. Alfred was one of the first to leave, having a home in his native Austria to return to, his almost completed manuscript tucked away securely in his bag.

"We'll be in touch" was all he could say as he embraced Martin, fighting back tears. "We'll be in touch."

Dr. Weiss left soon after, to join a shipment of Jews going to Palestine. Konrad was among the last to leave, accepted for emigration to Sweden.

Only Johann still remained.

◆ ◆ ◆

There was one other person Paul could not get out of his mind and he knew that he would look her up at the first opportunity—Margaret. He had had other relationships, even a very intense one with a girl with whom he was still corresponding. But through it all, overarching all his experiences like a sacred vision, hovered the memory of Margaret and of their few precious days together.

So it was that he left one Saturday at dawn in a mood of high excitement and anticipation, leaving early because he had only a weekend and it was a long trip halfway across the country. But as he drove along, his mood slowly changed and began to be invaded by a certain anxiety. Did Margaret remember him with the same intensity? What did he really want from her or expect from the trip? Was she really—or *could* she really live up to the fantasy that he had built up around her over the years? Maybe it was no more than the incompleteness of their brief affair that continued to haunt him.

As he drew close to the border, however, the peaceful, bucolic countryside helped him push his doubts away, leaving merely anticipation. He would see what he would see, feel what he would feel. It wasn't as if he was planning to march right up to the altar with her, now or maybe ever. What he needed was to see her again, to hold her and treasure her without the threat of termination that had hovered over their days.

He stopped by a bridge and walked down to the small stream and sat for a while, watching the water skipping over the rocks. It reminded him of the stream that had separated him from freedom on the fateful night of his escape. He remembered Margaret's shadowy figure waving to him out of the darkness as he plunged fearfully into the unknown of his new life. It was the sort of moment not a lifetime could erase. How much had changed! How radically different his life was now, beckoning with untold possibilites and promises!

Finally he got up and continued on his way. The little town of Stadtkyll was as sleepy as he remembered it. Not a house destroyed, not a shred of outward evidence that there had ever been a war. He drove through it without stopping and presently found himself on the road to her farmhouse. At that time he walked, he remembered, with a knapsack on his back which contained all his worldly belongings. He passed a few farmhouses, with chickens running freely about their yards. No, that wasn't her house yet. Then he passed a farmhouse that lay in ruins. Strange, he thought, there was no evidence of fire. Had there been fighting around here?

Presently he came to a house that looked familiar. Yes, that was the farmhouse, with the shed in back where her father had kept the pigs. He felt his heart beginning to drum in his throat as he eased his jeep down to the house and got out. What did Margaret look like? He suddenly realized that his image of Margaret had made no allowance for the passage of years! And he too had changed, perhaps even more than she. Would she even recognize him?

He hesitated in front of the door, trying to collect himself. Why the sudden fear? Yes, years had passed, but if what they had experienced then had been real, it would be real still. At length he knocked. No response. He knocked again, more loudly. Now he could hear steps approaching and in a moment the door opened.

He recognized her at once, even before she looked fully at him. As their eyes met, she gasped and a warm glow spread over her face.

"Paul."

He felt the past pulling him back through the years, erasing everything that separated them from the precious days they had spent together. At that time, Margaret had represented everything he didn't have.

"May I come in?"

Margaret nodded and was about to step aside when a little girl ran up. Half hiding behind Margaret, she eyed Paul with big, curious eyes.

"Louise," Margaret said. "She's four. And little Paul is two," she suddenly added as if in explanation.

"I see."

They stood looking at each other silently, each struggling with his own emotions.

"I thought of you many—*many* times, Paul . . . ." Her voice faltered.

"So have I."

Again they stood looking at each other. At length he said:

"And are you happy?"

"Yes," she said without hesitation. And yet Paul seemed to detect an ever so slight qualification in her voice. "And you?"

"Yes. Life has been good to me."

"I'm glad."

After a moment she said:

"Will you come in?"

He shook his head.

"No, I think I'll be moving on. I just wanted—I guess . . . ."

He fell silent.

She nodded. He began to turn but instead suddenly stepped forward and kissed her impulsively on the forehead. For a moment they leaned silently against each other.

"So . . . ." he whispered.

"Y-e-s."

Her voice was barely audible.

Then he turned around sharply and walked briskly to his jeep. Waving briefly, he accelerated and disappeared down the road.

◆ ◆ ◆

Despite Paul's consuming absorption in his work at Buchenwald, he found time to see Johann several times and in the process came to know Martin as well, for Johann continued to live in Martin's villa. The three talked about many things, including the future of Germany and particularly of Erfurt because there were rumors that the whole region would be vacated by the Americans and would be incorporated into the Russian Zone of Occupation.*

"How would you feel about that, Martin?" Paul wondered. "Are you afraid of the Russians?"

---

* It later was.

"Why should I be? Communists wear shoes too, don't they?"

"They wear shoes. But they don't have much use for the capitalists who produce them. Do you plan to leave if they take over?"

Martin shook his head.

"My life is here. I didn't run away from the Nazis and I'm not going to run away from the Russians."

"And you, Johann?" Paul inquired. "What do you plan to do?"

"I've offered him a job with me," Martin interposed. "But he won't take it. And it would be a good job too, Johann," he said, turning to him.

"I can't see myself cooped up in an office or factory. No offense meant, Martin. I need open spaces. Besides," Johann said with a smile, "I'm a *Münchner*, you know. I miss Munich."

"But what are you going to do? Go back to your old job?" Paul asked. Johann shrugged.

"I don't know. Maybe I'll just work on a farm for a while. Breathe fresh air, milk cows, roll in the grass, stare up at the sky."

They all laughed appreciatively, with quiet understanding.

"And when are you going to enter upon that idyll?" Paul asked.

"Any day now," Johann said. "Any day."

◆ ◆ ◆

The Buchenwald investigation was drawing to a close. Paul had requested a transfer to the International War Crimes Tribunal in Nürnberg and one day the transfer came through. He was to report there in two days.

That evening it was a Tuesday Paul set out for Erfurt to say goodbye to Martin and to offer Johann a ride as far as Nürnberg. From there he could take a train to Munich.

"Are you ready to launch into that idyll of yours, Johann?"

"I think so."

It was agreed that Paul would pick him up early Thursday morning. The three spent the evening together, celebrating quietly.

It was part celebration, part wake.

◆ ◆ ◆

Next day, Wednesday, the last contingent of the "Hammerschmidt KZ'lers" left the factory. Martin went to see them off and so did Johann. It was a tearful scene, with endless embraces, and yet joyful too: an end and a beginning. Martin and Johann stood waving after the two buses carrying the last of them away, the prisoners' tears and laughter and shouts of gratitude and anticipation still ringing in their ears.

When Martin finally turned around, Johann was gone. He felt a pang of sadness and regret, feeling lonely and restless. He would have liked to spend some time with Johann, to simply be in his presence. Tomorrow Johann too would be gone.

Instead of returning to his office, as he had intended, he turned back to the silent prison-factory, driven by a desire to be with "his" prisoners awhile longer. The old factory building lay deserted now. His footsteps echoed hollowly through the empty halls. He walked slowly through the building with a sense of bereavement, realizing suddenly how rich his life had been, how tremendously rich and full—with worry and fear but with joy and satisfaction too . . . .

Coming up to the infirmary, he saw that the door stood ajar and suddenly became aware of Johann sitting at a small table that he had used to take the prisoners' blood pressure and for various other purposes. His elbows were propped up on the table and he sat with his head supported on his folded hands. His eyes were closed and he seemed deep in thought. Hearing the door opening, he opened his eyes and, seeing Martin, made a small gesture toward the chair facing him across the small table.

Martin sat down. Both were silent. All at once Johann fumbled in his shirt and drew out a crust of bread.

"An old habit from camp," he murmured. "Would you share it with me?"

He broke the piece of bread in half and handed half to Martin.

They ate the bread in silence, chewing slowly, ever so slowly, neither saying a word.

◆ ◆ ◆

Next morning Paul arrived early to pick up Johann. It was a warm, intermittently sunny day in late June. They didn't talk much because it was hard to be heard in the open jeep and once they reached the Autobahn, where Paul accelerated to a steady sixty miles an hour, they had to shout to hear each other at all. Paul enjoyed the wind striking his face, blowing about his hair. Now and then he turned his head to Johann, who was looking steadily ahead, his close-cropped hair barely moving in the wind, and grinned with boyish relish and Johann smiled back.

At the Nürnberg exit of the Autobahn, Paul pulled to the side.

"Are you sure you don't want to take the train?" he asked again.

"I prefer hitchhiking. And I'd like to walk a bit."

They shook hands.

"See you in Munich," Paul said. "Be sure to let mother know where I can reach you. You have her address."

"I will."

"And if there's anything you need, Johann. Please."

"I promise."

Johann got out of the jeep, slinging his tiny bundle of possessions over his shoulder. Still Paul lingered.

"Well," he said finally. "I'll be seeing you."

He threw the jeep in gear, waved, and accelerated rapidly around the curve and in a moment was gone.

Johann began to walk along the broad Autobahn. A few cars passed by but he made no effort to flag them down. The movement felt good. The air was fresh. The sun was shining.

About the Author

PETER BRONER has had a varied career as a novelist, playwright, journalist, psychotherapist, and intelligence agent. Emigrating as a boy from Germany, he fought in World War II against Germany, serving in various branches of U.S. Intelligence. After the war, a bachelor's degree in journalism led to work as a foreign correspondent in Vienna and Frankfurt before returning to the United States to pursue a career in writing. In 1970 he obtained a master's degree in social work and worked for ten years as a staff therapist in a mental health clinic. He continues to maintain a private psychotherapy practice near Hyde Park, New York, where he lives with his wife and two children. Mr. Broner has had several plays produced Off-Off-Broadway and elsewhere, published a number of short stories and has twice won Samuel Goldwyn writing prizes. *Night of the Broken Glass* is one of several novels he has written.